THE DEVIL'S BRIGADE
(FORMERLY THE SLUSH PILE BRIGADE)

A NICK LASSITER-SKYLER NOVEL BOOK 1

In this first thriller in the Nick Lassiter-Skyler International Espionage Series, Mr. Everyman Nick Lassiter becomes an unwitting intelligence operative and encounters for the first time the beautiful female assassin Skyler, who plays a prominent role in Books 2 and 3 of the series. As he celebrates his thirtieth birthday with friends, Lassiter is also a man in crisis: he has lost his girlfriend and his job, is wanted by the police, and has discovered that his unpublished thriller, *Blind Thrust*, has been stolen and turned into a blockbuster movie called *Subterranean Storm*. Even worse, the movie is based on a soon-to-be bestselling novel by Australian thriller writer Cameron Beckett, one of the world's biggest brand-name authors. Rather than seek revenge through a financial settlement or public humiliation, Lassiter sets out for New York to obtain *mea culpas* from Beckett and his renowned literary agent, whom he is certain colluded with the Aussie in stealing his debut novel.

Once in New York, Lassiter, and his three fish-out-of-water friends who insist on accompanying him, instantly run afoul of the law and other powerful forces intent on thwarting them and their mission. As they encounter one thorny obstacle after another, the scope of their inquiries expands and they are soon in way over their heads, battling toe-to-toe not only against the mega-bestselling author and his agent, but a formidable army of antagonists, including the NYPD, Beckett's Big Five publishing house security squad, and the Russian mob. Collectively, these adversaries present Lassiter with the greatest—and deadliest—challenge of his life.

Unexpectedly aided by his CIA father, Director of the Russian Counterintelligence Desk, and his former girlfriend turned CIA-informant, Lassiter and his comrades take to calling themselves the *Devil's Brigade* in tribute to the legendary U.S.-Canadian First Special Service Force, an elite commando outfit that fought in Italy in World War Two. Outmatched and outgunned, they are foiled at every turn but still they are determined to win. But will justice be attained? Can they prove that Beckett and his crooked literary agent have stolen Lassiter's blockbuster novel and are undeservedly reaping the success? More importantly, can they solve one of the most important counterintelligence cases in CIA history and in the process honor the original Devil's Brigade?

Praise for Samuel Marquis

#1 *Denver Post* Bestselling Author
Foreword Reviews' Book of the Year Winner (HM)
Beverly Hills Books Awards Winner & Award-Winning Finalist
Next Generation Indie Book Awards Winner
& Award-Winning Finalist
USA Best Book Awards Award-Winning Finalist
Colorado Book Awards Award-Winning Finalist

"*The Coalition* has a lot of good action and suspense, an unusual female assassin, and the potential to be another *The Day After Tomorrow* [the runaway bestseller by Allan Folsom]."
—James Patterson, #1 *New York Times* Bestselling Author

"*Altar of Resistance* is a gripping and densely packed thriller dramatizing the Allied Italian campaign...reminiscent of Herman Wouk's *The Winds of War*."
—Kirkus Reviews

"Marquis is a student of history, always creative, [and] never boring...A good comparison might be Tom Clancy."
—Military.com

"In his novels *Blind Thrust* and *Cluster of Lies*, Samuel Marquis vividly combines the excitement of the best modern techno-thrillers, an education in geology, and a clarifying reminder that the choices each of us make have a profound impact on our precious planet."
—Ambassador Marc Grossman, Former U.S. Under Secretary of State

"*Blind Thrust* kept me up until 1 a.m. two nights in a row. I could not put it down. An intriguing mystery that intertwined geology, fracking, and places in Colorado that I know well. Great fun."
—Governor Roy R. Romer, 39th Governor of Colorado

"*The Coalition* starts with a bang, revs up its engines, and never stops until the explosive ending...Perfect for fans of James Patterson, David Baldacci, and Vince Flynn."—Foreword Reviews

"[A] combination of *The Great Escape*, *Public Enemies*, a genuine old-time Western, and a John Le Carré novel."
—BlueInk Review (for *Bodyguard of Deception*, Book 1 of WWII Series)

By Samuel Marquis

NICK LASSITER-SKYLER INTERNATIONAL ESPIONAGE SERIES

THE DEVIL'S BRIGADE
THE COALITION
THE FOURTH PULARCHEK

WORLD WAR TWO SERIES

BODYGUARD OF DECEPTION
ALTAR OF RESISTANCE
SPIES OF THE MIDNIGHT SUN (JANUARY 2018)

JOE HIGHEAGLE ENVIRONMENTAL SLEUTH SERIES

BLIND THRUST
CLUSTER OF LIES

THE DEVIL'S BRIGADE

A NICK LASSITER-SKYLER NOVEL BOOK 1

SAMUEL MARQUIS

MOUNT SOPRIS PUBLISHING

THE DEVIL'S BRIGADE
A NICK LASSITER-SKYLER NOVEL BOOK 1

Copyright © 2017 by Samuel Marquis

MOUNT SOPRIS PUBLISHING
Trade paper: ISBN 978-1-943593-00-2
Kindle: ISBN 978-1-943593-01-9
Epub: ISBN 978-1-943593-02-6

Third Mount Sopris Publishing Premium Printing: April 2017 (Previously published as *The Slush Pile Brigade*: 2015-2016)
Cover Design: Christian Fuenfhausen (http://cefdesign.com)
Formatting: Rik Hall (www.WildSeasFormatting.com)
Printed in the United States of America

To Order Samuel Marquis Books and Contact Samuel:

Visit Samuel Marquis's website, join his mailing list, learn about his forthcoming suspense novels and book events, and order his books at www.samuelmarquisbooks.com. Please send all fan mail (including criticism) to samuelmarquisbooks@gmail.com. Thank you for your support!

ATTENTION: ORGANIZATIONS AND CORPORATIONS
Mount Sopris Publishing books may be purchased for educational, business, or sales promotional use. For information, please email the Special Markets Department at samuelmarquisbooks@gmail.com.

Dedication

This suspense novel, my first, is dedicated to five remarkable individuals without whom I would never have written this book.

First and foremost, *The Devil's Brigade* is dedicated to my father, Austin Marquis (June 1924-April 2015), who served in the Pacific Theater in World War II and was a great dad.

Second, this book is dedicated to Thatcher "Claggebart" Claussen (November 1961-September 2008), my longtime irreverent friend and partner in mischief.

And finally, the novel is dedicated to Indie authors Barry Eisler, Hugh Howey, and J.A. Konrath, who inspired me, in the words of Eric Clapton, to "keep on keeping on."

There's a little Austie, Claggebart, Eisler, Howey, and Konrath in all of us. They are all true Devil's Brigadiers.

The Devil's Brigade
A Nick Lassiter-Skyler Novel Book 1

Far better it is to dare mighty things, to win glorious triumphs even though checkered by failure, than to rank with those poor spirits who neither enjoy nor suffer much because they live in the gray twilight that knows neither victory nor defeat.
—Theodore Roosevelt

It's not whether you get knocked down, it's whether you get up.
—Vince Lombardi

PROLOGUE

NEW YORK'S VERY OWN SHINING STAR—über literary agent Anton Fitzgerald De Benedictis—looked into the eyes of his *numero uno* client, the planet's second bestselling author of all time who hailed from the Australian bush country, and couldn't believe what the hell he was hearing. They were sitting in the agent's sumptuously appointed office on the thirtieth floor overlooking Sixth Avenue, a *sanctum sanctorum* where together he and his client had made literary history. Yet, it was as if he was talking to a complete stranger instead of the forty-eight-year-old cash cow that he had plucked from obscurity two decades earlier and pushed to the top through his creative genius. Seriously, he thought, shit like this was only supposed to happen in the movies.

He leaned his elbow onto his sprawling cherrywood desk, gazing fiercely at Cameron Barnaby Beckett IV, who was busy primping his jet-black, pomaded hair. The fifty-two-time *New York Times* bestselling author was not only his most important client but a close friend; yet, right now the Aussie bastard was vexing him in the extreme.

"What do you mean you have writer's block?"

"Strordnary, I know, but it's like I'm stuck in quicksand. I don't know what the hell to do for my next novel. I've been at the keyboard for weeks and haven't typed a single bloody word. I can't even muster a rough outline. I tell you I'm at a loss, stuck in a quagmire."

"You're one of the world's biggest literary brands—second only to James Patterson—and you don't know what the hell to write? Tell me this isn't happening."

"I'm afraid it is, mate, and I don't know what to do about it. I've tried everything."

"I don't see how this is possible. You've never had any trouble like this before."

"I know but it's quite real, I assure you."

Benedictis mumbled something under his breath and frowned darkly.

"Why are you looking at me like that, Anton?"

"Like what?"

"Like you want to cut my nuts off and feed them to a pack of feral dogs. It's not like I've done anything wrong. You're my agent and I'm trying to explain to you what I'm going through. This is a very difficult time for me."

"I'm just being realistic, Cam. You're a professional novelist so you need to be writing as opposed to…not writing. Get it? That's all I'm saying."

"Oh crikey, you sound like my damned father, *Sir* Cameron." He wrinkled his nose with a prodigal son's disdain. "I must say it's very disconcerting, Anton."

"I think you're blowing things out of proportion. All I'm doing is trying to come up with a solution to your problem."

"Problem? Is it a problem? I mean…do I really have a problem?"

"Are you hitting the booze and hookers again, Cam? Is that what this is really about?"

"No, my drinking…it's…it's under control."

"Bullshit, you're drinking like a fish. What about hookers?"

"I've cut way back. I'm down to one or two per month now."

He gave him a skeptical look.

"Okay, six or seven times a month, but I swear that's it!"

"Does your wife know?"

"Dear Lord no—and I must keep it that way! I don't know what I'd do if I lost Nicole!"

"What about the blow? Are you still snorting like a bloodhound?"

"No, now *that* I really have given up. I haven't had any since last summer in Perth."

"You wouldn't lie to me, would you, Cam?"

"No, I tell you liquid libation, sporting women, and cocaine are not the problem. I just have a bad case of writer's block and I'm terrified it's going to turn into a long-term problem."

"Look, first off you don't have a *writing problem*. We just need to Google it or get you a book…*The Idiot's Guide to Writer's Block* or some such thing."

"I've sat in front of a computer screen for the past two weeks and I haven't written a single bloody line. Not one. I don't know what to do—I think I need a break."

Benedictis felt a flutter in his chest. Did he just hear the taboo words he hoped never to hear? "A *break*? Did you just say you needed a *break*?"

"Yes, I need some time away to recharge my batteries and become sane again. This hectic pace is positively killing me."

He gave a time-out signal. "Okay, Cam, just hold on a second. I'm in the best position to know what you need and don't need, okay? I'm your literary agent, remember? Now, the last thing you want to do right now is make a rash decision and get this crazy idea in your head that you need a break to cure this minor little setback of yours. A break will only make things worse. Trust me on this. What you really need is a fresh new idea—something inspiring, something to allow you to grow and test new boundaries, something to light a fire inside you and help you rekindle your passion. Then you'll be fine, I promise you."

"I don't think so, Anton. I think I need a break. A long one."

Benedictis knew at this point he should say something consoling, but he couldn't bring himself to do such a stupid ass thing. For Beckett to take time off to recuperate or reconnect with his inner self or some other new agey crap was absolutely, positively not an option; he had to get that out of his client's mind right away. The guy was Chase-Manhattan Bank for crying out loud and you didn't close down Chase-Manhattan Bank for goddamned repairs or renovation!

There had to be a way to fix this.

He glanced around his resplendently furnished office, as if a cure for Cameron Barnaby Beckett IV's writer's block could be found in the antique cherrywood furnishings, finished oak wainscoting, gilded window trim, intricate ceiling of raised plasterwork, or the priceless Jackson Pollack hanging on the wall along with multiple Warhol's. Or the equally valuable, antique, .38-caliber machine-gun pistol and bullet-proof vest hanging beside the paintings, both of which had belonged to the Depression-era gangster "Baby Face" Nelson. The memorabilia—once brandished proudly by John Dillinger's fellow Public Enemy #1 and cherubic-faced partner in crime—had been gifts fifteen years earlier from Cameron Beckett, thanking Benedictis in commemoration of their tenth *New York Times* bestselling novel together.

He wracked his brains for a solution. As he pondered, the sunlight trickling in from the huge window overlooking bustling Sixth Avenue glinted off his Cartier watch like one of the precious jewels on prominent display at the American Museum. The light held there for a moment then reflected through his glass of water sitting next to the slush pile of query letters, synopses, and manuscripts stacked on his desk, a teetering mountain of submissions. He stared at the vast pile, pensively stroking his chin. Having risen to the top during what some considered the second "Golden Age" of book publishing in the 1980s and 1990s, he was old school and still printed out everything to read in hard copy; paperwork of one form or another covered virtually every square inch of his desk.

He suddenly lit on an idea. "Just for kicks, why don't we take a look at a few of these?"

Beckett's blood-red, puffy-lipped mouth opened in protest. "What, from the *slush pile?*"

"It couldn't hurt to take a look." Feeling a little tingle of hope—and a hint of danger—he plucked up the stapled query letter and synopsis lying on top that some poor schmuck had probably spent the better part of a month writing and rewriting and gushing to her friends about and praying over—yes fucking *praying* over!—until she thought she was poised to receive her lucky break and enter that venerated temple of temples, the holy sanctuary of the traditionally-published author that brought about instant credibility, not to mention nirvana.

"I don't know about this," said Beckett. "Is this...ethical?"

"Ethical, smethical...we're just taking a look." He glanced at the query. "Okay this one's about a transvestite vampire serial killer from Queens who—"

"Bogan, Anton, bogan. Plus I don't do vampires and you bloody well know that."

"Okay, okay, that wasn't a good choice. Let's grab another." He rifled through the pile, grabbing twenty or thirty submissions and erecting a second, smaller pile. "All right, here we go. Here's a legal thriller set in New Orleans. It's about a rich runaway debutante and her opulent antebellum family. Of course, they're concealing a steamy southern secret and—"

"I don't like the South or legal thrillers. I'm not Turow, Richard North

Patterson, or Grisham, Anton."

"I know, I know—you're much better. All right, just bear with me. Let's look at some of these." He took a moment to flip through several more query letters and synopses. "Okay, I've got thrillers on South American drug cartels, cyber criminals, Islamic terrorists, amnesiac CIA hit men, Chinese and Russian business cabals, an NSA spying scandal, more vampires and serial killers, and—"

"No, no, no!"

"Come on, just play along for a minute. There's got to be something in this pile of crap. How about this?"

He pulled from the slush pile a submission that was fatter than the others. It contained a query letter, synopsis, and, this time, a full manuscript. Somehow his assistant Natalie Perkins must have included the full novel with the query and synopsis, which meant that he, or one of his myriad subordinates, had requested it because it was promising enough for a full-length look.

"Okay, this one's called *Blind Thrust*."

"What's it about?"

"Oh yeah, now I remember this baby—the environmental thriller. It's about an illegal toxic waste operation that results in major earthquakes killing thousands of people. It was set in Colorado. I almost forgot about this. I took a look at it when it first came in a couple of months ago. It was promising but, unfortunately, I had to turn it down. Unpublished greenhorn, too much risk—you know the drill."

"Yes, but it sounds interesting."

"I thought so too. Like I said, it was close—just not close enough."

"Tell me more about it."

"Well, from what I recall, the hero is a Native American geologist and the villain is a corporate big shot that operates this secret, illegal waste operation. He pumps toxic fluid into the ground knowing he could generate small earthquakes. But he fails to control the tremors and they become much worse, killing thousands of people. Then, once all hell has broken loose with the earthquakes, people start getting killed left and right by the bad guys in the cover-up, and the Indian hero saves the day and solves the case. Overall, the characters were well-drawn and the story was authentic. The author—this Nick Lassiter fellow—is a real-life geologist, so all of the technical details are Clancy-like accurate."

Beckett's eyes brightened, as if a little light had gone off in his mind. He leaned forward in his chair alertly. "You know, I've always been *fascinated* with earthquakes."

"Twenty-two years we've known each other and only now do you tell me this? Do you have any more secrets I should know about?"

"When I left the God-forsaken Outback three decades ago to attend Oxford, I actually considered majoring in geology," confessed the Australian.

Good thing you didn't or today my net worth wouldn't be fifty million dollars. "Did you now? Well, you truly are full of surprises today, Cameron my friend."

"Just be a good mate and read me the synopsis."

He flipped through the submission until he found it. "All right here we go. It says:

The central dramatic question of Blind Thrust is will a young, rising scientist risk his life and career to vanquish his own powerful client whom he greatly admires and is professionally bound to protect? The large-stakes conflict takes place in Colorado's Front Range and pits two equally matched individuals: Cheyenne environmental geologist Joe Higheagle and billionaire "green" energy entrepreneur Charles Prometheus Quantrill.

The action begins as horrific earthquakes are devastating the Front Range between Denver and Colorado Springs in an area long believed to be seismically quiescent. They are being generated by ruptures along cryptic, mysterious, deeply buried thrust faults (or blind thrusts) that, unlike most faults, do not break the surface during large-scale seismic events. Somehow, the cause of the unusual earthquakes must be unraveled and the cataclysms stopped before they result in more carnage and devastation. But are they the result of regular crustal adjustments, hydro-fracking, conventional subsurface sequestering, or clandestine operations?

In his quest for the truth, the dogged everyman-sleuth Joe Higheagle determines that the earthquakes are, in fact, being carefully and systematically controlled through a secretive, highly profitable hazardous waste deep well injection program using abandoned oil wells by his own client, Charles Prometheus Quantrill. Except controlling nature is not humanly possible and the earthquakes catastrophically worsen. It, therefore, falls upon the Native American Higheagle to stop his client and save Colorado from total destruction..."

When he stopped reading, Benedictis looked up. Was it his imagination or had his pulse quickened as he was reading the opening paragraphs of the synopsis. It was a bit melodramatic, to be sure, but the idea of human beings trying to control earthquakes was certainly an intriguing concept. More importantly, it was fresh and unique. In his three decades in the business, he had never heard of such a story being done before, which was exceedingly rare. He recalled how the high concept had intrigued him right off the bat when he had perused the submitted materials last month. And the writing had been strong. Just not strong enough to be confidently placed with a publisher in his view given that it was written by a neophyte. But in the more financially secure hands of an established bestselling author, it was pure—

"I bloody well love it!" he heard Beckett blurt, startling him in his seat. "Give me that damned thing!"

The bestselling author extended both of his ham-like hands in a sudden movement, his stubby fingers clasping the query, synopsis, and novel in a flash and pulling them into his lap like a mother clinging desperately to her infant child.

"Earthquakes, earthquakes...I've always wanted to unlock the mysteries of the universe in one of my novels! Finally! Oh my God, is this exciting or what?"

For the next few minutes, Benedictis watched with a warring amalgam of excitement and deep uneasiness as his client flipped through the pages of the synopsis and manuscript, nodding and smiling in agreement every so often and finally pulling out his monogrammed gold pen and underlining passages of particular interest before nodding vigorously some more. Watching Beckett's visibly growing enthusiasm for the material made the agent more and more uncomfortable as the anxious seconds ticked off. He had only meant to spark some ideas, to liberate his bestselling client from his writer's block, to breathe some fire and passion back into him. But now it appeared as if he had opened Pandora's Box. Beckett seemed intent on adopting the project as his own and was apparently not going to let go until it belonged to him.

"Good on you, mate—I absolutely love it!" he announced five minutes later. "I'm taking this with me! You are brilliant, absolutely brilliant, Anton!"

He wanted to protest—in fact he had the sick feeling that if he didn't say something he was signing a Faustian pact that would come back to haunt them both—but no words came out. Nothing. Nada. He told himself that Beckett needed this; that, hell, he himself needed this! And besides, it wouldn't be the first time he had stolen from the slush pile. With the rare exception, the no-name schmucks in the heaps on his desk stood virtually no chance of publication in their lifetimes, so there was never any real damage. Unless, of course, they were bamboozled into self-pubbing with *Goddamn Amazon*, as he and his tony New York literary colleagues disparagingly referred to the rapacious behemoth that was killing their once-profitable industry. Who cared about some idiot way out in Oklahoma or Colorado or wherever the hell this pathetic little shit hailed from who had cobbled together a few complete sentences with actual punctuation. *Fuck him—he was a nobody!* If he knew what was good for him, he would consider himself lucky to be the source of inspiration for a genuine bestselling novelist—and leave it at that. New York was too big a town, and the literary marketplace here in the city too grandiose a stage, for the likes of some redneck, tale-spinning wannabe from west of the Mississippi, who knew a thing or two about seismological perturbations but little else.

"This is it—this is exactly what I need! You're right the guy that wrote this is a real geologist! What's his name again?"

"Nick Lassiter."

"Well, here's to Nick Lassiter! The details are fantastic! This is perfection!"

Benedictis took an invisible breath, keeping his eyes fixed on his client of twenty-two years, a man who had made him more money than he could count. He knew this was his last chance to speak out, but as he took in the glow of inspiration on Beckett's face, actual words of protest escaped him. The smiling Aussie from Narrambla—the birthplace of Andrew "Banjo" Paterson, the legendary poet who had written "Waltzing Matilda" and "The Man from Snowy River"—looked just like his daughter Rebecca had as a little girl opening presents on Christmas morning. How in the hell could he say *"No!"* to that! He felt like an anvil was pressing down on his chest, compressing his lungs. Yet, he couldn't bring himself to utter a peep, let alone an objection. Who was he to deny his most important client and the second bestselling author of all time a little shot in the arm, a tiny pick-me-up to ensure his continued success?

"Why are you talking to yourself, Anton? You're scaring me."

Oh shit, did I do it again? He was always talking to himself, and sometimes people thought he was crazy. *But Jesus H. Christ there's so much shit up there!* "I guess I'm just happy for you, Cam," he said affably, but inside he felt his stomach all twisted in knots.

"Don't worry. I'm not going to steal this Nick Lassiter's novel. I'm just going to borrow a few ideas. Of course, I'll have to create all new characters and change the story line, but this is a wonderful conceptual starting point."

"I'm just glad I could help, Cameron. That's what you pay me for: to be your advocate and look out for your interests."

"You are a true genius, mate. This time you truly have outdone yourself. How can I repay you?"

"You can start by writing another *Number One Bestseller*."

"Then let the literary journey begin. I won't let you down, Anton, I promise. This is going to be my best effort yet!"

"Then I can't wait. Here's to Nick Lassiter."

"To Nick Lassiter! Oi oi oi!" cried the Australian, and they pretended to clink champagne glasses.

But inside Benedictis was in agony. He heard a little voice and it told him that he, like the legendary Delta bluesman Robert Johnson, had indeed signed a pact with the goddamned devil.

THREE YEARS LATER

SATURDAY

JUNE 1

CHAPTER 1

BUCKHORN EXCHANGE RESTAURANT
1000 OSAGE STREET, DENVER, COLORADO

THE BUCKHORN EXCHANGE was Nick Lassiter's favorite restaurant in the Mile High City, a place where he dined only on special occasions—like tonight on his thirtieth birthday. He liked Denver's oldest drinking and dining establishment because it was the antithesis of postmodern political correctness. He liked it for the smoky, pungent aroma of broiled buffalo, elk, and rattlesnake wafting out of the kitchen. He liked it for its archaic museum-of-natural-history feel with the profusion of bear, moose, bighorn sheep, bison, and other wild animal heads displayed on the walls to go along with sepia-toned daguerreotypes and colorful oil paintings of the Old West. He liked it for the neat rows of glass cases that displayed an eclectic assemblage of antique rifles and pistols and the rusty wares of trappers and miners. The original proprietor, German immigrant Henry Zietz, had converted the two-story brick commercial building into a restaurant in the late 1800s, and the historic establishment had lost little of its rustic Western charm over the last century and a quarter. Which was another way of saying that it was cheesy as hell—but in that good old-fashioned heartland kind of way, like listening to John Cougar Mellencamp.

Stepping onto the creaky oak floorboards of the restaurant at 6:08 p.m., Lassiter informed the maître'd that he had a reservation. After scanning her list, she, in turn, informed him that his dinner guests had already been seated and led him to his table. There he found his three best friends—and frequent partners in mischief—already well-lubricated with a round of Fat Tires.

"Here he is—the man who's late for his own birthday party!" roared Frederick Najarian Welch, nicknamed 'Squelch,' a pony-tailed Professor of Anarchy Studies at the University of Colorado in Boulder. "Happy Birthday, Nicky! Have a brew…we already ordered you one! Sit down and imbibe, laddie!"

Squelch slapped him on the back and shoved a Fat Tire into his palm and then he and his two bibulous companions stood up from their chairs and raised their bottles, ignoring all the people at the neighboring tables gawking at them.

"One runs out of superlatives—here's to you, Nicholas!" cheered Morrison Frautschi Claussen, known as 'Claggebart,' the rebellious, independently wealthy scion of one of Denver's oldest and most venerated gold-baron families. "Here's to your thirtieth!"

Lassiter smiled bashfully.

"Hear, hear!" cheered Timothy Caleb Bermingham, nicknamed 'Bermolito,'

IT-nerd extraordinaire who literally never let his Apple iPad Air 3 tablet leave his sight and who proudly wore glasses with black frames so thick they would make both Patrick Carney and Buddy Holly proud.

They tipped back their beers, each of them swilling back a third of the amber fluid in their bottles as the nearby diners continued to stare at them in stupefaction. Then, amid much back-slapping and joking, mostly on the part of Squelch and Claggebart, they all sat down.

"You guys are genuinely crazy," said Lassiter, feeling a little embarrassed to be the center of attention, but also enjoying it. "But that's why I love you."

"And we love you right back, Nicky baby. That's why we're here to cheer you up," said Bermolito. "I heard about you losing your job. I'm really sorry."

"Come on, man, we're not here to talk about that," protested Squelch. "This is a night of celebration—we're going to light this town up!"

"I'll drink to that. The Queen City of the Plains will undoubtedly never be the same after tonight," echoed Claggebart, looking impishly dapper in his blue blazer and maroon ascot. "All references to employment, or former employment, are henceforth off limits during tonight's bacchanalian adventures."

"That's only because you don't have a job," said Bermolito.

"Why should I? I'm a man of independent means."

"And I'm both unemployed and lacking in independent means so I'm really fucked," said Lassiter with a wry grin. "But there's no reason for you guys to worry about me. I'll get back on my feet in no time. Hopefully, this will be my first and *last* lay off."

"Well, at least you've still got Alexandra," said Bermolito.

Lassiter felt an instant sting, but tried not to let it show on his face. Squelch and Claggebart shot Bermolito a frosty glance.

"What? What did I say?"

"Nicky broke up with Alexandra," said Squelch. "She moved all her things out this morning—the little wretch."

"Come on, Squelch, you don't need to talk about her like that. It takes two people to make a relationship work and I'm just as much to blame as her. And don't sweat it, Berm. I know you didn't know."

"I'm sorry, Nick. But man, what a bummer—first you lose your job and then your girlfriend. I mean, how much lower can you go?"

"Great Scott, some help you are, Berm?" snorted Claggebart. "We're supposed to be celebrating his thirtieth birthday and you have to say that? This is a toast not a roast, you lummox."

"Don't worry about me boys, I'm fine. I'm just happy to be here with you lunatics. Now why don't we order some dinner before someone says something that really does piss me off?"

"Attaboy Nicky, we're going to have a great night," said Squelch. "We've got it all planned. First dinner and copious imbibery here at the Buckhorn then it's off for a kick-ass movie at the Tivoli and a night of total debauchery at the Diamond Cabaret. The latter is guaranteed to take your mind off what's-her-name." He held up his hands and grinned mischievously. "You see, I've already forgotten!"

Lassiter couldn't help but smile; Squelch always knew how to cheer a guy up when he was down. "I don't know what I'd do without you crazy S-O-B's," he said as the waitress came to take their orders.

They went for another round of Fat Tires, appetizers of jerked venison and rattlesnake marinated in red chile and lime, and a mix of entrees to be shared: broiled elk medallions, smoked buffalo sausage cooked with a green chile polenta and spicy wild game mustard sauce, roasted duck enchiladas in a tomatillo-chipotle pepper sauce with black beans and rice, and buffalo meatloaf and garlic mashed potatoes smothered in brown onion gravy. When the waitress shuffled off, they talked and drank and laughed even harder than before. When dinner arrived, they pitched into the cornucopia and drank and prattled on goofily some more, having themselves a fine time. Gradually, Lassiter felt his recent disappointments vanish as the four friends, who had been best buddies since kindergarten, recounted their many escapades growing up in Denver. They had all attended St. Peter's Catholic School and East High before Squelch and Lassiter had gone on to Kenyon College together in Ohio. After an hour of feasting and ribaldry, they paid the bill and started out the door for the movie.

That was when he saw his ex-girlfriend, Alexandra Barrett, walking into the restaurant with Jason Cornwall.

His jaw dropped.

"Alexandra, what are you doing here?"

As soon as the words left his mouth, he felt like an idiot. It was obvious what the fuck she was doing here. But how the hell did she know that goddamned dick Jason Cornwall? She hadn't grown up in Denver, as he and Cornwall had, and he had never introduced them to one another.

Her face crimsoned.

"Oh, Nick. I didn't expect to see you here."

"Neither did I, Lassiter, or we would have gone somewhere else," sniffed Cornwall, stepping forward with his chest pumped out like a game rooster.

Lassiter glared at his hulking nemesis. Was the guy the reincarnation of Tom Buchanan from *The Great Gatsby* or what? They had once been friends, but Cornwall had moved out of the city by sixth grade and went on to attend the elite private school Kent-Denver south of Denver. From that point on, they had gone viciously toe to toe against one another in soccer, basketball, and lacrosse and, over the course of their competition, had become mortal enemies.

"So let me get this straight, Alexandra," said Squelch, pressing up close to Cornwall, whom he also detested. "You moved out of Nicky's apartment only this morning and already you're going to hop in the sack with this preppy, pompous ass after he buys you a dinner of elk medallions? What Gollum wasn't available?"

"That's not funny, Fred."

"Oh, you don't think so. How about this? Didn't you get the medical memo on Jason Cornwall? It reads like this: He's got crabs—really nasty crabs—from sleeping around with unsavory women and you're sure to get them if you get anywhere near the son of a bitch."

"We don't have to take this—especially not from a Professor-of-Absolutely-Nothing at a second-rate college like CU!" snarled Cornwall, and he shoved

Squelch hard in the chest.

But Pup Squelch was unfazed by the assault and merely gave a defiant grin. "Yes, but at least people refer to me respectfully as Dr. Welch," he retorted with aplomb. "Everyone still calls you Mr. Preppy Kent-Denver Dickwad—and you're thirty freaking years old!"

Cornwall took a step forward, both fists balled up. Lassiter looked at Squelch: his fists had tightened, too, and his face had scrunched up with that dangerous, D-pole search-and-destroy-mission look that Lassiter knew only too well from their high school and Kenyon lacrosse games together.

"Whoa there, big fella—I think that's enough," he quickly interjected, stepping between them and pulling Squelch away before he and Cornwall came to blows. "I'm sorry about this, Alexandra. I wish you the best." He was not going to acknowledge Cornwall. "Let's go, guys."

"Badly done, Alexandra—badly done indeed," snorted Claggebart, echoing Sir Darcy in *Pride and Prejudice* and shaking his head with disapproval as they headed out the door.

But Cornwall wasn't going to let it end there. "You're not good enough for her, Lassiter!" he snarled back at him angrily just before the door closed behind them. "That's why she dumped you! You're not good enough for her, you unemployed loser!"

As the door shut, Lassiter wanted to storm back inside and rip his head off, but instead he bit his lip, shoved his hands in his pockets, and headed for his car. He wished he could just crawl in a hole and die.

Bermolito was right: *How much lower could he go?*

CHAPTER 2

TIVOLI MOVIE THEATER
900 AURARIA PARKWAY

THEY DROVE TO THE TIVOLI for the 8 o'clock movie in two separate cars. Squelch had obtained special tickets to an advanced screening of an upcoming release called *Subterranean Storm*. They bought popcorn and sodas, took their seats, endured twenty minutes of nerve-rattling previews with Lassiter thinking the whole time about how good Alexandra had looked in her white silk blouse, cardigan sweater, and snug-fitting jeans, and then finally, mercifully, the movie started and he slowly put his troubled thoughts behind him.

And then, fifteen minutes into the film, he began to have a strange feeling of déjà vu.

And twenty minutes after that, he felt as if his world had been turned upside down yet again. At first, he thought he might be imagining things, like some sort of conspiracy theorist. But then he realized that what he saw on the screen could not possibly be a coincidence.

He tapped Squelch on the shoulder.

"They stole my book!" he said in a loud whisper.

"What are you talking about?"

"This movie—they stole it from my goddamned novel *Blind Thrust!*"

"What do you mean they stole it?"

"I mean the screenplay writer, producer, somebody co-opted my fucking book! This movie we're watching is my goddamned novel *Blind Thrust!* You know the book I've been trying to get published for the past three years. *Subterranean Storm* is different, but there's no doubt it was lifted from my unpublished work. It's a clear case of copyright infringement. There are too many similarities for it to be a coincidence!"

"Are you sure?"

"Yes, I'm sure! These bastards, whoever they are, took my original idea and forged it into this fucking movie we're watching!"

"Would you shut up!" a voice snapped in the row behind him. "We're trying to watch the goddamned flick!"

"You don't have to be rude, asshole!" hissed the hot-headed Squelch, jumping up from his seat and turning around. "We've got a situation here."

"Oh you do, do you? I'm getting all teary-eyed. Can I call you a fricking shrink?"

"Hey, Muttonchops, do you want me to—?"

"Just calm down you two. We'll be quiet," interjected Lassiter, and he reached out and gently pulled Squelch back down into his seat by his prodigious pony tail. A few seconds later, once everyone seemed to have recovered their composure, he leaned in close to his three friends and whispered. "We'll talk afterwards."

For the next hour and a half, he remained unnervingly gripped to his seat watching the film. The story line had been altered slightly, the characters were different, and the dialogue was not his; yet, in more than half of the scenes, he had a feeling of having been here before. It was like re-watching a movie you had seen ten years earlier. You couldn't remember all the scenes or how they unfolded, but when you watched the film you knew you had seen it before. This was not a simple coincidence. The skeletal framework, the original inspiration for *Subterranean Storm*, could have only come from one place—and that was his unpublished novel *Blind Thrust.*

When the closing credits rolled, they stepped into the lobby. Lassiter felt a mixture of outrage mingled with curiosity. How the fuck had someone pulled off such a brazen act of thievery? A crime had been committed—and now, shockingly, he had to figure out not only *who* was responsible but *how* and *why* the person had done it. Despite his anger, he found the idea of solving the nascent crime and getting his comeuppance on whoever had done this to him powerfully seductive. Or was he just kidding himself? Did he even have a legitimate shot at figuring out whodunit and getting some sense of justice?

"All right, Nicky," said Squelch. "Explain to us what the hell is going on here."

"I told you. That movie we just watched is based on my novel *Blind Thrust.* They stole my idea and repackaged it as their own."

"Wait a second, boy-o," said Claggebart. "Who are 'they'?"

"I should think that would be obvious," said Bermolito. "*They* are the people who managed to get their hands on a copy of *Blind Thrust* via email or hard copy. Or that snatched it electronically out of the Ethernet."

"Snatched out of the Ethernet? Is that really possible?"

"Happens all the time, but it's less likely than the former. Who did you submit the novel to via email, Nick?"

He pondered. "Let's see. There were probably a half dozen literary agents and the same number of large and small publishers."

"Is that it?"

"Yeah, I think so."

"What about hard copies?"

"Just you guys and my mom and dad. Oh, and ten or so people from my writers' group."

"Holy Wallace E. Stegner, that's a viper's nest right there," said Squelch.

"No, there's no way anyone from my writers' group did it. Those people are incredibly helpful and dedicated. It's like a support group."

"Gentlemen," declared Claggebart. "I feel it my duty to inform you, as the one and only bona fide Sherlock Holmes in this motley crew, that the principal culprit must either be the screenwriter of *Subterranean Storm,* or the original writer of the novel if it was an adapted screenplay."

"He's right," said Bermolito, who was already conducting a Web search on his ever present Apple iPad Air 3 tablet. "It says here that the film *Subterranean Storm* is based on the novel by bestselling Australian suspense novelist Cameron Barnaby Beckett. The release date for the novel and the early screening of the movie that we just saw were both today, the first of June. Bingo, there's who stole your idea: Cameron Beckett. The movie is based on his *just-released book*, not the other way around, so it has to be him. The question is who aided and abetted him. The guy didn't do this in a vacuum. There had to be others."

"You're talking about Cameron Beckett—the world's second bestselling novelist of all time?" muttered Squelch in disbelief. "Have you all lost your minds? Why would he steal anything? He has an army of researchers and team of agents, publishers, publicists, and bean-counters on call twenty-four-seven whose express purpose is to get him whatever the hell he wants. He doesn't need to steal from some unpublished hack—no offense intended, Nicky."

"None taken, I think?"

"Did you submit your novel to Beckett's literary agent, Nick?" asked Bermolito.

He felt all his senses on high alert. "As a matter of fact I did. His agent is Anton De Benedictis, the head of Benedictis Literary Associates. He's, like, the biggest agent in New York."

"That's where Natalie worked, right?" said Squelch.

He hesitated a moment before answering, drawing a mental image of the one great love of his life, his former girlfriend Natalie Perkins. She had gone to Kenyon with him and Squelch, and he had broken up with her three and a half years ago. He often wondered what she was up to, if she was happy, whether she still thought of him as much as he thought about her. He smiled with fond reminiscence as he thought back to their time together. He remembered her smell, that little devilish gleam in her eye, the way she used to—

"Nicky, are you all right, dude?"

"Sorry, I was just thinking."

"About what, man? For a second there I thought we had lost you to the zombie apocalypse."

"We were talking about Natalie, right? The thing is she's working again for Benedictis. But she's an agent now instead of just an assistant like she was three years ago. She left to work as an editor at a publishing house in London. This was maybe six months after we broke up and I had moved back to Colorado. But then, she returned to Benedictis's agency in New York a few months ago. She's now a full literary agent with her own client list. But you're right. She was the one who originally helped me get my foot in the door with my submission. She got *Blind Thrust* to Benedictis, but he ended up rejecting it. I sent him a query and synopsis and he liked the materials enough to request the full novel. She told me he read it, or at least most of it, but in the end he didn't go for it. He would never have looked at it at all if not for Natalie's recommendation."

"You should have married that girl. She was a keeper," said Squelch.

Lassiter felt a prickle of irritation; seldom a day went by that he didn't think of Natalie Perkins and he didn't want to be reminded, yet again, of what he had lost when he had more pressing problems to deal with at the moment.

"That's all well and good," he said, "but that's not what we're talking about right now. Look guys, I'm sorry to have dumped this on you when you've gone to so much trouble for my birthday. But I've got to go home and figure this out. I've got to find out who the hell did this to me. It could be Beckett and Benedictis, but the truth is we don't know."

"Nicholas, my dear fellow, you shall go nowhere without me," declared Claggebart with braggadocio. "Revenge is a dish best served cold and I am going to be with you every step of the way, starting right now. Of course, due to my extensive experience in crime-solving, I'll be playing the role of Sherlock Holmes, while you shall serve as my doggedly loyal companion and dear friend Mr. Watson."

"Looks like Clagge's Narcissus Complex is kicking in again," put in Squelch. "But this time, even I have to admit he's on to something. You are not alone in this, Nicky. The four of us have always been a team and I just want to say, on behalf of everyone, that we've got your back, man. We're going to figure this thing out together. Besides, in addition to young Sherlock here, you're going to need a Professor of Anarchy Studies to unravel this conundrum. I mean this is right up my fucking alley!"

"It is? I don't even know what an Anarchy Studies professor teaches?"

"All kinds of stuff, man. I'm not some frumpy, bespectacled wimp with tenure who teaches one course per year. I teach two kick-ass courses every semester—and my students love me. Of course, I do end up sleeping with half of the women in my classes, but hey I'm a single, thirty-year-old, heterosexual college professor. What am I supposed to do? Restrain myself?"

"Now there's a novel idea. So what do you teach exactly?"

"For starters, *From Nietzsche to Johnny Rotten: The Western History of Anarchism.* That's my freshman class for non-majors. Then there's *Collectivism, Anti-Capitalism, and Anarchist Nirvana.* Doesn't the title alone send tingles up your spine? No? Okay how about this, my senior seminar. It's called *Autonomy, Class Warfare, and the Environmental Liberation Front Movement?* Now that's a winner." They all just looked at him. "Come on, man, don't tell me you guys haven't even heard of any of those classes? Jesus, how did you all graduate from college?"

"I have no idea," replied Lassiter, grinning. "But I do know that you and Clagge are as dangerous as Hunter S. Thompson on Chivas and shrooms with a handful of M-80s and a loaded twelve gauge outside the Woody Creek Tavern. I always thought I was way out there, but compared to *you guys*, I realize that I am almost completely normal."

"I concur wholeheartedly," said Bermolito. "Listen, Nick, in addition to these two totally irresponsible maniacs, you're going to need a computer guru, which I've been successfully pretending to be for some years now." He smiled with geeky awkwardness as he pushed up his thick-framed, Khalib Gatez-brand glasses, which had broken in two places and were being held together by black electrician's tape. "Seriously, we should start by taking a look at your emails to this Benedictis fellow. I think that's the best place to start."

"Well, well, well, if it isn't Nick Lassiter and his Three Stooges," interjected a new voice.

He turned to see Jason Cornwall with Alexandra on his arm, looking embarrassed to see them for the second time of the night. The sight of Cornwall and his ex together again sent an instant thunderbolt of anger through his whole body.

"What's the matter, Lassiter, couldn't you and your loser friends get dates? Why you could always troll East Colfax for some skanky bimbos with—"

The words never had a chance to finish coming out of his flapping mouth as Lassiter erupted with violent fury. He knew, in the microsecond before his fist landed hard on Cornwall's nose, that he should just walk away, but animal impulse overtook him—or did he secretly allow it to overtake him?—and suddenly his bigger and stronger opponent, the cheap-shot asshole who had cross-checked him into the lacrosse turf, shoved him from behind onto the basketball court, and kicked him in the shins a dozen times during soccer games from sixth grade through high school, was a human punching bag with Lassiter striking blow after devastating blow. Then the situation turned even more irrevocable as he head-butted Cornwall in the face, knocked him off his feet to the sidewalk, and fell on top of him like a pouncing lion. Within a matter of seconds, he had him pinned to the pavement and was beating the holy crap out of him.

"Have you gone crazy, Nick! Stop it!" he heard Alexandra scream.

But he couldn't stop, or maybe he didn't want to stop, as his fists struck satisfying blow after blow after blow. For the first time in his life, he felt like a lethal killing machine. It scared him, but it also made him feel deliciously alive. Like some sort of Viking warrior.

And then, he felt arms clasping him, trying to yank him off. But he was in such a state of fury that it took more than a minute for Squelch and the others to dislodge him. He stood there restrained by three pairs of arms, fuming and puffing and red-faced, sweat pouring down his face as the fallen Goliath at his feet moaned and greedily sucked in air. Cornwall had a purplish-blue hue like a newborn infant deprived of oxygen. Blood gushed from his obviously broken nose in a crimson torrent.

"I'm going to get you for this, Lassiter!" he shrieked, blood spewing from his flapping mouth. "You'll be fucking toast when my lawyers get through with you!"

"How could you, Nick? How could you?" screamed Alexandra. "No wonder I dumped you! You're a monster!"

Am I a monster? he wondered. And then he looked at his homies. Even Squelch, Claggebart, and Bermolito appeared frightened of him. Which was the one thing, after all the crap that had happened to him today, that truly crushed him.

"I'm sorry," was all he said, and he walked unsteadily to his car.

CHAPTER 3

WHEN HE REACHED HIS LOFT, he grabbed a fresh Fat Tire, wrapped an ice bag around his bloodied knuckles, cranked up Eddie Vedder's *Hard Sun*, and stepped up to the window looking out onto a sweeping view of Lower Downtown and, beyond, the towering Rocky Mountains, silhouetted against a pregnant moon. The wind whistling along the railroad tracks rose up and gently stirred the glass. He stood there looking out at the winking lights of the city in silence, wondering how his life had been turned upside down so quickly.

Was there a reason God was somehow punishing him? Or was it a simple twist of fate? Or how about a case of plain old bad luck? Did he somehow deserve this shitstorm his life had suddenly become? Was he paying penance for some past wrong he had inflicted on a classmate or his pet turtle Alfred E. Neuman that he had lost when he was nine? Or how about Natalie? As Squelch had said, she had been a definite *keeper*—and yet he had completely screwed that one up. Was he getting his just desserts for messing up the best thing that had ever happened to him?

His mind went back to the fight.

"How could you, Nick? How could you?" he vividly relived Alexandra screaming at him, her lips quivering with outrage. *"No wonder I dumped you! You're a monster!"*

The painful truth was that she was right: he was a fucking monster. The way he had torn into Cornwall, like a demon possessed, was not something that a normal human did; maybe when Neanderthals were smashing Cro-Magnons in the head with spiked war clubs, but certainly not in the twenty-first century where people reveled in fighting their enemies, real and imagined, anonymously from afar via fiber-optic cable. Even he was stunned by the violent fury, the buried rage that had exploded from deep inside him and found daylight through his fists. They were weapons he didn't even know he had, and it was almost as if they hadn't belonged to him, but to someone else, Mike Tyson or Rocky Marciano perhaps. At least for two primeval minutes that had seemed a lot longer. He shouldn't have lost his self-control like that; Cornwall would, no doubt, press charges and the police would show up any minute to arrest him and haul his ass off to jail.

He was looking at assault and battery, probably two years minimum, even with good behavior. He would come out ten times worse than when he went in; if he wasn't a goddamned monster now, he most definitely would be then.

He was startled by the bleep of his intercom. Jesus, were the cops here already? With resignation, he realized that he should probably just give himself up peacefully.

He went to the intercom and pressed the button. "I surrender, officers. I'm coming down."

"*Surrender?* We're not the cops, you dumb fuck! It's us!" he heard Squelch roar. "Open up, we've got Beckett's new book!"

He felt a tingle of renewed energy, a modicum of hope, knowing that his buddies seemed to have his back and hadn't completely disowned him after all. He hit the button and, two minutes later, let them in. They were filled with frenetic energy as they elbowed and jostled their way inside. Claggebart was carrying a bottle of Don Julio tequila, two six packs of Boulder Beer, and a bag of commercial edible weed under his arm; Squelch was reading out loud from Beckett's book with a puissant gleam in his eye, like a minister at a pulpit; and Bermolito was hammering away at his tablet, a feat which the cyber-savvy multitasker was able to do whether stationary or on the move at any time day or night, as if the contraption was an additional appendage on his body. They immediately took over the living room like an occupying Napoleonic army, cracking open beer bottles and making themselves obscenely comfortable on the threadbare couch and side chairs.

"All right, here's the situation, Nicky," barked Squelch like General Patton as he closed the hardcover copy of *Subterranean Storm*, setting it down on the battered coffee table. "First off, Beckett's guilty as fuck. I've just skimmed the first hundred pages of this bad boy and it's more or less the same as the movie script. So the movie stuck closely to the book, which means that the script was optioned and sold based on Beckett's outline or an early draft. Second, Beckett's in New York this weekend and all next week to promote his book simultaneously with the early screening of the movie. So he's doing a shitload of publicity for the book as a movie tie-in, which means you've got a perfect public forum to hit him and hit him hard. Third, I've already contacted my lawyer, Peter Sturgis, and he says that the best approach is for you to—"

"I'm not going to get a lawyer involved," he cut Squelch off.

A stunned silence slashed through the room. Squelch and Claggebart stared at him as if he was crazy as Bermolito typed away at his tablet.

"Oh, don't be un-American," admonished Claggebart. "Of course a barrister is required. This is about vengeance, extracting a pound of flesh in the good old-fashioned American legal tradition, is it not?"

"I'm not suing anyone. I just want an apology."

The room again went anxiously silent.

"My God, Aliens really *have* taken over your mind," said Squelch, his mouth still half-open with disbelief. "Did they make you have sex with them too?"

"I'm dead serious about this. I don't want a dime of money. I just want Beckett to look me in the eye, admit what he's done, and say he's sorry. That's it."

Squelch and Claggebart continued to look at him in disbelief. The only sound in the room was Bermolito typing away at his Apple. His bony fingers fluttered across the keyboard like an army of tarantulas. Lassiter wondered if he was conducting a simple Web search, running software, or programming actual computer code as they sat there debating.

Claggebart tugged at his ascot and gave an exasperated sigh. "Well, that's all fine and dandy, Nicholas, if you happen to live in a dream world. But, unfortunately, the rest of us in this room live on a little planet called Earth and in a country called *Les États-Unis*. It is our country's proud heritage, not to mention God-given right, to proudly bear arms when we're mentally incompetent, make fun of our leaders on both sides of the aisle, and sue the holy crap out of anyone that pisses us off. Now, goddamnit Nicholas, where is your American spirit!"

"I'm not suing him. But I am going to New York this week and confront him."

"*Confront?* Oh, that's rich. You're just going to sashay on in to the Big Apple like Joe Buck and...*confront* one of the world's biggest-selling authors. Now, how in the name of St. Jude, the patron saint of lost causes, do you propose to do that?"

"He's right, Nicky, you've got to think this thing out."

"I have thought it out and I'm going to New York."

"You can stay with me at my hotel," said Bermolito, not even bothering to look up as he continued to hammer away at his tablet. "I'm going to be in New York on business Monday through Wednesday. Then I've got to be in North Carolina on Thursday and Friday. I'm upgrading the servers in our Manhattan and Charlotte offices."

Lassiter smiled. "You see? It's destiny."

Claggebart cringed. "The thing about destiny, boy-o, is...well, I don't actually believe in fucking—"

"Neither do I," interrupted Bermolito, "but I do believe in statistics."

"Don't be so cryptic, Mr. Geekmeister. What are you trying to tell us?" demanded Squelch, who had gotten hot and taken off his shirt to expose his six-pack abs, which he often did on a whim.

"I just ran a query on the twenty most recent litigation cases involving an unpublished no-name author suing a major brand-name author for literary theft. The no-name lost in every case and four of the cases were thrown out. Not one resulted in a financial settlement."

Claggebart devoured an edible in the shape of a gummy bear. "So you're telling us he should just give up?"

"No, I'm saying that if a big-name author steals your idea and massages it into something that can pass as being *just different enough* by slightly changing the plot, creating new characters, and the like, it's a virtual certainty that he's going to get away with it."

"That sucks!" rejoindered Squelch.

"Undoubtedly, but it's the way of the world. It doesn't matter if your case is strong or not. If the guy's a bestseller, he's going to get away with it. All you're going to get in return from taking legal action against him is a shitload of legal fees."

Claggebart shook his head in disgust. "I still don't see how that's possible. Where are you getting this from?"

"Multiple sources, so let's review. First off, Beckett covered his tracks.

According to Nick, he used some portions of *Blind Thrust* and discarded others. The characters' names are all different even though both novels have a seismologist and a scientific sleuth unraveling the earthquake mystery. Most importantly, Beckett's mechanism for the man-made earthquakes is different. Instead of deep well injection of liquid hazardous waste, he uses a special subsurface explosive detonation device used by major oil companies in geophysical exploration.

"But the most important thing, by far, is the new climate in these types of legal cases due to Tort reform." He nodded towards his tablet screen. "I just pulled this up. A new law was enacted last fall that makes the plaintiffs and their attorneys responsible for all legal fees and third-party costs if you lose a literary theft-plagiarism-copyright infringement case. The law was designed to discourage the little guy from making claims against big-name creative artists—bestselling authors, agents, screenwriters, producers, and directors—and to protect them from supposedly frivolous lawsuits. The only problem is that a large number of these types of lawsuits aren't frivolous at all. People, even entire countries, steal ideas every day. Look at China and Korea—they haven't had an original idea in decades. They steal everything from us and sell it outright or repackage it as their own."

Lassiter found himself nodding in agreement. "I'm not going to run the risk of paying hundreds of thousands in legal fees. I just want the Aussie to admit what he's done and apologize."

"Come on, Nicky, you know Rupert Murdoch Junior's not going to fucking do that," protested Squelch.

"He's right," said Claggebart. "Beckett and his agent, this Benedictis fellow, and whoever else is behind this will never admit a damned thing. What about your dad? Isn't he with the CIA? Maybe he could gather some dirt and threaten Beckett?"

"My dad is not with the CIA—or at least it's never been confirmed."

"Never been confirmed? That's a weird thing to say about your father, Nick," said Bermolito.

"Didn't you tell me he has an apartment in New York?" asked Squelch. "Why don't we stay there?"

"It's the size of a Mini-Cooper. And besides, getting my dad involved in this mess is absolutely not an option."

"What about Natalie?" asked Claggebart. "You don't think she's mixed up in this do you?"

Lassiter felt his breath catch in his throat. He had been wondering the same thing about his old girlfriend and one great love of his life. Could she be involved? Had she ultimately been the one to railroad him?

"I don't know," he said. "As I said before, she left Benedictis's agency right after my novel was turned down. She left to work as an editor with Excalibur Media in London for two years, but returned to Benedictis to work as a literary agent four months ago. I was surprised she came back. But he does pay really well."

"So she's in New York and can help you," said Bermolito. "Assuming she wants to.”

“I know how close you two were, Nicholas, but I’d be careful on this one,” said Claggebart. “I have a bad feeling she’s somehow involved. It’s just too much of a coincidence.”

“A modern day Mata Hari,” said Bermolito. “The intrigue grows.”

Squelch was vigorously shaking his head. “No way Natalie would do that. I swear, Nicky, you should have married that girl when you had the chance.”

The room went uncomfortably silent. Again, Lassiter tried not to think about what he had lost.

Eventually, Claggebart broke the silence. “You said she was the one who originally helped you get your foot in the door with Benedictis?”

“Yeah, like I said she got him to read my novel, but at the time I didn’t want her to reveal to him that we knew each other.”

“Why not?”

“I didn’t mind having a referral, but I didn’t want to use special contacts. I thought it might actually hurt my chances, or get Natalie in trouble, since we had had a relationship.”

“All I know is these bastards think they’re above the law and something needs to be done about it,” said Squelch with a determined expression on his face.

“So fly to New York tomorrow and confront Beckett at his book signing on Monday,” proposed Bermolito. He nodded towards his screen. “It says right here that’s where he’ll be. If nothing else, you’ll know for sure if he did it or not. The eyes can’t lie, not up close.”

“Wait a second, what are you saying?”

“I’m saying Beckett has a luncheon and book signing scheduled at the Excelsior Hotel in Manhattan on Monday. That’s two days from now. The Wednesday signing is sold out, but there are still tickets available for Monday at two hundred dollars per plate. And like I said, you can bunk with me at my hotel.”

“I must say a trip to New York could be rather exhilarating this time of year before the savage heat begins,” said Claggebart, thoughtfully scratching his chin. “Assuming, of course, that one has the proper seasonal attire.”

Lassiter shook his head. “You’re not going, Clagge. This is my bed and I’ll sleep in it by myself, thank you very much.”

“Like hell you will,” challenged Squelch. “If you go it alone, you’ll probably botch the whole damned thing. I’m not about to let you go all the way to the Big Apple and come away empty-handed. We have a stake in this too.”

“Yeah, how’s that?”

“You’re our best friend and we’re not about to let some Australian billionaire asshole-author steal from our homey and continue to be a hypocrite to his millions of unsuspecting, adoring fans. We’re going to expose the son of a bitch for the fraud he truly is. Remember Lexington, Concord, and Bunker Hill? Remember ‘Don’t fire until you can see the whites of their eyes’? Well, history is repeating itself, only this time we’re the Minutemen, motherfuckers. This is war, my fellow patriots, and we are going to rise up from behind the stone wall and shoot that bloated Aussie bastard’s head off! Give me liberty or give me death, that’s what I fucking say!”

"Magnificent hyperbole, Patrick Henry, but I'm afraid this isn't your fight. Besides, unlike poor, poor pitiful me you guys have actual jobs and girlfriends."

"Did you just say the word *job*?" gasped Claggebart. "Good Lord, please don't utter such a monumentally depressing term in my presence ever again. I might be inclined to faint."

"Schools out for summer for me. Libidinous coeds are nowhere to be found on the CU campus this time of year. And I'm afraid this old powder hound and Professor of Anarchy Studies needs to perform some pre-sabbatical research in Gotham. Call me crazy, but I'm going to the fabled city and I'm going to score an *I-Love-New-York* t-shirt."

"You guys have got to be kidding me."

"Do we look like we're kidding, boy-o?" snorted Claggebart. "Why I even insist on financing the bold enterprise." He withdrew his American Express black card from his wallet and handed it to Bermolito. "Will you be good enough to purchase four tickets for the Monday book signing?"

"It's going to have to be three. I'll be working that day, but I can rendezvous in the evening."

Squelch was beaming. "We're all in Nicky. There's no turning—"

His voice was interrupted by the sound of screeching tires down below on the street. They all dashed to the window to have a look.

Three police cars skidded to a halt in front of his apartment, red and blue lights flashing. The doors jerked open and six bullet-headed cops jumped from the cruisers. From the rear seat of one of the cars stepped Jason Cornwall and Alexandra Barrett, who pointed up to his apartment as she spoke to one of the policemen.

"Holy Jack D. Ripper, they're coming in hot!" shrieked Squelch. "I knew that little prick Cornwall would report you. But I didn't think they would get here this fast!"

Lassiter shook his head in dismay. "I shouldn't have done it. I totally lost it and now the game is up. Looks like I'm headed for a jail cell not New York City."

"Like hell!" snorted Squelch, throwing his shirt back on. "Did our great nation give up after the elite commando unit of the German Herman Goering Panzergrenadier Division destroyed Pearl Harbor? Hell no! We're going to N-Y-C—and that means all of us, goddamnit!"

Another police cruiser screeched to a halt out front, roof lights flashing, sending strobes of prismatic illumination across the street. Two cops hopped out and started for the front entrance along with the other group.

"Well, whatever we decide, we'd better do it quickly!" cried Claggebart. "They've got guns, batons, and pepper spray and they look like they know how to use them!"

Lassiter was torn. If he stayed here, he would be arrested. If he went to New York with these jokers, he would probably make a total fool of himself and they would all get locked away in jail without accomplishing anything.

"Which is it to be, Nicky? You've got to make a choice!"

"Staying here isn't a choice any more than a firing squad!" cried Bermolito, closing his tablet. "We'll make our getaway using the rear fire escape. It leads to

Larimer!"

Claggebart's eyebrows flew up. "Great Scott, how do you know that?"

"I just uploaded and scanned the building schematics! We can get to the street level in precisely 3.7 minutes!"

Lassiter hesitated. "I don't know about this, you guys…running away from the cops? This could affect the rest of my life."

Claggebart wagged an admonishing finger. "Now is not the time for wavering, Nicholas—now is the time for bold action. As the late great Lord Nelson declared, 'Five minutes make the difference between victory and defeat.' We must go now, boy-o!"

"All right, all right!" He crossed himself as they bolted out the door. *I shouldn't be doing this—may God help me. But if I stay here I'm screwed.*

They dashed down the hallway towards the outdoor fire escape, the sound of their running footsteps echoing off the walls. A young woman stepped out of her apartment with a load of laundry, only to be almost bowled over.

"Sorry, Janice, sorry!" cried Lassiter, grabbing her by the elbow to keep her from falling and gently guiding her back inside her apartment.

"Keep moving, keep moving!" cried Bermolito, prodding him along. "We have to hit the street in 1.6 minutes or the police will cut us off!"

They charged down the hallway, feet pounding like the hoofbeats of cavalry.

"I must say this is rather exciting!" pronounced Claggebart. "I've always wanted to be a fugitive from justice!"

"Be careful what you wish for, that's what my mom's always told me!" said Lassiter as they popped open the window and started scrambling down the metal stairs of the fire escape.

"New York City here we come!" cried Squelch in exultation a moment later as they touched down on the sidewalk with no sign of the cops. "Wait 'til they get a load of us!"

They dashed down Seventeenth. When they reached Larimer, they bolted across the street towards the parking garage where their cars were parked.

But all Lassiter could think was: *What in the hell have I gotten myself into?*

MONDAY

JUNE 3

CHAPTER 4

ARBORGAST ROOM, EXCELSIOR HOTEL
120 CENTRAL PARK SOUTH, NEW YORK CITY

CAMERON BARNABY BECKETT IV—who was counting on one day being *Sir* Cameron like his imperial father, the Lord of Perth—stood at the podium gazing at his customary adoring crowd.

He had just finished giving his rehearsed speech, and his worshipers sat at their exquisitely arranged dining tables clapping in adulation as an army of harried waiters darted to and fro serving espresso and deserts of tiramisu and chocolate mousse. The packed crowd boasted first-class authors, literary agents, editors, posh New York elites, celebrities, and devoted fans, but the vast majority of seats were occupied by a specific nondescript individual: the unpublished hack who foolishly dreamed of "making it big" and climbing to the top of the *New York Times* bestseller list, a freight-class dimwit just stupid enough to shell out two hundred bucks to listen to the Australian ramble on for an hour about how to publish that singular literary masterpiece, the blockbuster breakout novel that would land him or her on Oprah and secure a rightful place as a "published *Homo sapien sapien*" for all eternity. "There's a sucker born every minute!" Phineas T. Barnum is reported to have once proclaimed, and as Beckett stared out at his genuflecting audience, he knew it was just as true today as it was back in the great and cynical New York showman's times.

"Now are there any questions?" he asked pleasantly, keeping his eye on a nubile young woman with a Vassar-College-kind-of-look up front who appeared particularly smitten. Who knows maybe he could get her to come up to his hotel room after the book signing? At least then he wouldn't have to pay another $4,000 for a hooker tonight like he had last night!

The young woman raised her hand eagerly.

"Yes," he said, smiling down at her. *I want to ravage you repeatedly, you bookish little vixen. Crikey, I hope you're not a lesbian.*

"Mr. Beckett, what would you say is the single most important thing for a first-time novelist to do to write a great book that people will actually buy?"

Come to my room and I'll show you. Have you ever done it Aussie style? That's why they call me the Road Warrior, my dear.

"Uh, the most important thing is to get into high gear quickly and keep your tension level soaring throughout your novel."

"Can you elaborate further?" asked another audience member, an older balding man in a cardigan sweater who looked freakishly like Louis C.K.

"You've got to hook your reader right away. Grab his attention right from the opening page and don't let go for the next four hundred. My agent—the fabulous Anton de Benedictis who regrettably couldn't be here today—has hammered that concept into my brain for the last twenty-two years. Sometimes, I regret to say, I forget his sage advice, and when I do, believe me, he gives me a good tongue-lashing. Strordnary but true!"

Everyone laughed. He smiled winsomely, taking in the juxtaposition of the humdrum attire of the unpublished wannabes versus the lavish two-thousand-dollar business suits clinging to the supple bodies of the first-class movers and shakers in the audience, like silk sheets hung over priceless sculptures. Then he answered more questions, trying his best not to look bored after more than two decades of doing these stupid little publicity events. He delivered the usual jokes that made him appear humble and compassionate to the neophytes trying to break in, but it was nothing more than an act. The only thing that mattered to him was that he was one of the top-selling authors on the planet and everyone in the room not only adored him, but wanted, literally, to be *him*. When the question session was finished, the crowd showered him with hearty applause, amplifying his feelings of self-adulation but also self-loathing. After all, he was a total fucking fraud and he knew it.

It was then he noticed that a young man in the back had stood up.

"Excuse me, I just have one last question," the man said politely, looking a little nervous.

Beckett had been just about to sit back down for the book-signing portion of the event, but the young man was signaling to him and, unfortunately, he couldn't just ignore him. The fellow had a healthy, outdoorsy look about him and appeared to be coaxed by the two gentlemen sitting next to him. They were whispering to him in urgent tones, as if they were putting him up to it. Something about the three young men sent an alarm to Beckett's brain—was it their animated body language or the wild look about them?—but he forced himself to put aside his misgivings and serve up his most generous book-signing-event smile.

"Why I suppose there's time for one more question," he said, thinking he was doing the kid a favor.

"Yes, thank you," said the young man politely. "My name is Nick Lassiter and I was just wondering what gave you the original idea for *Subterranean Storm?*"

Though the tone was deferential, there was…something about the question and the person asking it that made Beckett's brain suddenly go all foggy. *Why the bloody hell is my mind not working and my body freezing up?*

"Uh, excuse me, what was the question again?"

His questioner's face remained neutral, reading like a blank slate. But he had the uncanny feeling the lad was up to something.

"My question is what gave you the original inspiration for *Subterranean Storm?* I'm a geologist and I was wondering how you got the original idea?"

The young man was probing for something, he was certain. He felt his face flush with guilt. Or was his imagination getting the better of him?

"Well, of course…of course I…I made use of…uh…many credible scientific sources of information for the novel."

"Oh, really which ones? I'm just interested in the original source material. It's kind of a hobby of mine."

With a feeling of dread, he noticed that the crowd was looking at them both intently. They seemed to realize that something unusual was happening, like sharks sensing blood in the water.

"Off the top of my head I can't recall the specific names, but...uh...I think there was a *Scientific American* article, or maybe it was *Nature*...or *Nature and Science*. I'm sure...I'm sure it was one of those."

"Can you please be more specific? If your tectonic focal mechanism for generating the earthquakes in your novels is based on geophysical peer review journals, then I would certainly like to know the specific citations. As I said, it's a fascinating hobby for me. Seismology and plate tectonics—great, great stuff. That is, if you happen to be a practicing earth scientist."

Now this was becoming both irritating and embarrassing. "No, unfortunately I...I don't know those things off the top of my head. But if you check my author's website or Wikipedia under *Subterranean Storm* I...I'm...I'm sure you'll find the answers to your questions there." He faked a polite smile, hoping that would put an end to it. "Well, if that's it, let's get to the book signing, shall we?"

But the persistent little stickybeak was still standing there like an immovable object.

"I just have one more question, Mr. Beckett."

He felt his heart pounding in his chest. "I...uh...I'm terribly sorry, but we really have to get to the signing."

"I'll be quick. I'm sorry, it's just that I've flown all the way from Colorado to see you. You know we all"—he gestured expansively to everyone in the room— "look up to you so much. It's truly amazing what you do for aspiring writers like me and all the other people here today." There were head bobs and nods of agreement from the audience. "It means so much to us all to see you in the flesh, to hear you describe your new, exciting book and all your great literary secrets. We're all just trying to soak it all up. So I hope you'll allow me one final question."

Beckett felt like Poland on the eve of the German invasion. The lad's voice was dripping with insincerity, but he seemed to be the only one aware of it as the crowd continued to nod and mutter in agreement. Nick Lassiter, Nick Lassiter— why did that name sound familiar? And then, he saw the little flicker in the young man's eyes and he realized that the bloody bastard knew—knew it all—knew the whole fucking sordid story of where *Subterranean Storm* had come from. In that revealing instant, Beckett knew that it wasn't his own face, words, or body language that had betrayed him—it was that the insolent little prick knew the answers before even posing the questions.

It had been a set-up all along!

He cursed himself for his mental lapse. The prickle of suspicion that had gripped him at the first sight of the lad now turned to panic. And yet, against his better judgment, he was curious to know what the obnoxious little Yank was about to ask. He certainly didn't want to be seen as timidly backing down in front of so many of his fans and peers.

"What is your question, mate?" he cheerfully acceded to Nick Lassiter's request, though he knew that he was most likely signing his own death warrant.

"Thank you, Mr. Beckett. Here's my question. Isn't the truth actually that you got the original idea for *Subterranean Storm* from my unpublished novel *Blind Thrust* that I submitted to De Benedictis Literary Agency over three years ago? Wasn't that your *true* source of inspiration, without which you could never have written your scientifically-challenged, copy-cat novel?"

The room went totally silent.

Looking out at the stunned audience, Benedictis felt himself freeze up. Like Hugh Jackman caught with his bloody trousers down.

CHAPTER 5

ARBORGAST ROOM, EXCELSIOR HOTEL
120 CENTRAL PARK SOUTH

"ALL RIGHT, THAT'S ENOUGH! STOP THIS RIGHT NOW!" shrieked David Sloan, Chairman and CEO of Excalibur Publishing Group, the renowned international publisher that had produced, vigorously promoted, and sold Beckett's last fifty bestselling novels, as well as orchestrated his last dozen Hollywood film and cable deals. *What the fuck took you so long, David?* seethed Beckett as Sloan turned towards Ruth Rothschild, the shrew-faced Excalibur publicist sitting next to him. "Go get Security right now, Ruth! Tell them there's a celebrity stalker on the loose! I'm calling the police!"

Sloan punched 911 and began jabbering into his iPhone. But to Beckett's dismay, Nick Lassiter was still striding towards him with an implacable look on his face, as if he would brook no opposition and was demanding a full hearing in front of the entire room.

Jesus Christ, this was a fucking disaster!

"Get the police! An unhinged man is disrupting our book signing in the Arborgast Room at the Excelsior Hotel!" screeched Sloan into his phone, his Waspish Upper West Side accent slicing through the room like a polo mallet. "He's physically threatening bestselling author Cameron Beckett!"

Finally, you incompetent twit, you're doing your bloody job. But how did you bollix everything up by allowing this stickybeak in here in the first place?

He wondered if he should just leave the room, but what would his legion of loyal fans say and where could he possibly go? Instead he kept his eyes fixed on Lassiter. The whole room was still in shock, every eye upon him and his opponent and no one else.

The young man continued to walk unwaveringly towards him.

"We need the police here on the double!" cried Sloan in a panic. "The stalker's name is Lassiter—Nick Lassiter—and he's threatening Mr. Beckett's life as we speak!"

Beckett wanted to command the young man to stop where he was, but his mouth and whole body had become immobilized. With everyone in the room staring at him, he couldn't bring himself to utter a single word.

It was Lassiter who spoke first as he came to a halt in front of the podium.

"You stole the idea for your novel from me and claimed it as your own. All I want from you is to admit that you did it and apologize to me right now. I know you were probably desperate or backed into a corner by your agent or publisher. So just tell me the truth and you will never see me again. Do you think you can do that? Please, all I want is an apology."

Beckett just stared at him in disbelief. Did this redneck idiot from Colorado actually think he was going to get an apology? My God, any sort of admission of guilt was a death knell, a fork in the road that would lead to public censure, or even worse, a permanently tainted legacy. He stood there, stunned, as Sloan continued to shout into his cell phone that a crazy stalker had taken the room hostage.

"You know perfectly well, Cam—you don't mind if I call you Cam do you?—that I am no stalker. I just want you to admit that you stole my book, *Blind Thrust*, and tell me you're sorry. That's all I'm asking and then I'm out of here. I may not be much of a writer, but I am a man of my word."

Still tongue-tied, he felt an overwhelming sense of desperation. But then he gathered his wits about him. The only face-saving course of action was stern denial. Ignoring the gaping-mouthed audience, he pointed an accusing finger at his accuser, hoping to turn the tables. His eyes blazed with feigned outrage.

"How dare you come here and ruin this book signing for me and all of these people? How dare you make such outrageous accusations? Just because you can't get published doesn't mean you can storm in here and create a scene by trying to blame me for your own personal failings. I'm sorry, but it's not my fault that you're a freight-class writer and your work isn't good enough to be published. What are you hoping to achieve in trying to embarrass me in front of my loyal fans and friendly peers? Is your goal to break into the industry by creating a public spectacle? You win hearts by great writing, Mr. Lassiter, not by trying to destroy other writers and manufacture excitement."

The young man gave a look of surprise and Beckett knew he had him off balance.

"Look, I understand how a person can be desperate for his fifteen minutes of fame, but this is ridiculous. This isn't *Dog Day Afternoon*, my misguided friend. This is not a public forum for you to invent lies and bring media attention to your imagined cause! I tell you, you are out of order, sir, and achieving nothing but making a bloody fool of yourself with these erroneous accusations!"

"But this isn't about me, it's about—"

"Oh, yes it is about you. You are a confused young man, Nick—I can see it in your eyes. Everything you've told us here today is a lie. You're desperate to be somebody—to be a *real* writer—and that's why you've come here to play the poor little unpublished-author card. But I'm telling you right now, in front of all these people, that you'll never get away with this...buggered-up travesty! Never!"

"You're a lying sack of shit, you Aussie fuck!" a voice in the back suddenly boomed.

Beckett looked up to see Lassiter's two companions charging towards the front. He gulped hard. My God, they were a curious-looking bunch: one of them had a pony tail and wore a tweed jacket like a college professor, and the other wore a ludicrous stars-and-stripes ascot and blue blazer that looked like something Austin Powers would have worn had he been born a bloody Yank. Dear Lord, could these idiosyncratic Americans be armed and dangerous as well? Everyone in this damned country, it seemed, carried a concealed weapon these days and blasted away at the slightest provocation.

"Stop immediately! You have no right to be here!"

"Oh yes we do—we all paid our two hundred bucks, though in my humble estimation your contrived little presentation wasn't worth one-hundredth of that!" It was the one out front, the one with the pony tail, who looked the most dangerous, but in a curiously academic sort of way. "You stole my best friend's book and thought you could get away with it! Well, you were fucking wrong, Crocodile Dundee!"

Suddenly, four hotel security guards charged into the room.

"There are the three troublemakers! Arrest them at once!" yelled Beckett, pointing at Lassiter and his two friends stomping up to his book signing table.

"No, you should arrest him!" yelled the one with the pony tail, pointing fiercely at Beckett. "For literary theft, copyright infringement, and plagiarism! He appropriated the architecture of my friend's book, *Blind Thrust*, and called it his own, goddamnit!"

Now the guards looked confused.

"No, they're lying! Arrest them!" screamed Sloan, pointing at Lassiter and his partners in crime. "They're celebrity stalkers and must be removed from the premises at once! Be careful, they're from Colorado—they're almost certainly armed!"

"We are not armed!" countered Lassiter. "We're just here for an apology because he stole my book!"

The audience was now up on its feet and murmuring excitedly, a low rumble navigating through the crowd, growing like a gathering storm. A handful of men and women up front began jeering and demanding for him to respond to his accuser. Beckett felt a desperate, sinking feeling in his stomach as several people glared and shouted at him.

"We're not stalking anyone! We've come here only for an apology!" protested Lassiter to the approaching guards in a loud voice.

Oddly, what pained Beckett the most was how honest and sincere the meddlesome little bogan looked. But thankfully, just as the room appeared like it was about to explode into total chaos, the security guards took Nick Lassiter and his two cohorts firmly by their arms.

"Come quietly with us, sir."

He jerked his arm away defiantly. "No, I haven't done anything wrong." He wheeled suddenly. "Do you really want to go this route, Beckett?"

The Australian again feigned a look of outrage. "You have disturbed the peace and made outrageous accusations. There is no option but for you to be removed from the premises and put in jail. What you have done here is an abomination!"

"Handcuff them! Handcuff them all immediately and hand them over to the police!" snarled Sloan, red with anger.

But more jeers and protests came from the men and women up front. The entire crowd was now on its feet, filling the aisles and emitting a steady roar of disapproval. Even the security guards looked nervous that a complete riot would break out.

"If you don't come quietly, we will have to handcuff you, sir."

"I'll go quietly," said Lassiter, and he looked again at Beckett. "But you and I aren't finished."

"Oh, you and I are quite finished, mate," said Beckett harshly. "I hope you have a good lawyer. You're going to need one."

"Nick, is that you? My God, what are you doing here?" a female voice suddenly interrupted them.

Startled, Beckett looked up to see Natalie Perkins, one of Benedictis's junior agents, who was supposed to pick him up after the book signing and escort him to his next engagement.

"Crikey, you two know each other?" he gasped in disbelief.

"We went to college together," said Lassiter, but by the way he was looking at her Beckett could tell it had been far more serious than that. "I'm sorry, Natalie. I should have called you before I..." The words spluttered off.

She stepped forward worriedly. "Mr. Beckett, I'm terribly sorry. Was he bothering you?"

"*Bothering* me? Why this publicity-seeking maniac has completely ruined the entire event. It's a total fiasco." He scowled at Lassiter. "I can't believe you two actually *know* each other."

Lassiter jerked his arm free from the security guard again. Beckett jumped back, suddenly fearful for his life. But he quickly saw that the troublesome lad wasn't after him.

"He's lying to you, Natalie," pleaded Lassiter. "I'm the one who has been wronged here, not him. You've got to believe me."

Beckett rolled his eyes as the security guard clasped his hand firmly around Lassiter's wrist. "Oh, that's what they all say when they're being arrested. I'm innocent, I'm innocent."

Again, the young man struggled to pull free, but two more security guards joined in and restrained him. "Don't give us any more trouble, sir. Just come with us and we'll settle this."

"All right, all right, you don't have to break my arm to get my attention." He turned again towards Natalie Perkins, pleading now with his eyes. "You've got to believe me, Natalie, I'm the one who's been wronged here."

She shook her head in dismay. "My God, Nick, what have you done?"

The guards began forcibly removing him and his two disruptive cohorts from the conference room. The one with the pony-tail was a handful; he kicked and screamed like a raving lunatic. *So much for going quietly into the night,* thought Beckett with a surge of triumph. How dare this lowly, unpublished hack and his incorrigible mates burst into his world of power and influence and ruin his book signing with these outlandish accusations? He would notify his army of barristers immediately of this unconscionable indiscretion and they would slap the insolent little shit with an injunction, restraining order, and whatever other legal land mines they could come up with in the next twenty four hours. Seriously, a man should know his station.

"Nicky, how could you?" he heard Natalie Perkins call out again as Lassiter was dragged unceremoniously towards the exit door. He saw that her face was flush with shock and outrage.

"Yes, *Nicky*, how could you?" he sniped sarcastically. "How could *you* indeed?"

And then, he watched with enormous satisfaction as four cops stormed into the room, seized Lassiter and his two partners in crime from the security guards, handcuffed them, and gruffly escorted them from the Arborgast Room of the legendary Excelsior Hotel.

Now this was truly top shelf. Maybe he would get that bottle of Veuve Clicquot champagne and a $4,000 hooker again tonight after all.

CHAPTER 6

MIDTOWN NORTH PRECINCT
306 WEST 54TH

NICK LASSITER stared out the window of the minuscule, glassed-in interrogation room and felt like a goddamned fish in a fishbowl. He had already been fingerprinted, photographed, and interrogated by both uniformed and plainclothed cops and was now waiting for…what? Another interrogation most likely. This time from someone higher up on the food chain. So far, no one had brought up his attack back home of Jason Cornwall. But how long before the cops learned about that? Then he would be totally fucked. Disturbing the peace, assault…what was next for him, attempting to foist a Ponzi scheme on some unsuspecting victim, armed robbery, or how about good old-fashioned murder?

Though he hated to admit it, he couldn't help but feel a sense of impending doom, as if he had somehow detoured off the road of normal, everyday life and steered into a world of desperate criminality.

Out of the corner of his eye, he saw a flash of movement in the corridor outside the interrogation room. The plainclothed detective who had questioned him earlier had reappeared and was talking to another plainclothed officer, an older skin-headed man with a puckered pink scar extending across his jaw like a policeman's badge of honor. They turned to look at him several times as they conversed; obviously, they were talking about him. Then the detective with the scar turned on a heel and entered the room, toting a spanking new Dell laptop. He sat down at the table, opened the computer, and typed away at the keyboard without saying a word for a full two minutes.

"You're in a lot of trouble, Mr. Lassiter," he finally broke the silence in a working class growl. It hailed from somewhere in the greater New York metro area that was definitely not Manhattan, the voice equal parts admonishing and casually flippant. "That is your name, isn't it? Nicholas Maxwell Lassiter of Denver, Colorado?"

"Yeah, that's my name and I already told the other two cops all of this."

"That may be, but you didn't tell *me*."

"Why am I in trouble? I haven't done anything wrong."

"Actually, you have. In fact, you've been doing a lot of dumb things, Mr. Lassiter. Like assaulting a man in Denver and fleeing across state lines. That is—as you no doubt are aware—a federal crime."

He gulped hard.

So the game was up: he really was going to prison to be ravaged mercilessly by a gargantuan, tattooed gang member.

"You're very fortunate the charges were dropped. It seems your *mother*—who I've just learned is a quite persuasive Denver lawyer—convinced this, uh, Jason Cornwall fellow to drop all charges against you. I must say, that's some mom you have there, Mr. Lassiter. A senior partner at Brooke, Kieger & Russell. Though I have to admit, I don't normally take much of a shine to those in the legal profession."

He was stunned. "My mother?"

"Apparently, she intervened on your behalf earlier today. You're one lucky S-O-B, kid."

So that's why she had left him four messages on his phone that, with everything that had happened today, he hadn't had the chance to listen to. He wondered how his mom had even gotten involved in the first place. Then he realized that Alexandra must have called her this morning and brought her into the fold. Maybe his ex wasn't so bad after all.

"The thing is, Mr. Lassiter, you made the mistake of coming to New York—my home turf, Kemosabe—and I'm afraid Mr. Beckett and Mr. Sloan are not as obliging as this Cornwall fellow. They are—how do I say this?—positively *eager* to press charges against you."

Lassiter looked at the detective. In the strong overhead lighting, the guy's bald-headed pate glimmered with white spots like distant stars.

"Who are you?"

"Detective Frank Stafford, Special Investigations."

"Can I see your official badge?"

"No, you may not."

He knew that he should have been intimidated by this guy, but he wasn't. More than anything else, he was angry that he seemed to be the one in trouble while the real guilty party—Cameron Beckett, the 'Aussie James Patterson' as the media referred to him on account of his mega-bestselling success—seemed to have gotten off scot-free.

"Special Investigations, huh. That must mean that you handle the most important cases—those involving celebrities, corporate big shots, or high-ranking government officials. Correct?"

The detective's puckered pink scar seemed to redden slightly. "Keep it up, kid, and I'll see to it that you have a one-way ticket to Riker's Island. It's a nice little hotel for the criminal element we have here in *the City*. You're from Oklahoma, so I'm sure you'll feel right at home."

"Actually, I'm from Colorado."

"Like there's a fricking difference?"

"They couldn't be more different. For starters, their capitols are seven-hundred miles apart, around the same distance New York is from South Carolina."

"Is that so?"

"Yep, and you might also be interested to know that Colorado and Oklahoma are as different culturally as New York is from South Carolina. I know that might be hard for a person from *the City* to grasp when all he or she knows about U.S. geography comes from a 1970s *New Yorker* magazine cover."

Now the scar definitely reddened. "Well, well, aren't you a regular sophisticate and wiseass all wrapped up in one? I guess this is my lucky day. Now, I understand you're a geologist."

"Unemployed geologist."

"Let me make a correction: *Unemployed* geologist." With a smirk on his face, he typed in the new information, updating Lassiter's electronic rap sheet. "This just keeps getting better by the minute. How long have you been out of work?"

"I already told you that."

"As I indicated previously, you didn't fricking tell *me*."

"The answer is a week. Are you really going to go over the same information as the other guys?"

"Probably at least a dozen more times. So are you married?"

"No."

"Homosexual?"

"Are you for real?"

"Why were you harassing Mr. Beckett?"

"I wasn't harassing him. He stole the idea for the book version and subsequent movie version of *Subterranean Storm* from my novel, *Blind Thrust,* without giving me the proper—"

"Where's your book published? I Googled it but couldn't find anything, not even on Amazon."

"It's not published."

"Not published? Then how could Mr. Beckett—one of the biggest-selling authors on the fricking planet—have stolen your book from you? Your *supposed* novel isn't even in print. So how did Beckett get his hands on it?"

"Most likely through his agent, Anton De Benedictis."

"And what evidence do you have of this?"

"My novel, query letter, and synopsis were written at least three years before his book came out. And there are more than a dozen events that appear in both his work and mine and in the same order. There are too many questionable similarities to be just a coincidence."

"So you flew all the way out here just for an apology? Man of principle, is that it?"

"Maybe I'm just stupid, Detective. Or maybe I believe in second chances, even for thieving assholes like Cameron Beckett."

Stafford kept typing, his eyes locked onto his computer screen. "It wasn't some sort of publicity stunt to draw attention to yourself?"

"That's a rather cynical point of view. But not, I guess, for someone who works for the NYPD. By the way, what am I being charged with?"

"Disorderly conduct."

"Disorderly conduct? For telling the truth in front of a bunch of book fans?"

"More specifically, breach of peace. And I don't like breaches of the peace taking place in my city."

"Breach of the peace, huh? Maybe here in the Big Apple, but not anywhere where the rule of law actually applies. Beckett stole my book, Detective Stafford, and if he had done the same to you, I'm sure you would be pissed off and want to do something about it, too."

"That's what lawyers are for and, apparently, you've got one in the family. I'm sure your dear mother the senior law partner will be more than happy to represent you. Hell, she'll probably be happy to do it *pro bono*. She can change your diapers, wipe your ass, and give you legal advice all at the same time. Now won't that be convenient?"

"Why I think it's you who are the comedian, Detective. Maybe you're in the wrong line of work."

The cop leaned back in his chair and blew out a heavy sigh. "Look, you don't seem like a bad kid—a little misguided, but definitely no dummy. But you're naive if you think you can come at an opponent in a frontal assault. Didn't you ever study your Sun Tzu?"

"Yeah, hit your enemy when and where he least expects it."

"That's right. But all you did was alert your enemy. That wasn't too fricking bright, was it?"

"Oh, so now you're helping me. Is this one of those cop-imparting-the-lesson moments like Sean Connery in *The Untouchables*?"

"I actually happen to like that flick—a lot."

"That makes two of us. An oldie but a goody."

"I don't think of it as old."

"I'm sorry, Detective, but that just shows your age."

"You know what I think, kid? I think you're a little too cute for your own good." His beady black eyes narrowed and his puckered scar throbbed like a snake. "I'm not fucking with you about Riker's. I will put you there in a heartbeat just to show you what the real world can do to you when you're young and reckless and have the misguided belief that the whole world is your oyster. Now listen up: I want you out of *my* city, got it?"

"You own New York City? Now that is impressive."

"You have until tomorrow to disappear. Or I'm going to slap you with a ten-thousand-dollar fine and lock you and your friends up for ninety days. That happens to be the most I can do within the letter of the law. But if you promise me that you and your buddies will leave—and don't come back for a very long time— I'll see to it that the charges against you are dropped."

"You can guarantee that?"

"I can guarantee a lot of other things too. But the rest of 'em are all bad."

Though the situation was deadly serious, Lassiter stuck out his chin defiantly. "I think I'm beginning to see what a Special Investigations Officer does, Detective Stafford. If it's your job to protect all of the scumbag movers and shakers in this spectacularly glitzy but nonetheless sleazy-ass town, then you must be one busy man. How do you do it?"

"This deal can be pulled off the table at any moment, so I wouldn't mess around."

"I'm not messing with you. I'm actually quite impressed. What you really are is a fixer, a mediator at the highest level of New York City. In a city where billions of dollars are at stake every day of the week, it makes sense that the NYPD would want to protect a brand-name, bestselling author like Cameron Beckett, even though he's not even fucking American. Because when it's all said and done, he's worth a half-billion dollars per year in revenue to Excalibur Media Group—and that is one multinational media empire that is not to be messed with."

Suddenly, instead of appearing hostile and sour-faced, the detective looked intrigued. "Beckett makes his publisher a half-billion dollars per year? You've got to be shitting me."

"He doesn't make the publishing arm of Excalibur alone that much. He makes the Media Group—the publishing division *and* the motion picture-television division that takes his thrillers and turns them into films, TV shows, and mini-series—a half-billion per year."

"So what's his take home pay then?"

"Around a hundred million dollars per year. Only one other author earns more."

"Yeah, who's that?"

"James Patterson. As the writer and creator, Beckett basically gets around twenty percent of the gross, with his agent getting fifteen percent of his total earnings. It's the publishing and the media groups—not the author—that make most of the money on his properties. But he still makes a shitload of money. So at least now it makes sense why you're protecting the bastard, Detective. Here endeth the lesson."

"And here begineth my lesson, wiseass. You are getting very close to that closet-sized cell at Riker's, kid. Is that really where you want you and your homies to end up? Because if you keep pushing me, that's what's going to happen. *Capiche?*"

"Is that a guarantee?"

"Lemmethinkaboutit. Yeah, that's a fricking guarantee."

"Then I guess me and my wayward amigos will be flying out tomorrow."

Stafford flipped shut his laptop and stood up, signaling that the interrogation was over. "*Arrivederci*, kid. Have fun back in Oklahoma—don't bother to write."

"It's Colorado—I'm from Colorado."

"Sorry, kid, but I don't see the fricking difference. But I was never good at geography. Now, get the hell out of here before I change my mind. Oh, and there's one more thing."

"Yeah, what's that?"

"There's a hot, young Jane Doe waiting for you downstairs."

Lassiter gulped. "Is that right?"

"Yeah, except her name happens to be Natalie and she's got some friendly advice for you."

He felt his heart leap in his chest. Natalie was here now? "What kind of advice?"

"The kind you'd better listen to. And I mean *really* listen."

"Is that all then, Detective?"

"No, there's one last thing."

"I'm all ears."

"I'm giving you one—and only one—chance here, kid. Don't fuck it up."

CHAPTER 7

CONSERVATORY POND
CENTRAL PARK

THE SETTING at Central Park's Conservatory Pond was picture postcard perfect—yet Natalie Perkins couldn't help but feel on edge. She was walking along the lake with Nick, whom she had once loved but hadn't seen in more than three years, since they had broken up. Which was ironic considering that she had been working for Nick's father, Benjamin "Austin" Brewbaker, for the past several months.

In secret.

The tension in the air was unbearable. It was as if they were randomly selected Internet daters—with nothing in common, accidentally linked by a computer glitch—instead of two people who had been serious for two years in college and lived together for nearly five more, first in Boston then in New York, following graduation. She couldn't believe she was furtively working for his dad, the head of the Russian Counterintelligence desk at the Central Intelligence Agency's National Clandestine Service, formerly known as the Directorate of Operations. If and when Nick ever found out, he and his father—her mentor and control officer—would have to have a serious father-to-son chat.

The early June sun shone down resplendently upon a flotilla of remote-controlled model yachts gliding across the pond. From the granite-lined banks, shrieks of delight came from children and toy hobbyists alike; and above the rolling, green, manicured lawns soared kites, balloons, and a squadron of famous Fifth Avenue red-tailed hawks. To the east, the Kerbs Memorial Boathouse shimmered in the late afternoon sunlight reflecting off its copper rooftop and the little model boat lake where Stuart Little, the beloved protagonist of E.B. White's classic tale about a mouse born to human parents, had skippered his fictional sailboat to victory. Beyond the boathouse, the majestic buildings making up Fifth Avenue's legendary skyline stood like sentinels along with a profusion of towering oaks, smaller cherry trees with pink and white blossoms, and clumps of birch and copper beech.

All in all it was an exquisite sight. But Natalie Perkins felt none of that, only a frisson of tension in the air, as she came to a stop and looked her ex-boyfriend in the eye. His two companions, Frederick Welch and Morrison Claussen, trailed behind them marveling at the statue of Hans Christian Anderson.

"In the long list of humanity's stupid ideas, Nick, this has to rank up there, don't you think?" she said to him as they took a seat on one of the boathouse benches next to a planter overflowing with perennials.

He nodded. "It's fair to say that significant strategic planning and flawless coordination were not part of the operation."

"Don't try and be cute with me. The only thing that stunt you pulled may end up doing is costing me my job."

"I can't even believe we're having this conversation. You know perfectly well that Beckett really did steal my book. If I had to guess, I would say that it must have happened just after we broke up and you left De Benedictis to work for Excalibur in London."

"I sincerely doubt, Nick, that Cameron Beckett *stole* anything. He's a fifty-time number one bestselling author. Why would he need to steal from you?"

"I don't know. Maybe because he also happens to be a drunken lout and cokehead."

"A drunken lout and cokehead?"

"Yeah, that became fixated on a promising original book idea from some lowly unpublished hack from Hayseed, Colorado."

"Oh yeah, right, like that's probable."

"I've read about Beckett's police blotter antics and dependency issues, Natalie. Don't tell me there's not more than just a grain of truth to what I'm saying."

"I think I'm talking to a confused and desperate young man."

"Is that so?"

"A young man who's willing to take irrational risks, for what purpose I don't know. You've always been that way. If it wasn't paragliding, swimming with Tiger sharks, extreme heli-skiing, or trying to climb the Eiger—I mean the Eiger, Nick, come on—then it was staying up all night partying with those frat-boy friends of yours." She pointed off at Squelch and Claggebart, who had moved on from the Hans Christian Anderson statue and were imitating a street mime beneath a giant Dutch elm tree. "I mean just look at them. They're never going to grow up. They don't even have real names. You guys live in a world of juvenile nicknames that I don't even understand. I mean Squelch, Claggebart, and Bermolito? What is that all about?"

"I've changed Natalie. I'm…I'm…"

"You don't even have a job, Nick. Is that what you call change?"

Again, they fell into uncomfortable silence. She stared out at the model sailboats cutting through the glassy surface of the lake, wondering how she could have ever loved him. Had he even grown up at all since college?

"Three years ago, your client stole my book and today I asked him to apologize," he said after a minute, his voice carrying an undercurrent of suppressed anger. "Getting that apology is the only thing that matters to me. That's why I'm here."

"You have no proof Beckett did anything."

"If you really believe that, why were you waiting for me at the police station? Even more importantly, why did you speak to Detective Stafford about me? Are you two friends or something?"

"That's not funny. I was…I was worried about you."

"Squelch thinks I should have married you. What do you think about that?"

41

She was taken aback. "Oh, that's a good one. As if I was waiting at your beck and call. Yep, all you had to do was ask me and I would fall into a romantic swoon. You guys will never grow up, will you?"

"Beckett stole my book, Natalie, and I want a fucking apology."

"Oh, I almost forgot I'm in the presence of Mr. Honor and Principle." She made her voice deep and authoritative, like a judge giving a verdict. "I just want an admission of guilt and a face-to-face apology, Mr. Beckett, sir, and then I will be on my merry way."

"He stole without giving me proper credit. That Aussie fuck may look like Hugh Jackman and be one of the world's biggest-selling authors of all time, but he's still a plagiarizing little shit."

"As I was saying, you lack just one crucial thing: it's called actual *proof.*"

"You want proof—I have plenty of proof. It's true that his characters are for the most part different, though we both have a scientist and a crime-solver with strikingly similar ages, ethnicities, and backgrounds. But there are at least a dozen story elements that are almost exactly the same, the language in more than twenty scenes was lifted directly from *Blind Thrust*, and then there's the timing. My query, synopsis, and full manuscript were submitted to Benedictis more than three years ago. I can guarantee Beckett didn't start his outline or first draft until after my novel was rejected. Ultimately, it's the chronology that provides the smoking gun. My novel came first."

"How do you know? You don't have copies of Beckett's drafts."

He smiled knowingly and she knew she was in trouble. "That's where you come in. You're going to get them for me."

She shook her head dismissively. "I'm not getting you a damned thing."

"Oh, so Claggebart was right. You are complicit."

"Fuck you. This is not a game."

"Why are you obstructing me from getting at the truth?"

She didn't respond, feeling all torn up inside. She didn't know for sure whether Beckett was guilty or not, since she had moved to London to take the job with Excalibur most likely around the time that he had begun *Subterranean Storm*. But she suspected that there was some merit to the accusations Nick was making against the famous Australian author. The truth was she did want to help her ex-boyfriend; but the other, more pragmatic side of her knew that such insufferable recklessness would only lead to trouble. She would probably lose her job, maybe even her whole career, or worse. After all, what he was so cavalierly proposing was going after one of the most powerful literary agents and authors in the world, both of whom were stolidly backed by the Excalibur Media Group, who would go to extreme measures to protect their long-term, multibillion dollar investment. Cameron Barnaby Beckett IV was a living, breathing gold mine and would be protected like Fort Knox.

"I can't believe I'm actually sitting here listening to you," she said. "You need to do what Detective Stafford told you to do and leave town. He's not going to give you a second chance."

"Did he instruct you to tell me that?"

"As a matter of fact he did. He's a smart man and a good cop."

"He protects 1% scumbags, Natalie, by keeping the little people who dare to challenge them at bay. He's about as noble as the Sheriff of Nottingham."

His eyes never used to blaze like that before, she thought. "When did you get so angry, Nick?"

"When your boss and his cash-cow client stole from me—that's when. I want my fucking apology and I'm not leaving town until I've gotten it!"

"If you go through with this, you're the only one who's going to be left without a chair when the music stops. Don't you see, this is too big for you?"

The challenge seemed to strike him like a punch to his stomach. "Too *big* for me?"

"Even if you took your case to court, there's a little thing called *scènes à faire.* Have you heard of it? You should have because it's your Achilles heel."

"All right, Clarence Darrow, enlighten me."

"It's a legal term meaning you can't protect or copyright information that is typical of a certain established genre and would, therefore, naturally follow from the narrative. Such as a gunfight or barroom brawl in a Western, or hacking a computer system, an assassination, or international intrigue in a spy novel. Based on established case law, most literary theft or infringement challenges lose on the grounds of *scènes à faire,* as well as on the fair-use principle. Check out Adair Lara, Lewis Perdue, and Vanity Fair 2006 on the Dan Brown *Da Vinci Code* case and you'll see what I mean."

"I told you I don't want to sue. I just want an apology."

"Well, you're never going to get one. You need to take Detective Stafford's advice and leave town. All of you."

She nodded towards Squelch and Claggebart, who had rolled up their pant legs and waded into the pond to untangle a pair of model sailing yachts that had crashed into one another. From the bank, two kids and their parents were laughing and cheering them on.

"I'm not leaving until I have my apology, Natalie. It's as simple as that."

"God, are you stubborn. You should listen to yourself, Nick. You sound like a Tea Party nut job. The world's not fair, or black and white. Remember, we learned that at Kenyon."

"Yeah, I remember. That's when I loved you more than life itself."

She felt a sudden swooning sensation. A lightheadedness, as if she was being swept off her feet, but not necessarily in a pleasant way. But Sweet Jesus was he still sincere and principled and good-looking! He blew away the vast majority of the creatures that tried to pass themselves off as men in this *Bright Lights, Big City* metropolis. Every guy who wasn't betrothed to another male seemed to be a hairy-chested, dark-haired Neanderthal who grunted *lemmehavethis* and *lemmehavethat* in that grating NYC dialect that, since she came from the Midwest, still physically hurt her ears. They were children in adult clothing who boorishly raved on about the Giants and Yankees and Rangers as if rooting on sports teams was more important than atmospheric oxygen and who had a dark five o'clock shadow at ten o'clock in the goddamned morning! With his laid-back outdoorsy vibe, hardy tan, and hint of blondish-brown stubble, Nick Lassiter had a rugged, adventurous, distinctly un-New Yorkish appeal that made her *want*—and want to run for

43

cover—at the same time. Damn *him* for looking so good!

"That was a long time ago, Nick," she said, suppressing her urge to reach out and kiss him on the lips, to salve her curiosity and return to the way things once had been, if only for a sensuous moment.

"It wasn't that long ago when we were still together. We only broke up three and a half years ago."

"Yeah, and I tried to help you get your book published. You can't call me a vindictive bitch—I was there lobbying for you after we broke up. For what it's worth, I thought *Blind Thrust* was a fantastic debut novel."

He looked sad for a moment and she realized how…emotionally serious…things had been between them. "I'm sorry I let you down, Natalie. I just didn't want to live in New York anymore. I like the open space, mountains, and endless sky out west. It's just not the same here."

"Well, I didn't want to live in Colorado. How could I when there's, like, three literary agencies total in the whole state?" She reached out and gently touched his hand, feeling all the old feelings rushing back, stirring her up inside. *Wait, I probably shouldn't have done that!* she admonished herself. "You've got to listen to me, Nick. You've got to stop this crazy witch hunt. Even if there's a grain of truth to what you say, it can only end badly for you. Just do what Detective Stafford told you and get on a plane home. The sooner you put this behind you the better."

There, she had said it. But did she really mean it? Or was it that, in her heart, she wanted him to stay? *My God,* she realized, *you still care about him, don't you? Oh shit.*

He said, "Is that what your boss Benedictis told you to say? You know that he's involved in this. Your golden-goose Beckett certainly didn't cook up this scheme on his own. "

She was so conflicted in his presence that she wasn't sure how to answer. She could see the pain in his eyes and it made her hate herself because she knew he was probably right. If so, then it stood to reason that the literary theft had happened around the time she had left De Benedictis Literary Associates and taken the job with Excalibur in London. Which meant that Benedictis and Beckett had most likely colluded together behind closed doors, stolen Nick's idea, and turned that idea into a blockbuster thriller novel, which, in turn, had been developed into a big-time Hollywood movie. Both the book and the movie were, at this very moment, making tons of money and would undoubtedly go on to garner hundreds of millions of dollars in profit globally. It was a travesty, but such things happened every day in both the literary and film industries. She knew they were part of the accepted collateral damage. It was virtually impossible to challenge success—the industry powers that be wouldn't allow it. As a veteran in the business, she knew that's how the game was played.

"Look Natalie, all I'm asking from you is to makes copies of whatever draft versions and correspondence you can track down at your firm on *Blind Thrust* and *Subterranean Storm*. Look them over for yourself and tell me what you think. If you don't believe that Beckett's version is a rip-off of mine then I promise to drop the whole thing. You're the literary expert and should be the final arbiter. But I need to know the truth."

"Do you realize what you're asking me to do? You're asking me to steal."

"No, I'm asking you to take back what is rightfully mine. You know Beckett stole *Blind Thrust* from me with your boss's help. Look, Natalie, there's no other way for me to know for sure how deep this all went. Don't you want to know if your boss is a crook or not? How do you know he hasn't done this to someone else? This may not be Benedictis's one and only time. He may steal regularly from the slush pile."

"I seriously doubt that," she said, but inside she was less certain. She knew that her boss was capable of a great many things that were not in the public eye. "I'm sorry about what's happened, Nick, really I am. But you just don't seem to care that I could lose my job. I signed a confidentiality agreement stating that I would never, under any circumstances, disclose information on our clients to outside parties. Anton's lawyers could sue me and then what would I do?"

"I understand the risks you would be taking, but I'm still asking you for this one favor. And I'm not doing it because we used to be together. I'm asking you because you're all I've got. I'm asking you because, at the end of the day, I need to know the truth. The drafts will answer that question. We have to hurry though because Benedictis, if he's smart, will probably try to get rid of them."

Suddenly, she felt in danger. Were they being watched? She looked around. Was there someone lurking in the trees or inside the boathouse shadowing them? What about Stafford? The VIP detective was not the type to mess around and probably had someone watching Nick to make sure he followed through with his promise to leave town.

"My God," she said. "I feel like I'm in *The Conversation* or *Enemy of the State* with Gene Hackman. We could both be destroyed by this thing and no one's going to be there to help us pick up the pieces."

"Are you part of this, Natalie? Is that why you're so eager to get me on the next train out of Dodge? Is that why you're refusing to help me?"

"Fuck you—I don't deserve this!" She stood up abruptly from the park bench. A pair of mothers with children shot her a glare for cursing, but she ignored them. "You know you're just like your father!"

"What do you mean I'm just like my father?"

"I mean...I meant from what I remember of your father. Just stop it, Nick...you've...you've just got to drop this whole thing. You're going to get not only yourself but everyone else in trouble."

His eyes narrowed on her. "Why did you bring up my father? You haven't seen him in years."

"Stop changing the subject, Nick. I can't help you."

He reached out and grabbed her by the arm as Squelch and Claggebart came strolling up in their rolled-up, now mostly soaked pants, carrying their socks and shoes in their hands. "Wait, Natalie, what is this about my father? What are you trying to say to me?"

"Just drop it, Nick—just drop it, goddamnit!"

"Sounds like you guys are definitely rekindling the old flame," said Squelch. "Are you going to throw rocks at one another now?"

45

"And afterwards will you be requiring the services of a romance counselor or a lawyer?" quipped Claggebart, fussily rearranging his ascot. "Luckily for you, I happen to have certification in both fields."

She glared at them both, feeling the blood boiling in her veins. "Get out of town—all of you! You don't belong here!"

"Sorry, Natalie," said Lassiter defiantly. "But I'm not leaving until I have my apology."

"Then you've signed your own death warrant—just don't expect me to be at the funeral!"

And with that, she turned on a heel and started back in a huff towards her office.

CHAPTER 8

DE BENEDICTIS LITERARY ASSOCIATES
DONALD TRUMP, JR. BUILDING, 1450 SIXTH AVENUE

"WHY DON'T WE JUST KILL NICK LASSITER? It sure as hell would save us all a lot of trouble. That's the way Baby Face would have done it."

Pointing up to the .38-caliber machine-gun pistol and bullet-proof vest that had once belonged to the legendary Public Enemy #1, Anton De Benedictis let the words hover in the air of his office, drawing out the moment like a master thespian. The über agent then calmly steepled his long, bony fingers and leaned back in his chair with a devilishly ambiguous smile spreading across his lean, hawk-like face. To his delight, his two guests seated in the chairs in front of his massive cherrywood desk—Cameron Beckett and David Sloan—appeared stunned by his pronouncement. They gave a nervous laugh.

"You're kidding, right?" said Sloan, Chairman and CEO of the Excalibur Publishing Group that depended on Beckett for more than fifty percent of its revenue. He looked at Beckett for confirmation. "He's kidding, right?"

Benedictis grinned. "Of course I'm kidding, David. Come on." But inside he was thinking *Am I though*? His smile widened. "Had you there for a second, didn't I?"

"Yes, you most certainly did." Sloan exchanged another nervous glance at Beckett and wiped a bead of sweat from his furrowed brow. "But I don't think this is a joking matter, Anton. These allegations that this *Nick Lassiter* has publically leveled are causing some consternation upstairs."

"So what, your bosses are edgy? They're always edgy."

"I have to answer to them, Anton, and right now they're nervous. That damned incident at the Excelsior is already out there on YouTube. This thing is building momentum as we speak."

"Tell them there's nothing to worry about."

"They're going to need more reassurance than that, Anton."

"Why's that? I mean, you're obviously going to get a friendly New York district court judge to issue a declaratory ruling that no copyright infringement has taken place and then file a defamation lawsuit against Lassiter and threaten to bleed him dry, right? He'll shut up quickly once you do that and this whole thing will be forgotten before the weekend. That is what you're going to do, right? Follow the standard playbook by going on the offensive and destroying the messenger?"

"I don't think we need to go after him. Boorstein and Bernstein are nervous, that's all," said Sloan, referring to the Excalibur Media Group, Inc. CEO and CFO that many in the Publishing Division sarcastically referred to as Tweedledum and Tweedledee. "You know how they can be. I just need the facts, Anton. Thankfully this Nick Lassiter fellow has agreed to leave town. But I still need to conduct a damage assessment to see what we may be looking at from a risk management standpoint."

"What the fuck do you mean you're not going to go after him? He's a raving lunatic. A common criminal who disturbed the peace and ruined the book signing. We didn't agree to drop the matter—that was your deal with Detective Stafford. I never bought into it."

"Come on, Anton, it was our call. The book signing was our event."

"I don't believe this shit. For a second, I thought you were talking about lightweights like King, Grisham, and Rowling—not Australia's answer to James Patterson. I mean, I don't think I need to remind you that the guy sitting to your right makes more moolah per year for Excalibur in combined U.S. and international sales than all three of the aforementioned wannabes put together. Only Patterson earns more and my client is closing in on him like a thoroughbred in the final stretch. The Chinese and Indians—they love Cam's books, read them like crazy. No one has come close to building up Asian readership like my client. So don't fuck with me, David. We can go elsewhere. As you know perfectly well, Simon and Schuster and HarperCollins are both offering more for my boy than—"

"Good on you, mate, for your advocacy on my behalf, Anton," politely interjected Beckett. "But I would prefer it if you didn't call me your 'boy' or talk as if I'm not even in the room." He gave a deferential smile before turning back to Sloan. "You see, David, all we're saying is that we can't allow this Lassiter fellow to dictate how we respond to the situation. He's already done serious damage because you and your people couldn't control the event."

Sloan's shoulder slumped into obsequiousness. "I know, I know, you're absolutely right. We should have had better security. My humblest apologies, Cameron. I promise it will never happen again."

Benedictis suppressed a gloating smile. "He's got a great point, David. It stipulates in his contract that Excalibur is to provide full physical protection during book signings and other publicity events—without exception. I think we're talking about a serious breach of contract here. How did these dangerous celebrity-stalkers get into the event so easily? That's what we both would like to know."

"Look, I know we screwed up, but you can't use this to gain leverage. I want to know about Lassiter's charges. Is there any truth to them?"

He felt his heart rate click up a notch: this was the reason Sloan was here and his response had to be handled convincingly. "None, absolutely none whatsoever," he answered quickly. "The charges are completely groundless."

"Groundless. Are you forgetting that I was there, Anton? I would be remiss if I didn't point out that there appeared to be some serious *heft* to the accusations."

"You have the gall to say that when you allowed three raving lunatics to break into my client's book signing and ruin the whole event? Just as it is the responsibility of the Secret Service to protect the president, it was *your* responsibility to protect my client. And you failed miserably."

Beckett nodded his concurrence. "He's right, you buggered it up, David. You let the situation get out of control and I had to sit there and listen to those vicious lies while you panicked. It took five full minutes before security arrived and order was restored. It was a very stressful situation for me, I assure you."

Benedictis watched as Sloan took a deep breath to steady his growing anxiety; after all, billions of dollars were at stake long-term, and if Beckett moved on to a different publisher, Excalibur would suffer a staggering blow. "Look, I understand how you both feel and want you to know that we have your back in this unfortunate matter. But I need the facts so we know how best to proceed."

"And we've relayed them to you, David. The charges are ridiculous. What this celebrity-stalker Lassiter claims are substantial similarities are nothing more than *scènes à faire*. It's that simple."

"So you're admitting that you did...*borrow*...something."

He held up his hands, irritated that Sloan was twisting his words. "Nobody borrowed a damned thing. I might have gotten the general story line from Lassiter's crap in the slush pile, but that's it. That's the extent of his contribution, which isn't jack shit. That's like plucking out a newspaper headline for crying out loud. It's fucking nothing."

"You're sure that's the extent of it?"

"Of course I'm sure."

But Sloan wasn't looking at him, he was looking at Beckett. "Cameron, is that true?"

The Australian slowly licked his blood-red lips. Benedictis had gone over the playbook with him for an hour before Sloan had showed up, making it abundantly clear that they could divulge nothing about how *Subterranean Storm* had actually been developed—even to their own publisher—or both their asses would be on the hot-seat and future advances, royalties, and electronic rights might be in jeopardy. So they had agreed to lie. After all, they were in this together; if one went down so would the other.

"Cameron, did you hear what I asked?" repeated Sloan.

"Yes, I was just thinking" he said, buying time. "The way Anton just described it is the way it was."

Sloan looked skeptical. "You're sure?"

Benedictis felt his heart hammering his chest. *Don't look so damned guilty, you pusillanimous Aussie shit!* Jesus, he wanted to reach out and shake him by the collar of his hand-stitched Versace business suit. *I made you what you are today, goddamnit, and you'd better not blow this!*

But thankfully, Sloan, despite his obvious skepticism, didn't press the matter further. "Well then, I suppose that's all I needed to hear, gentlemen. I'm sorry if I've appeared...nosy...but there are concerns at Corporate. I know you two are being above board with me, and I can assure you that Excalibur, most definitely, has your back."

You'd better have our back, David! We've made your company billions of fucking dollars!

Now that they had the ugly business behind them, Sloan seemed to relax. He crossed his pant leg over his one-hundred-dollar, patterned socks and sat back in his chair. "Will there be no end to these no-names coming out of the woodwork trying to ride the coattails of successful authors? These money grabbers just won't go away, will they? They tried to shake down J.K. Rowling and Dan Brown and now they have the audacity to go after you. It's pure extortion. But I guess that's the thing that puzzles me about this guy."

Benedictis felt something bad coming. "Puzzles you? How so?"

"The fact that Nick Lassiter doesn't want any money. He just wants an apology."

Again, he looked at Beckett and saw him make a nervous gesture. *Get a grip on yourself, goddamnit! We need the status quo to continue, so keep your mouth shut and don't muck things up with your stupid conscience!*

He looked back at Sloan. "Hell, it's just posturing. He's still a deluded no-name author trying to make a public statement out of some false sense of injustice."

"Yes, but don't you two find it strange that he isn't seeking some sort of financial compensation?"

"You're giving him too much credit. The guy is a complete—"

He stopped right there as the door suddenly flew open and in rushed four desperate-looking young men, one of whom was tall, bronze-faced, and long-haired. He looked like some sort of Greek God, Adonis or maybe Achilles, and Benedictis realized that he was staring at Nick Lassiter in the flesh.

He smiled inwardly: this was going to be fun.

CHAPTER 9

DE BENEDICTIS LITERARY ASSOCIATES
DONALD TRUMP, JR. BUILDING, 1450 SIXTH AVENUE

"WAIT, DON'T TELL ME," he said, jumping up from his chair and taking the offensive as his father the football coach had taught him, and taught him well, growing up in Hell's Kitchen. "You're Nick Fucking Lassiter from Dung Heap, Colorado, right? You're here to get your apology so you can fly back home tomorrow with a sense of accomplishment, a feeling of closure, right? And by the way how did you get past security and my receptionist? This is the goddamned Donald Trump, Jr. Building not the Dung Heap County Courthouse for crying out loud!"

He saw at once that he had caught his opponent off guard, and felt a delicious triumph turning the tables on him. There was no need to call security—no doubt they were already on their way.

"Oh crikey, it's him! It's Nick Lassiter!" cried Beckett as if he was staring at the devil himself, or maybe just Attila the Hun. "What are you going to do to us?"

Benedictis scoffed. "Why he's not going to do a damned thing. He's here for his apology, aren't you Nick? You're a man of your word, a man of honor, right? You just want your apology, right cowboy?"

The kid remained speechless and Benedictis knew he had him right where he wanted him. The only problem was his partners in crime weren't quite so easily flummoxed. One of them, a wild-yet-professorial-looking gentleman with a pony tail, had managed to fend off his secretary and receptionist, shut and bolt the door, and seal off the room with a heavy couch and credenza; while a second young man in an outrageous stars-and-stripes ascot had already posted himself at the window to scan for approaching police; and a third, nerdy-looking fellow with unusually thick-framed glasses that made him look like a young Roy Orbison was typing and scrolling away at his tablet, as if gathering critical information to be used by the intruders.

Jesus, these really were some crazy fuckers!

"Detective Stafford is going to be very angry at you, Nick Lassiter," hissed David Sloan, standing up from his chair. "What do you want, really?"

Benedictis grinned with bemusement. "I already told you what he wants. He's here for his apology, right Nick?"

Lassiter appeared to have recovered his composure. "Yes." He looked at Beckett. "I'm giving you a second chance to come clean." He then eyed Benedictis. "You, I'm giving only this one chance."

Benedictis laughed disdainfully in his face.

"Who do you guys think you are, barging in here like this?" demanded Sloan in his peevish corporate inflection. Urgent voices and loud knocking noises could now be heard on the other side of the barricaded door.

"Why we're the Slush Pile Brigade, boy-o," said the one wearing the tacky ascot and blue blazer. "Who the hell are you to question us?"

"You're the what?" howled Benedictis.

"The-Slush-Pile-Brigade!"

"What kind of name is that?" sniffed Sloan, wrinkling his nose distastefully, as if he had eaten an unpleasant batch of *foie gras*.

Benedictis gave a disparaging chuckle. "Yeah, that's got to be the stupidest name I've ever heard. You guys are a few cards short of a full deck, aren't you?"

"It is kind of a lame name," agreed Lassiter, looking at his three cohorts. "Couldn't you have come up with something a little more roguish and illustrious sounding?"

Ascot pondered. After several seconds, his face lit up. "Okay, I've got it! How about this?" Here he paused a moment, heightening the buildup. "We're the...the *Devil's Brigade!*"

Lassiter and his compatriots looked at one another and vigorously nodded. "Now you're talking, Clagge," said Lassiter. "That's us all right—we're the modern-day First Special Service Force!"

"First Special Service Force? Who the hell were they?" snorted Sloan, again wrinkling his nose.

"Only the most fearsome and elite commando unit of World War Two. Didn't you ever see *The Devil's Brigade*, the 1968 Hollywood movie starring William Holden and Cliff Robertson?"

"No. But I did see Holden in *Sunset Boulevard*, *The Wild Bunch*, and *Network*. Great films."

"You're telling me you've never even heard of the Devil's Brigade?"

"Is that a crime?"

"Yes, it is. It also explains why the literary industry is dying a slow death—you people don't know the first thing about history. The First Special Service Force was a joint American-Canadian brigade that fought against the Nazis during the Italian Campaign and Battle for Rome in 1943 and 1944. They were specifically trained for cold weather insertion, mountain combat, and covert operations behind enemy lines, and the Germans nicknamed them '*Schwartzer Teufel*'—the Black Devil's—because they would creep in at night with blackened faces and slit the throats of the Krauts. At Anzio, they became known by the Germans and the Allies both as the Black Devil's Brigade. And now today that's us, gentlemen. We are inheritors of a truly great legacy."

"I don't believe this," said Benedictis, shaking his head. "Are you guys on medication?"

"Of course not," cried Ascot. "The Devil's Brigade doesn't take medication except in the form of edibles and mild hallucinogens for purely medicinal purposes. As Nick just told you, we are an elite combat unit, and we are here in your office to do battle. So you had better treat us with the respect we deserve."

"That's telling 'em, Clagge." Lassiter gave a snarky grin that instantly produced smiles on the faces of all three of his cohorts. He then looked back at Benedictis. "As the *de facto* leader of this renegade outfit—and of course in the spirit of, and with deference to, the late great Bill Holden who in the 1968 movie starred as General Robert T. Frederick, the hard-fighting commander of the Devil's Brigade—all I want is an apology. That's the battle we have come here to wage. Come on, gentlemen, is it really too much to ask for a simple apology?"

Benedictis thought: *He is one principled son of a bitch. I have to give him that.*

But then he sneered: "Sorry, Nick. Of course, we'd love to help you and your fellow Brigadiers, but seeing as none of us here has done anything wrong, I'm afraid we're going to have to pass." He flicked his hand at the door, as if shooing away a pesky puppy. "So go on now, get on your flight, and don't even think about coming back here ever again."

"I told you I'm not leaving town until I have my apology."

"Um, let me see if there's a delicate way to put this. Fuck off!"

"Wait a second," said Sloan. "All he wants is an apology, Anton. Let's not make this bigger than it needs to be." He looked at Lassiter. "Unfortunately, we don't have time to prepare an official non-disclosure agreement. Would you and the Devil's Brigade here be willing to accept a generic apology without any admission of wrongdoing?"

"Who the hell is this guy, Alan Dershowitz?" cried Pony Tail, pressing his full weight against the barricaded door. On the other side, Benedictis now heard frantic banging sounds and yelling voices as his staff, or maybe it was Security, struggled to force their way into the room.

"No, sir, I am David Sloan, President and CEO of Excalibur Publishing Group. I think we can cut a deal and not have to involve a bunch of lawyers. Can you, Nick, accept my proposed terms of a generic apology? I assure you it will be delivered in—"

"Fuck that, David. Cameron and I aren't going to apologize. We haven't done anything wrong."

"Now just hold on a second, Anton. We need this problem to go away—and the sooner the better."

Beckett started to say something, but Benedictis cut him off with a chop of his hand and a look that said, *"Don't you even think about betraying me and giving in, you bastard! I was only helping you out when you needed a leg up!"*

The pounding on the door had grown to an infernal racket, and the literary agent could now hear security guards yelling, "Hold on, Mr. Benedictis! We're coming!" as they struggled to bust into the room. The pounding was so frenetic that Pony Tail had grabbed another chair and jammed it up against the barricaded door along with the couch and credenza.

Now the young man at the window wearing the ascot stirred. "Shit, our time is up—the cops are coming." He pointed down to the street below.

"Okay, we've only got only 3.4 minutes until they reach the thirtieth floor. You guys know the drill," said Young Roy Orbison, typing away on his Apple tablet. "If you're still bent on getting that apology, Nick, now's the time, buddy!"

"Anton and Cameron, just tell him you're sorry," said Sloan. "The last thing we need is another public spectacle. Just apologize."

Benedictis shook his head. "No fucking way. We didn't do anything wrong, and he's making all this up to get attention. He's a disturbed young man, can't you see that?"

"I'm not making it up, Mr. Sloan." Lassiter withdrew a padded envelope and handed it to him. "There's a copy of my query letter, synopsis, and manuscript in there with notations of all the places where Cameron Beckett plagiarized from my novel *Blind Thrust*. The infringements on protected material are listed in chronological order by the page numbers from both texts. I have submitted the novel along with a hard copy of *Subterranean Storm* to Dr. Howard Coltrane, Director of the New York Forensic Linguistics Institute. He will be performing a statistical and linguistic analysis to quantify the number and extent of infringements of protectable material. The package is sealed and will only be opened if I do not receive an apology before I leave tomorrow on my six p.m. flight to Denver—or, as Mr. Benedictis so eloquently referred to my home town, Dung Heap."

The pounding and yelling at the door reached an ear-splitting level.

The literary agent felt himself purpling with rage. "Don't take that envelope, David. There could be legal consequences...it's a setup...he's putting a gun to our heads...don't do it!"

Sloan cautiously drew his hand back.

Lassiter shook his head. "You're making a big mistake, Mr. Sloan. Take it. What have you got to lose?"

"Don't listen to him, David...it's some sort of trick...no one could possibly just want an apology... he's dangerous...don't fucking take it!"

The banging suddenly stopped and a woman's voice could now be heard. "Nick, is that you? You've got to listen to me! You can't do this, Nick. You'll go to jail!"

It was his junior agent Natalie Perkins. He looked at Lassiter, who had taken a step towards the door to listen. Following the debacle at the book signing, Beckett had informed him that Natalie and Lassiter knew one another; he had been meaning to confront her about it when Sloan had showed up unannounced. Well, she would have some explaining to do once the dust settled from this unseemly affair!

"We've got to go guys!" shouted Young Roy Orbison, snapping shut his tablet. "Our time has run out!"

"Wrap it up, Nicky! We can't hold them back any longer!" shouted Pony Tail, who, with the help of Ascot, was losing the battle at the door. It was slowly sliding open from the force of the growing crowd of people pushing on the other side.

"Are you guys going to apologize or not?" asked Lassiter with surprising calm, making Benedictis want to strangle him all the more. "This is your last chance."

"Hell no! Fuck you!" he screeched in reply.

"Well, I guess that's it then. If you change your mind, gentlemen, here's my card. I actually lost my job, but it does have my cell number on there. You have until six p.m. tomorrow."

Benedictis watched in astonishment as Lassiter handed a card to Beckett and Sloan. Then the kid tried to give one to him, but he threw it back at him. "I'm not taking that damned thing—you're fucking crazy!"

"Oh, you'll give in eventually. I'm sure of that."

And then, to Benedictis's surprise, the kid winked at him. *Winked!*

The pounding on the door and urgent voices grew louder. Suddenly, several pairs of hands poked through the crack and began to push aside the hastily erected barricade of furniture.

"All right, we're out of here!" cried Pony Tail, and he and Ascot shoved aside the heavy desk, allowing the frantic group on the other side to push their way into the room.

They were instantly blasted with pepper spray.

"Make way, make way!" cried Pony Tail, letting loose with a noxious cloud of the eye-watering chemical into the stunned faces of the two security guards up front.

The hallway dissolved into complete chaos as the security guards screamed and covered their faces, and a dozen employees scrambled to get out of the way. Benedictis watched with astonishment as the four young men quickly parted through the crowd with military precision, following in the path created by Pony Tail and Ascot out front as they sprayed an offensive cloud that scattered the hall like Moses parting the Red Sea.

To his left, he saw Natalie Perkins dashing to get out of the way from the spray, yelling, "How could you, Nick? I told you to leave town, damn you! How could you?"

"I told you I want my apology!" Lassiter fired back at her.

"Well, you're never going to get it like this! I can't believe what you've done!"

"I'll succeed, you'll see! I'm going to get what I came here for!" he cried, and Benedictis could tell that he meant it. The kid was one fiercely principled and determined son of a bitch—he had to give the little fucker that.

"Cheerio, literary chaps!" Ascot waved a jaunty goodbye and then suddenly the four Devil's Brigadiers were making a mad dash down the hallway for the elevators.

"You'll never make it out of the building, you bastards!" cried Benedictis. "You haven't got a chance! You're going to jail!"

And then, he heard the fire alarm go off and the ceiling sprinklers came on, showering him and everyone else with a wet spray.

CHAPTER 10

LANGLEY WAS AS QUIET AS A MAUSOLEUM. There were no hurried shoes scuffling down the hallways, no urgent voices scratching over the intercom, no telephones ringing in shrill unison, no anxious fingers flying across state-of-the-art computer keyboards. Even though it was broad daylight, tendrils of silence reached out to every room of the CIA headquarters, lending a sepulchral aura to the cavernous, military-like compound. Langley, Virginia, after all, didn't officially exist. Aerial photographs showed a balloon-shaped collection of buildings, towers, parking areas, lawns, woods, and a helipad bordering the serpentine Potomac. Despite this seemingly irrefutable evidence, there was no actual physical location bearing the prominent name known by every member of the U.S. and international intelligence community. Langley simply was—like a shark lurking beneath the surface.

Standing in a control room that smelled of stale air and bitter coffee, Benjamin "Austin" Brewbaker, whom everyone called by his middle name, quietly sipped his cup of old school java with two lumps of sugar and a dash of cream. His mind was impervious to the vacuum of silence as he gazed at a large color monitor, which at the moment showed nothing except wavy static. But the Director of the Russian Counterintelligence Desk, Counterintelligence Center, Central Eurasia Division of the CIA's National Clandestine Service (NCS) knew that an important transmission would be coming in at any moment.

He felt expectancy in the air.

Outside the sound-proofed walls of the windowless room, a slashing wind assaulted the building, pushing rain sideways amid thunder that boomed like a volley of musketry. Sturdy oak trees bearing closed-circuit television cameras groaned and rattled under the furious wind while scrawny weeping cherries and magnolias twisted about like pulled taffy. Brewbaker was deaf to the storm and blind to the security guards making their rounds as they dutifully patrolled the double chain-link fence topped with barbed wire surrounding the compound. With the collars of their jackets pulled up against the rain and their sniffing guard dogs on leashes leading the way, the sentries fought the foul weather with every stride as they trudged past signs bearing the standard "U.S. Government Property, No Trespassing."

Suddenly, the wavy lines disappeared on the screen and, in its place, an image of a well-appointed business office appeared along with a running time stamp in the upper left hand corner. A technician clicked away at his computer keyboard and the image began to roll at regular speed. Four young men in their late twenties to early thirties—who looked like typical millennial oddballs from an Indie Hollywood film—suddenly burst into the office, barricaded themselves inside, and appeared to hold three men in expensive-looking suits hostage, while one of the young men bantered on with the captives. As Brewbaker watched the exchange unfold, his secure coded mobile rang. He checked the caller ID and photo before turning to the technician at the screen.

"I'll take it from here, Daniel. I'll call if I need you."

"Yes, sir, Mr. Director, sir," and he left the control room.

Brewbaker took the call and spoke into his coded mobile. "It's funny you should call," he said with a trace of amusement in his voice. "I happen to be watching *your* son on my screen here at the office. If I'm not mistaken, he's about to get into a bit of trouble."

A stunned silence.

Followed quickly by a voice of outrage: "He's *your* son too, remember? And why does it not surprise me that you are in a control room in Virginia watching our son in real time when he is in the Big Apple? No wonder American citizens are paranoid about electronic eavesdropping and civil liberties violations."

"It's for a good cause. National security is at stake."

"Isn't it always with you? If I recall correctly that's the reason we got divorced."

"No, it was mostly because you threw cast iron skillets at me. Pots and pans I could have endured, but not cast iron skillets. They hurt like hell when they strike you in the head."

"Very funny, Austin. So you know where Nicky is and what he's up to. When did he call you?"

"About an hour before you. He actually called to ask my advice. He hasn't done that in years."

"So you also know that he assaulted Jason Cornwall in Denver on Saturday night and that I had to scramble to have the charges dropped?"

"I always detested that little prick Cornwall. He's just like his father."

"Yes, well we all know that the apple doesn't fall far from the tree. What is *your* son doing exactly at this moment?"

"Sorry, but that's need-to-know. I can't tell you without violating a dozen national security laws. But I can tell you that it is *slightly* over the top."

"You're scaring me, Austin. You've always had a tendency towards understatement."

"Don't worry, if things get out of control, I'll bail the kid out. After all, I work for the Company—our best perk is unlimited get-out-of-jail-free cards."

"You're still not exactly reassuring me."

"Okay, how about this. The New York skyline in the background behind Nick looks spectacular as a backdrop. It's a postcard-perfect day there. Not like here where it's raining cats and dogs."

"Are you going to be able to fly out of Reagan?"

"Yeah, flights aren't cancelled. I should be in New York by six."

"I still can't believe Nicky's on this little revenge tour. Honestly, I don't

SAMUEL MARQUIS

Brewbaker continued to watch the screen. His son was arguing some point with the subject—the illustrious Anton De Benedictis, who was so much, much more than just a literary agent—and Brewbaker couldn't help a little smile of pride that his son seemed to be holding his own.

"I think he's handling himself just fine," he said to his ex-wife.

"Now you're really worrying me. Can't you just put aside your national security protocols for one moment and tell me what he's up to?"

"I'm sorry, Vivian, but I just can't. However, I can report that if he keeps up what he's doing at this very instant, the little bastard will probably be in jail within the hour."

"Good heavens, Austin, you can't talk about *our* son that way!"

"He's more like you than me. I haven't exactly been around to serve as a role model for the past fifteen years."

"Seriously, what are we going to do about him? This Beckett-Benedictis copyright infringement case is a serious matter. I can't believe he was foolish enough to bust into Cameron Beckett's book signing. That took some proverbial balls. And now he seems to be up to more shenanigans. Can't you please put aside your precious Company protocols for one minute and tell me what he's doing?"

"I'm sorry, but I can't. But I can tell you that, while what he's doing is definitely over the top, it's totally justified."

"Justified? Justified how?"

"They stole his book, Vivian. You would be upset if that had happened to you, wouldn't you?"

"Of course."

"Good, then you understand why he has to do what he's doing. He told me all he wants is an apology. Can you believe that? He's either the most principled person on the planet—or the most naïve."

"Yes, but what are we going to do about him?"

"You let me worry about that. You're going to have to trust me, all right? If things get out of hand, I'll take care of it. Like I said, that's one of the advantages of working for the CIA: I have the authority to pull strings." He paused. "You know I've missed you, darling."

"You're not getting sentimental on me are you, Mr. Director?"

"No, I just wish you didn't have to cancel at the last minute and we could have had our little New York rendezvous. Instead, it looks like I may have to babysit our son."

"Well, when we do rendezvous next, I'll be sure to do something special for you. Victoria has no secrets. By the way where is Nicky staying?"

"The Hotel Elysée with one of his friends. He didn't tell me who."

"He's with Frederick Welch, Morrison Claussen, and Timothy Bermingham. Now if that isn't trouble with a capital T then I don't know what is."

"That's a motley crew all right. I may have to have a talk with not just Nick, but all of them."

"Nicky still doesn't know about us, does he?"

"I haven't told him anything."

THE SLUSH PILE BRIGADE

"Don't you think it's time we tell him?"

"I suppose we'll have to."

"Does he know you're coming to the city?"

"No, I haven't told him that either. You're right though, we do have to tell him about us. This sneaking around is beginning to feel like infidelity, even though it's with my own ex-wife."

"He'll probably be pleased to know we're back together again."

"Or, he might be angry that we've kept it a secret from him for the past six months. But we'll just have to deal with that when the time comes."

"I don't even want to know how you're watching a tape of our son, if it's from a surveillance camera or a public feed. But you have to promise me that you'll protect him at all costs."

He calmly watched as his son and his comrades-in-arms pulled the obstructions from the door, sprayed two security guards with pepper spray, and escaped into the hallway, scattering people left and right. Including Nick's old girlfriend and Benedictis's junior literary agent, Natalie Perkins, who, like her boss, represented so much more to Austin Brewbaker than she did to her unsuspecting literary colleagues. Nick and his partners in crime were dangerously close to a felony situation, if not already beyond it, but Brewbaker couldn't help but smile as he watched the hallway scene unfold like something out of a Charlie Chaplin movie.

"Don't worry. I'll take care of the kid, even if he is his own worst enemy. Now I've got to go—I've got a flight to catch."

"I miss you, you handsome devil. And be sure to look out for Nicky and those irrepressible cohorts of his. I have a bad feeling about this. Just like I did in ninth grade when they threw those snowballs at that RTD bus and it swerved out of control and decimated Mrs. Dines' crabapple tree. You do remember that one, don't you?"

"How could I forget? But don't worry, darling, I've got it covered. Bye." He punched off, smiled wistfully, and stared at the madcap chaos continuing to play out on the giant video monitor.

A fire alarm was now blaring and water was spraying down from ceiling sprinklers, throwing a mist onto the hidden camera in Anton De Benedictis's plush office.

CHAPTER 11

DE BENEDICTIS LITERARY ASSOCIATES
1450 SIXTH AVENUE

LITERARY AGENT NATALIE PERKINS was in her office drying off her soaked paperwork when her desk phone rang. She nearly jumped out of her seat. My God, was she on edge! Thanks to Nick, her life had suddenly turned unbelievably complicated—and far more dangerous.

She checked the caller ID: it was her boss, Anton De Benedictis. The phone rang again. Her hand started to move towards it, as if by a will of its own, before stopping like a car at the edge of a cliff.

Did she dare answer it?

Before she could tell herself *"No!"* her hand moved forward the last inch and carefully lifted the receiver.

The voice on the other end launched in without preamble. "Natalie, come to my office immediately! I need to have a word with you!"

He hung up.

As she set the phone back down, her breath seemed to leave her all at once. She felt a momentary paralysis. Did he want to talk to her about Nick Lassiter, or the other more important—?

Damnit, stay calm. He couldn't possibly know about that. Or could he?

No, there was no way. That's what Brewbaker had told her. Even if her boss did have suspicions, he wouldn't be able to connect the dots and put everything together; and in any case, Brewbaker had said he would pull her out long before that happened.

Austin Brewbaker.

Nick's father—how crazy was that? But he was the reason she had become a spy—actually the proper term was CIA asset or non-official cover agent—shortly after she had returned from London to Benedictis Literary Associates. This time as a real literary agent instead of a trainee. He was a very convincing man, but even she had to admit that she had been easy pickings. Like Roosevelt and Churchill before her, she had long harbored a secret and obsessive passion for all things clandestine. It had started when she had done a sixth grade term paper on Mata Hari, the Dutch-German exotic dancer convicted of spying for Germany during WWI and executed by firing squad in France. As Nancy Drew had been drawn to solving mysteries, she had been fascinated by spy games. Culminating in her recruitment by her old boyfriend Nick's father, Austin Brewbaker, this past winter upon her return to New York from London.

But she couldn't worry about Nick or his CIA father at the moment. She had to concentrate her efforts on protecting her cover by continuing to lie to her boss's face and putting on a false front as she had been doing for the past four months. But unfortunately, her ex-boyfriend was making things more difficult for her. Or was it just the opposite? Was he, in fact, providing the perfect diversion, a timely distraction?

She took a deep breath to steel her jangled nerves. There was no alternative but to meet with Benedictis and see what he wanted. Before she had a chance to talk herself out of it, she rose from her chair and headed out the door.

She walked down the still-damp carpet of the hallway to his office and knocked on the door.

"Come in!"

The voice boomed like a howitzer and she took an involuntary step back. Then, summoning her courage, she turned the knob and opened the door.

Benedictis sat behind his desk, shuffling through his soaked paperwork. The massive slush pile he always maintained on his desk had turned to a mound of papery mush. When he looked up at her, she felt herself shudder inside. She had the uncanny feeling that he could read her mind, but she told herself that she was just being paranoid. Still, the man was, quite simply, larger-than-life. She found him utterly captivating.

Part of his appeal came from his unique physical appearance and manner: his silver eyes, neatly trimmed snow-white beard, and the cultivated way he carried himself gave off an aura of intelligence and erudite gracefulness that provided an intriguing contrast to his brusque, edgy New Yorker personae. Part of it came from his rags-to-riches authenticity—he had been born and raised in a two-bedroom apartment in Hell's Kitchen, before the neighborhood had become gentrified in the early 1980s. Here was no bombastic, preppy, silver-spoon Ivy Leaguer following in Daddy's footsteps on Wall Street. Instead, here was a genuine native son from the mean streets who had been born to a working-class Italian longshoreman father and Irish homemaker mother, a blue-collar kid who had played stickball in the streets and run among gun-packing Irish gangsters in the summers of his youth, a guy who had started with nothing and gone on to make something of himself by graduating with a Creative Writing degree from Columbia and, through his own grit and determination, had risen up to become perhaps the most powerful literary agent on the planet. He was a veritable encyclopedia of knowledge on every conceivable type of fiction, and was regarded, quite simply, as the best in the business, second to no one, a kind of Harvey Weinstein of the Right Coast literary establishment. But what truly set him apart was the whiff of danger that he radiated like the musky scent of an apex predator. That was the defining character that Natalie found most awe-inspiring—and terrifying—about him. And yet, surprisingly, he also had his gentle side. He positively adored his daughter Rebecca and younger brother Danny, and it was said that he would do anything for them. Anything in the world.

"Natalie, please come in and sit down."

She licked her lips, closed the door, and walked to the chair in front of his desk, noting that it had been dried off.

"Is there something wrong?" he asked her. "You seem nervous."

Looking back at him, she involuntarily shrank back in her seat. "Um...no. Everything's fine." She gestured to his mushy slush pile. "Those sprinklers really soaked everything."

"Thanks to your friend Nick Lassiter."

The accusatory tone resonated in the room and his silver-tinted eyes narrowed on her. She gave a little gulp of relief; at least now she knew the reason he had called her into his office and, fortunately for her, it was the reason of lesser importance.

"I'm sorry, Mr. Benedictis. I tried to stop him. I told him to leave town, but he wouldn't listen to me."

"There's an APB out for him and his friends. That was quite a little stunt they pulled. They're going to go to jail, Natalie. Does that upset you?"

"Why should it? They broke the law."

"Because this Lassiter fellow is your ex-boyfriend, whose novel *Blind Thrust* you tried to help him publish. Why didn't you tell me when I first read the manuscript that you two were lovers?"

She knew without looking in a mirror that her face had turned two shades of red. "We weren't going out then," she answered feebly. "We had broken up."

"But you didn't tell me, Natalie. You kept it from me, and I find that disappointing. What about now? Are you two back together?"

"No, of course not."

"Are you sure?"

"Positive. In fact, I hadn't seen him in over three years until today."

"But you still keep in touch? You're still close?"

"I'm sorry, Mr. Benedictis, but I believe that's my personal business."

"Once upon a time it might have been, but not anymore. Not when your ex-boyfriend terrorizes our top client and unloads pepper spray in the faces of my employees. He's going down, Natalie, and the only remaining question is, are you going down with him?"

She felt it suddenly hard to breathe. He had only rarely been gruff with her and had never directly threatened her like this before; she was unsure how to react. She couldn't help but wonder what had she gotten herself into in returning from London to work here again.

"I'm sorry if you've gotten the wrong impression, Mr. Benedictis. As I've told you, I haven't seen Nick Lassiter in more than three years and we don't keep in touch anymore."

His eyes bored into her like laser beams. "And yet you waited more than two hours for him at the police station earlier this afternoon."

How in the hell did he know that? Did Detective Stafford tell him? "Yes, to warn him to get out of town. I was just doing what Detective Stafford told me to tell him. I was embarrassed by what he did at the book signing. It reflected badly on all of us here with the firm as well as Excalibur."

"So you told your ex-boyfriend to leave, but instead he storms into my office, threatens me and my associates, and causes a mass panic? Is he just a poor listener, Natalie, or do you not hold any sway over him?"

"I...uh...I'm not sure what you're..."

"I want to know if you can talk any sense into him. The first thing he needs to do is surrender to the police. They'll take care of it from there."

"Mr. Benedictis...I...I don't know if I should get involved. I might just make things worse. And, believe me, that's the last thing I want to do."

He gave an understanding nod, but somehow it seemed contrived. "I apologize if I've frightened you, Natalie. But you know how important it is to ensure the continued success, and maintain the confidence of, our top client, Mr. Beckett. I can tell you that you are an important part of that team. And remember, I went out on a limb for you when you wanted to return here four months ago after your stint in London. You're a literary agent with several of your own clients now because I made it happen. I'm not questioning your loyalty—I just want to remind you of my loyalty to you and make sure that it hasn't been misplaced. It hasn't been misplaced, has it, Natalie?"

She felt a chill up her spine at his directness and couldn't help but feel as though her life had entered dangerous territory. What had Nick gotten her involved in? And what was she going to do about him? She couldn't just throw him to the wolves and pretend that their years together had meant nothing. But more importantly, what was she going to do about his even more challenging and demanding father? Thus far, Benedictis hadn't even intimated at that more critical subject. But how long before he did? Then she would be in an even deeper hole than she was now.

"I need you to call your ex-boyfriend, Natalie, and convince him to turn himself in." He handed her a business card. "That's his cell number. Go ahead and call him."

"You mean *right now*?"

"Of course, I mean right now. I need you to do this for me."

Or what? she thought. *Or you're going to chop off my head like that crazy Wall Street psychopath in the novel* American Psycho?

"I know it's a tough situation, but I have confidence in you. That's why I took you back after you left and promoted you to literary agent. Because I've *always* believed in you."

"I'm sorry, Mr. Benedictis, I'm just not sure—"

"Oh, come on, Natalie. Be a team player. You are a team player, right?"

"Yes, of course, I am. It's just that—"

"Wait, I've got an idea. Instead of using your cell, why don't you make the call on my phone so we can listen to it on speaker? That way we can mute and I can prompt you if necessary. What do you say?"

She felt a combination of nausea and panic. It was bad enough that he was forcing her to make the call in his presence, but to do it on speakerphone? Too many damned things could go wrong and her cover might be blown. If that happened then Brewbaker would literally—

"Mr. Benedictis, I'm just really not—"

"Nonsense!" He snatched the card back from her hand. "We're calling him right now. Here we go." Before she could object again, he hit the *speakerphone* button and started to dial the number on the business card.

Shit, I have to get out of this! But what should I do?

"Wait, Mr. Benedictis, please—"

"I'm afraid it's too late, Natalie."

"But wait, wait, I have an idea!"

"Phone's ringing, Natalie. As I said it's too—"

"If I talk to him now on your phone, he's going to recognize the number and know that I've been compromised. Wouldn't it be better if he thought I was sympathetically in his camp, but was really gathering information and keeping tabs on him on behalf of you and the firm?"

He looked at her, his mind working it all through.

Suddenly, the voice came through on the other end. "Hello, this is Nick."

Her gaze remained fixed on Benedictis. She held up her hands in a gesture that screamed, "Tell me what you want me to do!"

But he said nothing. A little bead of sweat formed on his forehead, but that was all. Neither of them made a sound.

"Hello? Who is this?"

Still, Benedictis said nothing. She held her breath, frantically waiting. Then his chair squeaked and, though the sound was not loud, it seemed to echo through the room like a depth charge. But still neither of them murmured a peep.

"Hello, who the hell is this?"

Suddenly, Benedictis leaned forward and spoke into the phone. "This is Anton De Benedictis, Nick, and I have one piece of advice for you. Surrender yourself to the police right now!"

There was a moment's pause then: "Come on, Benedictis, you know I can't do that. I haven't done anything wrong."

"That's not true, Nick. You and your Little Droogies have committed a slew of felonies. The police took down a full report."

"Did you do the right thing and tell them that you and Beckett stole my book?"

"Nick, Nick, Nick—you know perfectly well that no one stole your book."

"You're a liar. But lucky for you, I still only want only one thing: a personal apology. Do the right thing and come clean. The truth will set you free."

"Listen to me, Nick. You need to get on that plane back to Denver and put all of these crazy ideas behind you. Because if you don't, you're going to see serious jail time and be about a half-million dollars poorer. Think about it. Once the assistant district attorney, who happens to be a very close friend of mine, and a dozen lawyers from three different law firms get through with you, you are going to be one broke, pathetic creature. An untouchable really. You've got to know when to fold 'em, Nick. That's what your own lawyer must be telling you. You do have a good one, right? I mean, after what you've done, you're going to need a good lawyer. You're in a lot of trouble, my man. A lot of trouble. Natalie's very worried about you. After you pepper-sprayed everyone, she left here in tears. Now why would you go and do a thing like that to someone as sweet as Natalie? She was just trying to help you, Nick. She still cares about you."

"Is that so? Did she tell you that?"

"As a matter of fact she did."

"Well, I'm glad we could have this little chat. But can you do me one favor?"

"I don't know. It depends on what it is."

"Don't call me unless it's to apologize."

"Nick, I don't think you're getting the—"

But the line had already gone dead.

She watched with a feeling of dread as Benedictis jabbed violently at the *speakerphone* button, making sure it was off. He shook his head in dismay, and again she felt herself shudder. Unconsciously, her eyes drifted up to the antique machine-gun pistol mounted on the wall behind him. It was her boss's pride and joy, given to him fifteen years earlier by Cameron Beckett to commemorate their tenth *New York Times* bestselling novel together. The Aussie thriller writer had reportedly paid over a hundred thousand dollars for the gun and vest at a Sotheby's auction.

"Find him for me, Natalie," he said through gritted teeth. "Find him, win him over, and make sure he does no further damage to any of our clients or this firm. Do this for me and I can guarantee you will be amply rewarded."

"And if I refuse?" she wanted to say. But she knew better.

CHAPTER 12

CONSERVATORY POND
CENTRAL PARK

THEY SWUNG IN FROM THE WEST, crossing East Drive, parting through a swarm of joggers, and heading for the Statue of Alice in Wonderland before nosing south and veering towards a park bench in the trees overlooking Conservatory Pond. Back when he and Natalie had lived in their cramped, exorbitantly-priced loft in the Upper West Side, Lassiter had treasured this little nook of the city. It was quiet, peaceful, and felt safe. Which was what he and his mischievous cohorts needed right now. He took a seat along the far right edge of the park bench with Squelch, Claggebart, and Bermolito squeezing in next to him. From a leather satchel, Claggebart withdrew four 24-ounce cans of local P.J.'s Bronx Brew tucked away in brown paper bags. He then solemnly handed one to each person, like a priest giving final rites.

They popped the tops and started tipping them back in peaceful silence, watching the day's dying sunlight reflect off the surface of the pond like a shimmering mirage. A pair of well-dressed elderly gentlemen sat on the park bench next to them quietly conversing. Lassiter was reminded of the old Simon and Garfunkel song that his parents used to play about the two old friends sitting on a park bench like bookends, quietly talking with the sounds of the city sifting through the trees. It seemed as if the song had been written for just this place.

He knew that he and his buddies were in a boatload of trouble, but he didn't want to worry about the future right now. Natalie had called him four times in the last half hour—each message more frantic than the last. *Where the hell are you, Nicholas? Uh, right now I'm watching Stuart Little sail his boat across the pond and tipping back a cold one with my irresponsible friends.* Like his mom, she only called him *Nicholas* when he was in the doghouse with her.

But before he had taken his second swig, the two old men sitting in the park bench next to them began to argue, jarring him and his companions from their silent reflection. The one on the left was short and plump, the one on the right tall and rail thin, providing a distinctive and amusing contrast. They both wielded stout walking canes.

"What do you mean Tom Wolfe is better than John Irving?" bristled the thin one. "Why that's a crock of dog poop if I've ever heard one."

"*Bonfire of the Vanities* and *A Man in Full* alone are better than all of Irving's works put together," retorted the fat one. "You just have crappy taste, Ezekiel—and you always have."

"Oh, I have crappy taste do I? Well, how about you and I wrestle. Irving's a wrestler, Morton, which you probably didn't know since you're an idiot. How about you and I take our business on the grass right over there and settle this like men? And the winner takes all."

"Of course, you have to turn to violence since you're not clever enough to win an argument. You're a schlep and you've always been a schlep."

Lassiter found himself grinning. These old coots were hilarious; they reminded him of the two grumpy old men from the old folks' home in the novel *Water for Elephants* he had read a few years back. He looked at Squelch and the others: they were smiling too.

"*A Man in Full* may have sold millions of copies, but it sure as hell isn't art or literature. I mean who gives a damn about some schlub developer from Atlanta. At least he could have been from New York."

"*A Man in Full* is a great American novel. Compared to *Garp* or *Cider House Rules*, it is the Holy Grail of U.S. literature."

"You don't know what you're talking about, you dumb schlub. Reading Wolfe is like reading a bad piece in *The New Yorker*. Having to endure a single page penned by that imbecile makes me want to toss my cookies. It's not even entertainment."

"And I say John Irving is a pompous ass who wouldn't know good writing if it snuck up and bit him on the ass!"

"Hah, it's Wolfe who is the pompous ass! There's something ludicrous about a grown man who wears a white linen suit in all seasons—especially in goddamn New York!"

"Oh and Irving's the serious literary author, is that it? We'll you're an idiot, Ezekiel, and I've had enough of your idiocy!"

"Good heavens, these New Yorkers certainly take their literature seriously," observed Claggebart.

"I'll say," said Squelch. "This is fucking great. I haven't seen anything like this since Tyson versus Lennox Lewis."

Lassiter too had been smiling whimsically at the passionate exchange, but now he felt a hint of danger in the air. As if on cue, the plump man, Morton, stood up abruptly from the park bench and rapped his friend hard in the head with his walking cane, knocking him from the bench onto the pavement.

"Holy Joseph Pulitzer!" cried Squelch. "Did you guys see that?"

But Lassiter was already up on his feet and running to break up the fight. While shouting an obscenity, the fat man, Morton, again raised his cane to whack his friend in the head.

But the blow never connected.

Lassiter clasped the man's surprisingly strong right arm, seized the cane from him, and forcefully directed him to the grass, where he kept him lightly restrained. The red-faced old timer howled in protest as Bermolito and Squelch helped his companion to his feet.

"Goddamnit, Morton!" cried the rail-thin Ezekiel, wiping away the blood from his gashed skull. "Look what you've done to me! You've cracked my noggin, you dumb schlub!"

"You deserved it, you old coot! John Irving better than Tom Wolfe? Why

I've never heard such malarkey in all my eighty years!"

"Yeah well, you've got the police to answer to now! Look, they're coming for you, you dumb schlub! And I'm pressing charges!"

He pointed to the west. Lassiter followed his gaze and watched in stupefaction as an unmarked police car and four black-and-whites burst through a copse of massive oak trees, lights flashing. The menacing convoy came to a screeching halt on the walkway bordering the pond. Everyone, including old Morton and Ezekiel, stood there gaping-mouthed as Detective Stafford and a dozen uniformed cops jumped out of their cars and trained their pistols on the group.

Lassiter gulped.

"Put the…is that a goddamned walking cane?" shouted Stafford. "Put the cane down, Nick!"

He dropped it and held up his hands. Slowly, Squelch, Claggebart, and Bermolito did the same.

"Looks like they're not here for you, Mort. They're after these young bucks," said Ezekiel. He then made eye contact with Lassiter. "What you'd fellas do, rob a bank?"

"No, we just wanted justice done."

"Oh, young fella, you'll never get that in this goddamned town."

Stafford strode forward with an air of authority as the cops quickly surrounded him and his friends like a pack of wolves. The detective then shook his head with a dark expression on his face that was rife with barely suppressed violence.

"You should have listened to me, Nick," he said, moving quickly—too quickly, Lassiter realized as he felt his stomach squeezed like an accordion. "I thought I told you to get your ass back to Oklahoma."

"It's Colorado—we're from Colorado. And you gave me until tomorrow, sir."

"Sir? Hmmm, I like that. Sir? So now you call me *sir*. Yet when I tried to warn you that you were your own worst enemy, what do you go and do? You break into a respectable literary agency and make a mockery of the entire NYPD—from the lowliest rookie to the commissioner himself. I just can't believe that you're actually that stupid, Nick. So stupid, in fact, that I'm beginning to think that you're not from Oklahoma or Colorado, but New Jersey or maybe even Boston. You see, Nick, I hate New Jersey and Boston. I absolutely hate 'em. So much so that I actually detest every individual from either of those places. I know, I know, it sounds crazy, but the mere mention of the Swamp or Beantown makes me violently angry. Kind of like you and your friends, Nick. You make me violently angry."

Lassiter said nothing, his heart racing. His gaze darted warily between Stafford, his fellow Devil's Brigadiers, the cops with their pistols pointed at him, and the two old coots staring at the unfolding scene with wide eyes and open mouths. The guy called Ezekiel was probably thinking: *Maybe we shouldn't have come to the park today, Mort.* Looking again at Stafford, Lassiter felt as if a quietly ticking time bomb had been placed beneath his feet.

"Keep your hands up and don't move," warned the detective.

"We're not moving. As you can see, we're surrendering."

"Shut up, Nick. You have severely disappointed me and I may have to cut your nuts off to feel any sense of satisfaction today. Call me crazy, but that's how I feel." Then to the cop standing next him. "Cuff 'em and read them their rights, Lieutenant!"

The officer's eyes lit up with pure malice. "My pleasure."

Four grim-faced cops drove Lassiter face down into the concrete. The lieutenant then stepped forward, yanked out his handcuffs, kneed him hard in the spine, jerked his arms back savagely, and clicked the cuffs into the locked position, making sure that they were painfully taut. Lassiter was then yanked to his feet, searched, and read his Miranda while the same was performed with equal aggression to Squelch, Claggebart, and Bermolito. The cops then shoved them, Gestapo-like, towards the police cars.

Just before they were thrown in the back, Stafford circled the handcuffed group like a barracuda. Lassiter could tell something bad was about to happen.

In a sudden flash, the detective yanked out a heavy black baton and jabbed him hard in the stomach. He delivered the blow quickly, precisely, like a featherweight prizefighter throwing a well-timed jab. In the next instant, he clasped his palm over Lassiter's face as one might handling a cantaloupe, shoved him into the back seat of his unmarked police car, and slammed the door shut.

He then leaned inside the open window, smiling savagely. "Oh, I almost forgot. How do you like our New York hospitality, Nick? Are you having a nice fucking day?"

CHAPTER 13

THE NATIONAL
557 LEXINGTON AVENUE

ANTON DE BENEDICTIS was in a foul mood as he stepped into The National Restaurant at nine minutes past seven o'clock. He was already under tremendous stress from the situation with his brother Danny and the Russians—and now he had this thorny plagiarism issue and pesky Devil's Brigade to contend with. There seemed to be a painful truth to the old adage that when it rained it poured.

As he stepped through the entrance, he almost bumped into his old friend and fellow agent Trevor LeStrange, head of the Trevor LeStrange Literary Agency.

"Trevor, how the hell are you?"

"Good Anton, and you?"

"Couldn't be better," he lied, knowing that, in reality, he must look as rundown as lowly Fredo in Mario Puzo's *The Godfather,* his favorite book growing up. "I can see you're on your way out. I'm sorry I missed you."

"We'll have to do lunch sometime—and I don't mean in freight-class." He winked.

"How about the Four Seasons next week? You can tell me all about your new book, *Tension Every Nanosecond.* Great title by the way."

"Thanks, it was my wife's idea. Oh wait, I just remembered, I'm going to see you tomorrow night at your party for Cameron Beckett." He raised an eyebrow. "How are things going by the way? I heard the news about the book signing fiasco and the break-in at your office. Sounds like you've been busy with this celebrity stalker...what's his name again?"

"Nick Lassiter."

"Do you think he's crazy?"

"As a loon. That's why I'd recommend staying away from him."

"You know, he submitted *Blind Thrust* to my agency too."

Oh shit, there are other copies out there? "He did?"

"Two years ago. I thought it was promising, but a hair short in terms of dramatic tension. I really liked his Native American protagonist, but when I heard about what happened at the book signing and your office today, I'm relieved that I passed on the novel. If I had signed Nick Lassiter back then, today I could very well have not only another freight-class freeloader but a first-class nut job on my hands—and I already have a dozen writers under contract who fall in that unfortunate category. But is it true that all he wants is an apology?"

"Don't believe everything you read in the newspapers or on the Internet, Trevor. That's all I'm going to say. It's been good to catch up with you. Sorry, but

I've got to run. I'm meeting my brother."

"All right, I'll see you tomorrow night, Anton. Good luck with everything."

Thanks buddy, but you don't know the half of it. I'm a goddamned criminal!
He stepped inside the restaurant and the maître'd escorted him to his table. His kid
brother Danny was already seated, a purple shiner ringing his eye like a raccoon.
He was skinny as a scarecrow and looked like he hadn't gotten a wink of sleep in a
week. Benedictis felt a bolt of anger surge through him. He thought back, for a
nostalgic flicker of an instant, to their halcyon days running together through
spraying fire hydrants, tossing around battered pigskins and Mr. Spalding's, and
feeling up Ruthie Wick and Sweet Bobby Bilello during those long, glorious
summers growing up in Hell's Kitchen. Danny sure as fuck hadn't looked like that
back in those days. Back then, Benedictis had been known as Jimmy, his given
name; Anton was an invention that had come later, when he was getting his
Creative Writing degree at Columbia and working part-time as an assistant to a
big-shot New York literary agent whom, a mere five years after graduating, he
would go on to totally eclipse. He had been smart enough to know that no posh
literary agency would hire some mick-wop brat from Hell's Kitchen named
fucking Jimmy.

In high school, his younger brother Danny had been a sight to see on the
gridiron. The star quarterback had signed with Syracuse and even gotten looks
from Giants' scouts until he blew out his knee late in his senior year. Benedictis
had never been prouder of anyone in his whole life than when he had watched
Danny single-handedly win the state 5A football championship his junior year of
high school. The kid threw for three touchdowns and ran in two more on naked
bootlegs. Their drunk-ass, football-loving father had worshiped him too—until
Danny had gotten hurt and lost his full ride to Syracuse. From that sorrowful day
forward, his dad had cursed his very name and kicked him around like a worn-out
dog. He eventually threw him out of the house. That's when Danny had become a
monumental fuck-up, making one bad decision after another. Until ten, twenty,
and now thirty years had gotten behind him and he still had nothing to show for
his life, except a high school football championship trophy and a quarter-million
dollars of debt.

Benedictis stared in disbelief at his brother's black-and-blue eye. "Who the
fuck did this to you? Alexei Popov, or one of his goons?"

"Does it matter?"

"To me it does."

"Just forget about it."

"I'm worried about you, Danny. I'm worried about *us*."

"Don't be. No one ever said life was going to be fair."

"Yes, but someone should have warned us that it was going to be a fucking
shitstorm."

"You've done pretty well for yourself. Last time I heard, you were topping
out at over fifty million. If I had known that a person could get that rich peddling
books, I would have become a literary agent, too."

"Yes, but you never liked to read, remember?"

"That doesn't seem to have stopped you, Big Brother."

He gave a shit-eating grin and Benedictis couldn't help a brotherly smile in return. Even as battered and haggard as Danny looked, he still had, even in his late forties, a gleam in his eye and a natural handsomeness. As a younger man, he had drawn the opposite sex to him like a magnet and had bedded more women than Benedictis could count. He still had the looks and the touch, but it wasn't the same. Something had broken inside of him and he seemed fragile now.

A waiter came by to take their drink orders. Benedictis ordered a Beefeater double martini, dirty with three olives, his brother a P.J.'s Bronx Brew on tap and an appetizer of chicken wings with ginger sesame sauce and pickled Daikon. Danny was only joining him for drinks and a quick appetizer as Benedictis was having dinner with his daughter Rebecca—his only child, his pride and joy—whom he hadn't seen in a week.

When the waiter moved off, Benedictis said, "We're both in a lot of fucking trouble, Danny. Why did the Russians beat you up this time?"

"Gambling. I lost a lot. Again."

"That doesn't give Popov the right to have his thugs beat you up. I don't understand how you got mixed up with a fucking Russian mobster from Brighton Beach in the first place."

"Do we really have to go through this again? You know how it happened. I messed with the wrong guy at the wrong time and now we're both in a fucking pickle. But I'm going to make things right, Anton. I'm going to make it up to you, I promise."

Benedictis knew that would never happen, but he gave a little nod, seeing the sincerity in his brother's eyes. "It just seems unreal is all, like this is all somebody else's life, not ours. Here I am paying Popov off and squaring up your debt, so why the fuck does he keep pulling this shit? I mean, Jesus H. Christ, do you know how big the operation has become? We're talking tens of millions, Danny. The guy's making money hand over fist and he has to bust your chops?"

"I know, I know. You don't think I feel guilty as hell about what *you* have to deal with?"

"I'm not trying to make you feel guilty about it. That's not the point. You're my kid brother, goddamnit. I would fucking die for you—that's why I'm doing this. You and Rebecca, I would die for you two—but you're the only ones. My kid brother and my beautiful young daughter. But no one else."

"Not your three ex-wives?"

"No, them I'd throw in a shark tank."

"Not Roxanne."

"Especially not her. There's a reason that my fourth wife and I are separated, Little Brother. We hate each other. All I can say is thank God I had a prenup each time."

"Well, I appreciate all you've done for me. I'm sorry that fat Russian piece of shit Popov has sunk his claws so deeply into us both. It's a fucked- up situation, that's for sure."

"We have to find a way to get rid of him."

"Yeah, right. Like that's possible."

"We have to do something. We can't go on like this forever, Little Brother.

Or we're both going to wind up at the bottom of the fucking Hudson."

The waiter reappeared with their drinks and Danny's wings. They talked some more and then his brother had to leave. Benedictis gave him a check for ten thousand dollars to help him out. It was the least he could do for his kid brother who had suffered through so many bad breaks.

As Danny rose to leave, Benedictis said, "You can't gamble that away, Danny. You've got to make it last this time. Promise me."

"I promise," he said, but Benedictis could tell it was a sham. "Thanks, Big Brother. I won't forget this."

"I love you, Little Brother." He felt the emotion welling up in him at the sight of his once proud sibling, the former star athlete and popular chick magnet, reduced to such a fallen state. "We're going to get through this shit together. We're going to beat Popov at his own game. It's going to take some time, but we're going to fucking do it, Danny."

"Yeah, but we have to stay alive in the process. Say hello to Rebecca for me."

"Are you sure you don't want to stay and say hi yourself?"

"Naw, I don't want her to see me like this."

Benedictis nodded, his heart all twisted in knots with conflicted feelings. God, he wished his brother had had the life he deserved. It made him ache to see how low he had fallen. But ten grand ought to take some of the sting away. As long as Danny didn't gamble it all away in a week like he had the last time. All the same, he had to wonder if he was truly helping his kid brother. Or, was giving him money all the time just making things worse?

When he left, Benedictis ordered another dirty double martini and mulled over his troubled thoughts. He felt on edge. But even more, he felt a deep melancholy at the unfairness of life. Between the Alexei Popov blackmail situation and now this Nick Lassiter fiasco, he was a very troubled man. But he was nowhere near as troubled as Danny and that made him ache inside. He wished he had done a better job protecting him all of these years. He ordered another dirty martini, tossed it back, felt the black anger coming on. But then, fifteen minutes later, the sight of his daughter Rebecca made all of his troubles instantly disappear. It was as if a cool sea breeze had swept through the room. She had just graduated from his *alma mater* Columbia two weeks ago and he was so damned proud of her.

He stood up from his chair. "Hi, honey," he said in that soft, fatherly voice he used only in her presence. "I'm so glad we could get together."

"Hi, Daddy," she said.

She gave him a warm hug and kiss on the cheek and he somehow felt cleansed and purified by her sweet innocence. He beamed at her radiance. He especially loved that she still called him *Daddy*.

"Are you all right, Daddy?" she asked.

"Yes, sweetie. I'm just…I'm just so happy to see you."

"Are you sure? You seem a little…emotional."

"It was a tough day at work. I'm fine."

"Does it have to do with this thing with Cameron Beckett?"

He felt himself stiffen. "How do you know about that?"

"Come on, Daddy, it's all over the Net and I've gotten like a hundred tweets. Did your client really steal his book from that young guy?"

He suppressed his vexation. Fucking-A, was this thing getting so big that his own daughter was questioning him?

"No, of course not, sweetie," he said with a dismissive wave of his hand. "This guy Lassiter is an angry celebrity stalker. You know how it is. Everybody wants to be a *New York Times* bestselling author and they'll go to ridiculous lengths to achieve it. The guy's from Colorado. You know how they are out there in the west...they're fricking nuts. Remember those crazy parents a few years back that pulled that publicity stunt claiming that their son had accidentally flown away in a hot-air balloon? And how about that maniac who gunned down those innocent people at the Batman movie opening in Denver, and that crazy abortion clinic murderer in Colorado Springs? I mean, that's the kind of unstable people that live out there in flyover country. They're either lunatics, or they want their fifteen minutes of fame without earning it."

"But did Nick Lassiter really send his novel to your firm? I mean, did you and your client Cameron Beckett read his novel *Blind Thrust* and then adopt it as your own as he says?"

He struggled hard not to look guilty, presenting a mask of disbelief. "Are you kidding me, sweetie? Would your dad really do something like that?"

"I wouldn't think so, but you should see what the blogs are saying. They're saying that this is a classic case of a big-name author stealing from the little guy. Screwing him over just like the Wall Street thieves at Goldman Sachs and Lehman Brothers who destroyed the whole country years ago. People are angry about this: it's turning into an Occupy Literary Movement."

Jesus, was the situation really that bad? No wonder Sloan was in such a panic. Benedictis was not an avid Internet searcher or blog reader and tended to rely on more traditional sources for his news, specifically the *New York Times* and *Wall Street Journal*, the only two media resources he trusted. He was old school, but he was well aware of how swiftly social media could take over a story, how a career built up over decades could be destroyed within a single twenty-four news cycle. Uninformed, axe-to-grind social media was the new technology of vindictive persecution and career destruction. The new Scarlet Letter.

"I'm sorry to tell you, sweetie, that there is no big corporate monster or smoking gun. I think this is all just a simple misunderstanding that will blow over within a couple days. These things happen."

"I'm sorry, Daddy, I don't mean to ruin our dinner together. I'm sure you wouldn't do anything to hurt a young author who is just looking for a lucky break."

He winced inside, hating himself for lying to his daughter. *You're a fucking bastard Benedictis,* he told himself. *You knew three years ago that you were signing a pact with the devil and yet you went ahead with it. You stood by and allowed it to happen. Well, now Judgment Day has come, you dumb schmuck, and you're sitting here lying to your own daughter. The only person in the world besides Danny that you actually give two shits about. You are a sublime moron—*

and so is that Aussie toad Beckett for putting you in this position in the first place!

His daughter was looking at him. "Are you all right, Daddy? You seemed like you were talking to yourself."

He concealed his embarrassment with an amused smile. "I was? I hate it when I do that. I'm sorry, sweetie…like I said, I just had a tough day." He reached across the table and took her hands in his. "Let's not talk about all that stuff, honey. Let's just share a nice meal together and reminisce about the good old days. Did I ever tell you that, on the day you were born, you were the most beautiful baby in the whole wide world?"

She smiled at him. God, did he love that smile? "As a matter of fact you did."

"And did I also tell you that the day you were born was the very best day of my life?"

She rolled her eyes with amusement and again smiled that sweetly innocent smile of hers. Suddenly, everything seemed all right. "Only a hundred times, Daddy."

"Well, sweetie, I'm sorry but you're going to have to hear the story one more time."

CHAPTER 14

DE BENEDICTIS LITERARY ASSOCIATES
1450 SIXTH AVENUE

NATALIE PERKINS—the great-granddaughter of legendary book editor Maxwell Perkins who, some say, was the true creative genius behind both Hemingway and Fitzgerald—sat in her still-damp office at De Benedictis Literary Associates in the Donald Trump, Jr. Building trying to unravel a literary crime. It was after eight o'clock. All of the staff except her had left for the day. The whole floor was dark. The only illumination emanated from her computer screen, the vending machines in the lunch room, an overhead exit light at the south end of the hallway, and another overhead light at the north end above the entrance to Benedictis's office.

Outside her window, down on the street, neon lights flashed red, yellow, and green, blinking off her computer screen like fireflies. Through the double-paned glass, she heard the muffled sounds of honking horns, blaring music, police sirens, and other less resonant pulses of the city transitioning from day to night. The sounds of the asphalt jungle were pleasant to her, familiar. She had been raised in Chicago, and fittingly, she had always thought of herself as a city girl.

She had spent the last hour running plagiarism-detection software developed by Professor Louis Renard, a physics professor from the University of Michigan. She had used the program to check Beckett's various drafts and the final WORD version of *Subterranean Storm* to Nick's WORD version of *Blind Thrust* submitted to the agency three years earlier.

In comparing the documents, she had found, not surprisingly, that several descriptions in both Beckett's early drafts and the final novel had been lifted, in many cases word for word, from *Blind Thrust*. It quickly became evident that the world's second bestselling author had not merely borrowed the premise and plotting of Nick's novel, he had actually purloined virtually complete sentences and strings of key words in dozens of passages directly from *Blind Thrust*. In many cases, he had tweaked the wording and made a concerted effort to disguise what he was doing, but the algorithms in the software revealed that such changes were mostly cosmetic, altering nothing more than superficial details.

She kicked herself for doubting Nick.

What Beckett had done went way beyond simple *scènes à faire*, which was a legal nicety that cleverly skirted the issue and ingeniously protected big-name authors, producers, and screenwriters, allowing them to steal from more obscure, unpublished, or long-forgotten authors with impunity. It was true Beckett had not copied the novel word for word, but there were dozens of plot parallels and pronounced similarities in sentence structure and verbiage. It was now an indisputable fact that Cameron Barnaby Beckett IV—beloved and lionized by hundreds of millions of readers across the globe—had stolen his latest and greatest bestselling novel from Nick's unpublished work.

What she still didn't understand, however, was why in the hell he had done it? Or why in God's name Benedictis had allowed him to do it, or somehow failed to recognize what he had been up to during the outlining, writing, and editing process? She had not worked on the novel when she was either at De Benedictis Literary Associates or Excalibur in London, so she hadn't been a party to the story development or editorial process. Had Beckett become lazy after so many years of success atop the *New York Times* bestseller list? Had he encountered writer's block? Had he simply fallen in love with the unique premise? Or, had Beckett stolen the unpublished novel because he was struggling and desperate for a new sure-fire hit? She knew he had had a severe drinking and drug problem back then; and it was well known in New York literary circles that he still liked his single-malt Scotch, Peruvian flake, and high-class hookers.

But somehow Anton had to be involved too; otherwise, how did Beckett get his hands on a copy of Nick's manuscript? Beckett couldn't have acted alone, which meant that Anton had to be culpable as well. Had it been a collaborative process whereby Anton had urged him to shoot for something big and spectacular and, after rummaging through the slush pile, they had both recognized the enormous commercial potential of *Blind Thrust*? After all, over ten million copies of *Subterranean Storm* had already been sold worldwide in less than a week and the pre-screenings in the eight U.S. cities where the blockbuster movie was playing were getting rave reviews and generating favorable buzz. Hollywood insiders were already projecting the film would earn more than a half-billion worldwide when it opened nationwide in two weeks.

To her surprise, she heard a sound coming from down the hallway.

Was it a footfall?

It sounded like it, but by whom? It was unlikely someone had come back to work this late in the day. Maybe it was the cleaning staff.

She rose from her chair, opened her door, and peaked to her right down the hallway. She felt certain the noise had come from the direction of Benedictis's office at the end of the hallway. She pricked her ear in that direction.

But she heard nothing.

Still, she felt a vague presence and had the feeling she was being watched. Her first thought was that somehow Benedictis was on to her. Maybe he had software that tracked her keyboard entries. Then he would know what she had been doing tonight. But the more she thought of it, she realized she was probably just being paranoid.

She stared down at his office at the end of the corridor, telling herself that she was worrying over nothing.

But just to be safe, she returned to her desk, removed her 50-gigabyte USB 3.0 flash drive, and quickly copied all of the files she had been running through the plagiarism-detection software. When she was finished, she stuffed the drive into a hidden pocket sewn into her purse and began shutting down her computer. But it seemed to take forever to power down and she couldn't help but feel a growing uneasiness. She couldn't shake the feeling that she wasn't alone. It wasn't just a presence; she felt like she was being stalked.

And then she heard, or thought she heard, a noise down the hallway again.

Slipping quietly from her desk, she poked her head out her door and peaked down the hallway again. This time she saw a faint light coming from beneath Benedictis's office door, a hint of a glow, and she heard whispering voices.

They sounded foreign.

Her heart lurched in her chest. She felt terribly vulnerable and all alone.

Why were the voices foreign? It couldn't be the cleaning staff—the voices were too stealthy and the cleaning staff turned on the lights when they cleaned. It couldn't be Benedictis—he wouldn't be talking in a foreign language. But maybe he had forgotten something and come back to the office with another person, a foreigner? That seemed unlikely. No, the most plausible explanation was that it was not Benedictis at all, but someone else breaking into his office.

Could it be the Russians?

But why would they be breaking into his office? She didn't know the answer, but she suspected Austin Brewbaker would.

She listened closely.

The voices were low, mere whispers, but the accents she could tell now were definitely Eastern Bloc. She still wasn't positive they belonged to Russians, but they sure sounded like it. She also heard rummaging noises as if someone was searching the desk drawers, sifting through paperwork, or perhaps even tinkering with Benedictis's computer. Maybe it was Brewbaker's people and he had forgotten to tell her they were coming. That seemed unlikely as they wouldn't be speaking in Russian. Unless, of course, the CIA was into recruiting foreigners to perform break-in jobs these days.

Whoever it was, she needed to get out of here since she couldn't very well call the police. If it was the CIA and Brewbaker had ordered the penetration, she didn't want to muck up the whole operation by calling in the cavalry.

Grabbing her purse, she started moving down the hallway towards the fire exit stairs in the opposite direction of Benedictis's office. She wasn't about to take the elevator; it was situated too close to her boss's office.

Halfway to the fire stairs, she thought she heard the sound of footsteps behind her. She froze in the shadows of the hallway and, breathlessly, chanced a look over her shoulder.

No one.

She breathed a sigh of relief. But still, she heard voices coming from the office down the hallway. She started off again, moving quickly but stealthily.

She hadn't gone five paces when she heard the footsteps again, this time coming from close by. There was a branching hallway fifteen feet back, and with sudden horror, she realized that there must have been a third party besides herself and whoever was in Benedictis's office.

Had that been the presence she had felt earlier?

She turned abruptly to confront her stalker, but again, no one was there.

She was gripped with a sudden urge to run—to flat out fly down the hallway, dash down the fire stairs, and never look back. But she knew it was best not to panic despite her overwhelming, primal urge to flee.

She turned and started down the hallway again, moving more quickly but still resisting the urge to run. She told herself not to be afraid, but instinct told her she was being followed.

She began to walk faster.

To her infinite horror, she heard the noises again. This time the source was unmistakable: methodical, carefully placed footsteps directly behind her.

She turned abruptly. As before, the sound stopped.

She probed the shadows of the hallway. "Who's there?"

No reply.

Continuing to search the darkness, she still saw nothing but felt a tickling sensation on the back of her neck, as if someone was watching her. She wanted desperately to dash to safety, but at the same time she wanted to know who the hell was back there.

"Mr. Benedictis, is that you?"

There was no answer.

Heart hammering in her chest, she demanded sternly: "Who's there?"

Suddenly, far down the hallway, she saw two men clad in black leather jackets emerge from Benedictis's office.

They were both carrying guns.

"Halt!" one of them shouted in a heavy, unmistakable Russian accent.

Stifling a scream, she turned and ran as fast as her legs would propel her.

She darted down the hallway, drove her shoulder into the heavy steel fire escape door, and, just before dashing down the stairs, she glanced back to see if they were coming after her.

They were!

Slamming the door closed, she looked for something to jam the door with but saw nothing.

Her only chance was to try to outrun them.

She scrambled down the fire stairs, her pumps clattering against the concrete, resonating loudly in the hollow stairwell and raising a note of terrified urgency.

Five floors down, she heard the fire door bang open and looked up. A pair of scowling faces peered down at her over the railing, and in the next instant her pursuers began to frantically chase after her down the fire stairs.

Oh my God! Oh my God!

Feeling her survival instincts kicking in, she moved at breakneck speed, taking the steps five at a time and swinging herself around the hand rails like a parkour champion. Reaching the ground floor thirty floors below, she was panting heavily, covered in perspiration, and terrified out of her wits. But she knew that she had at least a couple of floors of separation between herself and her pursuers because she could hear them still scrambling down from above. Flinging open the door to the lobby, she called out to the security guard at the front desk, but saw that it was now unmanned.

Where had the guard gone? Had they done something to him?

Telling herself not to panic, she started to run past the bank of elevators towards the front entrance.

One of the elevator lights flashed green and a door suddenly opened.

Her heart thundered in her chest as a burly, goateed, middle-aged man in a crisp business suit—a man she had never seen before in person but instantly recognized from CIA and FBI surveillance photographs Brewbaker had shown her—stepped out of the elevator.

"Hello, Natalie," he said with a thick Russian inflection.

It was Alexei Popov!

Oh shit, oh shit! She felt her heart nearly explode in her chest. How did he know her name? And more importantly, how was she going to get away from him? Then she noticed that he wasn't wielding a gun and was too far away to grab her.

Survival instinct took over as she bolted past him and darted as fast as her legs would carry her to the front entrance, her feet flying like a magic carpet across the marble floor.

"Wait, Natalie!" he called after her in his deeply Russian-accented voice that carried an undercurrent of violence. "I just want to talk!"

But she didn't stop. There was no reason to stop for Alexei Popov, unless you wanted to end up in a body bag.

She heard the fire stairs door crash open behind her and the two armed men that had been chasing her, Popov's henchmen, suddenly emerged. Catching only a quick glimpse of them as they ran up to their boss, she shoved her way through the door and ran out onto the street, frantically waving her arms and screaming at the top of her lungs.

"Help, I'm being chased! Help! Help!"

A white Mercedes suddenly pulled up at the curb and the passenger window rolled down.

"Natalie, what are you doing here?"

It was Anton De Benedictis.

She froze. She didn't know which was worse: her crooked boss or the Russian mobster!

"My God, Natalie, what is going on? What are you doing here?"

"There are armed men chasing me!" she cried, still not sure whether she could trust him. "They're Russian!"

Dawning realization flashed on his face. "Quick, get in!" He flung open the front passenger door.

She hesitated.

"Get in, goddamnit, unless you don't want to live! I know who they are and we need to get the hell out of here!"

Despite the warning bell in her brain, she hopped into the car and quickly shut the door. Benedictis slammed his foot down on the accelerator and sped off just as the Russians burst out the building's front door.

But she knew something wasn't right when she looked back at her pursuers in the rear view mirror.

Alexei Popov was smiling.

CHAPTER 15

"I KNOW THIS WILL COME AS A SHOCK, DETECTIVE," declared Benjamin "Austin" Brewbaker. "But these four young men you've arrested are critical assets in a CIA surveillance operation that poses a direct and current threat to U.S. national security. I'm going to need you to release them immediately." In a fluid motion, he pulled out his creds and held them up for Stafford to see. He flashed an official picture ID card with his name and CIA title—*Director, Russian Counterintelligence Desk, Counterintelligence Center, Central Eurasia Division, National Clandestine Service*—and followed up quickly by presenting a special gold shield denoting his seniority in the agency hierarchy. It was meant to be intimidating, but judging by Stafford's unimpressed face, Brewbaker could tell that he had not achieved the desired effect.

"You can pull out a hundred IDs, but none of them will mean a damn thing to me," fired back the detective insolently, his bald head gleaming in the artificial light, his puckered pink scar along his jaw line pulsing like a coiled snake. "You don't have any jurisdiction over local crimes committed in *the City*."

"*The City*? And which *city* would that be? Manhattan, or one of the other four boroughs stolen from the Lenape Indians in the 1600s?"

"What are you an anthropologist or just a wiseass? Don't play word games with me, Mr. CIA Big Shot. I don't like feds coming into my town and stirring the pot. All you guys ever leave me with is a bad migraine, collateral damage, and a buttload of paperwork."

Brewbaker nodded, pretending to be sympathetic to the administrative burden that outside agencies imposed, which he knew from experience was a valid concern. But still, this NYPD cop for VIPs was a punk of the first order—but maybe that was because he knew the son of a bitch's full history, and it was not pretty. The question was how was he going to crack him? Was he going to have to resort to the—

"I understand where you're coming from, Detective. I apologize on behalf of the Central Intelligence Agency for any…failings on our part. Of course, I cannot speak for the FBI, NSA, or any other governmental body, but I can offer you my full assurance that—"

"Sorry to interrupt, but my bullshit alarm went off eight seconds ago. That's usually when I boot people out of my office. Lemme clear up one thing right off the bat, Brewbaker. You can't guarantee a fricking thing, so don't try and con me with silky smooth talk. In fact, why don't you tell me why the fuck I should listen to you at all?"

"Because you are a patriotic American?"

"No."

"Because interagency cooperation is something the NYPD knows is beneficial to both parties?"

"Hell no!"

"Because with one phone call I can have you banished to Backwater, Alabama, or Nome, Alaska, for the rest of your law enforcement career?"

At this, a flicker of worry crossed Stafford's face, but it was swiftly suppressed. "No, the correct answer, Mr. Smarty Pants, is A, because you don't actually wield that kind of authority even though you would probably like to; and B, because in reality you'd have to jump through a dozen hoops with your own people to get approval for what you're doing. As a matter of fact, I would wager that your 'case,' as you call it, has not been officially sanctioned by your bureaucratic bosses at Langley."

"What makes you say that?"

"Because the jokers you're trying to bail out of jail are your wiseass son and his buddies, the Three Fricking Stooges."

"That's not a very nice way to refer to my progeny and his friends. After all, they are bringing tax dollars into *your* fair city."

"I was wondering who the kid would call, but I had no idea it was going to be his Government Agent Daddy. You're probably not even here on official business. You're just trying to bail your kid and his criminal friends out of trouble. But they got themselves in far too deep for even Mr. CIA Big Shot to pull strings. Now how do you like them apples?"

Brewbaker felt himself becoming increasingly agitated, but he refused to allow it to show. He gave a smile that said, "Touché, Detective Stafford, you sly dog, you really got me!"

And then he thought: *When the time comes, I'm really going to enjoy this one.*

He cleared his throat and leaned in closer to the detective's battered wooden desk. It was heaped high with paperwork and case files.

"Detective, I apologize for getting us off on the wrong foot. So let me ask a simple question. What is it going to take to get my prodigal son and the Three Stooges released in the next fifteen minutes?"

"You're not serious?"

"I assure you that I am quite serious."

"It's going to take until hell freezes over."

"Come now, Detective. All they did was sneak into an office, ask a few questions, and let loose with a little pepper spray on their way out to secure their escape."

"Aren't you forgetting that they illegally pulled a fire alarm?"

"Oh yes, and the fire alarm. But let's be realistic here. In the interest of national security and to relieve the burden on American taxpayers, the charges can easily be dropped and the four subjects in question can be remanded under my custody. From a procedural standpoint, it's quite simple."

Stafford shook his head, a stubborn look on his face. "No way. They're not getting off that easy. I gave them fair warning to get the hell out of town, but they didn't listen. And now they're going to have to pay the piper."

"For a harmless prank? You can't be serious? All my son wanted from that plagiarist Beckett was—"

"Alleged plagiarist."

"If you prefer, Detective, but please don't interrupt me again. As I was saying, all my son wanted from the *alleged* plagiarist Cameron Beckett and his *alleged* accomplice Anton De Benedictis was a simple apology. From that perspective, perhaps the end justifies the means?"

"It wasn't a fricking harmless prank. They sprayed innocent victims in the face with that pepper spray. Here in New York that's a goddamned punishable crime. Misuse of tear gas comes with state penalties of up to a one-thousand-dollar fine and up to three years in prison, as well as a potential felony conviction on the record. And that's just the pepper spray. Pulling that damned fire alarm was an even worse crime. New York Code Section 15-214 states that pulling a false fire alarm, or aiding and abetting in the pulling of a false alarm, is punishable by imprisonment up to one year or a fine not exceeding ten thousand dollars, or both. So it doesn't matter how you slice it or dice it, those four little pricks are in a heap of trouble."

"I'm sorry Inspector Javert, but at the end of the day, the charges will be dropped to misdemeanors, they'll get no jail time, and the fines will be $500 tops per person. So why waste your time on these small fish, Detective? They're not worth wasting countless hours and taxpayer dollars to interrogate, incarcerate, and judge in a court of law. Let them go and you'll be doing everyone a big favor."

"Why do you want them so bad?"

"I told you. They're working with me on a case that is of vital interest to our national security."

"I hear my bullshit alarm going off again."

"I know it's hard to believe, but it's true. I need them released posthaste."

"What's the CIA doing in New York anyway? You're not supposed to be spying on American soil."

"As you well know, Detective, in the post-9/11 world, counterintelligence has its domestic spheres of influence."

"Well, I don't like it, and more importantly, I don't like you or your cocky little son. *Capiche?*"

"I don't think you need to get personal, Detective. Unless, of course, you want to open that door. Is that what you want to do?"

He let the menacing words hang there a moment, like a cloud of acrid cigar smoke. The detective blanched, but only for a moment, before recovering his composure. *It's not quite time to stick in the knife,* thought Brewbaker, *but it is getting damned close.*

"You're going to have to give me more than this, Brewbaker—a lot more." He held up a hand. "I'm not saying that I would even consider releasing them. But if you don't give me the details of this...*case* of yours, then I can guarantee you won't get any cooperation whatsoever from me."

"Point taken. But I can't tell you anything specific about the case; only that it is here in New York and I am in charge of it."

"But it does involve the Russians."

"I don't recall ever saying that."

"Don't mess with me. You're the fricking Director of the Russian Counterintelligence Desk of the NCS. Let me guess, you're after the Russian mob and the case involves narcotics or the white slave market? Or maybe we're talking about international weapons dealers? Or maybe there's a diplomatic angle of some kind? Does it involve the UN?"

"I'm afraid I can't tell you anything more."

"That's unfortunate for you because now I won't be able to help you. *Capiche?*"

He looked at his watch; damn he was wasting too much time with this peon. It was time to get down and dirty. "I think it's time I talked to your boss, Frank."

"It's Detective Stafford to you. And I don't have a boss. I run this department."

"Is that so, Frank? That's unfortunate for you then."

"I'm just shaking in my shoes."

"You should be, Frank. Because now I'm going to have to talk with Internal Affairs—as well as your cuckolded wife—about your secret mistress."

Stafford's face went visibly pale. He made no attempt to protest.

"And how you've been on the take for the past four years from the appreciative VIPs you've managed to protect. That is what has allowed you to pay for the young woman's, shall we say, lavish accommodations and lifestyle choices. It is true, the money and other...*gifts*...you've received might not actually constitute violations of official New York statutes. But they nonetheless raise serious ethical questions. Are you prepared to deal with such inconvenient issues at this time in your life, Frank?"

Now Stafford looked as though he had become sick to his stomach. Brewbaker resisted the urge to gloat as he continued, though it was hard to suppress.

"Her name is Angelina Farmiga, age twenty-nine, mixed Italian and Irish heritage, which, to be honest, seems like a volatile combination to me. She was born and raised in Staten Island, went to NYU but dropped out, and is now an exotic dancer. She is very attractive and does a lot of yoga which is, of course, not just good for her but you as well. She has a happily married mother and father who still live on Staten Island and two younger brothers and sisters. You visit her in the apartment you pay for on the Lower West Side on Mondays and Thursdays. Though you sometimes sneak away for a weekend rendezvous by telling your wife that you have to go out of town on police business. Boy Frank, your wife Evelyn must be gullible to believe that crock. Should I go on?"

Stafford wasn't able to speak. He looked utterly stricken, as if he had just been informed of a death in the family.

"Now here's the good news. If you withdraw the charges and release my son and his three irresponsible, but hardly dangerous, friends in the next"—he looked at his watch—"shall we say, five minutes, then the damaging file I have in my possession shall remain in my possession, where it is highly unlikely, or dare I say, virtually impossible that it will ever see the light of day, except among a handful of federal government officials with too much time and budget on their hands." He blew out a sigh. "Wow that was a mouthful."

"You bastard," grumbled Stafford through gritted teeth.

"Actually, I'm a nice guy just like my son. But the difference between him and me is I am willing to do whatever it takes to achieve my objectives. And I mean literally *whatever it takes*, Frank. *Capiche?*"

"And what is your objective?"

"I already told you: to protect the national security interests of my beloved country."

"So you're a Boy Scout, is that it?"

"Not really. I'm more of a renegade Boy Scout. The kind that sneaks a toke of weed or a kiss from an equally naughty girl behind the Club House. But, of course, you wouldn't know about that, Frank, since you're just a cop on the take who's housing and banging a young woman who happens not to be your wife. Poor Evelyn, I'm beginning to wonder why such a sweet woman could have possibly married a lying sack of shit like you."

"You and that damned son of yours. I can see now that the apple hasn't fallen far from the tree."

"Yes well, that's my fault, not Nick's."

"You're going to get in trouble just like him, you know. This is all going to come back to bite you in the ass."

Brewbaker stood up from his chair, signaling that he was finished and there would be no more debate. "Not as bad, Frank, as you're going to get bitten in the ass if you don't do exactly as I say."

"All right, all right, I'll let them go. But I want it in writing that you're taking them on your recognizance. If those bastards screw up again, it's going to be your ass, not mine."

"Very well, Frank. Now that we've reached an understanding, I need you to do one last thing for me."

Stafford looked at him with dread.

"I need you to apologize to my son for striking him in the ribs with your baton. That was an application of excessive force, and you're going to apologize. Please tell me that you're not going to have a problem with that, Frank."

The detective gave him a stubborn look, as if he wouldn't do it.

"If you don't apologize—and I mean like you really and truly mean it, Frank—then your wife and Internal Affairs will be getting a rather graphic notification."

Now the cop for VIPs looked genuinely scared.

"You're going to do it, right Frank? If you don't, I'll make sure your wife gets my full report on young Angelina, with photographs of you two in the act, along with the NSA and FBI reports. Whoops, I forgot to tell you that there's more than one federal agency interested in you, Frank. So far our interest has been at the documentation level because you are peripheral to our objectives. But of course, that can change in a heartbeat."

Stafford gulped hard. Then, in a voice that was more of a defeated croak than an actual human utterance, he said, "Okay, okay, I'll do it. Just please leave me and my wife alone."

Brewbaker smiled. "Why thank you, Frank. That means a lot to me and I know it will mean a lot to my son, Nick, too. So, please see to it that the four subjects in question are released. You have five minutes so you had better chop, chop."

Stafford almost tumbled onto the floor he was out of his chair so quickly. "Yes, Mr. Brewbaker, sir. I'll have them out of here in no time. And on behalf of the entire NYPD, I'd like to offer my sincerest apologies."

"Now that's more like it, Frank. Please give my regards to your wife, Evelyn, when you see her this evening. I know you two have some catching up to do."

CHAPTER 16

SIXTH AVENUE TO FDR DRIVE

THE TIRES of Benedictis's cirrus-white Mercedes-Benz CLA 45 AMG squealed and smoked as night fell upon the city. They blasted up Sixth Avenue, took a hard right onto West 57th, and headed southeast towards Lexington Avenue. The car was still gripped with a tense silence. He looked over at Natalie Perkins. She had not yet uttered a word since they had sped away from the Russians and still appeared frightened. He knew that she didn't trust him—in fact, he knew it went far deeper than that—and that was something he had to work on. Starting right now.

He smiled sympathetically. "Are you hurt, Natalie? Did those thugs harm you?"

"No, I'm fine." Her arms were wrapped tightly around herself beneath her seatbelt. "They just chased me."

"You were working late?"

She nodded. "Why would they be in your office, Mr. Benedictis? Were they looking for something?"

It was an important question, and he knew there were many ways he could answer it. But he had already decided on a course of action—and it had to be handled delicately since he would be, for the most part, telling the truth. But it was the truth, he felt certain, that would enable him to get what he needed from her.

"They're with the Russian mafia, Natalie," he said. "They're blackmailing me. I owe them a lot of money."

Her face showed genuine astonishment, which was what he had been both expecting and hoping for. Or was it possible she was bluffing? No, she couldn't be that good.

He slammed his foot down on the accelerator and ran a yellow light. Out of the corner of his eye, he saw her tense. *Good,* he thought, *I have to keep her on edge.*

She looked at him again. "The Russian mob is after you? For what?"

"It has to do with my brother Danny. They said they would kill him."

"Your brother's mixed up with the Russian mob?"

"And now so am I. They've threatened to kill us both if I don't repay my brother's debt."

He turned right onto Lexington, tires screeching. Out of the corner of his eye, he discreetly studied her. As he had expected, her skepticism was slowly turning to sympathy.

"For your own protection, Natalie, I can't tell you any more than that. These guys are serious. It's enough for you to know that my brother screwed up and now I'm on the hook for a lot of money."

"But why would they be in your office?"

"Isn't it obvious? To get damaging information in order to continue blackmailing me. This whole situation with Beckett has stirred the pot. Half the country has already seen the book signing fiasco on YouTube, or learned about it on the Internet and Twitter. The Russians smell blood. They're never going to let me go, Natalie. Once they sink their hooks into you, they don't let go. That's how the Russians do things. They are a tenacious people."

She was looking ahead. "Are you driving me to my apartment?"

"Yes."

"But how do you know where it is? You've never been there before."

"One hundred and twenty-eight Broome Street, Lower East Side. I guess I just know."

They fell into an uncomfortable silence. He could tell that she still didn't completely trust him, but she appeared to be coming around. By rescuing her, he had shaken her moral compass. She was no longer sure if magnetic north was truly north, or maybe, by some trick of nature, actually south. Inside she was torn, wavering, and she still didn't have a clue about what was really going on, why he had come from out of nowhere and rescued her. She was a clever, clever girl but still an amateur spy; she had been conflicted and uncertain for the past several months at the office and that was how he had to keep her. Telling her at least the partial truth now was going a long way in achieving that.

She was looking at him again, trying to read him. "It was fortunate that you happened to drive up just as I ran out of the building. Were you coming to the office?"

He suppressed a knowing smile. He had to answer this one carefully. Even though she had probably received no professional training from her handlers— whoever the hell they were, he still didn't know—she had a meticulous appreciation for detail. That was what made her a good spy.

"As a matter of fact, Natalie, I was visiting next door with my lawyer, John Mahoney. I had dinner with my daughter and then I met with my lawyer to examine the legal options regarding this...Lassiter situation. You do recall our previous conversation in that regard, don't you?"

He again slapped his foot down hard on the accelerator as he veered left onto East 42nd Street. They both leaned into the turn as the Mercedes' tires churned and squealed. As before, the aggressive maneuver was meant to unsettle her, and judging by the look on her face, it had done precisely that. To the south, the spindly crest of the Empire State Building, softly lit up with lights, stood out like a rocket ship against the winking backdrop of the big, brawny city.

"I was able to find out that he and his friends were arrested," she said, clutching the hand grip tightly, her knuckles close to alabaster. "That was why I stayed late at work—to find out what had happened to them."

"Well done, Natalie. I told you to keep an eye on young Nicholas and you have done precisely that. Your loyalty to the firm is unquestioned. But just to be the nosy boss for a moment, was that the only thing you were doing at the office?

Were you finishing up your line edits on the Link Nicoll thriller?"

"No, I was busy trying to track down Nick, just like you asked me to do."

He knew she was lying, but still, it was reassuring to see her body language confirm his suspicions. He made a mental note. He knew that she had actually spent two hours running plagiarism-detection software and that she had copied several documents to her flash drive. He knew this because he was set up, via his company IT chief, Ben Paddock, to track every computer keystroke, every Internet search, every email composed, sent, or forwarded by every single one of his employees twenty-four hours a day, seven days a week. Nothing anyone did at Benedictis Literary Associates went unmonitored. This evening, he had known that Natalie was working late on things she shouldn't have been working on, and he had driven to the office to confront her. But he had not anticipated that tonight, of all nights, Alexei Popov and his nefarious Russians would be on the prowl.

"I believe you, Natalie," he said sympathetically to gain her trust.

They fell into silence again as he turned right onto the on-ramp for the FDR Drive. The scenic, ten-mile long, six-lane strip of battered asphalt ran along the entire length of the East River, all the way from the RFK Bridge bordering Harlem to the southern tip of the Manhattan borough at Battery Park. They were heading south with the moonlight-dappled expanse of the wide river on their left.

"Can I ask you something, Natalie?" He waited for her to respond affirmatively. "Are you afraid of me?"

"I'm not sure what…what you mean?"

"Is it my imagination or have you been frightened of me ever since you returned from London?"

"I've just got a lot going on with my clients. It's been a busy time for me, Mr. Benedictis."

"I shouldn't have let Beckett do it, Natalie. I shouldn't have let him rummage through my slush pile and co-opt Nick's project like that. It was a mistake. And then, to make matters worse, I failed to check Beckett's first draft or the final product of *Subterranean Storm* against *Blind Thrust*. At that point, it was all out of sight, out of mind, I'm afraid."

She said nothing, just watched as the Mercedes raced past the towering buildings along the FDR in a blur. She seemed more relaxed, but he could tell that her mind was still feverishly working. She was still unsure whether he could be trusted.

"I know I should have checked the two versions. I should have cleaned up *Subterranean Storm* and removed all of the similarities between it and *Blind Thrust*. Actually, I should have reined the son of bitch in from the beginning. But I didn't Natalie. The fact is I felt sorry for him. His drinking and coke consumption were out of control and I took pity on him. Subconsciously, I think I wanted to see him get back on his feet and have another big hit. I failed to do my job as an agent. I let the damned genie out of the bottle, and now it's too late and I can't coax the little bastard back in."

She gave no reply. The only sound was the purring throb of the engine as the sleek Mercedes knifed through the scattered traffic on the FDR with the dark East River on the left and the flickering lights of Stuy Town on the right. Smoothly accelerating the high-performance luxury vehicle up to 70 m.p.h.—thirty miles above the posted speed limit—Benedictis now went for the jugular.

"I should have checked the documents against one another, Natalie, but I didn't. However, it has been brought to my attention that you have."

The words hung there. A renewed sense of tension quieted the air and he saw her body stiffen.

"I'm going to need that flash drive, Natalie."

She said nothing, but he could see her mind working frantically for some way out. She wrapped her arms tighter around herself.

"Remember, Natalie, you signed a very strict confidentiality agreement—an agreement that you will recall contains no whistleblower protection provisions with regard to the disclosure of information on our clients. Client confidentiality, Natalie, is our lifeblood just as it is in the legal profession. If our clients knew we were handing over sensitive information on their private lives, foibles, addictions, sexual relationships, family situations...well we'd be out of business in a heartbeat. There would be no literary agents, and you and I would be out of a job."

"I don't think...I don't know what you're talking about."

"Don't lie to me, Natalie. I've always treated you well as an employee. And God help me, I've just confided in you. I'm in a lot of trouble, but believe me, the least of my worries is the situation with Mr. Beckett and your ex-boyfriend Nick Lassiter. Nonetheless, I would be remiss in my duty to my client if I failed to maintain strict confidentiality. I've got the Russian mob after me. The last thing I need to worry about is some two-bit plagiarism case. So you're going to have to hand over that flash drive. You'll find it zipped into that special pocket in your purse there."

She hesitated, clutching her purse tautly. He saw that her hands were trembling. He felt cruel and manipulative, but he had no other choice, really.

"Please just hand it over, Natalie. It's illegal to steal information on our clients and you know it. You signed the agreement."

She clutched her purse even tighter, her mouth set in a stubborn line. Slowing down to sixty miles per hour, he withdrew a folded piece of paper from his pocket, and handed it to her.

"Take a look at that, Natalie."

Slowly, she unfolded the piece of paper as they approached the massive steel girders of the Williamsburg Bridge to the southeast. He could feel the fear radiating off her like a feverish sweat. She didn't want to look at the sheet of paper, but of course she had no choice.

"You bastard," she hissed after reading it over.

"Come on, Natalie, I just want to make sure that my employees take their client confidentiality responsibilities seriously. Note that the email is from you and has a date stamp from three years ago. Along with it is your brief letter to Cameron Beckett referencing that you were attaching an electronic WORD version of *Blind Thrust* along with the query letter and synopsis. No other conclusion can be reached other than you were the one who passed on *Blind Thrust* to Cameron Beckett."

"How could you do something like this? I have always been loyal to you."

"And I to you. I made you a full agent, didn't I? But the reason for the subterfuge was because I knew you were moving on to Excalibur. I didn't want there to be any…shall we say, questions, regarding the origin of what would turn into *Subterranean Storm*. This way, I figured if you ever raised the issue, there would be this little piece of evidence to explain. To be honest, it was about the only smart thing I've done in this whole sordid mess."

"But you faked it all. I never sent this email."

"It has your name, email address, and a date stamp. Try explaining that it's not yours to a judge or jury."

"My God, you're a cold bastard, Anton De Benedictis."

"And you're no Mother Teresa yourself, my dear. You betrayed my trust and smuggled client documents out of the office for your boyfriend, or whoever you were planning on giving the information to. So I'm going to have to ask you again, Natalie. Please hand over that flash drive."

"And if I refuse?"

"You don't want to do that," he said as he took the slip of paper back from her and stuffed it back in the pocket of his pearl-white linen suit.

"Damn you. I shouldn't have come back to work for you."

"You have my permission to move on then. With this letter tucked safely in a secure place, I'll be happy to give you a sterling reference."

"This is pure blackmail. You really are a cold-hearted bastard."

With bitter resignation, she pulled the flash drive out of her purse and handed it to over him. He gave a winsome smile as he slammed his foot down hard on the accelerator, ran a red light, and blew past the Williamsburg Bridge on their left.

"You know, I think you're right, Natalie—I am a cold-hearted bastard. But what can I say? I'm a New York literary agent."

TUESDAY

JUNE 4

CHAPTER 17

BREWBAKER FLAT
44 WEST 56TH STREET

LASSITER WAS SOUND ASLEEP, in the midst of a strange dream, when the external sound registered in his unconscious mind. It didn't even sound real, which is why he thought it was part of his dream. But then he thought he knew what it was: the sound of jiggling keys outside the door to his father's apartment. Or was it a set of lock picks?

The sound wasn't particularly loud or obtrusive—in fact, Squelch's and Claggebart's snoring on the floor next to him almost overwhelmed it—but it was still enough to awaken him. Opening his eyes, he listened for a moment half-consciously, hoping the noise would stop so he could roll over and go back to sleep. He remained silent and motionless, casting an ear towards the front door, trying to separate out the noise from his cohorts' snoring.

But something about the foreign sound must have touched off his primordial instinct. Because when he tried to tell himself that it was just his imagination, his primitive being told him not to just lay there or go back to sleep like some Darwin-Award-winning numbskull, but instead to get up and see what the noise was about because maybe, like, the future of his gene pool was at stake.

Then he heard a light chuff of shoes across creaking floorboards and the sound of a key—or, again, was it a lock pick?—probing the lock and he knew he was in serious trouble.

Someone was breaking into the apartment!

Crawling quietly off his sleeping mat, he slipped on his pair of jeans hanging from the nearby chair and reached for the heavy flashlight on the table. It wasn't much of a weapon, but it would have to do.

He moved stealthily to the wall next to the door, gripping the flashlight like a billy club. There it was again, a soft footfall. Every sense was suddenly acute.

The noise outside the door stopped.

He waited for what seemed like an eternity. But there was nothing.

Then he heard the floorboards creak again and the sound of something scraping and being lifted. Something heavy.

On the floor, Squelch changed positions, ground his teeth together, mumbled incoherently, and stopped snoring for a moment as his lips smacked together. He was probably in the arms of Lara Woodley back at Kenyon and having a good old time right now. Lassiter stepped up next to the door, clasping the flashlight in his right hand. Carefully, he slid his hand along the bumpy wall, feeling for the light switch.

It was then he saw the door slowly start to open.

His entire body froze as a tremor of fear lanced through him. Who the hell was it, Stafford again?

The door inched open a crack. Then some more, slowly.

He felt a taut knot of muscle squeezing his chest.

A shadow of a figure fell across the open doorway.

Pressing himself against the wall so he could jump out at the last second, he hoped to take the intruder by surprise. He felt his heart palpitating like an A-10 Thunderbolt in his chest, threatening to explode. Jesus, he didn't know the fucking thing could beat so fast. He glanced down at the flashlight, felt the solid heft of it in his hands. It held four D-sized batteries, which wasn't bad, but he still wished he had something heavier.

Summoning all of his courage, he edged closer to the slowly opening door, the flashlight gripped tightly in his right hand.

He raised the weapon to strike.

Suddenly, the light turned on and he was momentarily blinded.

Then he heard a stunned voice.

"Don't shoot, man! Don't shoot!"

He looked to his right to see Squelch standing there in his boxer shorts with his hands raised in the air, a look of shock mingled with fear on his face. And then he followed his friend's gaze to the object of his astonishment.

"Dad, what the hell are you doing?"

His father stood inside the door with a Smith and Wesson M1911A1 .45 semiautomatic pistol, which he now, thankfully, pointed up and away instead of at Squelch. He was wearing a lengthy trench coat turned up at the collar, a French beret set at a rakish angle, and dark-black reflective sunglasses, as if he were a 1950s jazz bassist-expatriate living on the Left Bank, or a spy trying to disguise himself.

But from whom?

Lassiter looked at him with bewilderment. But his father said nothing, just stood there staring back at him and Squelch. Then he tapped his right heel against the door, shutting it closed with a firm click.

"Dad, are you going to tell us what the fuck is going on or do we have to guess?"

"I'm sorry, Son. I didn't mean to frighten you." He quickly stuffed his gun into his trench coat. "I thought I heard a noise outside in the hallway. I didn't want to wake you guys so I went to check on it by myself."

"Yeah, and what did you find?"

"Nothing. I didn't see anything."

"Are you sure?" asked Squelch skeptically, his Caribbean buccaneer-blue eyes glittering with anticipation now that he was wide awake.

"Yes, I even checked the maintenance room and the fire escape. There was no one there."

"I don't know," said Squelch, shaking his head. "Are you sure, Mr. B, that you're not actually embroiled in a clandestine, spy-versus-spy, black-on-black op and you're just not telling us to protect us? Is your code name Condor by chance?"

"No, Professor Squelch, my code name is not Condor. Seriously, you all go back to sleep now. It was nothing."

Lassiter wasn't convinced either. "You wouldn't have taken your gun, Dad, if it was nothing."

Now Claggebart and Bermolito were awake, wiping the sleep from their tired eyes. "Is that really you, Mr. B?" ventured Claggebart. "Good heavens, it is. For a second there, I thought I was staring at Max von Sydow."

"Yes, there's a lot of that going around. Now go on back to bed."

"Go back to bed? How on earth can I do that when you're wearing a trench coat, a French beret, reflective sunglasses, and have a bulge signifying the presence of a handgun in your pocket? A bulge so prominent, in fact, that it resembles flute-and-sax player Chris Woods' prodigious testicular Battle of the Bulge on the cover of my favorite Traffic album, *The Low Spark of High-Heeled Boys*. I say, did you just go for a stroll through Central Park? It can't be very safe at three o'clock in the morning—even with a gun."

"I thought I heard a sound and went to check on it. But it was nothing."

"That's what they always say. Then in the next scene a murder takes place with nothing but a faint susurrus of wind and a tiny gasp of expelled breath at the curtains," said Bermolito. "I'll bet it was Detective Stafford or his men prowling around and trying to scare the bejesus out of us."

Claggebart nodded. "Suspicious shadows in the night, rogue policemen giving fright. Yes, yes, I can sniff Stafford all right. These bloodhound nostrils of mine don't miss a bloody thing, my dear Watson."

Bermolito nodded, grinning impishly. "Whoever it was, gents, we definitely have a little shadowy intrigue here in Gotham." He simulated talking into a radio. "Broadsword calling Danny Boy...Broadsword calling Danny Boy. Come in Danny Boy."

"Okay, that's enough, you guys. You've been watching too many movies. Go back to bed."

Lassiter wasn't so sure. "If it was nothing, Dad, then what do you think you heard?"

"I thought I heard footsteps and creaking floorboards. But like I said, when I checked there was no one there. So let's just all go back to sleep."

"But why did you need the gun then? And why the full disguise?"

"That's enough of the questions, all right. I'm the senior CIA officer here, not you rapscallions I just bailed out of the slammer. So I'll be the one to ask the questions from here on out."

"But is there someone specific that you're afraid of? Or were you meeting with someone? Someone that you don't want us to know about."

"Okay, that's enough of the conspiracy theories for one night, Agent Condor. Go to bed, gentlemen—and that's an order."

"I just want you to be honest with us, Dad. We have a right to know if we're in danger."

"Okay, I'm going to be completely honest with you. Totally transparent. Are you ready?"

All eyes were fixed on him with rapt attention. Lassiter gave a little nod and held his breath.

"Despite the noises I heard, there really was no one out there when I checked. No one at all. And I have no idea who it could have been, if there actually was someone lurking in the shadows. Furthermore, I was not secretly meeting with anyone."

"And that's it?"

"Yes, that's it. Well, not exactly all of it."

"Not exactly all of it? Exactly what part did you leave out?"

"It's true that I wasn't meeting with anyone in secret tonight. But at the same time, it is also true that I have been meeting surreptitiously for the past several months with someone else. In fact, it's someone very dear to you."

Lassiter looked at his buddies, who appeared as stunned as him. "Okay, this is getting weird, Dad. What the hell are you trying to tell me?"

"The truth. And the truth is, well, your mom and I are..."

"Mom and you are what?"

"Your mom and I are back together again."

Lassiter's jaw dropped. "What?"

"We've been carrying on a secret romance for the past six months, right here in my apartment in New York. I know...it sounds crazy, right?"

He was rendered speechless. It was as if his mouth had been wired shut. His mom and dad were back together? That was the last thing he had expected.

"I know your mother and I should have told you before now, but we didn't want to let you down if it didn't work out. So we decided not to tell you. That is, until this afternoon when your mom called me at Langley. I'm sorry, Nick. We just didn't want to let you down like we did the first time around."

Lassiter felt overcome with emotion. "You and Mom are really back together?"

"We're trying. In fact, we're trying really hard."

"This fucking rocks, Nicky!" roared Squelch. "Your mom and dad are putting the band back together—how cool is that? Now that's what I call rekindling the old flame. They're coming in hot, baby—they're coming in hot!"

"Okay, Dr. Squelch," said his dad. "I appreciate your tendency for hyperbole, but after everything that's happened today, you've got to dial it down a notch."

"I'm sorry, Mr. B, I just get a little over-the-top exuberant sometimes. I guess that's why I'm a college professor."

"Yes, of Anarchy Studies. Is that really an actual college major in this country?"

"Actually it is," said Bermolito as he checked to make sure that his computer tablet was tucked safely beneath his pillow. "And you're not going to believe this, but it's one of the most popular undergraduate majors—with enrollment increasing at 9.4 percent per annum."

His father rolled his eyes. "Now I know why this country's going to hell."

They all laughed, Claggebart the loudest, a little comingled howling-wheezing utterance that sounded like a contented wolf baying at the moon. Lassiter looked at his dad and they smiled.

"We'll talk some more in the morning, Son. I'm sorry that you had to find out like this about your mom and me. But at least now you know the truth."

"Yes, now I know," he said. He felt a little disappointed that his parents had kept their relationship a secret from him, but his dissatisfaction was swamped out by the pure joy and sense of hope he felt inside. In fact, it was the same happiness he had experienced as a kid when his parents were together, that warm and fuzzy feeling that everything was all right and the universe was a fair and orderly system because he had two loving parents that cared deeply about him and one another.

"Night, Dad," he said with feeling. "I'm actually really glad you and mom are back together."

"We're trying, Son, that's all. Don't get your hopes up too high."

"I won't. But I'm still happy for you both."

"Your mom and I are happy too. Goodnight. I love you—and, believe it or not, I love your crazy ass friends too." He tipped his head towards the giddily-smiling, boxer-clad Squelch, Claggebart, and Bermolito—who looked like poster children for the Hunter S. Thompson Fan Club.

Squelch extended his arms and stepped towards his father, as if to hug him. "Mr. B, that's the nicest thing anyone has ever said about me. I love you man, I really mean—"

"Okay, Professor Squelch, that's enough. I love you too, but if you come any closer I'm going to have to put you in a full nelson."

Lassiter smiled. "You'd better do as he says, Squelch. He's not kidding. He was an All-American wrestler in high school."

"Cool beans! I had no idea! That rocks, man!"

His father laughed and rolled his eyes. "Night boys," he said, and he disappeared into his bedroom.

Lassiter let out a little sigh. Yes, there seemed to be order in the universe again. As crazy as it seemed, his parents were back together, at least kind of.

And that was something. That was really goddamn something.

CHAPTER 18

DE BENEDICTIS LITERARY ASSOCIATES
1450 SIXTH AVENUE

THE FOLLOWING MORNING AT 7:52 A.M., Anton De Benedictis suppressed a yawn, stepped from the lobby of his office building into a crowded elevator, punched the button for the thirtieth floor, and politely pressed two more buttons for three other passengers. When the doors clicked shut, he discreetly studied his reflection in the shiny, metallic panel of the elevator. A lean, dashing gentleman in a sleek, blue Louis Vuitton business suit and colorful Jerry Garcia tie gazed back at him through chestnut eyes and a hawk-like countenance that carried a trace of mischief. *Lord, you are a handsome devil,* he thought, and then, suddenly and unexpectedly, the light for the fifth floor flashed and the elevator doors opened up.

"All right, this is the end of the line, everybody out!" boomed a foreign-sounding voice from the rear of the elevator. Suddenly, there was pushing and shoving and everyone was being herded out of the elevator by three bulky men in the back whose faces Benedictis couldn't see.

"Come on, we don't have all day, everybody out—everybody except you!"

He felt a tug on his jacket. He was yanked towards the back of the elevator at the same time a dozen shocked and angry people were herded out the door in the opposite direction, mumbling and cursing at the three strange interlopers who had commandeered their elevator. Stunned, he wheeled around to see Alexei Popov—thickset, goateed, skin fleshy and pink as pig skin—smiling devilishly. The Russian mob boss looked dapper in a dangerous way in his gray Versace blue-stripe, wool-blend, two-button suit with a maroon silk tie and contrasting cream-colored silk pocket square tucked neatly into his breast pocket.

"My apologies, ladies and gentlemen, but you will need to take the next one up," he declared to the stunned crowd. "We have to inspect this elevator and talk to this gentleman. Have a nice day."

The doors closed. The elevator started up with Benedictis, Popov, and the mobster's two beefy goons wearing matching glossy-black leather jackets. Benedictis took a deep breath, summoning his courage and doing his best not to look frightened even though he felt like he was about to soil his Louis Vuitton trousers.

"This is not very smart, Alexei. We shouldn't be seen together in public like this."

Popov smiled like a crocodile. "*Da*, you are probably right. But what can I say? I needed to talk to you, my friend. I thought this would be a good way to get your attention. What do you think?"

"You already know what I think. I think you're fucking crazy. Why did you break into my office last night?"

"I think, my dear Anton, that I will be the one asking the questions. But I will tell you this much: I have been watching you closely and I do not like what I see."

"What's that supposed to mean?"

"It means that you are bringing unnecessary attention to your firm with all this trouble over your Aussie. The bloggers and tweeters are buzzing like busy bees. It is drawing attention at a time when we want things to be all quiet on the literary front."

"I don't see why you're keeping an eye on me or trying to gather blackmail material. There's no need for it and, besides, that's so old-school KGB."

"I always liked the KGB. They were like phantoms in the night: you knew they were there, but you could never see them."

"Look, Alexei, the operation is still going smoothly. You're making as much money as Vladimir Putin's five best friends that he hasn't snuffed out yet or sent to the gulag. So why do you want to mess things up by snooping around my office after hours and scaring my employees?"

Popov made a sudden jab at the *Stop* button. The elevator came to a shuddering halt between the twenty-second and twenty-third floors. Benedictis noticed that Popov's smile had disappeared.

"What was that girl doing at your office late last night?" asked the Russian, his squat body tense like a hungry bulldog.

"She was working. That's what my employees do—they work. I know it's different in Russia, but it's how we do it in the U.S."

"For the sake of our lucrative business arrangement, I will pretend I did not hear that. But I will say this: I do not like that girl. I think she's up to something."

He felt a little twitch at his jaw at the accusation. "She was just working late, Alexei. If you and these lunkheads of yours had bothered to check all the offices first, you would have seen that she was already there working."

The two bodyguards stiffened and took an aggressive step towards him. Popov held up a hand, halting them in their tracks like a pair of thoroughly-trained Dobermans. They calmly folded their hands together and backed up a step, returning to the rear of the elevator.

"The hallway was dark and the lights were off," explained the Russian. "We thought everyone had left. But, of course, I do not have to tell you any of this."

"Well, you shouldn't have been there in the first place. I still don't know how in the hell you three got past the building security staff."

Popov took one of his stubby thumbs, stepped forward, and jabbed it into Benedictis's chest, causing him to cry out in pain. He staggered back from the blow, clutching at his chest. Jesus Christ, it felt like he had been struck by a Mack truck.

"I'll bet you did not know you can kill a man using just a thumb."

He doubled over in agony. *Holy shit, a fucking thumb did that?*

The Russian raised the weapon again. "You did not answer my question, Anton."

"Fuck you! Why did your men beat the crap out of my brother?"

The two beefy bodyguards stepped forward. Again, Popov held up a hand to restrain them.

"Your brother is fine. In fact, he is moving up in the organization. I look forward to a long and prosperous relationship with the man. But he does need to watch his gambling. If he does not, his face will be seeing a lot more black and blue, I think."

"This is blackmail, Alexei. I don't fucking like it. How long am I going to be your serf?"

The Russian smiled, exposing a pair of sharp incisors. "For as long as you make me money, my friend. For as long as you make me money."

"Why don't you just let Danny go? I've already paid you back ten times over for what he did. The longer we keep in the game, the greater the risk we all get caught."

"No, Anton, you are the only one who has made things risky. By stirring up a hornet's nest with this nobody Nick Lassiter and allowing all this public fuss over Cameron Beckett."

"The situation is under control. It's nothing."

"Funny, it does not seem like nothing. That book signing disaster has already gone viral, and the attack at your office is in the news too. I would not exactly call that maintaining a low profile. It is also my understanding that Lassiter and the other mischief-makers responsible have been released."

"Yes, I heard that."

"Yet, you did not bother to tell me?"

"I didn't…I didn't think it mattered to you."

"You didn't think it mattered? What are friends for, Anton, if not to share problems with and open up your heart to? I could have easily solved your little problem."

The Russian meant killing, of course. Benedictis felt a flare of panic. "No, no, there's no reason to *solve* it like that. I tell you, the situation is under control."

"It does not sound under control, Anton. We have a saying in Russia: 'Little thieves are hanged, but great ones escape.' You see, my American friend, I am not a little thief. I am a great thief because I do not merely do what is necessary. I go beyond what is necessary, and in the process, I not only solve the problem but send a long-term message. What I do, these are not extreme measures. They simply ensure a permanent solution as well as the proper respect."

"You can't kill them, Alexei. That will only make things worse. I'm telling you, I've got the situation under control. We're meeting at lunch today to put the whole matter to rest. It's all set."

"Oh, so you have everything under control? That is indeed good news."

In a movement that was so quick it came to Benedictis as a blur, Popov's thumb again turned into a weapon, jabbing him this time in the eye.

He jerked back, screaming in agony.

Popov circled him in the elevator like a shark. "I think you need to treat me with more respect, Anton. I think sometimes you do not appreciate the full extent of my authority."

"Jesus Christ, you could have blinded me!" he yelled, holding both hands over his wounded eye.

Popov released the *Stop* button and pushed the button for the thirtieth floor. The elevator started moving upwards again. "Stop your whimpering. You Americans are such weaklings. When I was a little boy, before I moved to Moscow, I had to survive for a week on the steppes in December with no jacket and only a blanket and straw to keep me warm. Our farm was burned to the ground and a winter storm raged all across our province. My ancestors were Cossacks and we have always been taught to fight to the death rather than surrender or cry out in pain."

Benedictis looked at him sheepishly, still covering his eye. But inside he was thinking: *I'm going to kill you for what you've done to me and my brother, you fucking fat Cossack. And it's going to be sooner than you think!*

"So, Anton, are we clear on what is needed going forward? You will resolve this matter with your Aussie quickly and efficiently."

"I told you I'd take care of it, didn't I?"

"*Da*, you did. But we Russians have another saying: 'Poverty is in want of much, avarice of everything.' I don't want any more attention here at Benedictis Literary Associates, do I make myself clear? I am a greedy bastard—you know that quite well by now. So let there be no more...*obstacles*...to fulfilling my greed."

"I said I'll take care of it."

"You are meeting with this Lassiter today at lunch, you say?"

"Yes, it will all be settled then."

Popov smiled. "I will be at the book reception party tonight and you can tell me all about it then."

"You're coming here to Beckett's party? I don't think that's a good idea, Alexei."

The Russian mobster held up his thumb. "Did you want to say hello to my little friend again? No? I did not think so."

He felt weak and powerless, but again he vowed to find a way to eventually get even. He could not allow himself and his brother to continue to be held hostage by the Russian mobster, even if it did garner him an extra million or two per year. He and Danny could not keep on going like this; the stress was becoming unbearable.

The elevator light flickered, a bell sounded, and the doors opened.

Benedictis started to step from the elevator, but a powerful, talon-like hand reached out and clasped him by his suit jacket, spinning him back around.

"Remember what we talked about," warned Popov, smiling like a modern-day Stalin. "No need to invite us inside—we are headed back down. *Da svtriechi*," he then said in parting, his steely-gray eyes simmering with menace.

See you soon.

CHAPTER 19

BREWBAKER FLAT
44 WEST 56TH STREET

LOOKING AT HIS DAD standing in front of the framed photograph of his mother, Lassiter's mind reached back to when he was thirteen and he, his mother, and father had still been a family. His mom and dad had seemed like the perfect D.C. power couple, and he recalled how fun it had been growing up in the historic city. He had fond memories of playing soccer and lacrosse games at St. Albans, sailing off Carolina's rugged Outer Banks in his dad's twenty-seven-footer, cheering on the Redskins on Sundays in both victory and defeat, and treading through the hallowed fields of Antietam, the Wilderness, and Gettysburg.

And then somehow—for reasons that he had never been able to fully fathom—everything had fallen apart. His parents had split up when he was in seventh grade. He and his mother moved to Colorado where his Aunt Leelee lived, his mom went back to her maiden name, and he took her name and dropped his father's out of youthful anger. For the past seventeen years, Austin Brewbaker and Vivian Lassiter had lived apart, and in the intervening years, neither of them had remarried. They had remained civil to one another, but for Lassiter the damage had been done and his world had never been the same. He typically visited his dad twice a year and, for more than a decade and a half, that had been the extent of their relationship.

Until now.

Now everything had changed and his parents were, by some miracle or unusual twist of fate, back together again.

He was still coming to grips with the strange, new reality.

"Are you sure you don't want me there with you at the lunch, Son?" said his father as he sat down on the couch. "I might be able to advise you in case Beckett or Benedictis have a sudden change of heart or try to pull some kind of trick."

He shook his head. "No, Dad, I need to do this alone. It's gotten out of hand and it has to end. All I ever wanted was an apology and now apparently I'm going to get it."

"At least let me take a look at what you've got on Beckett. If he did plagiarize as you say, you might want to follow up later with a legal challenge. In case you change your mind."

"I suppose I could let you take a look at my notes and highlighted pages of *Blind Thrust* and *Subterranean Storm*. Would that satisfy you, Clarence Darrow?"

"Yes, it most certainly would."

"Are you also going to want to run my stuff by your geeky number-crunchers at Langley?"

"Nope. But you can send the materials to your mom if you want. She's the actual lawyer—I just have a law degree."

"That's funny I thought she was your hot, new girlfriend."

His dad laughed then glanced up lovingly at the photo of his mother. Lassiter thought to himself: *Jesus, maybe I'm not quite ready for them to be back together again.*

"You know, Nick, your mom and I totally support you in all this. We understand that you are sticking to your principles. But please promise me that you'll control yourself and those loose-cannon friends of yours and not get into any more mischief. If I hadn't intervened last night, you and the Three Stooges would be on your way to Riker's Island courtesy of Detective Stafford. His job is to protect the old New York bluebloods and new-money VIPs in this gilded town. Needless to say, he takes his job very seriously."

"I appreciate what you did for me, Dad. But you and mom both are going to have to let me handle this myself. I just want my apology and then I'm out of here."

"You've always been a man of principle, Nick. I can respect that. But you do have to be careful. You can't say or do anything that could be misconstrued as a threat or get you thrown back in the slammer."

"Is this my dad or the CIA spy talking?"

"Technically I'm just a senior-level intelligence officer."

Lassiter raised a brow. "That's more than you've ever told me before. Does this mean that you're finally going to come clean and tell me what you really do at the CIA?"

"It's not such a big secret nowadays. I'm the Director of the Russian Counterintelligence Desk, in what we now refer to as the National Clandestine Service. It used to be called the Directorate of Operations. Before I wasn't allowed to tell you even that, but now I am. It's all part of our new policy of semi-transparency."

"National Clandestine Service, eh. Okay, I have to admit that sounds pretty cool. But that still doesn't tell me what you actually do."

"Unfortunately, I can't tell you that. To talk about my clandestine responsibilities is officially a violation of the National Security Act. I could lose my job."

Lassiter shook his head. "Wasn't that the main reason you and Mom got divorced in the first place? Because of your job?"

A rueful nod. "Your mom couldn't stand not knowing what I did every day and why it seemed to be more important to me than you or her. I was an insensitive, sexist shit."

"So what's changed now?"

"Your mom and I both realized that the only person on the face of the earth that we would ever be able to truly love, with all our heart and soul, was each other." He sighed. "We both finally realized what we had lost—and out of mature consideration—we both decided to give it a second chance."

He was still skeptical. "After seventeen years?"

"After seventeen years of *being alone*."

His father looked genuinely sad. He felt empathy for the man and couldn't help but feel happy that his father and mother were back together again, as crazy as it sounded. To find love at any age was a blessing. Still, he was irked at them for keeping their relationship a secret from him, as if he couldn't be trusted.

"But why all the secrecy? Here you two have been rendezvousing in the Big Apple for the past six months and I only learn about it this morning? Don't you think that's a little deceptive?"

His father looked ashamed. "I already told you why. We didn't want to let you down a second time. We thought we had hurt you enough and didn't want to make the same mistake twice."

"I guess I can understand that," he said, feeling conflicted inside. On the one hand, he wanted them to go for it and take the risk that it would work out this time between them; on the other, he didn't want to get his hopes up and then have everything fall apart again. Either way, after so many years it was weird to think they were holding hands and having sex together like two hot-blooded teenagers.

They were interrupted by the sound of the downstairs buzzer. His dad went to the intercom, hit the button.

"Hello Mr. Brewbaker, it's me, Natalie."

"Oh, yes, Natalie. Nick's been expecting you—come right up." He hit the button. Two minutes later, she appeared at the door and Lassiter let her in. He was instantly struck by how jittery and haggard she looked.

"Are you okay?" he asked her.

"Why don't we get you a cup of coffee?" his dad put in quickly, taking him by surprise. "It's good to see you again, Natalie." He started guiding her towards the kitchen. "Thanks for bailing Nick out of jail yesterday. So I understand that you have some new information regarding this copyright infringement business?"

Why were his father and Natalie acting so weird? It was almost as if they had their own private agenda.

"Dad, I know you want to help, but this is between Natalie and me."

His father shook his head. "Uh, sorry Son, but when I had to bail you out of jail, you got me involved. I'm on the team too."

"The team? We're not a team."

"There's no '*I*' in the Devil's Brigade, Son."

"The Devil's Brigade? What's that?" asked Natalie.

"That's what our literary Robin Hood here and his three Merry Men are calling themselves: the Devil's Brigade."

"I like it. Definitely has a ring to it. Where did it come from?"

"The Devil's Brigade is the nickname the Germans gave the U.S.-Canadian First Special Service Force," responded Lassiter, as if reading from a military press release. "They were the first American elite Special Forces' unit ever to fight in combat as well as the greatest fighting unit of the Second World War. We're following in the legendary footsteps of Commanding General Robert Tyrone Frederick and the original Devil's Brigade. As you might expect, I'm playing the role of the general."

"Oh, you are, are you?"

"Yes, ma'am." He gave a crisp salute and clicked his heels together with military precision. *"The Devil's Brigade* was also 1968 World War Two movie featuring William Holden, who played the role of American General Frederick, and Cliff Robertson, who played a senior Canadian officer. It was pretty much *The Dirty Dozen* does the Italian campaign."

"I must have missed that one. My apologies, General."

She saluted him back and gave a radiant smile. Lassiter realized how much he had missed that smile during the past three years. In that revealing instant, it suddenly struck him that he had never cared half as much for Alexandra as he had Natalie. Though that, in itself, wasn't surprising considering he and Alexandra had been together less than a year compared to seven years for he and Natalie, what was significant was that the way he felt about Natalie was totally different, not even remotely comparable.

"By the way, where are the Three Stooges?" she asked as his father added a dash of cream to her coffee.

"The responsible one, Mr. Bermingham, is at work, while Dr. Welch and the irrepressible Morrison Claussen are out getting bagels," replied his father. "They should be back any minute—that is if they can manage not to get arrested. Now please, Natalie, tell me what you've managed to find out."

Feeling irritated at being left out, Lassiter stepped forward. "I'm the one that invited Natalie here, Dad."

"Yes, I'm aware of that, Son."

"And as you'll recall I'm the commanding general in charge of this unconventional outfit. To put it in terms that you can actually understand, this is my op. Which means that if you're going to serve in the Devil's Brigade then you're going to have to obey your superior officer. That's me, your commander, Brigadier General Nicholas Maxwell Lassiter."

His father saluted. "All right, Son, you're in charge, just like old Robert Tyrone Frederick. But don't screw it up—those are some awfully big shoes to fill."

"Don't worry, I won't. Now what did you find out, Natalie?"

"Last night, I stayed late at work running plagiarism-detection software developed by a Professor Louis Renard. He's a University of Michigan physics professor. I used his program to check Beckett's various WORD drafts against the WORD version of *Blind Thrust* you submitted to Benedictis three years ago. In comparing the documents, I found that the basic premise, plotting, and several descriptions in both Beckett's draft and final novel had been lifted from your WORD version of *Blind Thrust*. Beckett clearly changed a lot of the wording in an attempt to disguise what he was doing. But the software was able to give probability distributions that quantitatively show what he plagiarized versus what is original. From a statistical standpoint, that is."

"That's great. Do you have the results with you?" asked his father.

She shook her head. "Benedictis took them from me."

Lassiter felt a jolt of outrage. "What? How did he get them?"

"He drove me home last night and took my flash drive from me. He claimed that it was confidential information."

"But how did Benedictis know you had copied confidential information?"

His father answered: "He's likely set up to track all internal company keyboard entries, including computer input files, run and output files, documents, and emails."

Natalie nodded. "Big Brother is apparently alive and well at De Benedictis Literary Associates."

"Did he say anything about terminating your employment over this?"

"No, but I'm not staying with the firm. Not after what I've found out."

She exchanged a glance with his father; something about the exchange struck Lassiter as odd. Then his dad said, "Let's say that you are serious about leaving the firm. Is there still a chance that you can you get back on your computer today, run the plagiarism detection program again, and regenerate the information? New York State has very strong whistleblower protections, Natalie. Benedictis can't touch you and I'm sure that my wife, Nick's mother, will be more than happy to represent you, *pro bono* of course."

"I don't know what the hell you're doing, Dad. I've already told you this is not a legal matter, and look at how much she's risked already. I really just want my apology and then I'm out of here. This has gone too far. Things have gotten out of hand."

"Oh come now, look at what these people have done to you. They need to pay for this."

"You don't think I want Beckett and Benedictis to pay for this just like you? Why do you think I'm allowing you to compare the two manuscripts? Why do you think I submitted both novels to Dr. Coltrane, the best forensic linguistics analyst out there, to determine the extent of Beckett's infringements on my copyrighted material? You don't think I want revenge? I want it more than anybody, but what is revenge ultimately going to accomplish? *Subterranean Storm* has been written. I don't care about bringing Beckett and Benedictis down—I care about getting *Blind Thrust* published. The first inclination of most Americans is to sue, sue, sue for damages. Well, I think that's bullshit and I don't want any part of it. I don't want revenge—I want a fucking apology. You remember what Confucius said about revenge, don't you?"

"'Before you embark on a journey of revenge, dig two graves.'"

"That's right. I just want to start out with an apology, and that may be enough for me."

A tense silence gripped the room. His father bowed his head in contemplation.

"This is my problem, not anyone else's. I know the Devil's Brigade has got my back, and I appreciate that, but how this all plays out is still my call. And right now, all I want is an apology, okay. Is that too much to ask?"

"No, it's not," said Natalie, and she reached out and took him by the hand.

In the emotion of the moment, he pulled her to him, and then realizing what he had done, he awkwardly pulled away. But, to his surprise, she seemed to want him to touch her. She reached out and touched his hand again. Her hand was soft, warm, smooth.

He looked into her gentle blue eyes. "Thank you for understanding," he said.

106

"And thank you for researching all of this for me. I know you took a tremendous risk getting this stuff. I'm just glad you didn't get hurt last night."

"Me too," said his father, and Lassiter could tell that he meant it.

He noticed that his father was staring at him and Natalie and smiling, as if remembering back fondly to when he and Nick's mother were together at thirty. *My God,* thought Lassiter. *What am I doing? Am I falling for Natalie again?*

His thoughts were suddenly broken by a rowdy voice. "Yo man, what's going on here? Is this *The Love Connection* or what?"

Lassiter turned to see Squelch and Claggebart stomping into the apartment carrying two big grocery bags and a jug of orange juice.

Claggebart sniffed the room and gave a knowing smile. "Yes, yes, I definitely smell a whiff of romance in the air." He looked suspiciously at Lassiter, who couldn't help a guilty grin. "Oh, you naughty boy-o, Nicholas. I knew you two would rekindle the flame of Victorian passion. What did the great-granddaughter of Maxwell Perkins do? Read you a passage of Jane Austen? Recount a deliciously scandalous scene from *Lady Chatterley's Lover?*"

Natalie blushed, and Lassiter thought, *I could get used to that again, too.*

"You know what I see," said Squelch, grinning from ear to ear like a Cheshire cat. "I see a fucking smoking hot young couple who just *have got* to make it work the second time around. That's what I see, man."

"Okay, that's enough," said Natalie, her face crimsoning. "I have to get to work."

"I'm serious," Squelch persisted. "You are, like, the best-looking couple I have ever seen. You can't let it all slip away. You've each found your soul mate. You've just got to run with it and get it right this time. I'm telling you, man, I know about this kind of stuff."

His father crossed his arms. "If I may be so bold as to ask, Professor Squelch, what makes you such an expert?" he asked with a wry grin. "The fact that you're a professor of Anarchy Studies at the University of Colorado?"

"No, because I've gone out with more co-eds than there are ants in an anthill and I know the real thing when I see it. I mean, what I've mostly indulged in is instant gratification—which, believe you me, ain't half bad. But I know true love when I see it. And I can tell by the look in your son's and Natalie's eyes that what they're feeling is something truly special. Nicky's not still looking for that blue jean, baby queen, prettiest girl he's ever seen. He's already found her, and Natalie's found her soul mate too." He beamed proudly at them both. "You've both already found what you're looking for, and it's right here staring you in the face, man. Hey kids, rock and roll, rock on!"

"The great Lothario has spoken," declared Claggebart. "Who needs Sartre, Gandhi, or David Essex when you've got Pup Squelch?"

"Okay, I'm definitely out of here now," said Natalie, laughing.

"I'll walk with you," said his dad, stepping forward. "I'm headed in that direction."

"What are you doing, Dad? Are you a dirty old man trying to hit on my old girlfriend?"

"No, I just need to talk to Natalie. Let's just say this old spymaster needs to find out more about this plagiarism-detection software. And also a bit more about our mutual friend Detective Stafford, who is likely keeping an eye on us all. I'll be back in less than an hour. That will give you some time to catch up with your partners in mischief here."

Lassiter could tell something was up, but decided not to press the issue. Instead, he reached out and touched Natalie's hand again. "Thanks for everything. Please be careful. I don't want anything to happen to you. You've already done more than enough for me."

"Looks like we're both going to have to stay out of trouble," she said with a wink. "Now that we're part of this new team, the Devil's Brigade."

"Oh dear, where's the bubbly when you need it?" cried Claggebart. "All right, raise your imaginary glasses and let's give a toast. Lady and gents, to the new and improved Devil's Brigade!"

A cheer went up. "To the Devil's Brigade!"

They all laughed. When the laughter had settled down, Lassiter said, "You know you're all a bunch of crazy misfits just like the original First Special Service Force that trained in Helena, Montana, and fought in the cold mountains of Italy, don't you? But of course that's why I love you—every goddamned one of you!"

"Well spoken, boy-o—well spoken, indeed!" pronounced Claggebart ebulliently. "I can tell that, as a burgeoning author, you have taken to heart the immortal words of the South's greatest literary practitioner, Mark Twain, who proclaimed: 'The difference between the *right* word and the *almost right* word is the difference between lightning and lightning bug.'"

Lassiter chuckled. "Any comparison to the late, great Samuel Clemens I will take as a definite compliment. Thank you, Morrison—I must say you are one eloquent and well-dressed scalawag!"

"And I must thank me dear Irish mum for that."

The room erupted in more laughter. Lassiter looked at Natalie and smiled. And then, to make sure she knew how he truly felt, he leaned over and kissed her on the lips.

She tasted like wild mountain strawberries.

CHAPTER 20

DE BENEDICTIS LITERARY ASSOCIATES
1450 SIXTH AVENUE

FROM THIRTY FLOORS UP, Anton De Benedictis stared out the window of his plush office overlooking Central Park, clenching and unclenching his hands. In the foreground, the majestic view opened up onto The Pond; and, in the distance, spread a manicured grassy landscape interspersed with densely packed stands of Japanese cherry, globose European hornbeam, and a dozen species of oak and elm. It was a familiar and exquisite sight to Benedictis—yet he still felt on edge. The early June sunlight shimmered off the surface of the water a stone's throw from the towering statue of South American General Simon Bolivar; and the colorful carousels of the Victorian Gardens Amusement Park sparkled through the gaps in the trees beyond. But he was too anxious to take in the beauty. Still rattled by his run-in with Popov, he was now, to his chagrin, being given the third degree by David Sloan, Chairman and CEO of Excalibur Publishing Group.

"We need this situation resolved today, Anton," said Sloan in an admonishing tone, his head assuming the tilt of a lecturing schoolmaster. "It has dragged on too long and needs to be taken care of pronto."

"I already told you I am taking care of it," fired back Benedictis. "Today at lunch."

"Boorstein and Bernstein are very nervous."

"Tweedledum and Tweedledee are always nervous."

"I'm nervous too, Anton," said Stanton Greenbourne, Excalibur's in-house lead counsel, who was also sitting in a richly-upholstered Corinthian leather chair in front of Benedictis's massive cherrywood desk.

He continued staring out the window at the miniaturized green world below. "Why should you be nervous, Counselor? Beckett and I both are going to follow your script. You want us to issue an apology to Lassiter, alone and in person, without any admission of guilt, right? Well, in three hours' time, that's exactly what you're going to get. Hell, we're even doing it with you present, Stanton. Isn't that good enough for you?"

Sloan and Greenbourne looked at one another. "Since we last talked, Anton," said Sloan, "we've discovered some *irregularities* that have added to our level of concern."

"Irregularities?"

"Our security people compared *Blind Thrust* and *Subterranean Storm* using Plag-Checker plagiarism-detection software and found more than fifty clear-cut examples of direct line-by-line copyright infringement. Then there's the overall premise, structure, plot, and scene development. That's harder to qualify, but the correlation coefficient was over seventy-five percent. Again, these do not appear to be statistical outliers."

He felt his face go red; he had been violated. "How the fuck did you get a copy of *Blind Thrust*? Did someone on my staff give it to you? Because we have no record of the document here at Benedictis Literary Associates. So how the hell did you get it?"

"That's not important, Anton, though I will say it wasn't from anyone on your staff," said Sloan, his eyes as narrow as archer's slits. "However, what *is* important is how the hell *you* let this happen? You're supposed to be a reputable literary agent that vets this shit so that our overworked editors don't have to. Tell us what really happened, and this time don't try and bullshit me."

He smoothed his suit jacket and loosened his tie, stalling for time. *Should I lie?* But what was the point, really? Both Natalie and Sloan knew the truth: the software was like DNA analysis—and Beckett, and by extension himself as his literary agent, was one hundred percent busted.

Sloan gritted his teeth. "Well, Anton, what do you have to say for yourself?"

"What can I say? Beckett was desperate and I didn't catch it until it was too late. Having said that, I still think it can all be passed off as *scènes à faire.*"

"That *has* worked for us in the past," said Sloan. "But this goes way beyond anything we've ever seen before. My God, it's as if he took the electronic version of *Blind Thrust* as the starting point and *then* began to write his fucking novel. I want to know how the hell that happened. You gave it to him, right?"

He had no choice but to lie. "I didn't give him a damned thing."

"Then who the hell did?"

He feigned a look of disappointment. "Unfortunately, it was someone on my staff. I checked our archived email records and it appears a communication was sent without my knowledge. Beckett must have requested it based on our brief discussion of the project. You know that Cameron was going through a difficult time back then. Between all the booze and coke, it's a wonder he's still alive."

"Well, who was this employee? I certainly hope that you've fired the son of a bitch."

"I've taken care of it."

"I don't like the sound of that."

"Neither do I," echoed the attorney Greenbourne.

He felt a sudden constriction at his throat and again loosened his tie, this time to relieve pressure instead of stall. "What's past is past and it's time now to move forward. This matter will be resolved and behind us by this afternoon—and that is the best that can be accomplished. So you're going to have to accept that, the both of you, or I will take my billion dollar client elsewhere."

Sloan blinked several times. "You wouldn't dare do that."

"The fuck I wouldn't. I've already told you that Simon and Schuster and HarperCollins are both offering us an extra five percent on domestic sales, a seventy-thirty split on electronic rights, and a half-million more in advances for each novel. Do you really want to be the guy who lost Cameron Beckett, David, because I can make that happen quicker than your boss can say, 'You're fired!'"

You failed to protect my client when he was in physical jeopardy at Excalibur's book signing event. That, my friends, is a specific breach of contract."

"So is plagiarism, Anton," pointed out Greenbourne.

"That axe falls on you, the publisher, and Beckett, the author, not on me, asshole. But if you want to persist in this little witch hunt of yours, I will gladly take my golden goose elsewhere. There once was a little author named J.K. Rowling, who even at her peak only earned for her publisher half of what my boy does for you at Excalibur. Who do you think makes that happen? You think it's all smoke and mirrors? No, I make it happen—I'm the engine that runs this gravy train and don't ever fucking forget it!"

Sloan gave a skeptical expression. "Oh, so you're the great Maxwell Perkins responsible for the *'Aussie James Patterson'* bestselling phenomenon, is that it?"

"You're damn right," said Benedictis, and as the words left his mouth he drew a mental image of Natalie, great-granddaughter of Maxwell Perkins, the editorial legend behind the moody Hemingway, boozy Fitzgerald, and intractable Thomas Wolfe, who fought over individual words of text like a spaniel fought over dinner scraps. Why hadn't he been able to throw her under the bus to Sloan and Greenbourne? After all, she was the cause of all this.

He instantly knew the answer: she was a damned good employee, perhaps his best and brightest. She was a fine agent and editor of both commercial and literary works. She was also equally adept at upmarket fiction and non-fiction, had an instinctive knack for the literary marketplace, was an incredibly hard worker, and had the most long-term potential out of all of his junior agents. And with the editorial and marketing skills she had learned with Excalibur in London, she was actually sharper, more social media savvy, and overall more promising than several of his senior agents, whom he was certain she would soon eclipse as she built up her burgeoning client list.

Oh, Natalie, Natalie, what were you thinking in bringing Nick Lassiter and his dangerous novel into our lives? Even worse, I know you are spying on me, damn you. But for whom?

Sloan was looking at him funny. "You still with us, Anton?"

"Yes, I was just thinking."

"Well, think on your own fucking time. We're on the clock here. There are other issues at stake that need to be addressed."

"Really, and what might those be?"

"We want you to offer him this." From his briefcase, he pulled out a check and placed it on Benedictis's desk. "We want this matter put to rest today. *Today*, Anton."

Stepping away from the window, he took a seat at his desk again and looked at the amount on the check. Both eyebrows involuntarily shot up. "You're going to hand over a quarter-million dollars to this guy? You've got to be fucking kidding me!"

"I told you we're serious. We want this to be over…with no admission of guilt, of course. We want him to sign a non-disclosure and non-litigation agreement. As long as he signs it, he gets the money. It's that simple."

"If you try to buy him off, you're just going to piss him off. I know this kid—all he wants is his apology." Again, he thought of Natalie. "I have inside information in that regard."

"We want the agreement signed," said Greenbourne. "We need future liability protection."

"You do understand that this plan could blow up in your faces."

"We don't care what you think anymore, Anton," said Sloan. "This is our show now."

"Spare me the tyrannical tone, David. And what if he refuses to sign?"

Sloan looked at Greenbourne. "Then there will be an escalation."

"Oh, that's just perfect. Don't tell me, you're going to call in your Excalibur Security goons?"

The two corporate suits said nothing.

He rose from his chair again and stared out the window. The low-hanging cumulus clouds had dampened the sunlight. Central Park below looked bleak and uninviting, covered in a gelid pewter shroud.

"You want a scandal? Then have at it. But I'm not going to be a party to this crap."

"We've heard rumors, Anton," said Greenbourne, "that you're mixed up with the Russian mob here in the city. Mind you, so far there's only been whispers. But they seem to be picking up."

"With these rumors, we're wondering how much longer you're going to be around," said Sloan in a voice that was tempered, but still filled with unmistakable menace. "Just as your boy can have any publisher he wants, he can also have any literary agent he so desires. He doesn't necessarily need *you*."

"Listen up, you two. I made Beckett what he is. When he wanted to do his epic Swords and Sandals crap, I begged him not to, and he started his Jackson Preston modern detective series instead that has sold more than two hundred million copies. And when he wanted to do his Cold War spy trilogy, *Shadows of Empire*, I told him to wait until after his tenth book and the trilogy has sold over a hundred million copies. I've rewritten half of his damned novels for Christ sake! Now if that isn't pulling a Maxwell Perkins, then I don't know what the fuck is! Through calculated thematic choices, judicious plotting, and exhaustive editing, I've made Cameron Beckett the blockbuster he is today—and even he acknowledges it!"

"That may be, Anton," said Sloan perfunctorily. "But you were asleep at the wheel on *Subterranean Storm*."

"Bullshit, it's Excalibur that's been asleep at the wheel. You're the one that allowed Nick Lassiter into that goddamned book signing and now just look at what a thorn in our side he's become. The guy is a major lawsuit just waiting to happen."

"All right, all right, you've made your point," said Sloan, pulling at an invisible thread of his pin-striped suit. "Just stay out of trouble and keep Beckett in line."

"Or what?"

"Just stay out of trouble, Anton. This Russian mob stuff doesn't just sound like hearsay anymore. It's getting too close for comfort."

"I hope you have good legal representation, Anton," said Greenbourne with a challenging smile. "From where I sit, you're gonna need it."

Sloan leaned across the desk, took the check back, stuffed it in his briefcase, and stood up, signaling that the meeting was over. Greenbourne rose from his seat too, still smirking. Benedictis felt his world slipping away, as if he had been skating in Central Park in wintertime and tumbled to the ice. *Shit,* he wondered, *how have I allowed myself to get into this goddamned pickle?*

"Good luck with the lunch," said Sloan with false politeness. "And for God's sake, Anton, take my advice and stay out of fucking trouble. There's too much at stake—for all of us."

CHAPTER 21

WEST 56TH AND SIXTH AVENUE

FEELING LIKE A SPY, Natalie Perkins took a moment to smooth her black leather moto as she and Nick's father emerged from Brewbaker's apartment building atop Uncle Jack's Steakhouse. "So, you haven't told Nick about what's really going on?" she said to him. "That business about Stafford was just so we could talk?"

Brewbaker nodded as they started walking up the sidewalk along West 56th Street. Commuting workers, looking as if they were thirty minutes late for an appointment, hurtled past in steady streams, while clumps of rubber-necking tourists gawked up in awe at the skyscrapers as if gazing upon a Martian landscape. Yellow taxis, limousines, and cars of every color sped past in a blur—the drivers as flamboyantly aggressive as Dale Earnhardt, Jr. on crack.

"This situation has thrown a wrench into things and has forced me to move up the timetable," said Brewbaker, who though in his early-fifties, Natalie noted, was lean and spry-looking, still moving like a much younger man.

"Meaning what exactly?" she asked.

"Meaning we have to move tonight."

"During Beckett's party? You've got to be kidding me."

"We have no choice, Natalie. As you said yourself, the Russians are growing restless."

"Getting you inside without detection and then stealing away from the party is going to be tricky. The reception is being held in the Avanti Room on the twentieth floor. Security will be tight."

"We'll just have to find a way to slip away quietly."

Jesus, I really am a spy. This is getting freaking crazy.

"I need to take another look at Benedictis's hard drive. So far, the bastard has been too clever. We haven't been able to get anything on him that will stick."

"Not for lack of effort on my part."

They had to pause a moment to dodge a clump of tourists. Damnit, why did they always stop in the middle of the sidewalk and hold a family conference when they were lost?

"Look, Mr. Brewbaker—"

"Natalie, please don't call me that. I'm Austin, remember? We're in this together."

"Okay Austin, I just don't know how much longer I can last. I already told you earlier this morning when I called that Benedictis is onto me."

"He's not onto you, at least not about Popov and the Russians. He only knows about the copyright case with Nick—and we're going to keep it that way."

"How do you know he doesn't know?"

"Because if he did he would have questioned you more about what you saw last night."

She looked at him closely, trying to read him, but as always his face was inscrutable. "What are you not telling me, sir? I know you're keeping things from me."

"You can't call me *sir* either, Natalie. Remember, I'm Austin and we're in this together as a team. Look, I've always been up front with you since the day I recruited you. I've told you precisely why we have your boss under surveillance."

"I know, I know. His money-laundering operation on behalf of Popov poses a serious threat to the national security of the United States. But for reasons of bureaucratic red-tape, that surveillance does not include hacking into Benedictis's company computer. That's why you have eyes on him and know every move he makes at home or the office, except what can be accessed only by computer."

"Bravo, you would have made an excellent spy, Natalie."

"I'm already a spy, at least unofficially."

"Indeed you are. And that's why you know perfectly well that we need to take another look at that hard drive—and we need to do it tonight. The Russians must have been looking for something specific and we need to find out what that was. Benedictis may very well have something on Popov. This could be the big break we're looking for."

"I understand what you need me to do. I'm just not sure I'm cut out for this kind of work anymore."

"No one's cut out for this kind of work, Natalie. You and I both want to help our country—and that's it. It's not any bigger or smaller than that. It's our sense of duty that drives us and that's all we need to keep on going."

"I don't...I just don't know. I mean, I can't even sleep anymore."

"I'm sorry about that, but it's because of this thing with Nick not the Russians. You have to understand that, Natalie."

They crossed Sixth Avenue, taking their first step across the street the microsecond before the light turned from yellow to red, cheating the curb to beat all the out-of-towners waiting for the "walk/don't walk" sign to change. Just before their second step, a final convoy of taxis and cars raced past to beat the light, engines gunning. When Natalie and Brewbaker hit the curb on the far side, they knifed smoothly in and out of the pedestrian traffic, two abreast, as they passed beneath the sign that read "Avenue of the Americas," a name which no true New Yorker called anything but Sixth Avenue.

"You've done well, Natalie," Brewbaker reassured her. "We're almost at the finish line. I just need you to hang in there a few more days. We're getting very close."

She said nothing, just kept walking. She wondered, when all of this was over, what she wanted to do with her life. Did she even want to work in the literary field anymore? Did she want to work for the CIA? My God, even thinking such a thought sounded like heresy! And yet, since she was a little girl she had secretly dreamed of being a female James Bond with an array of gadgets, protecting her imperiled country from terrorists, rogue governments, and clever saboteurs. *You know you love the danger, damn you. Just admit it.*

Brewbaker broke through her thoughts. "There's something else I need you to do, Natalie. Get me a copy of the non-disclosure agreement you signed as well as your company HR policy. I told you I'm going to protect you, but I want to take a look and see what we've got."

"Oh, now you're really freaking me out."

He stopped and gently pulled her over to a fire hydrant where the sidewalk wasn't so crowded. "Look, I'm sorry if it seems that I took advantage of the fact that you and my son had a relationship when I recruited you. But you were my only in with Benedictis and I knew I could trust you. I know what I've put you through has been difficult. Playing the role of a planted agent is hard enough for a well-trained government professional, let alone a civilian. And at the end of the assignment, we won't be congratulating you on a job well done and pinning a medal on your chest. But know this: the sacrifice you are making for your country is a great one, and there are people, important people, who are going to be grateful for what you've done. Alexei Popov is a criminal arms-dealer and a seller of American military secrets. Thanks to you, the son of a bitch is going down. Soon, very soon."

"And Benedictis? Is he bad too? After all, he's just trying to save his brother."

He turned away and stared at the copse of giant oak trees lining the southern edge of Central Park, almost as if he was avoiding her. "He and his brother Danny have gotten mixed up with the wrong people. I know it's a tough situation, but they're going to have to pay the piper."

"Will Benedictis be given a deal if he can provide evidence against Popov?"

"You're asking too many questions again, Natalie. You need to find satisfaction in the fact that you're doing the right thing. Most people go through their whole lives and can't say that."

She felt a stab of irritation. "I think you've been playing me, Mr. Brewbaker. You knew all along I'd spy for you because of how I felt about Nick."

He looked away again. Was it shame or regret on his face, she couldn't tell? "No, I did it because I know how much Nick cared about *you*. And didn't I tell you to call me Austin?"

She stared into his intelligent, sensitive, but still non-revealing eyes. "What do you mean you knew how much Nick cared about me?"

He took her by the elbow and they started walking again, maneuvering through the crowd like a pair of barracudas darting in and out of a coral reef. "It means," he said, "that my son loves you more than any woman he has ever known. In fact, he hasn't stopped talking about you for the past three years, since you two broke up."

She stopped him again, feeling her head spinning. "What...what are you saying? Why are you telling me this?"

"I'm telling you this because the irrepressible Dr. Welch is actually right for once: you and Nick are made for one another. My wife and I feel the same way and we just don't want you to make the same mistake we did. Make it work—find a way. You won't regret it."

"So, that's why you wanted me to spy for you? So you could get Nick and I back together?"

"No, of course not. I needed you because you were the only person that I knew I could trust inside the literary agency. But the reason I have never doubted my decision is because of how Nick feels about you. And the way Vivian and I feel about you. You're the daughter we never had, Natalie. More importantly, you're the girl our son should marry if he knew what was fucking good for him."

She was so deeply touched she felt like she was about to cry, but she forced herself not to give in to her emotions. Nick and his parents cared far more about her than she could ever have imagined. My God, why had she allowed Nick to slip out of her hands? Or, looking at it from his point of view, why had he let her go? Did it really come down to the fact that he didn't want to live in New York and she refused to move to Colorado because of her career? In hindsight, it seemed so petty when the most important thing was to be together.

"I've got to get to work," she said, feeling torn up inside.

"Hang in there, Natalie. We're almost in the clear," he said, and she could tell he meant it.

But she still wasn't convinced. "That's what they always say—and then someone dies."

"Not this time. There's something else. I need you to get me on the guest list for tonight so we can sneak through the security pillbox. Put it under Mr. Courtney Brown of Tuxedo Park."

"Got it."

"The FBI has enough to worry about staking out Popov. He's the big fish they're after. I don't want the FBI meddling in our surveillance of Benedictis. We'll be in and out in fifteen minutes and no one from the party will miss us."

"Somehow, I don't think it's going to be that easy."

He shrugged, gave that inscrutable smile of his.

"I don't know what you've gotten me into, Benjamin Austin Brewbaker, but I feel like I'm in danger."

"Yeah, but it makes you feel alive, doesn't it? Remember, Mr. Courtney Brown of Tuxedo Park."

And then, like a specter, the veteran CIA officer disappeared into the crowd and was gone.

CHAPTER 22

THE VICTORIAN CLUB
1 WEST 77TH STREET

AS NICK LASSITER was escorted by the maître'd to one of the four private dining rooms at The Victorian Club, he found himself in awe of the restaurant's ostentatious elegance. Located in the Upper West Side, a stone's throw from the American Museum of Natural History, the establishment showed off a décor that was decidedly 1880's bordello chic. The large, open dining room and smaller private rooms boasted hand-crafted rosewood tables, chairs, and sideboards sporting tassels, fringes, and trimmed in silk and gilded leaf; ornate wooden carvings; decorative friezes; maroon velvet flocked wallpaper; curved moldings; and various polished brass antiquities lovingly imported from old ballrooms and castles of the United Kingdom. The interior was intended to recreate the ambiance of the Victorian-era "gin palaces" that had once flourished in the industrial cities of Northern Ireland and England and had later been faithfully recreated in the 19th century New World. As Lassiter passed the curved walnut bar, he couldn't help but feel as if he had been transported back a century and a half to the Gilded Age New York of Astor and Rockefeller.

The door to the private dining room was open and the maître'd led him to his table, where he found Beckett, Benedictis, and a third man in a suit with a miser's face and a small pile of paperwork in front of him. Benedictis, smartly dressed in a Savile Row suit, rose instantly from his velvet-backed seat with a smile and extended a hand.

"Nick, so kind of you to join us," he said, in a voice so welcoming that it instantly sent an alarm to Lassiter's brain.

He took the proffered hand and was pointed to the lone empty chair ringing the big rosewood table. He took a seat and looked at the third man. "And who might you be?"

"This is Stanton Greenbourne," said Benedictis by way of introduction. "He's Excalibur Media Group's in-house lead counsel. You know, to dot all the i's and cross all the t's. Just a formality."

Lassiter nodded warily. He glanced around the room, noting the handsomely authentic Victorian decor. "I hear the food here is great."

"This old dining establishment has an interesting history, Nick. It was a former Cabinet of Curiosity operated by P.T. Barnum. It is said to have a network of secret passageways running all along the walls of the various rooms. Back in Victorian times, these Cabinets of Curiosity were the precursors to natural history museums."

"Interesting."

"The one here in this building before The Victorian Club took up residence was exceptional. In the era of Boss Tweed, it housed the city's most rare and exotic paleontological and anthropological collections before the American Museum of Natural History was born. I'm kind of a New York history buff, Nick—that's why I'm telling you all this. Back in those days, there were more than a dozen parlor-style viewing rooms for the ancient fossils, wax figures, Medieval battle armor, exotic human and animal species, shrunken heads, precious gem stones, and the like. And as I said, running all along the perimeter of these rooms was a network of secret passageways with hidden doors and panels. The passageways allowed the proprietor to, shall we say, ramp up the scare factor by making ghostly sounds, rustling the curtains, and clanking tin cups. All in the name of enhancing the experience for the paying customers. P.T. Barnum operated his cabinet here before he set up shop at Barnum's American Museum, which eventually burned down, setting the stage for the American Museum of Natural History that we see today."

"Well, I feel fortunate to dine in such a historic place," said Lassiter pleasantly. "And, as I've said before, all I want today is an admission of guilt and an apology."

The room went silent. They sat there looking at him.

"What'd I say?"

"*Admission of guilt*, Nick? Why that's just the kind of loaded language that gives Esquire Greenbourne here indigestion. Don't get me wrong, you're going to get your apology…it's just that we need to honor certain legal niceties."

A waiter appeared, topped off their water glasses, and took their drink orders. Unfortunately, the upscale establishment didn't carry P.J.'s Bronx Brew, which Lassiter had grown fond of during his stay thus far in the city, so he went for a Guinness on tap. When the waiter shuffled off, he took a moment to look over the menu, noting that all three of his lunch companions—but especially Beckett who, in his view, was the most responsible for stealing *Blind Thrust*—appeared nervous.

"Why are you all so tense?" he asked innocently, peering over the top of his menu. "Don't tell me it's because I underdressed?"

A thrum of nervous laughter. "No, Nick," said the lawyer Greenbourne, speaking for the first time. "We're just surprised that all you want is an apology. Are you sure you don't have some clever trick up your sleeve?"

"I wish I could say I did, but I really just came here for the apology." He smiled at Beckett, who looked as though this was the last place on earth he wanted to be. "Though I have to admit I would like to know how and why you did it. My book was good, but it wasn't that good. So why did you steal it, Cam? You don't mind if I call you Cam, do you?"

Benedictis raised a hand to interject. "Again, Nick, that's the kind of question that's going to be tough to answer. We're not prepared to discuss the matter in that level of detail. I'm sure you can understand."

"But there must have been some reason you two were digging together through the slush pile? Were you just out of book ideas, Cam, or did you just cotton to my idea?"

119

Silence.

"Okay, how about this? Whose idea was it originally to steal my book? Was it you Cam, or"—he tilted his head towards Benedictis—"your literary agent?" He gave a shrug. "Was it the author or the agent, the chicken or the egg? Or was it a mutual decision?" He looked at Greenbourne. "Or what about Excalibur, Stanton? Was it perhaps your people? Is that how we came to be where we are today, Stanton? You don't mind if I call you Stanton, do you?"

"Actually, Nick, I do mind. You can call me Mr. Greenbourne."

"Sorry, but I like Stanton better. It has kind of a *J. Pierpont Morgan* feel to it that I think is particularly appropriate in our current one-percent setting." He gave an innocent shrug. "Come on, are you guys going to work with me here or not?" He looked hard at the bestselling author. "Think about it, Cam. I flew all the way out here from Colorado specifically to hear you apologize. As I've told you, I don't want money or fifteen minutes of fame. I'm also not one of those losers who gets some perverse sense of *schadenfreude* by dragging famous people through the mud, or cheering while another overpaid billionaire who made his fortune by fleecing the little guy gets his well-deserved comeuppance. Unlike most Americans, I don't derive pleasure from the misfortunes of others, even if those said others happen to be supreme assholes.

"To me, stealing from the little guy is the fundamental principle, the very backbone, upon which this great nation was founded. I mean think about it: how would the transcontinental railroads ever have been built by the robber barons that used to visit this old Cabinet of Curiosity if *fleecing* the little guy wasn't part of our national heritage? I don't want to mess with the American way, Cam. I just want an apology—and, I guess, a little explanation."

Greenbourne removed a document from his pile of paperwork. "Before we can do that, Nick, we're going to need you to sign this…uh…non-disclosure agreement and litigation release we've drafted up."

He pushed the clipped agreement across the dining table.

"Lawyers, guns, and money, Stanton—lawyers, guns, and money. You litigious fellows always have to have an agreement in place, don't you?"

Greenbourne frowned but said nothing. As Lassiter started to flip through the five-page legal document, the waiter reappeared with their drinks and asked them if they were ready to order.

"I think we need a few more minutes," Benedictis said to the waiter.

"No, we don't, I'm starving," said Lassiter, chucking aside the agreement and quickly scanning the menu again. "I'll start. They'll be ready by the time I order." He gave the waiter a conspiratorial grin. "I'm going to start out with the Oysters Rockefeller, a bowl of lobster bisque, and a fresh buffalini mozzarella tomato salad. For an entrée, I'll go with the pan-seared tuna with toasted black and white sesame seeds, watercress, seaweed salad, teriyaki sauce, and wasabi with a special topping of charred portabella bordelaise. For my sides, I'm thinking the five cheese mac and the sautéed asparagus will be a winner. And for dessert—I know, gentlemen, I'm decadent—I'm going to be so bold as to request the authentic New York cheese cake." He snapped the leather-bound menu shut with a resounding flourish. "I don't think I've ever had a one hundred and fifty dollar lunch before, so I want to thank you up front, gentlemen, for buying. By the way which one of you superrich, one-percent cocksuckers is footing the bill?"

"That'd be me, Nick," said Benedictis with visible irritation, and he proceeded to order his lunch of lobster avocado salad, followed by his two companions who both went for surf and turf of ten-ounce prime filet with a Brazilian lobster tail.

The waiter moved off and again they were alone. Lassiter could feel the tension at the table about to explode into something truly ugly, and wondered if he had been wrong to come to New York. How was an apology going to change anything or help him get his pilfered book published?

He returned his attention to the non-disclosure agreement and litigation release. He carefully read it over while his three adversaries looked on with growing anxiety. By the time he had finished, he still wasn't sure what the hell he would be agreeing to by signing the papers. He shook his head and took a big gulp of his Guinness, hoping the alcohol would loosen him up.

"So, let me get this straight," he said. "You want me to sign this five-page legal document that says you didn't do anything wrong. And then, once I do that, you're going to apologize to me for plagiarism and copyright infringement. Does that make sense to you guys because, to be honest, it doesn't make any sense to me?"

They looked as if someone had died. No one said a word. He noticed that Beckett's hands were trembling. Jesus, was the guy going to wet his pants?

"Let me ask another question. If I don't sign this, are you refusing to apologize?"

"Yes," said Greenbourne. "You need to sign it." The lawyer then gave an unctuous smile. "But I am also authorized to give you a little incentive for your signature."

He made a big show of pulling an unlabeled, white envelope from his suit coat and pushing it across the table as he had done with the agreement. Lassiter opened the envelope, pretended to blow off some dust, and withdrew a check made out in his name from Excalibur Media Group, Inc.

He nearly jumped out of his seat. "A half-million dollars? You're offering me a half-million fucking dollars?"

Benedictis immediately shot Greenbourne a hard stare. "A half-million? But I thought we were only—"

The counselor cut off the words with a raised hand. "That's your money, Nick. Now please sign the agreement. All it says is that you agree not to disclose any information to any outside parties or to pursue litigation against us, or any other third party, in regards to your unpublished book."

"So you're offering me a half-million dollars to keep my mouth shut."

No one said a word. They all just sat there looking guilty.

And then, frantically and without warning, Beckett jumped up from his chair. "I am dreadfully sorry, Nick—I know I shouldn't have done it!" he cried. To Lassiter's surprise, genuine tears burst from his eyes like a cloudburst. "I bollixed everything up…I was a fool…I was an idiot…I was a drunk, drugged-up buffoon and if I could take it all back I would do it in a—"

"Shut up, Cameron!" shrieked Greenbourne. "He hasn't signed the damned agreement yet!"

"I tell you, I don't even want to be a writer anymore, Nick…I'm done, I'm done, I quit…between the story development, pay-through and bonus clauses, the deadlines, the nitpicky line editing, the disputes over electronic and subsidiary rights, and the endless promotion…sometimes I just want to fucking die, Nick…I just want it all to fucking end!"

"You don't know what you're talking about, Cam!" cried Benedictis. "Everything's going to be all right! Now just settle down!"

"My God, look at what you've done to him, Lassiter!" snarled Greenbourne. "Now sign the damned agreement!"

"I am sorry, Nick…I am genuinely sorry…it wasn't Anton's fault either…I was the one who pushed it…all he did was show it to me, I swear…it was my fault…he did it out of pity and a sense of loyalty to me…he was just doing his fucking job. And that's the bloody truth!"

"Shut up—that's enough!" cried Greenbourne, and he leaned across the table, grabbed the check, and waved it aggressively at Nick. "You're not getting this until you sign, damn you! Now what's it going to be?"

Lassiter looked down at the legal document that he didn't understand at all except that it went against everything he stood for. Then he looked at Beckett. He couldn't believe the man was having a nervous breakdown before his very eyes. He looked so pathetic that Lassiter couldn't help but feel sorry for him. Maybe being a mega-bestselling author wasn't such a great thing after all.

Against both his publisher's and agent's wishes, Beckett blubbered on with his confession, the spittle flying off the crazed Aussie's livery lips like windshield washer fluid. But his contrition, Lassiter could tell, was genuine.

"I didn't know what else to do, Nick…I read your synopsis and full-length manuscript and I just couldn't help myself…I stole it…stole the whole bloody goddamned thing and made it into my own…it was a little raw, but I knew as soon as I read it that I could turn it into a blockbuster…I was a mess back then…my God, what am I talking about, I'm still a knackered mess…I don't even want to be a goddamned writer anymore…oh crikey, what's the fucking point?"

Benedictis was up out of his chair rushing to Beckett's side, and Lassiter could tell that he genuinely cared for the pathetic little man. "It's going to be all right, Cam—everything's going to be all right! But you've got to keep quiet now! You're going to be all right!"

Greenbourne was up on his feet, frothing belligerently at the mouth. "Sign it, Lassiter! Sign it now, or you're finished! Do you hear me, finished!"

"Oh, he's finished all right," said a new voice, and Lassiter looked up to see his father strutting casually into the private dining room. But before he could utter a word of surprise or acknowledgement, he heard Benedictis cry out in shock: "Austin Brewbaker, what in the hell are you doing here?"

Lassiter's mouth fell open.

"Hello Anton, long time, no see," said his father nonchalantly. "How are you and my son, Nick, getting along?"

"Your son? Really? Now how can that be when he doesn't have your damned last name?"

"Because he chose not to keep it. When Nick's mother and I were divorced and he and Vivian moved to Colorado, Nick took his mom's maiden name. You see, my son was angry at me—just as he is angry at you right now."

"Dad, what the hell is going on? You actually know this guy?"

"We all know each other, Nick," said Beckett, who seemed to have recovered his senses. "We went to Oxford together."

He looked frantically at his father. "What the hell is he talking about?"

"It's true, Son. Anton and I were there for a year as exchange students. He was at Columbia when I was at Yale. I didn't know Beckett very well at Oxford—we were only acquaintances—but Anton did. That's when their future profitable relationship first began."

"Why the hell didn't you tell me?"

"You didn't ask."

Lassiter just sat there openmouthed, trying to process it all. His father stepped forward, calmly reached into his pocket, and withdrew his iPhone—except it *wasn't* an iPhone at all, Lassiter realized with shock.

"Congratulations, Son, you just recorded the whole conversation—and I must say it was most illuminating." The voice was so smooth yet incisive that it could have belonged to James Bond, only with an American accent. He then glowered at Greenbourne. "Did you really think, Stanton, you could buy off my son for a half-million dollars?"

"Wait, we can cut a deal," said the lawyer, a note of panic in his voice. "It's not too late."

"Oh, but it is too late, Stanton. Nick and I have everything we need now."

His father hit a button on the fake iPhone and Beckett's desperate voice resonated like Pavarotti: *"...I read your synopsis and full-length manuscript and I just couldn't help myself...I stole it...stole the whole bloody goddamned thing and made it into my own...it was a little raw, but I knew as soon as I read it that I could turn it into a blockbuster..."*

"You can't do this!" cried Greenbourne. "I tell you we can cut a deal. This is New York, goddamnit—that's what we do best here! Listen to me! We've got to cut a fucking deal!"

Lassiter felt torn. What Beckett and Benedictis had done was unconscionable, but his manipulative father was hardly any better. He glowered at him, feeling that, under the circumstances, he was almost equally as culpable.

"Goddamn you, Dad! You shouldn't have tricked me!" he snarled at him. "All I wanted was a simple apology—on my terms and no one else's—and you had to go and do this." He then let his rage fall on the others. "All of you should be ashamed. You had to twist this thing all around without once taking into account the simplicity of what I wanted. Goddamn you all—except you, Mr. Beckett. I feel sorry for you. As far as I'm concerned, you and I are square. But for the rest of you—fuck you!"

And with that he stormed out of the dining room just as the waiter brought his Oysters Rockefeller, bowl of lobster bisque, and fresh buffalini mozzarella tomato salad.

CHAPTER 23

CENTRAL PARK

SILENTLY FUMING, Lassiter passed the sprawling, rusticated brownstone building and towering white columns of the American Museum on his left before waiting for the light to turn at the Central Park West crosswalk. He went over in his mind what had just happened. Had he really just thrown away a half-million dollars? Had his father really just rushed in and made a fool out of him? And couldn't he have at least tucked away an Oyster Rockefeller or two and a few steaming spoonfuls of lobster bisque before running out the damned door? I mean, he was goddamned starving and The Victorian Club was one of the most legendary dining establishments in New York City. But most importantly, what the hell was he going to do now that his father had tricked him into secretly recording Beckett's admission of guilt on what looked like an ordinary iPhone?

He looked back at the shimmering bronze statue of Theodore Roosevelt mounted on horseback. "What do you think, Teddy?" he posed rhetorically. "Got any ideas? Am I a complete fucking moron for stampeding out to your old stomping grounds to get an apology? Should I just sue the shit out of the bastards and call it a day?"

The light turned. He crossed the street into the park, quickly finding a paved path winding through the trees and heading south. Before he had gone a hundred feet, he saw his father dash out of the trees ahead of him and come to a halt on the path. Jesus Christ, should he turn and walk the other way? But he could tell that his dad wasn't going to be deterred. So instead of avoiding him, he walked right up to him, noting that the son of a bitch looked relieved that he was even willing to speak to him.

"All right, you can start apologizing now, dickhead," he said without breaking stride.

His dad jumped in beside him on the left. "I'm sorry, Nick," he said right off the bat. "I know I should have told you about the recording, but I didn't want you to be nervous in case they searched you. Plus I…I can't lie…I wanted to stick it to Benedictis and Beckett for what they did to you."

"So you had to trick me? You could have at least had the dignity to include me in the subterfuge."

"I know it was a bad idea." His father was panting, still out of breath from running after him. "But for the record, it was your mother's bad idea, not mine."

"That fiasco back there was Mom's idea? That's just great. You guys have been secretly back together for only a few months and already you've got her thinking like a spy. Even though that's why she left you in the first place. Nicely done, Dad."

"You don't know the man you're dealing with here."

"What's that supposed to mean?"

"It means that I didn't just *know* Anton de Benedictis in college. I knew him well."

"How well?"

"Enough to know that he is a formidable adversary and not to be underestimated."

"Is that so? How the hell do you know him so well? You were only at Oxford for a year and that was a long time ago."

"Because he was my best friend."

"You've got to be shitting me. Anton De Benedictis was your best friend?"

"He was until I got kicked out of Oxford on account of the son of bitch. That's when he became my worst enemy."

He came to sudden halt. "I don't fucking believe this."

"I knew this was going to be difficult."

"You're an asshole, Dad. Don't talk to me like that. That's why Mom left you, you know, because you used to talk like that."

"Like what?"

"Like a superior prick."

"I'm sorry," he said, and Lassiter could tell that he meant it. "But you've got to understand who we're dealing with here."

"I don't know who I'm dealing with when it comes to you. You never told me you got kicked out of Oxford. All you said was that you were there for your junior year abroad. What did you get kicked out for and how was Benedictis a part of it?"

"It's complicated."

"Then you'd better start talking."

"I took the fall for him."

"What?"

"Like I said, he was my best friend over there, but he betrayed me. I took the wrap for something he did. God help me, but that's what happened."

He shook his head in disbelief. "Jesus Christ, the plot thickens. I don't believe this shit."

"Well, you'd better start. I've been trying to catch the bastard for years."

"What do you mean...with your work at the CIA? But he's just a *literary agent.*"

"He's a hell of a lot more than that, Son. I'm sorry, but I can't tell you anything more than that. At least not yet. It's for your own protection."

They went silent. His father scanned the trees to their right, like a deer picking up the slightest sound, and Lassiter wondered if they were being watched or followed. He felt a vague presence that was disconcerting.

"We should keep moving," said his father, studying the trees to their left now as well as the commuters, tourists, and joggers moving along the footpath, the people sitting on the park benches lining the path, and the picnickers sitting on the blankets spread out on the grassy lawn. Suddenly everyone looked suspicious,

125

SAMUEL MARQUIS

even the young couple making out beneath a leafy oak tree and the septuagenarian reading the *Times*.

They started off again, walking at a brisk pace along the asphalt footpath. Dappled sunlight trickled through the leafy branches of the overhanging trees. But the trees made him feel hemmed in, threatened. Shit, were they really being followed? Lassiter kept a vigilant eye out, feeling increasingly paranoid.

"How did you get kicked out of Oxford?" he asked his father. "What did you do?"

"Benedictis and I got rip-roaring drunk one night and drove through campus at high speed in his car. We ended up tearing up a bowling green and almost killing two young British girls. They were the twin daughters of a shipping magnate and major college donor. They had to jump out of the way on a stone footbridge that we were racing down and were badly hurt in the fall. One of them broke her back and was in traction for a month, and the other had major reconstructive facial surgery. It was Benedictis's car and he was the one driving, but at the inquest I said that it was me and I was alone."

"Jesus, Dad, why in the hell did you do that?"

"Because Benedictis said that his father would kill him, or at least disown him, if he was expelled. His father was an Italian longshoreman from Hell's Kitchen and he had used his connections with both the Catholic archdiocese and the local alderman to get his son into Columbia. It would have been a major humiliation for him to have his son kicked out of Oxford as an exchange student after all the strings he had pulled. Benedictis was convinced the son of a bitch would actually kill him. To this day, I'm not sure he was exaggerating. He was my best friend and, rather than have us *both* kicked out of school, I decided to take the rap. At the time, I thought it was the right thing to do since it had been my idea to play Mario Andretti and race around campus snot-slinging drunk in the first place. Benedictis didn't want to do it and I talked him into it. I was going to be the one to drive, but at the last second he shoved me aside and climbed into the driver's seat. Neither one of us had any business being behind the wheel that night. But I insisted. I was the one that pushed it. I was the one who made it all happen, so I thought I should be the one to take the rap."

"So you were kicked out for protecting your friend?"

"I wasn't just kicked out of Oxford. I was booted from Yale, too. I had to take a year off performing community service and then reapply for admission. Thankfully, I was readmitted and finished two years later. Needless to say, I wasn't asked to join the Skull and Bones Society."

"Why didn't you just tell the truth?"

"You don't think I wanted to?"

"Well, why didn't you?"

"Because I swore an oath to my friend and didn't want to blow it for him with his martinet of a father. I figured that it was my fault for talking him into it in the first place and there was no reason for us both to go down. Except, as I found out later, he wasn't my friend at all. He used me."

They stopped again. He looked his father in the eyes, shaking his head with disappointment. The old man was clearly ashamed and he couldn't remember him

126

ever looking so vulnerable and ordinary.

"I apologize for not telling you the truth sooner, Son. And I'm sorry for letting you down. Again."

"So what you did back there at lunch was about getting even with Benedictis for what he did to you back at Oxford?"

"No, that's not it at all. I mean, yes I wanted to even the score I suppose but…but it's a lot more complicated than that. I shouldn't be telling you this, but the truth is I'm running a top-secret CIA operation that involves spying on Benedictis."

"Jesus. But I thought the CIA was only supposed to spy on foreigners? Or at least on foreign soil? I thought it was the FBI that handles domestic security threats?"

"Since 9/11, our mandate has changed, Nick. I can't tell you anything more. I've told you too much already."

"Why can't you?"

"You know why. I could lose my job and go to prison."

"Yeah, but you've already gotten me involved. The moment you snuck that recording device into my jacket, you made me essentially an agent acting under your orders."

"Now let's not get this all mixed up. Your unofficial copyright infringement case and my official covert operation have nothing to do with one another. As a matter of fact, your untimely involvement with Benedictis could blow my whole op if we're not careful."

"Then why the hell did you storm in and threaten them with the recording?"

"Because your mother and I both wanted more for you than just an apology. We both know what Beckett and Benedictis have done, Nick. It's a flagrant case of plagiarism and copyright infringement—and I'm sorry but we weren't about to let them get away with it."

"But it wasn't your decision to make. They stole my book, not yours."

"I'm sorry, but your mom and I both feel strongly about it. At least now we have the recording. Now you're in control of the situation and can threaten them with legal action, if that's what you choose to do. Mark my words, they're going to be desperate to cut a deal—and it's going to be for a hell of a lot more than a half-million dollars."

"But it wasn't your goddamned decision to make. This is my life we're talking about here, not yours."

"We just couldn't let you do it. And to be quite honest, I'm thinking that what you're doing will ultimately prove helpful to my case. Right now, you're shaking things up and creating the perfect diversion. If Benedictis is worried about recorded conversations regarding copyright violations, he's going to be distracted from other concerns. Plus I don't have much time—I have to move quickly."

"Why? Why do you have to move quickly? What has Benedictis done that involves national security?"

"I've already told you I can't tell you that. I've told you too much as it is."

Suddenly, a pair of onyx-black Lexus 570 SUVs ripped out of the trees and screeched to a halt in front of them. The doors of the vehicles popped open and six insanely fit men wearing gray suits and radio headsets jumped out.

Oh great, now what?

But before he and his father had a chance to react, the men in the gray suits surrounded them and shoved semiautomatics in their faces.

CHAPTER 24

CENTRAL PARK

"GET IN THE CAR NOW!" snapped an older, bald-headed man with a glossy patina of wax on his hairless cranium, gunmetal-gray eyes, and thick bulging biceps that rivaled those of a silverback gorilla. There was no doubt that Wax Head was the one in charge.

"Okay, okay, we're getting in," said his father. "Just take it easy."

Easy be damned—they were grabbed violently and hurled like ragdolls into the back seat of the lead Lexus. Then the doors slammed shut and they were off. A driver and Wax Head sat up front. Two suits sat behind Lassiter and his father in the third row of the monstrous SUV, insolently pointing guns at them.

"I don't know who you are," said his father, "but you should know that kidnapping is a felony offense that carries a decade of prison time."

Wax Head squinted disapprovingly. "I'll ask the questions if you don't mind, Mr. Brewbaker. Where's the recording device?"

His father said nothing.

Wax Head tipped his head towards one of the men in the back. Out of the corner of his eye, Lassiter saw the butt end of a pistol crack hard upon the back of his father's head.

What the fuck!

Lassiter swung his fist back angrily and popped the guy in the nose. "Don't fucking do that to my dad!" he cried, and he was instantly knocked in the head by the other enforcer in the back.

For a moment he saw stars.

"I will not ask you again, Mr. Brewbaker. Hand over the recording device."

"Okay, I'm doing as you say. Just don't hit my son again." He slowly reached into his pocket. "Just tell me one thing. Who are you guys? Do you work for Excalibur?"

Wax Head said nothing. His expression remained emotionless. The Lexus blasted through a copse of leafy trees and raced down a crowded path, scattering panicked commuters and joggers in all directions. Lassiter watched in anxious silence as his father withdrew the iPhone from his jacket pocket and handed it over to Wax Head, who took a moment to inspect the device before calmly slipping it into his own pocket.

"What are you doing in New York, Mr. Brewbaker? You work at CIA headquarters in Langley, Virginia, and yet we find you here. Why?"

"I must say that Excalibur does hire top notch private security to handle its problems. The associative word *Blackwater* comes to mind. But to answer your question, I'm here to visit my son."

"Is that so? So this is all a little father-son reunion. How lovely."

"Who the hell are you? Because I am a senior federal officer and what you're doing *is* kidnapping."

"And what you just did back at The Victorian Club could be considered both a misuse of government resources and a form of entrapment by the Office of the CIA Inspector General. You're not supposed to be spying on American citizens, Mr. Brewbaker. And you have no business in the city that can, in any way, be considered lawful. So why don't you make it easy on everyone and just leave. Take your son on a real vacation, say to Bermuda."

"But we don't want to leave the city. We like it here just fine."

Wax Head signaled his men in the back seat again. Lassiter heard a loud *Thwack* as the goon directly behind his father again cracked his pistol down on the back of his head. Lassiter cringed in vicarious pain as the cracking noise echoed through the Lexus along with the strain of the gunning engine. Reaching back, he raised his arm to protect his father from a second blow, but was dealt a savage knock to his own head. At the same time, his father was struck again. This time Lassiter saw blood dripping from the left side of his father's head, and he felt himself cut open too. They promptly stopped resisting.

"That's enough for now," commanded Wax Head to his men, his stentorian voice bringing instant silence to the vehicle. "Now Mr. Brewbaker, I need you to tell me that you will be leaving the city to go on a nice, long vacation with your son. If you do that, further violence can be avoided."

Lassiter still saw a trace of defiance on his father's face as the Lexus veered off the asphalt path and onto Center Drive, heading south. "You have the recording. What more do you need?"

"As I've made quite clear, I need you both to leave town." His gunmetal-gray eyes were as cold and brittle as winter ice as he shifted his gaze to Lassiter. "That's what Detective Stafford told you to do in the first place, Nick. You should have listened to him."

His father smiled with challenge. "So Stafford's on the payroll too. I don't know for sure who you're working for—though I'd put my money on Excalibur—but I am going to enjoy seeing you in a jail cell. With that well-honed physique of yours, you're going to be a very popular fellow."

Lassiter tensed in anticipation of the next blow. There was a lengthy silence, pregnant with anticipation, as the Lexus darted in and out of traffic and came upon Sixth Avenue, but neither of them was struck again. Every nerve and fiber of his body wanted to fight back, but he knew in the end it would be to no avail. Wax Head was making no idle threat. The entity the man represented was obviously powerful and highly motivated. Even more ominous, that entity could crush him and his father like insects, if the suits in the corporate board rooms giving the orders so desired.

With sudden clarity, he realized that his pursuit of justice here in New York had always been a pipe dream. From the beginning, he had been severely overmatched. In the long term, billions of publishing dollars were at stake, not to mention the professional reputations of highly influential movers and shakers in

America's most powerful mega-metropolis. How naïve he had been to think that he could traipse into the Big Apple and obtain a sense of justice, however small, without a grueling fight and without suffering countless setbacks.

Wax Head exhaled. "You have one chance and one chance only to make this right. Leave town by tomorrow and you will all go on to live happy lives. But come five o'clock, if you all are still here, well, I don't want to even contemplate how unfortunate that would be. Have we reached an understanding?"

The Lexus turned left onto West 56th Street. "Yes, we read you loud and clear," said his father, taking Lassiter by surprise. He had thought that his old man would resist to the bitter end. Or was his father bluffing, setting himself up to fight another day? "We'll be out of town by five tomorrow. You have my word on that. Now please let us go."

Wax Head looked at Lassiter, waiting for his answer. Though Lassiter wanted to kick the living shit out of the guy and not concede a thing, he nodded his head. Maybe it wasn't such a bad compromise, all things considered. After all, the skin-headed bastard had the firm upper hand.

Wax Head smiled the smile of a man who was used to winning. Looking at him, Lassiter could only imagine how much worse tomorrow would be if they were still in town and the grinning son of a bitch managed to find them. At that moment, Wax Head raised a liver-spotted hand and tapped it against the driver's headrest. The Lexus came to a halt at the curb at precisely 44 West 56th Street.

"Well, well," he observed sarcastically. "What do you know? We're already at your apartment, Mr. Brewbaker. Just in time for you and your son here to start packing your bags."

One of his suited thugs jumped out and opened the rear door, his movements surprisingly cat-like. Lassiter started to get out, but was held up by Wax Head as his father stepped from the vehicle on the other side.

Brewbaker saw what was happening and quickly protested. "You've got to let my son go, or there's no deal!"

"Is that so?" said Wax Head, and the doors suddenly shut and auto-locked.

Lassiter tried to push open the door, but his hand was smacked with the butt of a gun by one of the goons.

The Lexus peeled off down 56th.

Wax Head stared mutely out the window, his face expressionless. And then suddenly, the passenger door next to Lassiter popped open.

"We're going to be watching you, Nick—so don't do anything stupid," Wax Head warned as the Lexus screamed down the street. "Oh, and have a safe landing."

He was shoved out the open car door and jettisoned from the racing vehicle. Tumbling violently onto the sidewalk, he took out a pair of pedestrians waiting at the crosswalk at the knees like a bowling ball. He didn't come to a stop until he crashed into a stout metal light pole, feeling a shockwave of pain ripple up his back and through his head.

The last thing he saw before he blacked out was Wax Head glaring down at him through the front passenger window as the Lexus tore off down the street.

CHAPTER 25

AMERICAN MUSEUM OF NATURAL HISTORY
CENTRAL PARK WEST AND 79TH STREET

AFTER THE DEBACLE AT LUNCH, Cameron Beckett was resistant at first to taking some time off to regroup and visit the legendary American Museum; but after a concerted effort, Benedictis was able to talk him into it. They entered from the Theodore Roosevelt Rotunda at the top of the Central Park West steps—named for the vigorous outdoorsman and twenty-sixth president who had helped found the museum—and passed a series of thick pink marble columns and the skeleton of a huge *Barosaurus.* The long-necked plant-eater was being attacked by an *Allosaurus* while rearing up to protect her young. Stepping inside, Benedictis paid for two tickets, grabbed a map, and they quickly headed for the elevators to the fourth floor containing the dinosaur collections. Even after more than a century, the Saurian overlords of the Mesozoic Era still remained the museum's top attraction.

Unfortunately, Beckett was still a wreck. He had to be brought back from the brink before tonight's gala in celebration of the perennial bestseller. Otherwise, he might become an even bigger liability—and that had to be avoided at all costs. After the lunch at The Victorian Club, David Sloan had phoned to inform Benedictis that Lassiter's recording had been recovered by Excalibur's private security team. But Sloan also issued a strong warning: get their mutual cash cow Beckett under control or face serious consequences.

On the fourth floor, they watched a short video on the history of vertebrate paleontology and the celebrated museum from the first major fossil-hunting expedition in 1891 to the present day. The American Museum was founded in 1869 by a group of New York's Gilded Age elite, businessmen who hoped a museum packed with paleontological and ethnological curiosities would bring prestige to their city to match London and Paris, as well as educate the labor classes about the laws of this newfangled thing called *Science.* From humble beginnings, it had evolved into the largest natural history museum in the world, displaying more than thirty million specimens from all branches of natural history, along with a wealth of anthropological artifacts, in a vast complex of interconnected buildings. Most of the collections of mammalian and dinosaur fossils were concealed from public view and tucked away in storage vaults buried deep within the vast Museum complex.

Since he was a little kid growing up in Hell's Kitchen, Benedictis had loved coming here. Back then, the cavernous building and dinosaur exhibits had a dank, musty-old-bones atmosphere that was nothing like today's dazzling interactive displays. All the same, he had relished coming here on school fieldtrips and on the occasional Sunday afternoon with his parents and younger brother Danny.

When the film was finished, he and Beckett began a prehistoric journey that traced the evolution of vertebrates by means of a walking tour through the Hall of Vertebrate Origins, Halls of Saurischian and Ornithischian dinosaurs, and Halls of Primitive and Advanced Mammals. Many of the fossils on display represented unique and historic pieces that were collected during the American Museum's "Golden Age" of worldwide paleontological and archaeological expeditions from the 1880s to the 1930s. The Museum's roster of renowned fossil-hunters included such past luminaries as Barnum Brown, Roy Chapman Andrews, and Henry Fairfield Osborn.

"This is top shelf, Anton. Thank you for doing this," gushed Beckett, who seemed to have returned to his saner self since the lunchtime disaster as they halted before the massive skull of a 66-million year old *Triceratops*. "But I'm afraid I've made up my mind."

"Made up your mind? Made up your mind about what?"

"I don't want to be a goddamned writer anymore. I've bollixed up my life and I don't want to write bestselling novels any longer."

Benedictis held up a hand. "Now just hold on, Cameron, let's not make any rash decisions."

"I'm telling you the 'Aussie James Patterson' is kaput. I can't take it anymore and I want out."

My God, Beckett was worse off than he had thought. "Listen, I know how you feel and I want you to know that I've got your back. Why don't you consider taking some time off and see how that goes first?"

"I've already made my decision. I want out—strordnary, I know, but I'm done. I just don't have the fire in my belly anymore."

"You're just upset. You know you're not supposed to make life-altering decisions when you're in an agitated state. Mark my words, you'll change your mind in a day or two."

"No, I just don't give a bloody damn anymore. I want out. Hell, you can take my name and write my novels. I've already given you full control of my work, as well as the right to use my name in the event of my death, or God forbid, incapacitation. It's written in my will as you bloody well know. So why not just let me quietly step away and allow you to take over while I'm still alive? There's no real difference. I'm done, Anton. I can't do it anymore."

He thought for a moment. His initial reaction was that it was an outlandish idea, but the more he pondered the more intriguing it sounded. But could they actually pull it off?

"I understand that in the event of your death or incapacitation, I am authorized to carry on writing, or to arrange for ghostwriters, under the name Cameron Beckett. But you're alive, Cam. I can't very well start penning novels under your name when you're still alive. That would be a little creepy, don't you think?"

"No, because I want out and you're the only person I trust to carry on my legacy. We've spent the last twenty-two years building up my brand, but now I'm finished. I'm only too glad to pass it on to you."

"But what about your family? What about Nicole and your two boys? And what about your mother? What will they think about this?"

"I don't know and I don't care. My will already gives you one hundred percent of all future proceeds of the novels you write. After everything you've done for me since you plucked me from obscurity, I owe you that much. My family and I are already sitting pretty with well over a billion dollars in the bank. Why the hell do we need more?"

"I don't know, you tell me."

"The answer is we don't. So why don't you just do it? Take over as me— Cameron Barnaby Beckett IV—starting tomorrow. Hell, you've practically written half of my books with all your rewrites anyway. And without you, I would never have become a bestselling author. You not only gave me my first shot, I can honestly say you made me what I am today."

Benedictis had long known that to be true, but he appreciated his client, once again, acknowledging the pivotal role he had played in his meteoric rise to the top of, and continuing #1 ranking on, the global bestseller lists. He thought about what Beckett was saying as they moved on to the exhibit of a duck-billed hadrosaur. The odd-looking herbivore with the skull capped by a crescent-shaped helmet had lived in the river valleys and swamps of Western North America 70 million years ago.

"Cameron, I don't know about this. This sounds like crazy talk."

"Why? Why is it crazy? You and I have always talked about the possibility."

"But again, you're not dead or incapacitated."

"So what? I can still hand over my rights. Hell, look at the success of the continuing Robert Ludlum, Tom Clancy, Vince Flynn, and V.C. Andrews series. Some of those authors have sold better dead than when they were alive!"

Benedictis considered a moment. Though what Beckett was proposing sounded terribly far-fetched at first blush, the truth was that for a branded suspense series, the author didn't really matter. The James Bond and Bourne series had continued on quite nicely on the *New York Times* bestseller lists long after the deaths of both Ian Fleming and Robert Ludlum despite being written by no-name authors. And the same went for the Jack Ryan and Mitch Rapp series originally penned by Clancy and Flynn. Furthermore, sometimes the boldest feats in the history of mankind had started out as oddball notions. But could they really pull it off? What would Excalibur's reaction be? Then again, this might be his chance to stick it to them and renegotiate. After the atrocious treatment Sloan and Greenbourne had subjected him to, the thought sent a delightful shudder up his spine.

"So let me get this straight," he said as they walked into the next room, the Hall of Saurischian dinosaurs that included both the plant-eating longnecks and the meat-eating theropods like T-Rex and the lethal, fleet-footed raptor *Deinonychus.* "You're saying you would step down and I would take over as Cameron Beckett, bestselling suspense novelist? I would do all of your series and independent works?"

"Like I said, you already do half the writing anyway. Why only take fifteen percent when you can get one hundred percent? I'm a brand that will extend far into my afterlife. But why not get started now?"

"You would do this for me?"

"Of course. As I said, I've spent the last twenty-two years writing suspense novels and building up a loyal audience. I don't want my name to disappear. I just don't want the hassle of writing the books anymore. I'm done—I've taken my last breath. But my name will always live on. Just like him."

He nodded towards the massive specimen of *Tyrannosaurus rex* towering above them. They came to a stop and Benedictis felt his breath taken away. The skull was enormous, more than five feet long, with a huge gaping mouth and dagger-shaped teeth serrated like a butcher's knife. With its battery of powerful jaw muscles, the monstrous creature, in life, must have been able to easily puncture bone and rip off huge chunks of flesh in a single bite. Not surprisingly, the specimen he stood gawking at had given him a thrill ever since he was a little kid growing up in Hell's Kitchen. It was, quite simply, the most stupendous thing he had ever seen.

"Crikey, he truly was the Tyrant Lizard King," remarked Beckett, staring up with wide eyes at what was, without a doubt, the fiercest predator on land of all time.

"That's you, Cameron—you are just like him. The biggest literary giant of all time."

"No, my friend—it's you. You're the new literary titan who will carry on my legacy for the next half century. I want to give a press conference tomorrow to make the announcement. Let's do it at, say, four o'clock. That ought to give me enough time between now and then to talk to my lawyer and settle my affairs. I'm anxious to get on with my new life."

"Cam, come on, how long have we known each other? Are you sure you want to do this?"

"I'm a dinosaur, Anton. My time has come to an end. All that remains is my legacy and the brand I have built up all these years. But I want one other thing from you as well."

Benedictis continued to be stunned by his sudden change in fortune. Excalibur's security people had recovered Lassiter's recording and now his client was anointing him as a long-term, billionaire, bestselling author! My, how quickly Lady Luck changed hands; this was positively Dickensian! Of course, if he went through with this, he would need to get someone to run the office and take all of his clients so he could be freed up to write full time, which was what he had always dreamed of one day doing but had been putting off for years.

"Whatever you want, Cam," he said, feeling a flicker of euphoria at how suddenly his situation in life had changed for the better. "Just tell me what it is."

"I want you to set up another lunch meeting with Lassiter."

The request came like a blow to the head. "What? I don't think that's a good idea. We're through with Lassiter."

"I'm going to give him a million dollars and apologize in person—like I should have done from the beginning. And I want you to apologize as well."

"Look, we've been through this, Cam. We agreed that we should both stay as far away from that son of a bitch as possible."

"I'm asking you to do this for me, Anton. If you want to take my place as the 'Aussie James Patterson' then you'll do this one simple thing for me. Nick Lassiter deserves that much."

He couldn't believe what he was hearing. He had the same ominous feeling as he did three years ago when they had originally stolen *Blind Thrust* and set the stage for Nick Lassiter to alter their lives. It was déjà vu. He was signing a pact with the devil—and, once again, it would come back to haunt them both.

"I think it's a bad idea, Cam," he said, trying not to sound like he was pleading. "I'm just being honest with you. The kid is bad news, and you know what his dad is like."

"I hardly knew him at Oxford. But you obviously did."

"Austin Brewbaker was my best friend, next to you, of course."

"He's certainly not anymore—you could see that as plain as day. What happened between you two? You weren't involved in that reckless driving scandal that got him kicked out of Oxford, were you?"

"No, of course not," he lied. "Let's just say we were young and mistakes were made."

"All right, fair enough. But I still want you to set up the meeting with his son. I'm giving Nick a million dollars and you and I are going to apologize to him. Alone of course. I don't want that bastard Greenbourne or any other Excalibur suits to be there."

"All right, I'll set it up. But I still think you're making a big mistake."

"That very well may be, Anton, but it's high time you and I quit mucking around and do the bloody right thing. After all, we don't just have to answer to ourselves, mate."

"Then to who?"

"You know very well who. To that all-powerful, cheeky fellow in the sky who stands ready in waiting for Judgment Day."

CHAPTER 26

AUSTIN BREWBAKER answered his coded mobile after the second ring. It was a private number with no caller ID showing up on his digital display. However, he instantly recognized the voice on the other end. It belonged to Franklin Harcourt, Deputy Director of the CIA's National Clandestine Service. The no-nonsense mandarin, a thirty-five year Company veteran, was his immediate boss at the agency.

"And to what do I owe the honor, sir?"

"Oh, cut the crap, Austin. You've been running around the Big Apple like Jesse James and I want to know what the hell you're doing."

He hadn't seen this kind of trouble coming and was taken off guard. He took a moment to collect his thoughts before responding as he stepped into his bedroom. Nick and his buddies had gone out and he was all alone in the apartment.

"It's complicated, sir. Is this a secure line?"

"Would I be calling you if it wasn't? I want to know what the fuck is going on, Austin, and I want to know now," snarled the deputy director.

"I got a little sidetracked. A diversion unexpectedly popped up."

"You're talking about your son."

"Yes, sir."

"Bringing family members into the fold and putting them in harm's way goes against Company protocols. You know that, Austin."

"Yes, sir, I'm well versed in agency protocol."

"And yet, you deliberately misused Company resources by unlawfully recording a meeting involving your son?"

"Who told you that?"

"That's not important. I'm telling you this so you realize the hornet's nest you've stirred up. Are you familiar with Vortex Security?"

"Of course, second only to Blackwater."

"Well that bald-headed gentleman that interrogated you and took your recording device is Mark Maupin, second-in-command over there. He and I happen to have worked together during Desert Storm back in '91. He called me a half hour ago and filled me in on your little covert op."

"The son of a bitch should be locked up. He kidnapped me and my son."

"No, you're the one who was out of line. You used special agency developmental technology and resources to pursue a personal, non-agency matter involving a family member."

"The cases are related. I'm using my son to get at Benedictis and Popov."

"*Using your son?* Do you realize how wrong that sounds? What's next Grandma Brewbaker and Uncle Fester?"

"I just thought that this copyright infringement business between my son and Cameron Beckett had given us an opportunity."

"An opportunity?"

"To stir the pot. Benedictis is getting pressure now from Popov and the Russians. They broke into his office and I need to find out what they were after. I tell you, I'm getting close, Franklin. If you want Popov, you've got to let me finish the job."

The phone went silent. Excruciatingly silent.

Brewbaker felt a sense of desperation wash over him as he stared out the window at the dirty, bustling city below. He couldn't be shut down now—not when he was so goddamned close!

"I can see your thought process now, Austin. But you have to understand, you're not authorized to fight your son's battles using agency resources or to cause friction with local law enforcement personal. The Company can neither authorize nor condone that type of renegade approach. We have to answer to too many people, especially when it involves domestic resources. If the FBI catches wind of this, we'll be hauled before the Justice Department, or a Senate oversight committee, as fast as you can say the word *scandal*."

"I understand what you're saying, sir, but Vortex Security isn't law enforcement. They're a questionable private security firm making gargantuan profits by sticking it to the United States government."

"What are you, some bleeding-heart liberal in the U.S. Senate? If you want to play Diane Feinstein then go get a job at the goddamned EPA. We use Vortex all the time for crying out loud. Whether you and I like it or not, they are an extension of the United States intelligence community. So when I hear a report that my Russian counterintelligence director has gone off the reservation and turned into King Kong wreaking havoc in New York City, excuse me if I fly off the fucking handle!"

He knew it was time to shut up; he couldn't allow himself to lose sight of the big picture. More than anything else, he needed to stay on to finish the job. If Harcourt pulled the plug, he would really be screwed.

He needed to apologize.

"I'm sorry, sir. You've made your point. But as I've indicated, I was using this incident with my son to make a move on Benedictis and Popov. I'm close, very close. I know who the key players are and how the system operates. But I still don't have the electronic paper trail I need to put them both away. I just need a little more time. Especially since Popov has diplomatic immunity as a Russian national, with the full international legal protections that title conveys."

"I told you up front that you should use a full-scale surveillance squad and tactical black ops team. And yet you wanted to go this one alone without any operational ground support and only limited video surveillance."

"You know that I like small teams, sir. At least until I have all the facts. And I don't have all the facts yet. What I'm doing is checking up on and reassuring my assets, performing the necessary field reconnaissance, and gathering critical intelligence. A big team will only attract attention, sir."

"You seem to be attracting plenty of unnecessary attention all by yourself. You've already pissed off a lot of people, and I don't—"

"What do you mean a lot of people? I thought it was just your friend Maupin at Vortex?"

"No, this morning I also received a call from a Detective Stafford. Does that name ring a bell?"

"Yes, I met with the detective."

"And you bailed your son and his radical friends out of jail by claiming they were working on a big national security case. I'm wondering what case that would be, Austin?"

"I needed them out of jail so they could bring the necessary outside pressure upon Benedictis. It's the perfect diversion, sir. The two cases are unrelated, the parties that are involved don't know about my op, and the whole thing has complete authenticity since the left hand doesn't know what the right is doing. That's what makes it perfect. It's shaking things up—radically."

"You're using your own son as a guinea pig, as bait? Why you're an even more cold-hearted son of a bitch than I thought, Austin. And what about your ex-wife? She's a lawyer and an ACLU member for crying out loud. Please don't tell me that you've got her mixed up in this too?"

Brewbaker felt suddenly ashamed; the deputy director was right. What the hell was he doing getting his own son and his ex-wife, whom he was back together with, involved?

"I'll tell you flat out, Austin, I'm beginning to wonder how I could have possibly authorized this surveillance operation in the first place. I'm wondering why I haven't already pulled the plug. What you're doing isn't senior level analyst work—it's sounding more and more like your own special op. I've just been informed that you and Benedictis went to Oxford together and that he somehow screwed you over and got you kicked out of both Oxford and Yale. Are you sure this whole Benedictis money-laundering scheme isn't a figment of your imagination and you're just trying to find a way to get revenge after all these years?"

He took a deep breath to steel himself. The accusation made him feel like a small-minded, vindictive little shit—but there was no way that he could entirely deny it. He did want revenge on Benedictis, not only for what the bastard had done to him back at Oxford, but now also—and even more importantly—for what he had done to his son. Beckett was to blame as well, to be sure, but in his mind the theft of *Blind Thrust* would never have occurred if Benedictis hadn't rummaged through his slush pile and handed over Nick's unpublished novel to the desperate Aussie. From what he could tell, Beckett was incapable of tying his own shoes without the help of his all-powerful agent. It was Benedictis who was the key decision-maker in the partnership, as well as the invaluable behind-the-scenes mechanic that kept the literary machine clean and running.

"I just want to protect our national security interests, sir. And to do that, I'm going to bring down both Popov and Benedictis. Popov is a confirmed arms dealer and a spy, selling missile and laser guidance system plans and specs to his mother country. He's using Benedictis's agency to launder the money and we need to catch the son of bitch. I'm close to doing that, sir—but I can't if you pull the plug."

Silence. Even more excruciating than before.

"You have until tomorrow."

"Tomorrow, sir, but that's only—"

"Twenty-four hours. I'm giving you twenty-four hours."

"But, sir, twenty-four hours isn't—"

"Get it done, Austin. If you really care so much about the national security interests of the United States, you're going to have to get what you need quickly and put these bastards away once and for all."

"Yes, sir, I copy."

"Good because Director Brennan and I are both counting on you."

He gulped. *The Director of the CIA knows about this? Jesus Franklin, why the hell didn't you mention that before?* "I understand, Mr. Deputy Director. I promise I won't let you down."

"You'd better not, Austin. I don't even want to talk about the goddamned consequences if you should fail."

CHAPTER 27

THE POND
CENTRAL PARK

HE AND NATALIE crossed Central Park South at Sixth Avenue. After his hostile encounter with Wax Head and the Excalibur security goons, the city suddenly seemed oppressive and dangerous to Lassiter. Was it his imagination or did the pedestrians on the streets look like spies and the cars waiting at the intersections appear poised to run them down? He glanced at Natalie as they reached the far sidewalk and headed north on Center Drive. He could tell that she, too, felt the razor's-edge paranoia. She looked even more agitated and haggard than she had this morning, as if she was a fugitive on the run.

He kept these thoughts to himself as they reached the sidewalk on the other side of the street, looking back over their shoulders and to their left and right several times, like retreating footsoldiers hounded by enemy snipers. After all, he was the one to blame for her current state. Why did he have to stubbornly insist on coming to New York in the first place? What good could come out of his quest for justice in the form of a simple apology when everyone seemed to want to settle the matter with lawyers, guns, and money?

He felt her touch his arm and lean in close, so close he could feel the warmth of her breath. "Nick, the reason I wanted to talk to you...there's something I haven't told you."

He couldn't help but continue to scan the streets and pathways all around them, as if he was being followed in the park again, like before with his dad. Jesus, was it the city itself that brought out the paranoia, or was it everything that was happening? He felt like he was in a Barry Eisler, Daniel Silva, or John le Carré spy novel.

"Are you listening, Nick? You seem distracted."

"Yes, yes, I'm listening," he said, scanning the trees to their right as they ducked onto the footpath that led to The Pond and Hallett Nature Sanctuary. The wall of trees to the south dampened the noisy clatter of the city. "But to be honest, you're so on edge that you're scaring the crap out of me."

"I'm sorry. I'm just worried. And frightened."

"Of what?"

"Everything, but especially what I'm about to tell you."

Noticing that her hands were shaking, he came to a halt and took her gently by the arm. "What is it, Natalie? You've got to calm down and talk to me."

"No, they could be watching. We need to keep moving."

She started off again at a brisk pace. He quickly followed and pulled even with her.

"*They*—what do you mean *they*?"

"The Russians. They could be out there."

"The Russians? What the hell are you talking about? What Russians?"

"So he hasn't told you. Then it's good that I'm talking to you now."

"Natalie, I'm sorry but you're not making any sense."

"It's your father, Nick. I'm working for him."

"My father, what are you talking about? You're...you're..."

"A CIA asset. I'm working for your father as a spy."

This time he grabbed her arm hard and flung her around. "My father recruited you to spy on Benedictis? Is that what you're saying?"

"Yes," she replied.

He noticed her studying a pair of men in business suits talking on radio headsets up ahead. Shit, were they day traders, executives, or intelligence operatives like his father? Jesus, how the fuck could you even tell the difference?

"We need to keep moving, Nick. Come on."

They started off again. The glossy surface of The Pond appeared on their left, broken by clumps of green reeds, quacking ducks, diving turtles, and massive slabs of Central Park's famous Precambrian schist. Lassiter felt like Jason Bourne on the run with the massive knot of tension that had taken root in his stomach. Only three days ago he had been an ordinary Joe from Colorado—now he was trying to evade Excalibur security goons and Russian spies in Central Park. How crazy was that? Jesus, would his life ever return to normal or was this the new paradigm?

"I'm really sorry that I didn't tell you earlier, Nick. But I didn't want to jeopardize the operation. I was sworn to secrecy, but now I can't take it anymore. Everything seems to be coming to a head."

Operation? Did she just say operation? "Jesus, what has my father done to you? This is exactly why my mother left him."

"Your father didn't twist my arm. I wanted to do it."

"You wanted to become a spy?"

A suspicious-looking man in a green jogging suit with headphones passed them on the left. She eyed him closely and waited for him to move down the path before resuming the conversation. "Well, sort of...I mean, yeah I did. Four months ago it sounded exciting."

"But now it's all changed."

"That's right. Because last night the enemy that I had never seen before in person and was nothing but an abstraction broke into my office, chased me from the building, and was prepared to kill me."

"You're talking about the Russians?"

"There were three of them."

"My God, I had no idea you were involved in something like this."

"I told you, I want to help your father. I want to help my country. But it's gotten crazy and I wanted to let you know what's going on even though I'm not supposed to. Your father's going to be angry with me, though deep down, I think he would probably like to tell you himself."

"How did he recruit you?"

She took a deep breath to steady her nerves before speaking. "It happened a few days after I had returned from London. I was in a little coffee shop on Forty-Sixth. He calmly slipped into the seat across from me, told me that he knew where I worked, and asked if I would help him catch unsavory Russian criminals living in America and acting as spies. He said it was vital to U.S. national security."

"What did you say to him?"

"I told him that I'd think about it—but the instant he asked me I secretly knew I wanted to do it."

"Why?"

"Because ever since I was a little girl I've been fascinated with spies."

"That's right. I remember now from college."

"It all started in sixth grade when I did a term paper on Mata Hari. Then in high school and at Kenyon I read books and wrote papers on espionage during the Civil War, World War Two, and the Cold War. One of my favorites was the breaking of the German Enigma code and the British Double Cross spy system that fooled the Nazis into thinking that the main Allied attack on D-Day would come at Pas de Calais instead of Normandy."

He remembered reading her paper about Tar Robertson, the Scottish MI5 intelligence officer responsible for Double Cross. It had been an extraordinary paper and she had received an A+ from her History professor at Kenyon. But even though he was aware of her interest—after all, they had gone out together in college and lived together in New York and Boston after graduating from Kenyon—he hadn't realized the full extent of her passion for espionage. Until now.

"So that's why you've been taking all these risks?" he said, with a trace of skepticism in his voice. "Because you were fascinated with spies growing up?"

"No, of course it's not that simple. This isn't about some little girl obsessed with tradecraft—this is about me wanting to do something genuinely important and meaningful in my life. Believe it or not, I did it because I wanted to help my country. I wanted to help protect America from her enemies."

"And that's it?"

"I suppose a part of me also wanted a little excitement, an element of danger. You know, that's the reason most men become spies. Unlike women, they certainly don't do it out of patriotism. I'll bet you didn't know that."

"You're right, I didn't. But I must say you've become quite the patriot since we broke up. I'm surprised you haven't joined the Tea Party."

"Very funny."

"As I recall, you used to criticize America all the time. You used to say that we were a bunch of global bullies for foisting American exceptionalism onto the rest of the world. You thought that flag-wavers were morons."

"I still do. But that doesn't make me any less patriotic than them. In fact, it makes me more patriotic—because I know the difference between *real sacrifice* and being a partisan, obstructionist blowhard who waves a flag and calls for the impeachment of the President just because he doesn't agree with him. Stupid assholes like that are the ones that are fucking un-American."

My God was she still passionate or what? "So my dad reeled you in hook, line, and sinker, is that it?"

She gave a guilty shrug. "Given my predilection towards international intrigue, it probably wasn't all that hard. But I have to admit he's a very persuasive guy. Kind of like you."

"He has that effect on people. My mom stayed married to him for nearly fifteen years before she saw the light."

"Yeah, and what's that?"

"That he put the Company ahead of me and her. That's why they got divorced and my mom and I moved to Colorado, as you well know."

"That might have been the case back then, but what about now? You told me they've been secretly rendezvousing at his apartment here in New York and are back together again."

"I think they're looking for a little excitement in their pathetic, middle-aged lives."

"Or, maybe they just realize that they made a mistake and they were always meant to be together."

Is she trying to tell me something? he wondered.

They walked on in silence. He felt the power of the quiet between them wrack his body with angst. He looked at her again. Her eyes were soft as a doe's. He remembered back to the times they had made love and traipsed about Europe with nothing but backpacks on their backs, and the times they had hiked the Appalachian Trail and raced down the slopes of Vail and Aspen when she had visited him in Colorado. Jesus Christ, who the fuck was he kidding? He had never loved anyone more or been happier with any woman in his life than her!

They rounded the southeast corner of the pond and came to a massive, sloping outcrop of weathered schist covered with jubilant children scrambling to and fro. Bird-watchers with binoculars were out in force along with the usual stream of park hikers, commuters, joggers, roller bladers, and mothers navigating their babies in strollers. Was one or more of these people actually spying on them? He didn't see anyone that looked particularly Slavic, but maybe they were in disguise?

"What about these Russians?" he asked, as they kept to the right on the recently refinished asphalt path. "What's their connection to Benedictis?"

"They use Benedictis Literary Associates to launder the money they make through their arms trafficking and drug empire. The kingpin of the Russian mob— or the Odessa Mafia as it's officially known—is Alexei Popov. The Odessa Mafia is the most powerful Russian criminal group operating in the U.S. The group's headquarters is just south of here in Brighton Beach."

"But how did Benedictis get caught up with the Russian mob? I mean, he's just a literary agent."

"Reportedly through his brother Danny. Believe it or not, Benedictis told me about it himself last night."

"Why would Benedictis tell you anything?"

"I'm not sure. All I know is he confided to me about his brother when he drove me home last night after the Russians broke in. He says that Popov is blackmailing him because of something Danny did. Apparently, his brother stole something important from Popov. Given that Popov is a known arms dealer, it's most likely some sort of weapons system, though your father hasn't made me privy to the details. But Benedictis did tell me why the Russians broke into his office. He thinks they did it to get some dirt or keep tabs on him to make sure he doesn't double-cross them."

"So Popov and Benedictis are running a money-laundering operation? That's what you and my father have been working on together these past four months?"

"It's a joint FBI-CIA operation. The FBI is tracking Popov and the Russians. Your father and the CIA are keeping tabs on Benedictis. The two agencies share information, but I also think they compete with one another and don't report everything. But like I said, your father hasn't told me much."

"Money laundering. I would never have suspected that Benedictis was up to something that big. Do you think Beckett's involved?"

"I doubt it. But you're right the operation is big. Popov's not just an international arms dealer—he also owns several legitimate and illegitimate businesses and is a trafficker in U.S. military secrets. He's apparently using Benedictis to launder hundreds of millions of dollars in illegal funds."

"Then why haven't the FBI or CIA arrested Popov or Benedictis?"

"Isn't it obvious? They don't have enough evidence to secure a conviction or extradition. What we've been able to obtain so far are just scraps. They've both been very clever. But lately Popov has become careless. I had never seen him before last night, but now I know what he looks like."

"Which is what?"

"Hannibal Lecter with a bristly goatee and a heavy Russian accent."

"Maybe when he's behind bars you'll get to hear him say *fava beans* and *Chianti* in Russian. So what are you going to do about my father?"

"I don't know. I just wish he would come clean to you about what he and I are up to because I think it could be getting dangerous. Popov is a scary man, Nick. I don't want him coming to my apartment in the middle of the night."

"I don't blame you," he said. "We need to talk to my dad."

They came to a halt on the native-schist fieldstone arch of the Gapstow Bridge spanning the narrow northern neck of the pond. The bridge led to the Hallett Nature Sanctuary, home to hundreds of migratory bird species, enjoying a brief stopover in Central Park as they navigated the Atlantic Flyway. They stared out to the south over the gently rippled surface of the pond. It was an idyllic scene, the perfect escape from the hustle and bustle of the city. For the first time since they had entered the park, Lassiter didn't feel paranoid, as if someone was following them or lurking in the shadows. In that moment, all his troubles seemed to disappear.

The pond was filled with diving turtles and sprouting water lilies and squawking ducks and blocks of shimmering schist. Trim grassy lawn and lush oak, elm, crabapple, and forsythia nosed right down to the water's edge. Serving as an appropriate backdrop in the distance was the iconic, twenty-story Plaza Hotel, framed against a massive rampart comprised of even taller buildings south of West 59th Street. All in all, it was a majestic scene, a magic wonderland, a verdant undomesticated nature preserve tucked away in the woods—all of it a mere stone's throw from the grime and noise of the city. When he and Natalie had lived together in New York, visiting the Pond had always made him homesick for Colorado.

Suddenly he turned, took her in his arms, and kissed her on the lips.

She looked at him and they smiled. They kissed again, more passionately this time. He felt a warm feeling envelope him, clouding his brain, but it felt good, and dangerous, as if he was a young schoolboy again stealing a kiss behind Mrs. Bisbee's classroom. She snuggled in close to him, willingly and desperately, and he felt himself spinning in a wonderful way, like taking a whirl on the carousel at the nearby Victorian Gardens Amusement Park. Then, after a moment, they pulled apart for air.

They were both smiling, but a little shocked by what had just happened.

"That brings back memories," she said, looking suddenly vigorous and alive instead of haggard and afraid. He knew that he must look like that too, and he was happy for it.

"Being with you brings back the best memories of my life," he confessed.

"Well then, let's make a new one."

She kissed him again. Like before at his father's apartment, she tasted fresh like wild mountain strawberries. He felt as if he was under some sort of magic spell as her bosom pressed against his chest. When she gently pulled away, his body tingled all over.

She smiled up at him mischievously; he felt the power of her emotions. "I've missed you," she said simply.

"I've missed you too." He pulled her close again and they French kissed.

A moment later, they again drew apart. "Okay, that was nice, but what are we going to do now?" she asked him.

"Honestly, I don't know. But I do know one thing."

"What's that?"

"We need to talk to my father."

"What, do I need his permission to kiss you?"

They laughed. Then they took each other by the hand and started west on the path leading to the Hallett Nature Sanctuary and the bustling city beyond.

CHAPTER 28

BREWBAKER FLAT
44 WEST 56TH STREET

"SO, NOW YOU ALL KNOW THE TRUTH," declared Austin Brewbaker, wrapping up his introductory speech. "The question is do you still want in?"

Here he paused to look over his multifarious audience: his loyal inside asset Natalie, who was beginning to feel the strain of being a spy; his fiercely-determined but nonetheless naïve son Nick; and his son's zany yet fearlessly devoted friends Squelch, Claggebart, and Bermolito.

The Devil's Brigade.

If they consented, this would be his infiltration team, this would be his working army, and he needed them to be sharp and ready for the clandestine battle to be waged—and hopefully won—tonight. After all, he had no one else to turn to without alerting the FBI or unwanted branches of his own agency. And he only had until tomorrow to get what Deputy Director Harcourt wanted. Or else he was seriously fucked.

Hell, who was he kidding? He was already seriously fucked.

The Devil's Brigade?

Was this some kind of joke? Why the goddamned Bay of Pigs had had a better chance of success than this clandestine disaster-waiting-to-happen! He pictured Robert Tyrone Frederick rolling over in his grave. The youngest general to command a division-size unit in WWII, the legendary Frederick was awarded two Distinguished Service Crosses and several other decorations during the war, was the only U.S. serviceman to receive eight Purple Hearts, and was called "the greatest fighting general of all time" by none other than Winston Churchill, who proclaimed that "if we had had a dozen more like him we would have smashed Hitler in 1942."

"So, let me get this straight," said Squelch, taking off his tweed jacket with the elbow patches to expose his Phish t-shirt, then making a big show flipping his pony tail over his shoulder, as if he was about to address a class of awestruck undergrads. "Natalie, your son's former lover, has been working for you as a spy for the past four months trying to crack a secret arms- and money-laundering ring run by this Russian mobster Popov...and now you want us, a bunch of untrained amateurs with no experience in espionage, to go to a gala tonight celebrating Beckett on the twentieth floor of the Donald Trump, Jr. Building, create a diversion, break into Benedictis's office on the thirtieth floor, and download all of his computer files without being caught or leaving a trace. I mean, come on man, you had me at *covert op*!"

Brewbaker nodded. "Very good, it appears our resident Professor of Anarchy Studies is on board. Anyone else?"

"I have just two questions," said Claggebart, looking appropriately patriotic in his star-spangled-banner ascot. "First, do we get to use guns and special gadgets? And second, is it black tie, because if it is, I must say it is awfully short notice?"

He couldn't help but suppress a little smile. "Special gadgets yes, guns no. And there's a tuxedo rental place right down the street a half block west of Uncle Jack's Steakhouse."

"Wonderful," said Claggebart. "I believe I'm all in then."

"This is awesome. Professor—I mean Captain—Squelch reporting for immediate duty, sir." He snapped a surprisingly crisp salute that would have made the "Fighting General" Frederick proud. "Even though I don't have a shred of military or spy training, this is right up my goddamned alley. You want to know why? Because you said yourself we're going to be breaking every CIA rule in the book. Man, what's not to love about that?"

"Ditto, count me in too," said Bermolito. He set down the black electrician's tape he had used to repair his broken Khalib Gatez-brand glasses, picked up his tablet, and began to toggle his way through a series of screens. "I'm just doing a quick rundown on the building schematics, power and utility grid, and the process flow diagrams for the elevators and security systems."

"Good, we're going to need all that," said Brewbaker. He then looked at his son and Natalie. "Well, as expected, the Three Stooges are all on board. What about you two? What do you think?"

"I think you should have told us sooner," said his son. "And I don't believe you should have taken advantage of my previous relationship with Natalie as a recruitment tool, or used me as a human recording device at lunch. I also think you owe Natalie an apology. After all, you did coerce her into taking part in this little spy game of yours."

"He didn't coerce me," she said. "I told you I wanted to do it—just like I want to do it now."

Brewbaker looked at her. She was a courageous young woman to take the risks that she was taking, and his son's words made him feel like a prick. But he had never thought of her as just an intelligence asset. In his mind, she was the best thing that had ever happened to Nick and, all along, he had trusted her to work successfully and discreetly on behalf of her country. And that was saying something since he didn't trust a lot of people, even many he worked with on a daily basis at the CIA.

"Well, I appreciate you saying that, Natalie," he said. "But Nick is right about one thing. I have put you under strain. I want to tell you here and now that I'm sorry about that." He then turned towards his son. "And I apologize to you for being unnecessarily secretive. Old habits die hard. I'm a Company man through and through, but as I said before, that ends today if we decide to move forward with this. Today, I'm a pledged member of the Devil's Brigade and there are no more secrets."

He continued to look apologetically at his son.

"That's good enough for me," said Nick. "I'm in."

Squelch was nodding vigorously. "I just want to say that I love you all, man. I also want to say that your mom, Nicky—your wife, Mr. B—made the best damned chocolate chip-peanut butter cookies when we were kids. I mean *the best* I've ever tasted." He looked at Lassiter. "And Mama L was always our favorite mom. We always thought you were the luckiest kid on the planet to have a mom as cool as her. Plus she was mega-hot. Sorry, Mr. B, but it's true."

"I believe, Captain Squelch, that you have what's technically referred to as a *Mrs. Robinson complex*. Have you sought treatment for the disorder?"

"It's better than an Equus complex," said Morrison Frautschi Claussen, aka Claggebart. "Remember, it took me a whole year to overcome my fear of horses after I fell off that spotted Indian pinto during our sixth-grade field trip to the Four Corners."

"Ah yes, the spry little paint named Thunder—you were trampled underfoot and almost won a Darwin Award. I remember that trip quite well," observed Bermolito. "But let's get back to the subject at hand. Where do we go from here? Because personally, I'd like to know more about Popov, Benedictis, and Benedictis's brother, Danny. I still don't quite understand how they're all connected?"

Brewbaker nodded to indicate that the question was a good one. "That's the problem: we don't know all of the details of how they're connected. That's why they've all been able to evade the law despite joint FBI-CIA surveillance."

Bermolito's forehead wrinkled. "Wait a second. This is a joint FBI-CIA operation?"

Again, Brewbaker nodded. "Popov and his high-level lieutenants are under round-the-clock FBI surveillance. But since Popov is a Russian national with diplomatic immunity, an international arms trafficker, and a seller of secrets on American-made weapons, anti-missile defense systems, and bomb guidance and tracking systems, we keep an eye on him at the CIA too. Except we watch his contacts and business associates. That's why we track Benedictis's suspected money-laundering operation. We have both his home and office bugged and under audiovisual surveillance. But so far, between the FBI and CIA, we still don't have enough to lock away Popov or Benedictis."

"What the hell's this Russian's backstory?" asked Squelch. "How did he become such a bad ass?"

"Alexei Popov is the *Krestnii Otets*—or Boss—of the Odessa Mafia. It's the most powerful Russian criminal group operating in the U.S., headquartered just south of here in Brighton Beach. Popov is basically the Godfather, except there is one big difference between him and Don Corleone: like a general who likes to lead from the front, he enjoys hitting the streets and getting his hands dirty, at least on occasion, which means that he takes unnecessary risks. He is believed to be responsible for the deaths of more than a dozen people."

"So how does Popov's network operate?" asked Bermolito, fingers flying across his tablet keyboard.

"The *Krestnii Otets* controls four criminal cells in the Odessa through an intermediary called a 'Brigadier.' Working for the Brigadier are the *Boyeviks*, which literally means 'warrior.' These are the mid-level action guys that handle specific criminal activities, similar to *soldiers* in Italian-American Mafia crime families and Sicilian Mafia clans. A *Boyevik* is in charge of filling in personnel needs and making deals to facilitate criminal actions. They are the main strike force of a *bratva*, or brigade. This is how De Benedictis's brother Danny got into trouble. He was a small-time professional thief, a weapons and narcotics trafficker that wasn't even on our radar. Then one day he made the mistake of getting too big for his britches. He stole a crate load of FIM-92 Stinger surface-to-air missiles from one of Popov's brigadiers, who happened to be the Russian crime lord's nephew. That's how Popov first came into contact with Danny De Benedictis three years ago. Except instead of killing him, which he normally would have done without batting an eye, Popov came up with the creative idea of holding him up for ransom to his rich and famous literary agent brother. This, in turn, led to the launch of New York City's first major money-laundering operation at a reputable literary agency that, to this day, we still haven't cracked."

"Holy Grigori Y. Rasputin," exclaimed Squelch. "The guy sounds audacious as hell. I'll bet he likes his vodka too."

"That's an understatement. He washes it down with Molotov cocktails and beluga caviar. Seriously, he's believed to be worth almost a half-billion dollars and to have ordered the execution of more than a dozen people in the United States alone. It was reported that several years ago he beat up his exotic-dancer girlfriend in the parking lot outside a New York club and made her eat gravel."

"This guy sounds nuts to me," said Nick, looking at Natalie. "No wonder you were so freaked out by him last night."

"That's not the worst of it," she said. "He knew my name."

Squelch raised an eyebrow. "He knows who you are? Shit, that can't be good."

"Thanks a lot, Fred. Now I definitely won't get a wink of sleep tonight."

"Please tell me this Popov isn't going to be at Beckett's party tonight," said Claggebart, verbalizing out loud what everyone else was dreading.

Brewbaker shook his head. "No, there's no reason for him to be there. But that doesn't mean we don't have to be careful."

"What else do you know about him?" asked Lassiter. Like everyone else, he was both frightened and intrigued by the Russian mob boss.

"Alexei Popov was once a Soviet military translator and intelligence operative. He fought in Afghanistan before turning to a life of crime in 1989 when the Soviet Union collapsed. Through his family connections, he worked his way up quickly through the ranks of the *Solntsevskaya Bratva*, a powerful organized-crime gang based in Moscow. Named after the *Solntsevo* neighborhood, it's considered one of the most dangerous criminal organizations in the world. It's the largest faction of the Russian mob. Over a decade ago, Popov somehow managed to secure diplomatic immunity as a New York security attaché to the Russian diplomatic corps in the U.S.—specifically the Consulate General of the Russian Federation in New York—and he set up a base of operations in Brighton Beach. He's amassed a personal fortune in arms and narcotics trafficking, his three air transportation companies, and selling classified military secrets to the highest bidder. But, as I've said, we haven't been able to prove anything to date. He's never actually been convicted of arms smuggling or any other offense."

"This guy is definitely crafty as hell," said Bermolito. "As we've been talking, I've been pulling up classified WikiLeaks documents and I must say that your analysis is spot on."

"Uh, thanks Bermolito. As head of the CIA's Russian counterintelligence desk, I truly appreciate having WikiLeaks validation. May I continue?"

"Please do, you are a most riveting speaker."

"Okay, Comrade Bermingham here is right about Popov being a very crafty fellow. He's created multiple layers between him, his *bratva*, and his contacts as well as a number of offshore companies that do happen to abide by U.S. banking laws. He also owns a large number of legitimate U.S. businesses, and he discreetly moves in the highest social circles in the city. He makes huge donations to New York arts and charities, including The Metropolitan Museum of Art and The Guggenheim. He's friendly with a number of important political figures and business entrepreneurs. He is alleged to have connections to ranking Russian officials, including Putin himself. But despite all of his glittering connections, he's still nothing but a common hood. Which is precisely why we have to nail his proverbial ass to the wall."

"So what you're saying is that you've never been able to make anything stick against him." said Lassiter. "He's basically been able to do as he pleases."

"That's right. We've had a few close calls, but that's it. In 2011, Popov was brought to trial by the Justice Department on terrorism charges, after having been accused of intending to smuggle arms to the Revolutionary Armed Forces of Colombia to use against U.S. forces. But he was acquitted by a jury in a Manhattan federal court. The specific charges were conspiracy to kill U.S. citizens and officials, conspiracy to provide material support to a foreign terrorist organization, and conspiracy to acquire and deliver anti-aircraft missiles. Additional charges against him were filed for illegal purchase of aircraft, wire fraud, and money laundering. But Popov's diplomatic immunity, powerful connections, ownership of legitimate companies, and layering between him and his *bratva* and illicit contacts has made it hard for us to make a case against him. He also frequently changes his company names and re-registers aircraft and other capital resources to throw us off the scent. He has never even been charged for the alleged weapons trafficking to which he owes his fame. Furthermore, Russia's Ministry of Foreign Affairs has repeatedly denounced Popov's arrest and trial as 'a political vendetta' against Russia for America's failed foreign policy. That's another reason we've been cautious.

"But you know what? I'm sick and tired of playing it cautious. The Russians must have raided Benedictis's office for a reason and tonight we need to find out what that reason was. Benedictis may very well have something on Popov that could bring him down. We need to move quickly to find out what that might be."

"Looks like Benedictis and his brother got mixed up with the wrong Russkie," said Claggebart, in a flawless imitation of a nuclear missile-riding Slim Pickens in Kubrick's *Dr. Strangelove.*

"You can say that again," said Lassiter. "So what's the plan for tonight? How is the Devil's Brigade going to pull off this little intelligence caper?"

Austin Brewbaker smiled, presenting a mask of confidence which he, unfortunately, did not share inside. But the Brigade was all he had, and he had only one shot.

"Huddle up and I'll tell you, Brigadiers. It won't be easy, but here's my plan. And trust me, we will bring honor to our legendary predecessors who fought in the ice-cold Apennines and at Anzio against the Boche."

CHAPTER 29

DE BENEDICTIS LITERARY ASSOCIATES
1450 SIXTH AVENUE

LOOKING INTO the cold-steel eyes of Alexei Popov, Benedictis gave an involuntary shiver—as if a Siberian wind had suddenly whipped in and gusted through his bedroom window. The Russian Mafia don of Brighton Beach shouldn't even be here, he thought, but that was just like Popov to take unnecessary risks by flexing his muscles and showing off his power. Though dapperly dressed for the black-tie occasion, he gave off an aura of danger and casual violence as he calmly took a seat in the chair in front of Benedictis's desk. Behind him, two bodyguards stood in stone-faced silence with their backs to the wall and hands folded neatly at their crotches. They looked out of place in their jet-black tuxedos, their muscles almost bursting the seams of their jackets and pants. They also happened to be wearing black leather gloves, which meant that they were either making some kind of fashion statement or anticipated having to use their fists to pummel him.

"I apologize for crashing your party for your big client, Anton my friend," began Popov in his honey-smooth but always-threatening voice. "But I thought it would provide us a good chance to talk. I hope you do not mind."

Benedictis continued to look at the mobster in concealed awe and trepidation. Of course he minded, but what the fuck could he say? The son of a bitch was an emperor beholden to no one, not even the powerful U.S. government. Furthermore, the Russian had him and his brother both by the balls.

"What did you want to talk about?" he inquired mildly, though he secretly dreaded what the answer might be.

The Russian smiled, withdrew a manila envelope from his jacket pocket, leaned his barrel-chested frame forward, and tossed the envelope on the desk in front of him. Benedictis looked warily at the envelope before slowly reaching across and picking it up.

"What do you think my men and I were looking for here last night?"

"I don't know, Alexei. My secret recipe for cooking a great New York strip?"

"I see you have retained your sense of humor in these troubled times. That is good. But no, I am not here for your secret recipe. I am here because of what is in that envelope. I would have told you during our brief meeting in the elevator this morning, but I wanted to see how your meeting with Mr. Lassiter went first. Now I know the answer to that question."

Benedictis looked down at the envelope. He didn't want to open it.

Popov smiled knowingly and nodded towards it, signaling for him to open it or suffer the consequences.

He felt his fingers shaking as he began gently tearing open the envelope, and cursed himself for appearing weak. But holy shit, Popov was like a ticking time bomb or stalking serial killer; just being in his presence was unnerving as hell. When Benedictis had the envelope open, he pulled out a sheath of papers—papers which he instantly recognized.

"It is interesting that you should have a signed copy of Beckett's last will and testament," said Popov with a gleam of malice in his eyes. "You two are very close—closer than a husband and wife, it seems."

He said nothing. *Where is he going with this?* he wondered. *Wherever it is, it's not going to be pleasant.*

Popov continued: "It says that, in the event of Cameron Beckett's death or incapacitation, you will be the one to write his novels and will have full creative and artistic control going forward. The will further states that Beckett's family will retain all royalty payments and rights to his previously published work minus your fifteen percent commission."

"You broke into my office for this? This is what you were after?"

Popov didn't respond.

"What do you want from me then, Alexei? You already roughed me up and threatened me this morning, so I assume you haven't come to do that again. You want something from me and I'd like to know what it is."

"You are perceptive, comrade. That is the reason why you are such a successful literary agent."

"Until you came into my life I was. Now I'm a fucking crook. What do you want from me? You want me to start laundering money for your eight cousins in Brighton Beach?"

At this, Popov's two meaty thugs gave a twitch and stepped forward to deliver instant punishment. But a simple raised hand from the *Krestnii Otets* of the vaunted Odessa Mafia quickly halted them in their tracks. They stepped back near the wall again, refolded their hands, and looked on impassively. Benedictis wondered how long it would take for the two goons to kill him with those powerful, black-gloved hands of theirs. *Ten seconds tops,* he decided.

"No," said Popov. "I want something else from you."

"Jesus Christ, haven't I given you enough already? What do you want now, my soul?"

"Not exactly. You told me over the phone that you and Beckett are planning on meeting with Lassiter tomorrow at lunch to settle your dispute once and for all. That is good—it will give you a chance to be alone together."

"I don't know what you've got in mind, but I don't like the sound of it."

"I want you to *become* Cameron Beckett. Not in the future, but *right now.*"

"I'm not sure what you mean."

"I want you to kill him, Anton. And it must look like an accident."

"You're kidding, right? Come on, Alexei, you can't be serious."

"I couldn't be more serious."

"This is madness. You've gone off the deep end."

"No, it is merely business. You will terminate Beckett tomorrow at lunch, take over as author of all of his series immediately, and earn one hundred million dollars per year instead of your measly fifteen percent of that number. Of course, as your literary advisor, business partner, and real life example for your novel's villains, I will take a reasonable percentage—let's say fifty percent—of all of your earnings."

"You can have your fifty percent. But there's no way I'm doing this. You'll have to get someone else."

With a subtle inclination of his head, he signaled his two goons. Benedictis gulped as they coolly and deliberately took a moment to adjust their black gloves, making little squeaking noises as the leather tightened around their knuckles, before covering the distance to his desk in three quick strides. Once upon him, they each delivered two stunningly quick jabs to his stomach as he, belatedly, stood up from his chair and tried to protect himself. The force of the blows took his breath away and sent a flame of burning agony through his midriff. He fell to one knee, gasped for air, and gripped the desk hard with both hands to keep from collapsing.

"As you can see," said Popov, "Grigori and Yuri know how to inflict the maximum possible amount of pain without leaving a mark. You should appreciate the fact that I told them not to strike you in the face, since you are hosting an important party tonight. Just think, Anton, tonight could be Cameron Beckett's going-away party—and *your* coming-out party."

He didn't respond. He was in too much agony to even draw breath.

Popov signaled the closest goon. Benedictis braced himself for another blow, but instead of assaulting him the man calmly pulled out a pair of semiautomatic pistols—a Glock and a Beretta—and laid them on the desk in front of him along with a pair of magazines, one for each gun.

"Those are the weapons you will use. They are untraceable. The laser serial numbers have been removed and the barrels have been re-grooved so that the police cannot make a ballistics match to the original weapons."

"But why…why two guns?" His voice was a croak.

"Because you will need one for Beckett, the other for Lassiter. You see, they are going to kill one another, or at least that's what the police will think."

"You're stark raving mad."

"*Da*, I can see how an American Yankee might think that. But in Russia this is simply the way we do business. We go about things differently, that is all, my friend. The most important thing for you to remember is that if you want to see your brother again—or your daughter for that matter—then you will do as I say."

"You leave Danny and Rebecca out of this, goddamnit! This is between you and me!"

"I'm afraid it is not that simple. But I admire you for your devotion to your family. Though I doubt you would be as upset if I threatened to kidnap one of your ex-wives or your current separated spouse, Roxanne. By the way, what do you think of using The Victorian Club again?"

"You've thought this all out, haven't you?"

"What can I say, I love to make arrangements. Were you aware that the restaurant was a former Cabinet of Curiosities with a network of secret passageways?"

"Yes, I know all about it."

"Then you know that these secret passageways lead to and from the four private dining rooms to the rear of the restaurant on West 76th Street."

"Yeah, so?"

"Quite a nice little escape route, wouldn't you say?"

"But I...I've never killed anyone in my life."

"You *do* know how to shoot a gun." He pointed up at the .38-caliber machine-gun pistol mounted on the wall that had belonged to Baby Face Nelson. "Otherwise, why do you have that? There would be no point."

He laughed with malicious delight and, after a moment, his two goons joined in with him. But it wasn't really like laughter at all, thought Benedictis, more like Kodiak bears groaning while shitting.

"Do you even realize what you're asking me to do, Alexei? You're asking me to kill the author I have worked with for the past twenty-two years."

"I'm not *asking* you to do anything. I'm *telling* you that your brother Danny and daughter Rebecca will be terminated if you do not do as I say."

Benedictis shook his head in dismay as the horrible words sank in. "And what if I told you that Beckett has agreed to step aside and let me write his novels in his name?"

The Russian raised an eyebrow. The room remained silent for several seconds as he thoughtfully stroked his silver, Leninesque goatee.

"He told you this?"

Benedictis nodded. "Today after lunch. He's tired of the mega-stress and wants out. He said he wants to amend his will and his contract with his publisher to allow me to take over for him as soon as possible. He's built up the Cameron Beckett brand—at this point the actual author of his various book series is immaterial."

The room again went silent as Popov thought it all through. After a moment, he shook his head. "I don't like it. Too many things could go wrong. His wife and sons may worm their way in and challenge the will in court. His publisher could intervene. No, I believe I like the will as it is. It will be cleanest if you just terminate Beckett and Lassiter and make it look as if they killed one another. It will tie up all the loose ends quite nicely."

"I refuse to do it. You're asking the impossible."

He nodded towards his two goons, a barely perceptible signal. They were on Benedictis in an instant: three quick blows to his kidneys followed by a series of punches to his stomach that sent him to the floor in a fetal position. Before the punishment was administered, he was able to tense his stomach to protect himself, but the blows were so hard that he knew right away that they had cracked a rib or two.

He lay there, groaning in misery, for two full minutes. Wondering why he and his brother had the misfortune of getting mixed up with Popov and his goons in the first place? In his mind, the only good things to ever come out of the former Soviet Union were exceptional novelists with lengthy unpronounceable names, vodka, and *matryoshka*, the painted wooden nesting dolls. Everything else was shit—and most especially Alexei Popov!

The two goons hoisted him to his feet and unceremoniously stuffed him into his chair at his desk again. He knew he wasn't going to be able to take much more of this physical punishment.

"So," said Popov, as if they had been having nothing more than a friendly debate, "you will kill Beckett and Lassiter with the weapons I have given you and then you will become a bestselling author and we will make hundreds of millions together and I will not have to kill your brother Danny and daughter Rebecca. How does that sound? That is a good deal, no?"

He shook his head in dismay, unable to believe the nightmare he had gotten himself into. Popov was, quite simply, an unstoppable force, a raging maniac beyond the reach of any law. He was—the literary agent thought dismally— Cormac McCarthy's twisted brainchild, Anton Chigurh, on fucking steroids.

The Russian looked at him bleakly, as if life and death were simply the giving or not giving of commands.

After a moment, Benedictis found his voice. "You have given me no choice, Alexei. But I think you're forgetting one thing: I've never shot a gun at a person before. I'll probably blow the whole damned thing and then where will we all be?"

"Oh, I will have a little lifeline for you if you need it."

"A lifeline?"

"Detective Stafford. What, you didn't think I was going to let you go it alone like a cowboy?"

"Stafford will be there?"

"And others. You won't see them, of course. But if things get dicey, they will be there to make sure the job is done right."

"Is Stafford on your payroll?"

The Russian didn't answer.

He shook his head disconsolately. *How in the hell am I going to get out of this?*

And then he wondered: *But what if I go through with it?*

Then he would become the new Cameron Beckett—a world-renowned billionaire and bestselling author. How huge would that be?

He cleared his throat, forcing himself to steel his nerves. "If I do this, Alexei, you and I are going to have to have a different financial arrangement."

"I don't think you are in the position to be cutting deals."

"I don't give a shit. From now on, everything is between you and me and no one else. My brother and the rest of my family are strictly off limits. Also, you don't get fifty percent—you get forty percent and not a dime more. That's the deal or you might as well kill me now and call it quits with your money-laundering operation, because the real Cameron Beckett is done. He's not going to write another novel. He just doesn't have it in him anymore. Hell, I've practically been ghost-writing his last dozen novels anyway."

The room fell silent again as the Russian thought pensively.

"Do we have a deal, Alexei?"

Silence.

"Tell me, do we have a fucking deal or not?"

The Russian nodded slowly. "*Da*, we have a deal." His expression turned thoughtful, like a daydreaming kid. "I've always wanted to be in the literary business."

"Well, lucky you, now you are." But all he could think was: *What the fuck am I doing? Am I really going to go through with this?*

If he didn't, Popov would hound him the rest of his life. But if he killed Beckett, as regrettable as that would be, he would save his family, be an international rock-star author instead of an unknown agent that no one gave a shit about except the New York literary establishment, and he would make the kind of money that even most Wall Street tycoons could only dream about. On the flip side, he would still be a slave to the incorrigible Russian, a piece of chattel whose fate was out of his hands.

"To think that I am now a literary man," said Popov, still with that dreamy look on his face. "Just like my heroes Tolstoy, Dostoyevsky, and Solzhenitsyn."

He would have thought the bastard's heroes would instead have been the brutal Lenin, Stalin, and Putin instead of those glorious Russian writers, but he said nothing. What could he possibly say to such mental derangement? What could he say when he knew that his life, as he knew it, was over and he had been reduced to a serf banished to the Siberian hinterland, a living fucking dead man.

A living dead man who wrote bestselling novels for a Russian crook.

CHAPTER 30

AVANTI RECEPTION ROOM
20TH FLOOR OF DONALD TRUMP, JR. BUILDING
1450 SIXTH AVENUE

AS NATALIE handed the group's guest cards to the check-in staff and they stepped through the black-velvet ropes into the elegant reception room, Lassiter felt like a spy on the verge of toppling a foreign government.

The Avanti Reception Room was filled with New York's finest *literati* and *glitterati*: bestselling authors, literary agents, publishers, and editors mingled with politicians, movie stars, Wall Street tycoons, film directors and producers, academic elites, journalists, foreign dignitaries, business royalty, wealthy patrons of the arts, and kings and queens of the food and fashion industries. They were all here, shimmering like precious diamonds in their most resplendent "formal" attire, as waiters darted to and fro with glasses of French Veuve Clicquot Ponsardin champagne and hors d'oeuvres of foie gras, beluga and sevruga caviar, tomato and basil bruschetta, and smoked salmon croistinis.

"Split up like we talked about and keep a sharp eye out," said his father as they stepped into the bustling room. "We go in half an hour, eight sharp."

"Copy that, Commander," said Lassiter with a wink.

He took Natalie by the arm. They scuttled left while his father veered right and Squelch, Claggebart, and Bermolito, looking dapper in their rented black silk ties and tuxedos, made a beeline straight for the bar. At his father's insistence, Natalie had managed to obtain guest cards for every member of the Devil's Brigade and their plan had been synchronized to the minute.

All the same, Lassiter couldn't help but feel anxious and wanted a cocktail to loosen up. A white-jacketed waiter flitted past carrying a silver serving tray loaded down with glasses of champagne. He grabbed a pair of crystal flutes, handed one to Natalie, and they sipped while watching the crowd.

"Don't look," she said, "but there's Mayor Buckley talking to Martin Scorsese and fashion designer Donna Karan."

He, of course, swiveled his head and gawked at them like a complete idiot just for the fun of it and to embarrass her.

"Stop it," she chided him, unable to restrain a little smile. "Haven't you heard about being subtle? Now this time control yourself." She was glancing discreetly to his left. "Over there is Alec Baldwin speaking to Antonio Banderas, Anna Wintour, and Tina Brown."

"Okay, I'm going subtle this time." He craned his neck and waved at them frantically like a crazed celebrity stalker.

They looked away worriedly—all except Antonio Banderas who seemed to think it was funny and waved back.

"Stop it. You're embarrassing me." She took him by the arm and herded him towards the middle of the room.

"Okay, I'm going to give you one last chance," she said. "There's Cameron Beckett talking to Jane Freidman, Eric Simonoff, Trevor LeStrange, Douglas Preston, and Scott Turow."

He turned to look, this time restraining from acting like a complete nut job and drawing undue attention. "Oh, I recognize that guy."

"Trevor LeStrange?"

He nodded. "I sent *Blind Thrust* to him two years ago after I had submitted it to Benedictis, but he rejected it too."

"That doesn't surprise me. Trevor LeStrange is a top literary agent and takes on very few new clients."

"No, he's just another snobby, superannuated gatekeeper—a fucking dinosaur—who's about to be struck down by an asteroid hurtling towards earth called *the digital revolution*. His writers' caste system—dividing up novelists into freight-class, coach-class, and first-class like the passengers on the Orient Express—is total bullshit. So fuck him and the train he rode in on."

"My, my, someone has anger issues tonight. Have you forgotten that I'm a gatekeeper too, Nick? From my perspective, all LeStrange is trying to do is spark a legitimate debate on the pros and cons of both indie and traditional publishing."

"But he's not in a position to do any such thing. He's part of the entrenched aristocracy that doesn't want to change. He's King Louis the Sixteenth hiding out in his royal chambers when the peasants are storming the Bastille. I have to admit, though, that I did like his latest How-To-Be-A-Bestseller-Book, *Tension Every Nanosecond*."

"Oh, so the truth comes out. You may have more in common with the literary establishment than you think, Mr. Indie. Seriously though, do you think it's actually possible to do what he says in his book? I mean, can a writer really create tension *every nanosecond* in a novel?"

He shook his head. "It's hard enough to get tension on every page, let alone in every paragraph. I mean, even LeStrange's so-called 'first-class' authors, best sellers like Beckett, *never* do that, so what the hell is he talking about? Does the little weasel even know what the fuck he's talking about?"

"Not according to Barry Eisler, Hugh Howey, and J.A. Konrath, but that's another stor—"

"Good God, what are you doing here?"

They looked up in startlement as David Sloan, President and CEO of Excalibur Publishing Group, glared at Lassiter through a chewy mouthful of *foie gras*.

"It's all right, David," interrupted Anton De Benedictis, rushing in from their right. "I invited this mischief-maker to the party and instructed Natalie here to keep an eye on him." His hand extended gracefully. "Hello Nick, can you promise me you'll be a good boy and not pepper-spray any of my guests?"

Lassiter was taken aback; the last thing he had expected was to be treated civilly by Benedictis. He glanced quickly at Natalie—noting that she looked as surprised as him at her boss's congeniality—before taking the proffered hand.

"Hello Anton, we meet yet again."

As they shook hands, the literary agent leaned in close and whispered so Sloan couldn't hear. "Once again, you have surprised me, Nick. How did you manage to get on the guest list?"

"You'll have to thank, Natalie," he whispered back. "She's the one who invited me. She said you wanted her to keep an eye on me—so she insisted I come."

"Oh, she did, did she? Well, she's quite right." Benedictis turned towards her and now spoke in a normal-decibel voice. "Thank you, Natalie, for bringing Mr. Lassiter to our little gala. Now if you don't mind, I'd like to have a private word with him."

"That's fine by me. He's a handful."

Benedictis smiled: he seemed to enjoy the quip. Then he looked at Sloan, who was scowling with antipodal disapproval. "If you'll excuse us, David, Nick and I won't be but a minute."

Benedictis quickly took him by the arm and ushered him towards the buffet. As he did so, Lassiter delivered a parting glance to Natalie, who gave a nod and quickly disappeared in a crowd of people as the sourpuss Sloan stomped off in the opposite direction with his heaping plateful of food.

"He doesn't seem too happy," said Nick.

"He'll get over it," replied Benedictis.

"Are you sure about that? He may decide to send his Excalibur goons to kidnap us again."

"I don't know what on earth you're talking about, Nick. But I can say that I seriously doubt anything like that will happen going forward because we're all on the same page now."

"We are?"

"You bet. What if I told you that I'm sorry we got off on the wrong foot yesterday and that Cameron Beckett and I want to buy you lunch tomorrow to make it up to you? Same time, same place—and this time you get to actually enjoy your lunch."

"The Victorian Club? Are you serious?"

"I most certainly am—and this time we're going to do it without Excalibur's damned lawyer."

"So you want to hold the meeting again? Is that what you're saying?"

"This time we'll do it right. Just you, me, and my client. Of course, there will be a large financial disbursement for just showing up, which you can humbly accept on your behalf or give to your favorite charity. Mr. Beckett leaves that up to you."

He grabbed a plate and handed it to him. Lassiter found the cornucopia laid out on the table mouth-watering: an assortment of fine bread and cheeses; silver platters overflowing with chilled Georgia rock shrimp, Virginia bluepoint oysters, and Florida stone crabs on shaved ice; a platter of dilled Alaskan King salmon; cheese blintzes; herbed lamb meatball dumplings; miniature Australian rock lobster eggrolls; and a dozen other delicacies.

"Tuck in there, Nick, my man. Quite a spread, huh?"

"It sure is." He took the plate and began loading it up with peeled shrimp, oysters on the half shell, and stone crabs. "Tell me, Anton, why the change of heart?"

"My client and I never changed heart, Nick. We both would have preferred to have taken care of business at lunch today. But Excalibur got its legal team involved and that's what created the cluster fuck. Plus your dad didn't do any of us any favors with that secret little recording. So your father works for the CIA—I must say that's quite an ally to have. By the way, were you able to patch things up with the old man? You looked pretty angry when you stormed out of there."

"Yeah, we're good. He's my dad, so he can't help but meddle."

"Where is he by the way?"

"Oh, he's around here somewhere. Probably talking to Mayor Buckley, Martin Scorsese, or Donna Karan. You know, he just loves hanging with politicians, movie moguls, and fashion designers. But he wants to talk to you too. He wants to catch up with you again…you know, since you're old friends."

"You don't have to be sarcastic, Nick. Your dad and I are old friends."

"That's good to hear because speak of the devil, here he comes now."

His father walked up carrying a glass of champagne, looking elegant in his black-tie attire.

"Good evening, Austin, old buddy," said Benedictis, extending a hand. "You look like you're enjoying yourself."

His father took the extended hand and squeezed it hard, making Benedictis wince. "Thanks, Anton, old pal," he replied, clearly enjoying inflicting pain on the literary agent. "I hope you don't mind that we crashed your party."

"Now at least I know where your son developed the habit." Benedictis pulled his crushed hand away and waggled it. "That's some grip there, Austin. If I didn't know any better I'd say that you were trying to break my hand."

"If I was, old buddy, it would be broken."

"I have no doubt. By the way, Nick here and I were just talking. We have decided to put aside our differences once and for all tomorrow at lunch."

"Is that so? Well, that's certainly a pleasant surprise."

"I was thinking the same thing. Needless to say, my client will bring his rather *ample* checkbook to commemorate the occasion. But I must inform you up front that there will be no lawyers or hidden recording devices allowed. Right, Nick?"

"Hey, don't forget who you're talking to. I'm the one who insisted on nothing more than a simple apology from day one. You guys are the ones who complicated everything."

"Indeed, we are. I'm sorry about that," said Benedictis.

"I am too," said his father. "From now on, kid, you're on your own."

"Well then, let's drink to success," said Benedictis, and they raised their champagne glasses in a toast.

"What are we drinking to?" asked a new, foreign-sounding voice.

Lassiter looked up to see a bear of a man with a well-trimmed silver goatee, the veiny piggy-pink skin of a heavy drinker and gourmand, and steel-gray Slavic eyes that hinted at barely suppressed violence—all of which he knew had to belong to none other than Alexei Popov. The barrel-chested Russian gave a slight bow and held aloft a flute of straight-up vodka.

"Why, we're toasting to success," said Lassiter, pushing aside the shudder of fear that had seized hold of his body at first sight of the legendary mob boss.

"Ah, success," declared Popov with a gleam in his eye as he looked at Benedictis. "Now that is worth toasting. To success then!"

Natalie appeared at Lassiter's side. "Wait a second—I want to get in on this!" She gave him a mischievous look and raised her glass. "To success, everyone!"

"To success!" the group echoed in unison, and they clinked flutes and sipped their champagne while Popov tossed back his vodka.

Despite the convivial atmosphere, Lassiter felt a new underlying frisson of tension in the air with the unexpected arrival of the Russian. Popov clearly changed the dynamic, radiating an aura of violence like the musk of a wild animal. Nick noticed that his father, in particular, seemed on high alert in the mobster's presence. He wondered if they were going to scrap the whole operation now that Popov was here. He also noticed, for the first time, the presence of Detective Stafford standing along the margins of their group, as if eavesdropping. He looked again at his father and saw that he too had noticed the NYPD special VIP detective on the prowl.

"Now, Anton, my friend," said Popov with an obvious flair for the dramatic gesture. "If you would please formally introduce me to your friends, especially this enchanting young woman to my left." He gave Natalie a salacious smile.

Benedictis stepped forward politely, but even he seemed uncomfortable. "Oh yes, of course. This is Austin Brewbaker, his son Nick Lassiter, and Natalie Perkins. Natalie's a very promising agent who works in my office. She and Nick used to be *quite* an item." He winked conspiratorially at them both.

Popov's salacious smile grew. "Is that so?" With exaggerated chivalry, he stepped forward, bowed gracefully, took Natalie by the hand, and kissed it. "I am pleased to meet you, Natalie."

The mob boss then turned and shook hands vigorously with Lassiter and his father.

"So this is the Nick Lassiter I have heard so much about. Do you have Russian blood per chance? It appears you have Slavic features."

He looked at his father. "Uh, I don't think so, but maybe."

"Well, it is a pleasure to finally meet you face-to-face."

When the introductions were complete, they continued to make small talk about the party and Beckett's new book. Lassiter noticed that his father was scanning the room along with Stafford. Following their gaze, he quickly realized what they were both doing: making a count of Popov's bodyguards. There were six of them. Two stood with their backs against the east wall, two against the west wall, and two on the other side of the buffet line. If there were more, he couldn't see them.

He looked at his father. *Those guys are going to give us problems,* his dad's expression seemed to say. *And so might Stafford.*

"And how do you all know each other, if I may ask?" asked Popov with false innocence.

"Austin and I went to college together," answered Benedictis. "We spent our junior year abroad at Oxford together."

"Oh, what a wonderful experience that must have been. And what about you, Nicholas and Natalie? When did you two first start sleeping together?"

"Excuse me?" said Lassiter.

"Actually, more importantly Nicholas you numbskull, why did you *stop* sleeping with her? Young Natalie here is quite ravishing."

The Russian reached out, touched her cheek, and began gently stroking it.

Her face crimsoned. "What are you doing? Please get your hands off me." She politely pushed his hand away and moved closer to Lassiter.

For a moment, everyone was too stunned to speak. Then Benedictis said, "Alexei, I don't think that's—"

"The way a gentleman treats a lady," Lassiter finished for him.

He stepped forward and shoved Popov hard in the chest.

"Don't you have any manners you bloated, vodka-swilling Cossack?"

"That's enough, Nick," said his father. "I'm sure Mr. Popov didn't mean it."

"Really? Because I think the fat fuck did." He again shoved the burly Russian hard in the chest, this time nearly knocking him down. "Don't you ever talk to or touch my...my *girlfriend* like that again, you Russian piece of shit!"

Despite the packed reception room, the harsh words echoed through the crowd like a gunshot, bringing the party to a sudden standstill. Lassiter retreated a half-step, stunned by what he had just done, as a collective gasp and murmur of voices went up from the guests closest to him. The still-life tableau stood frozen for a moment as Popov's face reddened with naked fury from the public embarrassment. All around them mouths opened in shock, people stopped talking, and others craned their necks to have a better view. It was as if a knife had suddenly sliced through the reception room. As Lassiter struggled to regain his composure, he saw Stafford step forward and Popov's hulking bodyguards moving in quickly from three directions.

"Jesus, what have you done, Nicholas," muttered his father, and he started to grab him by the elbow as Stafford quickly closed the distance and was suddenly at his side.

He's right, what the fuck was I thinking?

He gulped as he saw the detective's hand slide inside his tuxedo jacket where his shoulder rig and NYPD firearm of choice would likely be. And then, all of a sudden Squelch, Claggebart, and Bermolito were there beside them.

"Yes, what have you done, Nicholas?" admonished Claggebart, looking first at him and then at Popov and shaking his head like an Etiquette School instructor. "Here the boys and I leave you alone for five minutes and you are already rude to our esteemed Russian guest? Good heavens, don't you remember your Tolstoy? Never lose your temper at a lavish cocktail party—it's unbecoming of a true gentleman."

Popov gave a curt nod of agreement and looked to Lassiter for an apology. When it didn't come, he puffed out his chest, patted his tuxedo, and adjusted his black silk tie. At that moment, his men came running up, ready to go for their guns or start breaking limbs at his command. But to Lassiter's surprise, the mobster called them off with an abrupt chop of his hand as soon as he saw Stafford. The goons halted in their tracks and started shifting sideways to form a protective wall around him, but he waved this off too and glared at Lassiter for a long moment.

The room went totally still. Lassiter held his breath.

Slowly, Popov's mouth creased into a cautionary smile. "I admire you for protecting your woman, my brazen young American friend. But with a temper like that, I do not think you will be on this earth for very long."

"I don't give a damn what you think."

"That is a mistake, I can assure you. Enjoy the evening with young Natalie here, Nikolai, because it could very well be your last."

And with that, he signaled his bodyguards that they were leaving, cut a swath through the stupefied crowd, and stalked out of the Avanti Reception Room with his fierce-looking entourage in tow.

CHAPTER 31

DE BENEDICTIS LITERARY ASSOCIATES
1450 SIXTH AVENUE

EXACTLY ELEVEN MINUTES LATER, Brewbaker watched impatiently as Natalie entered the access code to the electronic-entry keypad at the front door on the thirtieth floor. He then glanced at his watch: 8:03 p.m. He set his timer for fifteen minutes with a vibration alarm. That was all the time he would allow for the computer file acquisition—not a second more.

Fortuitously, the outcome of the confrontation with Popov had eliminated the most obvious threat to the plan. Had the Russian mob boss and his men not left the party, out of professional habit they would have certainly continued to vigilantly track who came and went and closely monitor any suspicious activity. However, although Brewbaker was relieved that Popov and his crew were out of the picture, he knew that he and Natalie still had to move quickly or they might be missed from the party.

The door clicked as the code was accepted and unlocked. He checked the hallway one last time before they darted inside, the door relocking automatically behind them. Darkness enveloped them. They quickly pulled out their flashlight-equipped smartphones and checked the hallways and offices before heading for their target, Benedictis's office, which had a standard key lock.

While Natalie shined her flashlight on the door, he carefully removed the two tools he needed to pick the lock, a tension tool and feeler pick. He inserted the tension tool first, which held the pins inside the lock down, then began to delicately probe with the feeler tool. Finally, after managing to align each of the pins along the shear line of the cylinder, he felt a solid click. With what seemed like a will of its own, the cylinder turned and the door unlocked.

No alarm sounded. They were in.

They slipped inside quickly, closing the door behind them. He felt along the wall and turned on a light.

"All right, we need to move fast," he said. "We need to be out of here in less than fifteen."

"Do you need help or do you want me on lookout?"

"Keep an eye on the front door and hallways. If someone comes and we get separated, we'll maintain quiet contact via our cell phones."

"Got it." She turned on her flashlight again and left the room.

He went to Benedictis's computer, turned it on, and quickly circumvented the literary agent's first level of antitampering protection by using a specially-adapted, portable log-in scrambling device that bypassed the thumbprint ID system and then logged on manually with the password *TheCore*, which happened to be the title of Beckett's first *New York Times* best seller. Benedictis had been using the same password since Brewbaker had first started working the case. His surveillance team had obtained the password the old-fashioned way: by breaking down, one pixel at a time, the video recording of the agent's keystrokes.

Once he had logged in, he breezed into Windows and clicked his mouse several times until he was into the C:\ and H:\ drive folders that were not on the local area network. These drives contained Benedictis's personal files. From the pocket of his tuxedo, he withdrew a 500 GB USB portable external hard drive. Compact as a smartphone, the external drive would be used to copy all of Benedictis's computer files and hopefully lead him to what the Russians had been after. He clicked the mouse on the C:\ drive folder first and the computer began humming. All the files in the folder were being copied, one file at a time. It took several minutes and then he began copying the files from, first, the H:\ drive and then, second, the other non-network drives that only Benedictis had access to directly from his computer.

That was when his coded mobile vibrated. He looked at the caller ID. It was his male assistant, CIA Officer Peter Brooke. He punched a button, accepting the incoming call.

"Peter, I'm in. You see me, right?"

"I'm sorry, Mr. Director, that's why I'm calling."

"You're telling me you're blind?" He looked at the camera concealed in the overhead ceiling sprinkler system just above the door. "I'm waving to you right now."

"We're not getting the feed, sir. It's been short-circuited."

"Damn, you're getting nothing?"

"Just static. And that's not all. We video-recorded a conversation from an hour ago between Benedictis and our boy Popov. But it got cut off a few minutes in. I was called upstairs so Beck Fisher was the only one in the control room. He just showed me what we got. It wasn't much because we lost transmission early on, but it looks like they were arguing."

"About what?"

"Apparently, Popov got his hands on Cameron Beckett's will. The will states that, in the event of the author's death or incapacitation, Benedictis will continue to write Beckett's novels under his name. The two must have worked out some kind of arrangement. The will also states that Benedictis has full creative and artistic control over all future writings, but that Beckett's family will retain all royalty payments and rights to previously published work."

Brewbaker hit a button on the keyboard and began copying another of Benedictis's encrypted folders. *Is that what Popov was after when he broke in? Or, is there something else?*

"Thanks for the update, Peter. But I need you to do something else for me. Can you uplink the Benedictis-Popov footage that you did manage to get to my secure site so that I can take a look at it?"

"Yes, sir. I'll get right on it. I'm really sorry about the lost footage. They were just starting to get angry when we lost the feed."

"What do you mean?"

"Well, Popov was trying to get Benedictis to do something for him. Something that Benedictis didn't want to do."

"They didn't say what it was?"

"No, sir. We lost audiovisual right then. It seemed like Popov was about to say what it was and then it cut out."

"Maybe I can figure it out when I take a look at the uplink."

"Yes, Mr. Director. I'm sorry, sir. I think it must have been those damned fire sprinklers that shorted-out the camera or messed up the link somehow. It was acting a little touchy even before we lost audiovisual, but an hour ago we lost it completely. I wanted you to know, sir."

"How soon can we get a team in here and fix the problem?"

"Tomorrow night. Nobody will know we were ever there. But there is something else, sir. I wanted to…uh…I wanted to warn you that Deputy Director Harcourt has been asking a lot of questions."

"Questions?"

"Yes, sir, a lot of them. I think you'd better wrap up what you're doing as soon as possible. He seems to be on the warpath."

"I copy, Peter, and I want to thank you. I'll be in touch on that uplink if I have any—"

Suddenly, the door blasted open and Natalie darted back into the room. "Someone's coming!" she whispered urgently.

"Sorry, Peter, gotta go." He punched off and looked at Natalie. "You saw them?"

"No, but I heard the elevator bleep and the doors open. Then I heard voices."

"Did you recognize them?"

"No." She nodded towards the computer. "How much longer do you need?"

He reached down to the keyboard, clicked on the final folder to copy, and looked at the time-stamp display. "Three minutes."

"We don't have three minutes. We need to get out of here."

He heard the voices down the hallway. She was right, they couldn't stay here. From the military-style shoulder holster beneath his tuxedo jacket, he withdrew his Smith and Wesson M1911A1 .45 semiautomatic pistol that carried a seven-round magazine.

"You've got a gun? Jesus, I should have known it would come to this."

He gave a shrug, threw his foot up on the glossy cherrywood desk, yanked up his pant leg, grabbed out his snub-nosed Beretta hideaway, and handed it to her. "Now you've got one too."

She looked at it with amazement.

"Welcome to the National Clandestine Service, Miss Perkins. Undo the safety, rack the slide, and you're good to go."

She did as instructed, making a sharp clicking noise as she racked the Beretta's tungsten, cerakote-stripped slide.

"Okay. Are you ready?"

She gripped her finger around the trigger and peered down the sight, surprising him by how comfortable she looked with the pistol in her hands. "Oh yeah, I'm ready all right," she said with a glint in her eye, as if she had suddenly transformed into Bonnie Parker.

"I'd say you're definitely field operative material. I think you might have picked the wrong profession, young lady."

"No, I haven't," she said, taking aim at Baby Face Nelson's bullet-proof vest on the wall. "I have two professions: literary agent and spy."

She smiled wickedly.

"Oh boy," he said, and he pulled out the external drive and killed the light.

CHAPTER 32

BENEDICTIS LITERARY ASSOCIATES
1450 SIXTH AVENUE

NATALIE felt her heart beating wildly in her chest as they crept down the hallway in the opposite direction of the voices. Now she could hear footsteps, too, approaching Benedictis's office, the door to which they hadn't had time to lock and had left partially open. They quickly passed her office on the left and came to the lunch room.

The voices and footsteps stopped.

Brewbaker came to an abrupt halt and grabbed her by the arm, pulling her into the lunchroom. They listened closely, ears pricked in the direction of Benedictis's office, where the noises had come from. He held his pistol in a two-handed hold and she imitated him, gripping her Beretta tightly. Despite her bravado a moment earlier when first handling the weapon, she wondered if she could actually pull the trigger and shoot down another human being if she was forced to defend herself. After all, it was one thing to hold a gun in your hand and feel its power wash all over you like a magic potion; it was quite another to fire at a living target and kill it dead.

The truth was she had never shot anything in her life. Not even with the BB gun that she had snatched from her older brother's room one summer when he was away at ice hockey camp. If her life was in peril and bad guys were shooting at her, she wanted to believe that she would have no problem firing back at them. But in the end, she was untested and unsure how she would react if bullets began flying.

After a tense moment, Brewbaker motioned her forward and they started moving again. They crept through the lunchroom and came out the other side into a parallel hallway that led back to her boss's office. But why were they going back there?

As if reading her thoughts, he whispered, "I need to see who it is."

Why? she wanted to challenge him. *Why risk going back there?*

But he was moving down the hallway already. More afraid of being left alone than confronting a potential enemy, she kept closely behind him. Thankfully, the Beretta felt solid and compliant in her hands.

They veered down another hallway that led directly to Benedictis's office.

Her hands started to tremble slightly. Playing the part of the gun-toting spy with armed adversaries prowling around you like stalking wolves wasn't as easy or romantic as she had thought. But the sight of Brewbaker in front of her steeled her nerves. His movements were wary and deliberate, but also confident, the consummate veteran-CIA operative in action. She understood why soldiers and spies had to undergo such rigorous training: it was so they could keep a cool head without freaking out in times like these. His eyes were watchful, like an animal on the hunt. She told herself to remain calm, follow his lead, and everything would turn out all right.

When they reached the adjoining hallway twenty feet away from the office, he peered cautiously around the corner.

She couldn't see what he saw, but she heard a light footfall and saw a blade of light slice through the darkness as the door to Benedictis's office slowly opened. She also heard whispering voices coming from the office. Suddenly, the hallway was blasted with light as the door flung open all the way.

Brewbaker jumped out from behind the wall. "Freeze!" he yelled, pointing his gun at the intruder.

"Dad, what are you doing? We've got to get the hell out of here!"

My God, Nick? She jumped out from behind the wall behind Brewbaker so that Nick could see her, feeling like a kid after surviving a scare on Halloween night.

"Goddamnit, Nicholas?" demanded his father. "Why are you up here? You were supposed to wait at the party and call us if there was a problem!"

From behind Nick, Claggebart appeared. "We couldn't call, Mr. B. They were watching us."

"Who?"

"The same guys who kidnapped and threatened us in the car," said Nick. "The Excalibur security people. So we pretended to leave the party and go to the lobby, but then we saw Popov and his thugs coming back so Clagge and I took the elevator up here to warn you. There's no phone reception in the elevator. That's why we came here to tell you in person. Squelch and Bermolito are downstairs waiting by the car."

"Popov came back? We have to get out of here and I mean right now."

Natalie noticed that Nick was looking at her with stupefaction. "Is that a gun you're carrying?" he asked her.

"I gave it to her," said his father. "And now I'm giving you one too."

He pulled up his pant leg to reveal a second compact hideaway gun, plucked it out, and handed it to Nick along with a spare magazine. "It's a Beretta nine-millimeter. Annie Oakley here can show you how to use it."

"Hey, wait a second—why don't I get one?" protested Claggebart. "I'll have you know that I happen to be a crack shot at the East Aurora paintball range. I joined this club, you see, and I've won several competitions. In fact, I happen to have won both my pro marksmanship certificate and my—"

"Save it for later, Clagge," Brewbaker cut him off as Natalie snicked off the safety on Nick's gun and showed him how to rack the slide. "We've got to get the hell out of here. Everyone, let's go now!"

He waved them forward. They moved swiftly down the hallway. When they reached the front glass door, Natalie opened it, waved everyone through, and then they started for the—

The elevator bell dinged for the thirtieth floor and the doors started to open.

171

"Shit!" cried Brewbaker. "All right, everyone back inside! Quick, quick!"

Natalie almost fell over Claggebart, but was able to turn around, reach out, and keep the door from closing shut.

"Go, go, go!" she cried, holding the glass door open as the elevator doors parted and Alexei Popov and his terrifying crew of six oversized, thick-necked thugs stepped from the elevator.

"Halt!" cried the Russian mob boss.

"Natalie go!" yelled Nick, and he shoved her through the open door along with his father and Claggebart.

Then he turned to face the Russians with his Beretta.

"He's got a gun! Shoot him! Shoot them all!" bellowed Popov.

Oh shit, thought Natalie. *We're all going to die.*

CHAPTER 33

BENEDICTIS LITERARY ASSOCIATES
1450 SIXTH AVENUE

IT WAS THE RUSSIANS' SPEED THAT STUNNED HER. She couldn't believe how quickly Popov pulled out his Makarov and his men yanked out their 9mm semiautomatic pistols and had them all pointing at Nick. He raised his weapon to fire, but the odds were a suicidal seven to one until she and his father could bring their weapons to bear. "No!" she cried, and she reached out and yanked him inside the glass door. They dove to the floor just as the door and partition exploded in a maelstrom of glass, wood, lathe, and plaster, raining down fragmented shards upon them like a Vesuvian eruption.

Austin Brewbaker stepped forward to cover them and was answered by another salvo from the Russians pouring into the lobby. Taking one in the arm, he grunted in pain and dropped his pistol. It went sliding across the floor as several more reports sent a shuddering staccato through the lobby and he and Claggebart were forced to take cover behind the receptionist's desk. More glass shards exploded all around the Devil's Brigadiers from the Russian onslaught as the reception area window was almost completely destroyed.

A moment later, there was a brief lull as the firing slackened and the Russians were forced to pull back and reload. Natalie and Nick, too, took advantage of the momentary cessation to pop in fresh magazines. Meanwhile, Claggebart scrambled across the floor like a fast-crawling baby, snatched up Brewbaker's pistol, ripped off a quick burst to hold the enemy at bay, dashed back behind the receptionist's desk they were hiding behind, and handed the weapon back to its rightful owner, who had managed to improvise a dressing from his torn shirt to staunch the flow of blood from his gunshot arm.

The firing quickly resumed on both sides.

Natalie took careful aim and let loose at Popov, but missed. Instead, the lobby painting of Donald Trump, Jr. clattered to the floor riddled with bullets through DTJ's face like a Mad Magazine cover. The Beretta bucked in her inexperienced hands, but with her, Nick, and Nick's father now firing in concert they were able to force the Russians into again taking cover.

But unfortunately, the enemy had more firepower and was able to quickly regroup. A dozen answering blasts from the Russians tore the couches Natalie and Lassiter were hiding behind to shreds, forcing them to duck down and pull back behind another bigger couch.

"Go! I'll cover you!" cried Nick. "We've got to get out of here!"

He fired again and this time one of the Russians gave a loud grunt and went down.

"I said go, goddamnit! Now!"

But just as she was about to make her move, one of Popov's men rounded the corner and smashed through the still-intact portion of the lobby window. The pane of glass exploded upon impact and the Russian fired at her. She felt her hair swish as the bullet whizzed past her ear like a hornet and buried itself in the wall behind her. A second later Nick popped up like a jack-in-the-box and put the Russian down.

"Are you all right?" he then called out to her.

"Yes, but that was damned close!"

"We're outgunned and have to fall back!" commanded Brewbaker, waving at them on their right from behind the receptionist's desk. "Follow me!"

But before they could obey the command, they again came under heavy fire. They delivered an answering burst to keep Popov and his goons at bay, but they were now in a precarious position. Even though the Russians had lost two men, they were still trained professionals and it was still five guns against three since Claggebart didn't have a weapon. Adept at keeping up a steady gunfire and moving forward and laterally after each burst, the Russians were also beginning to win the battle of position. When she again chanced a look over the couch at the enemy, she saw that Popov had moved away from the protective cover of an ornate pillar and drawn a bead on Nick's father, who was now exposed on his right flank.

"I know who you are, Austin Brewbaker!" shouted the Russian mob boss. "You're head of the CIA Russian desk and now you're going to die!"

Baring his teeth like a wild animal, he squeezed the trigger several times in rapid succession. Brewbaker ducked and pushed Claggebart to the side to shield him from gunfire as Natalie and Nick opened up. They instantly drew Russian fire away from their two cohorts. Bullets screamed past their ears and thunked into the wall, exploding drywall and stucco chunks and spewing chalk-like dust all around them. Brewbaker popped up and returned fire once, twice, then a third time with his Smith and Wesson. By some miracle, no one on either side was hit.

But their position was now untenable.

"We have to fall back!" cried Brewbaker. "Let's go!"

Natalie and Nick let loose with a covering burst and then all four of them were up and running, legs pumping furiously, dashing down one hallway and then another. Behind her, she could hear the sound of the Russians' feet crunching on the broken glass as they followed in hot pursuit.

"We need to get to the rally point," said Brewbaker as they ran. "Nick, get Bermolito on the phone and have him guide us to the service elevator on the twentieth floor. We're taking the fire stairs."

"Got it!"

"Natalie, is this the right way?"

"Yes, just keep on going." She saw the fire door at the end of the hallway.

"Good heavens," cried Claggebart. "I don't know what we've gotten ourselves into, but I don't want to die in New York City, of all places. I always wanted to take my last breath on the French Riviera, in a Belgian brothel, or on the slopes of Stadt, but not in a big, dirty American city."

"I'm sorry, Your Worship, I'm still working on it," replied Nick's father.

Now Natalie heard voices again and they were once again under fire. A pair of shots rang out, whistling past and driving into the heavy metal door to the stairwell, ringing out like a jackhammer. Nick's father turned to give cover fire and shouldered the door open as another fusillade of bullets slammed into the steel door and tore gaping holes in the wall. After a brisk exchange of gunfire, the firing paused a moment as both sides reloaded. Lassiter took advantage of the lull to receive escape instructions from Bermolito on his iPhone, which he had cleverly stuffed into the jacket pocket of his tuxedo so he could listen on speakerphone and talk into it while running and shooting.

"Brewbaker!" yelled out Popov from down the hallway. "What are you doing here, Brewbaker? Have you gone rogue?"

With a fresh magazine, Nick's father answered with a blast of gunfire.

"You missed Brewbaker! You and your son are going to die and your seed will disappear from this earth! You should not have brought these people here tonight! What kind of fool are you?"

"Fuck you, Popov!" yelled Nick and he fired off three quick shots in rapid succession.

While father and son held the Russians at bay, Natalie and Claggebart pushed their way into the stairwell. As they flew through the opening, Natalie chanced a look over her shoulder.

It was a mistake.

A bullet slammed into her side and she dropped her Beretta. She felt a burning sensation as if someone had thrown boiling water on her, followed quickly by another. She realized straight away that the two bullets had struck her upper ribcage and at least one of them had probably pierced her lungs.

"Natalie! Jesus, you're hit!" she heard Nick cry as he turned around to follow them into the stairwell.

"I'm okay—I'll make it," she cried back, but she knew she was hit badly and would only slow them down.

While Nick's father delivered rearguard cover fire, Nick and Claggebart helped her down the stairs. To her dismay, they had to practically carry her. It was then she realized that she was going to slow them down so much that she was a major liability.

"You have to go on without me," she said, feeling a horrific burning in her lungs.

"No fucking way!" retorted Lassiter. "We don't leave our own behind— we're the Devil's Brigade!"

"All right, I get it," she said. "You actually want me to live."

"Yeah, you got a problem with that? I happen to love you!"

"I love you too!" She smiled then grimaced as she felt a searing pain in her chest.

"Just hang in there," he said, taking off his tuxedo jacket and placing it over her two closely spaced wounds. "Keep both hands on there for pressure. We're going to get you out of here."

He leaned her against the hand rail, dashed up onto the landing, and fired off two quick bursts with his Beretta as Claggebart scrambled forward to retrieve her dropped pistol.

Nick and his father fired one final salvo to cover their retreat, slammed the fire escape door shut, and then all of them paused a moment to regroup while his father handed out fresh magazines. They popped the metallic clips into place with loud clicking noises.

Brewbaker waved them down the stairs. Blood poured from her wounds, dribbling onto the floor, leaving a trail. But she was able to move at a steady clip with assistance from Nick and Claggebart. Forcing herself to gut it out, she was able to press onward quicker than she had thought possible while keeping pressure on her wounds with Nick's jacket. When they reached the twenty-sixth floor, she heard the fire escape door above them blast open followed by shouting voices.

A shot rang out from above, the bullet ricocheting off a steel guardrail.

They kept moving downward, floor by floor.

Soon, she could feel herself getting weaker. The air just wasn't coming anymore and she felt as if she was ascending a monstrous Colorado Fourteener like she and Nick used to climb together. He and Claggebart were still helping her along, but she was slowing the group down badly.

But, with an effort, they were able to reach the twentieth floor.

Brewbaker shot off the door handle so they could get inside, and they dashed down the hallway. All the while listening to Bermolito's instructions over the speakerphone on Nick's cell.

"Now turn right! The elevator is down the branching corridor!"

They did as instructed and soon reached the service elevator. "We found it, Berm, we found it!" cried Lassiter. He punched the *Down* button.

But behind them, out of sight but not more than thirty yards away down the branching hallway, Natalie heard the thumping footsteps of Popov and his thugs.

The Russians were coming up fast.

She saw Claggebart reach out and hit the button again as Nick and his father crouched to one knee and opened fire on the enemy.

"You're going to be all right, Natalie," said Claggebart, as if by the conviction of his voice he could will it so. "Just hang on. Hang on so everyone will know your brave story just like your great-grandfather Maxwell Perkins. You know, of course, that he was the true genius behind both Fitzgerald and Hemingway."

"Thanks, Clagge, but is this really the time to be discussing this? If I'm not mistaken, I think I'm about to take my last breath."

"No way, you can't die, my fair lady. Not until you and Nicholas are properly wedded and the Devil's Brigade can partake of your splendid nuptials. And also note that Dear Uncle Clagge expects at least three adorable, rosy-cheeked children from you two before either of you can even contemplate kicking the proverbial bucket. I'm talking about little smiling-faced devils that I can toss around a pigskin with and recount tall tales to and make laugh so hard that the soda pop bubbles out of their nostrils like a Roman fountain."

"I...I don't know, Clagge," she croaked. "I think you might be asking too much."

"Like hell I am! Nicholas will never love anyone as he loves you. And you will never love another as much as you love him. So you see you must live, damn you!"

She gritted her teeth, fighting back the pain. "Okay, I'm going to live, damnit! I'm going to live!"

"Now that's more like it, luv! We're getting out of here—and that means every fucking one of us!"

But even as the inspirational words left Morrison Frautschi Claussen's mouth, Natalie knew she was slipping into unconsciousness.

Her life was in God's hands now.

CHAPTER 34

DONALD TRUMP, JR. BUILDING

WITH A PRETERNATURAL CALMNESS he didn't know he possessed, Nick Lassiter slipped in a fresh magazine, took down a granite-jawed Russian with two rounds from his Beretta, and found himself thinking: *Maybe instead of an unemployed geologist and unpublished hack writer, I should be a spy like my father and Natalie.*

The elevator doors started to open.

"Quick, everyone inside!" cried Austin Brewbaker.

From the branching hallway that led to the Avanti Reception Room, Lassiter saw Detective Stafford materialize and open fire on the Russians, forcing them to take evasive action and retreat down the hallway. The detective must have heard the gunshots at the party and raced out to see what all the commotion was about. Lassiter tilted his head so he could talk again into his iPhone stuffed into his jacket pocket.

"Bermolito, pull the van up front!" he shouted into the phone.

"Okay, got it! But is that gunfire I hear?"

"Yep, it's coming in hot. Is Squelch with you?"

"He's heading to the van now."

"Tell him to meet us at the service elevator in the lobby! We're coming down now and Natalie's badly wounded!"

"He'll be there. I'll be waiting out front with the van."

The Russians opened fire again, this time on his group and Stafford both. As they pulled back, Lassiter delivered a rearguard salvo before helping Claggebart carry Natalie the last few feet into the elevator. As he hit the button for the lobby, his father let loose with one final burst and ducked inside with bullets buzzing like hornets, shredding the mahogany paneling and a pair of antique Edwardian chairs in the hallway like a wood chipper.

The elevator doors closed.

As the elevator hummed and rattled downward towards the lobby, Lassiter surveyed the damage. Though Claggebart was applying pressure on Natalie's wounds, blood still gushed from her like a breached dam. She was limp, but thankfully Lassiter could see that she was still breathing. As for his father, he too was bleeding profusely even though he had managed to secure an improvised bandage from his torn shirt around his arm. Yet, Lassiter had to admit it could have been far worse. All the same, he was worried about Natalie. Shouldn't they try to keep her conscious?

His father echoed his thoughts. "Natalie, stay with me!" he beckoned, holding her head up as he tried to revive her. "Come on, stay with me!"

Nothing.

He pulled up her chin and spoke more urgently this time.

"Come on, Natalie, stay with me! You've *got* to stay with me!"

To Lassiter's surprise—and infinite relief—her eyes opened. But she still looked pale as a ghost from the traumatic blood loss. Jesus, they had to get her to a hospital quickly or she might not make it!

The elevator slowed. A moment later, the bell rang signaling their arrival to the lobby. The doors opened onto the marble-topped ground floor. Squelch was waiting for them as planned.

"Holy Doc Holiday!" he gasped with surprise at the sight of all the blood. "What the hell happened, the gunfight at the OK Corral?"

"You bet your ass, and all that was missing was Ike and Billy Fucking Clanton." Lassiter leaned down. "Hang in there, Natalie—we're going to get you out of here, all right?"

But she was unconscious again.

"Here, I got her," said Squelch. He took her from their hands, hoisting her up along with the blood-soaked jacket onto his shoulder to carry her. "Quickly, this way to the van!" he cried, and he started leading the way.

They made a beeline for the front entrance. Through the glass, Lassiter saw Bermolito sitting in the rented Dodge van idling on the street outside the building.

A hundred feet. That's all they had to do was make it a hundred lousy feet!

Suddenly, two security guards poked their heads up from their pillbox. "Hey, where are you going? That woman's bleeding!" one of them shouted.

His father had his government-issue credentials out and flashed them to the two men. "Director Brewbaker, CIA! We're being pursued by an armed group of Russian nationals! Call the police immediately and take cover! If you try and stop them, they *will* kill you!"

They stood there openmouthed before one of them snapped into action and jumped for the phone at his desk.

Lassiter pushed open the front door and started waving the group through. *Come on, come on, faster, faster!*

The main lobby elevators opened.

Popov and four of his men burst out onto the marble floor, guns blazing.

The wall of glass at the front entrance exploded into fragments and cascaded to the floor. Lassiter and his father stepped forward to return fire. Then, with bullets buzzing and ricocheting all around them, the group ran to the van, Squelch lugging Natalie over his shoulder like a slab of beef. Bermolito had thrown open all the doors and they were able to quickly pile into the van and drive off.

Unfortunately, the Russians had anticipated their move. A pair of sleek, black Range Rovers screeched up in front of the Donald Trump, Jr. Building.

Looking back, Lassiter saw Popov emerge from the front entrance, step carefully over the shards of broken glass, and bark out orders to his drivers and crew. In a flash, he and his heavily-armed bodyguards had packed into the two SUVs and were following in hot pursuit.

CHAPTER 35

CENTRAL PARK

WITH BERMOLITO BEHIND THE WHEEL, the Dodge van tore through a yellow light at West 59th Street and raced north into the park on Center Drive. The dusky sky overhead was blood-red, framing the massive skyscrapers standing at the edge of the New World's oldest and best known park in bold relief. A horse-drawn carriage packed with a group of tourists was just pulling onto the drive. Bermolito swung the wheel hard left to keep from mowing the conveyance down.

"Jiminy Crickets, be careful!" warned Claggebart. "We don't want to run anyone over, and we've got to get Natalie to the hospital in one piece! By the way, where are we going?"

"Mount Sinai Medical Center, 1176 Fifth Avenue," answered Bermolito. "It's the closest hospital."

"Are the damned Russkies following?"

"Unfortunately, yes," said Lassiter, peering back again at their pursuers. Both Range Rovers had run the red light and nearly crashed into oncoming traffic as they crossed West 59th and barreled into the park. "Do we shoot at them?" he asked his father.

"Only if they shoot first."

As if on cue, the front passenger-side window and rear-left window of the Range Rover out front rolled down and a pair of semiautomatic muzzles poked out.

"Shit, get down!" cried his father.

The first two shots clanked harmlessly against the rear bumper, but the third and fourth rounds found more critical targets, blowing out both the driver's side mirror and the rear window. Seated in the way back, Squelch was instantly showered with shattered glass.

"Holy Elliot P. Ness, I need a gun, goddamnit!" he cried. "I'm a sitting duck back here!"

"I'm sorry but we only have three," answered his father.

"And Claggebart gets one of them! Jesus Christ, he's more likely to shoot one of us than the Crazy Ivans!"

At that moment, they were suddenly rammed from behind by the lead vehicle.

Lassiter felt his neck whiplash violently forward. Out of the corner of his eye, he saw Natalie hit her head hard against the back of the seat and tumble with a heavy thud onto the floor of the van. Her eyes were closed and her body was limp and he wondered how she was going to possibly survive this terrible ordeal.

Bermolito hit the accelerator to pull away from their pursuers. But within seconds, the fleet Rover began to flank them on the passenger side. Soon they approached the 65th Street Traverse that bisected the southern segment of the park.

With the sound of revving engines hammering his ears, Lassiter looked up front at the speedometer. Eighty-seven mph—and in Central Park no less!

The Rover swung towards them like an enraged rhinoceros. To his credit, Bermolito swerved hard left to avoid the impact, but it wasn't enough as the van caromed off the SUV, the heavy scraping sound of metal against metal filling the Manhattan night. Hitting the brakes just as they came to the traverse, he swung the wheel hard to the left to pull away and gain some separation, as they headed west towards Central Park West.

But now they were going in the opposite direction of the hospital.

Both Range Rovers accelerated and suddenly the van was sandwiched between the two vehicles with Russians pointing guns at them.

"Duck!" cried Lassiter.

From both sides, gunfire poured into them like a Spanish treasure ship blasted port and starboard by buccaneers. Glass exploded—yet another eruption of jagged shards—and everyone but Bermolito was forced to dive to the floor. The cool, calm, and collected Timothy Caleb Bermingham then gave a clever smile, adjusted his electrician-taped, Buddy Holly-like glasses perched on his nose, and pressed his foot onto the accelerator as the Russians attempted to draw a bead on them a second time. He quickly pulled away by several car lengths but his speed, Lassiter saw, was now over a hundred miles an hour just as darkness was descending upon the city of Gotham.

At their new warp speed, they quickly came upon a traffic bottleneck and were forced to zigzag dangerously through the cars.

A moment later, they came upon two policemen mounted on horseback and a handful of pedestrians waiting to cross. There was no way Bermolito could avoid hitting them unless—

He yanked the steering wheel hard to the right, turning onto West Drive, scattering the two horses and swarm of panicked bystanders in all directions. One terrified horse pitched hard left and reared up on its hind legs, its nostrils flaring and hooves tearing sky; another threw its policeman rider and bolted down the road in panic. The bystanders scrambled for cover, stumbling over their feet and crashing into one another. Peering back at them through the broken rear window, Lassiter saw the lead Russian Rover plow over a hapless pedestrian who dodged the wrong way, pitching him into the bushes like a ragdoll.

Gunshots licked after them again from behind, peppering the van. Lassiter, his father, and Claggebart now leaned out the windows and returned fire, forcing both drivers to take evasive action by slowing down and dropping back. Then, without warning, Bermolito veered hard left onto the grass and charged the van up a gently sloping hill to the west.

"Where the hell are you going, Berm?" cried Lassiter.

"I just thought we should go this way, Brigadiers."

"Why, what's up ahead?"

SAMUEL MARQUIS

"Why the 7th New York Infantry Civil War Memorial, of course."

"Yeah, and the significance of that is?" demanded his father.

"The bronze statue was created by American sculptor John Quincy Adams Ward to commemorate the fifty-eight officers and troopers of the Seventh Regiment who died defending the Union during the Civil War. It depicts a Union soldier and was placed in this portion of the park by Frederick Law Olmsted, the designer of Central Park, in 1874 during—"

"Okay, okay, we get it!" shouted Lassiter. "What are we going to do with it?"

"Oh, I've got a little surprise for the Crazy Ivans."

He smiled devilishly as he came upon the bronze statue, cornered tightly around it, and drove straight at the lead Rover, playing chicken. The Russians came directly at him, but at the last second Bermolito pulled hard to the right.

The Rover crashed into the heavy pedestal of the giant Civil War statue. The front of the vehicle crumpled like an accordion and the statue toppled off its pedestal and smashed through the broken windshield.

"Goddamn Bermolito, you're a genius!" shouted Lassiter.

"Tally ho!" echoed Claggebart. "And my humblest apologies for all my deprecating remarks over the years! That was some serious gamesmanship!"

The whole van gave a rowdy cheer. But the celebration was short-lived as the second Rover raced up, windows down and guns firing.

Everyone ducked. Again Lassiter, his father, and Claggebart returned fire as Bermolito swung the van around again and started for the thick cover of the trees, trying to make it to Central Park West. The second vehicle stopped next to the fallen Civil War statue to pick up Popov, who was visibly fuming.

Bermolito quickly pulled away from the scene, but by the time they had reached Central Park West, a third vehicle had joined the chase. Out ahead of the Rover that Popov had jumped into, it came up quickly upon their rear, whipping through the traffic, engine gunning. The new Rover's occupants were an odd-looking bunch. The man in the passenger seat looked like an exact replica of Alexei Popov, so much so that he could have been his identical twin brother. The driver was a big, muscle-bound circus freak of a man with a shaved head, thick black goatee, and veritable swarm of arm and neck tattoos. The two Russian badasses in the back seat were also skin-headed and bore ample tattoos, but one of them also had a long slashing scar across his mouth that gave him an asymmetrical, misshapen lower jawline like an evil cartoon caricature. As if on cue, Popov's twin and the two men in the back seat began to open fire with their semiautos from their rolled-down windows.

Thunk! Thunk! Thunk!

"Jesus Christ, where did these new guys come from!" cried Squelch. "I feel like I'm in fucking Moscow!"

"I don't know," said Lassiter, "but they're not very friendly."

"Their green cards or visas should most assuredly be revoked," agreed Claggebart. "I don't believe they'll ever be able to adapt to our American legal system. Not with manners like these."

Police sirens now screamed from the north. It sounded like a whole fleet of vehicles was heading their way.

182

This would certainly change the equation.

The van's front left tire hit a huge pothole, forcing Bermolito to swerve hard right to keep the vehicle under control. A moment later, they were blasted with more gunfire, the bullets shattering what remained of the rear window, pinging off the metal bumper, burrowing into the van's seats.

"Goddamnit, I can't shake them!" cried Bermolito.

"Well, you've got to do something!" implored Lassiter. "They're about to ram us from behind!"

"Turn left onto Seventy-Fourth Street!" he heard his father command. "There's road and sidewalk construction there!"

"The Dakota? You want me to turn at the Dakota?" said Bermolito.

"No, I want you to turn two blocks past it at the San Remo, where there's heavy street construction and barricades. Do you have a better idea?"

"Not at the moment."

On their left, they passed the Central Park West entrance to the historic Dakota apartment building. The gabled and turreted bastion of the rich-and-famous twinkled and glittered in the night lights of the city. Down the 72nd street entrance where John Lennon had been shot in 1980, Lassiter saw the proud Dakota Indian figure carved into the south façade, standing watch over the city like a lone sentinel.

"All right, we're approaching 74th Street and I've got a mega-kick-ass idea!" cried Bermolito.

"Oh dear, we're in for it now," lamented Claggebart.

"That's right, *baby*, we are truly in for it! A little razzle, a little dazzle!" cackled Berm in his best Austin Powers impression, his thick-framed spectacles riveted to his head like a twin eyebolt. "Hold on tight, *baby*! This is going to be rather bumpy!"

As the renowned twenty-seven-floor, twin-towered San Remo came into view on the left, he sped up, and then, as he passed an oncoming car, he swung the wheel hard to his left onto West 74th, keeping to the far right lane as the tires screeched into the turn. Then suddenly, with the skill of Mario Andretti, he slammed on the breaks and jerked the van into reverse.

Lassiter saw the sheer genius of the maneuver the instant before it unfolded.

With oncoming traffic heading straight at them from the other lane, the pursuing Russians were forced to swerve hard to the right, towards the San Remo. The Rover leapt the curb and smashed into the heavy wrought iron gate at the 74th Street entrance to the historic apartment building, instantly dislodging several giant blocks of rusticated Devonian limestone and sending a white-gloved doorman scurrying to the pavement. The last thing Lassiter saw before the crash was four pairs of Russian hands flying upwards to cover their faces.

The force of the impact sent a tremor down the street. The Range Rover instantly burst into an orange-red eruption of flames, lighting up the night sky above West 74th and Central Park West like a signal flare. The flames rose thirty feet into the air, licking at the cartouches and intricate terra-cotta above the entrance. A swelling, black fuel cloud mushroomed up towards the San Remo's famous twin towers capped with colonnaded lanterns reminiscent of a Mayan temple.

On the street below the choragic temples framing the suddenly smoke-filled New York skyline, pedestrian spectators gawked in awe. The fire crackled and roared as an army of police sirens shrieked from the north. There was no movement inside the vehicle that Lassiter could see as the Rover was engulfed in an inferno, the flames billowing upward like a giant head of fiery brain coral.

"Good Lord, do you think they're all dead?" asked Claggebart over the sound of the sirens coming their way.

"There's no fucking way anyone could survive that," said Squelch.

"What should we do?" wondered Bermolito, staring at the blaze in awe.

"We've got to get Natalie to the hospital," said Lassiter. "We also have to get the hell out of here before the cops arrive and start asking questions. Right, Dad?"

But his father didn't respond.

"Dad, what is it?"

His father pointed up Central Park West where the third black Range Rover was barreling towards them. "Popov's coming—and, as good a driver as Bermolito is, I don't think we want to try our luck outrunning the Russians a second time."

Lassiter glanced up the street at the new interlopers. "Oh shit, he's right—let's get the hell out of here!"

And they were gone.

CHAPTER 36

SAN REMO AND BENEDICTIS APARTMENT AT THE DAKOTA
CENTRAL PARK WEST

ANTON DE BENEDICTIS peered over the police barricade thrown up across West 74th Street at the still-smoldering car crash at the San Remo. It was like the set of a disaster movie. The black Range Rover with the Russian diplomatic tags had smashed into the south entrance of the historic building, crumpling like an accordion, demolishing the wrought iron gate, and dislodging blocks of limestone from the high-speed impact. The front end of the SUV was so badly incinerated that the hood and a portion of the engine block had melted into the sidewalk.

Benedictis shook his head at the macabre sight. It seemed unthinkable that whoever had been inside the vehicle could have survived the crash. He took a whiff of the night air: it was redolent of gasoline, smoke, and the stench of burnt flesh. It was a smell of death, a miserable stink that brought back long suppressed memories of a meat-rendering plant he used to drive past as a kid on his way to Coney Island. Popov and his crew must have roasted in the flames like witches burning at a stake. Or, was Popov even in the vehicle? That had yet to be confirmed.

He had heard about the crash from Stafford. After prematurely breaking up the party at the Trump Building, the Russians had reportedly engaged in a high-speed chase through Central Park that had ended up with the horrific crash at the San Remo. The black Range Rover with the diplomatic plates had been identified as Popov's, but it hadn't yet been verified by the police whether the mob boss had actually been behind the wheel or even in the car during the collision.

Benedictis and the detective had quickly driven to the crash site to assess the situation firsthand. After speaking to a pair of cops, Stafford was able to ascertain that the four badly-burned Russians involved in the wreck had already been removed from the scene of the accident and hauled off to the morgue. It was obvious to the detective that Austin Brewbaker, Nick Lassiter, and the rest of their motley crew had been the cause of the accident. In fact, he had already put out an all-points bulletin on them.

Staring at the crumpled Range Rover, Benedictis didn't feel anything for the Russian bastards. In fact, in his mind, it seemed sacrilegious that a bunch of brutal criminals had died a mere two blocks away from the spot where the man who wrote *All You Need is Love* and *Give Peace a Chance* had been struck down.

He surveyed the scene up the street. A second set of barricades and crime scene tape had been laid out around what remained of the vehicle. Barricades had also been thrown up along the southbound lane of Central Park West. A fleet of police cars, ambulances, and fire trucks were parked all around the building with red, white, and blue lights flashing. Phalanxes of cops and firemen packed the sidewalk along the 74nd Street entrance to the building. Half the city's government work force appeared to be on hand for the spectacle, chattering on radios, phones, and walkie-talkies while the rubbernecking rabble stood gawking at the edge of the police barricades.

Realizing that there was little more he could learn here, Benedictis decided to return to his apartment. He walked two blocks down Central Park West to the front entrance of the Dakota, passing the prominent sentry box on his right. He was greeted ruefully by Jackson, his white-gloved doorman, who ushered him into the gabled and turreted building via a *porte cochère* that had once led to a central courtyard that served as a turnaround for carriages. He took the gold-leafed elevator to the tenth and top floor, where his $18,000,000 apartment commanded a sweeping view of Central Park with Strawberry Fields in the foreground. Since separating from his fourth wife, Roxanne, a still-stunning thirty-six year old former model, he had lived alone in the luxuriously appointed apartment. Originally tailored to her specifications, the residence was spacious, equipped with a lofty 14-foot ceiling, and floored in Carrara marble.

Flipping on the light, he went into the kitchen, poured himself a glass of Saint-Aubin Chardonnay, tossed his dinner jacket on the couch, and walked out onto the narrow balcony overlooking the park, leaving the sliding glass door open behind him. To his left, right, and above his head loomed lofty gables, balustrades, and terracotta spandrels. Here at the Dakota, too, the air still reeked of smoke and gasoline as he stared up the street at the policemen scurrying about like ants outside the San Remo. He shook his head in amazement at the spectacle, quietly sipping his Chardonnay.

He couldn't help but think that the damned Russians had gotten what they deserved. He found himself hoping that Popov had been in the crash so he could be through with the mob boss. But could he possibly be that lucky?

"Hello, Anton," said a gravelly voice behind him.

He nearly dropped his wine glass over the balcony. Slowly, and with trepidation, he turned around.

There sat Alexei Popov on his couch without a single scratch on him. He was holding a semiautomatic pistol in one hand and an open bottle of Stolichnaya in the other. *My God, how did he sneak up on me so quietly? He had to have already been inside the apartment—the creepy bastard.*

"I can see by your expression that you are surprised to see me. Is it because you thought I was dead?"

Benedictis stepped back inside, trying to conceal his surprise and fear behind a mask of outrage over the intrusion into his home. "No, of course I'm not surprised to see you. I'm getting quite used to you breaking into my office and figured it was only a matter of time before you invaded my home. What are you doing here, Alexei? Are you here to threaten me again?"

The Russian calmly took a sip from the bottle and waved his pistol at him. "I will ask the questions if you don't mind. Why didn't you call me to see if I was hurt in the crash? Are you not worried about the health of your executive business partner?"

"How do you know I was at the crash?"

"Because I was at the scene and saw you drive up with Detective Stafford. I left to come up here. I have always wanted to see your apartment. I must say it is exquisite."

"I was about to call to see what happened to you."

"Sure you were."

At that moment, he heard the toilet in the bathroom adjoining his bedroom flush and a few seconds later, one of Popov's thugs came walking in.

"I believe you know Drago."

Benedictis nodded. In truth, he couldn't tell any of Popov's bullet-headed, thick-muscled, tattoo-covered henchmen apart. He turned back to the mob boss.

"How did you get in here, Alexei? Don't tell me you have a key to my apartment?"

"As I said, I will ask the questions. Now, why didn't you tell me about this Austin Brewbaker?"

"What do you mean?"

"Why didn't you tell me that he was a CIA man and that he is Nick Lassiter's father?"

He slid closed the balcony door behind him. "I only just found out myself. But how do you know for sure that he is with the CIA?"

"I am in the intelligence business. It is my job to know such things. I think that Austin Brewbaker and his son have been in this together from the beginning."

"I don't see how that's possible. Nick Lassiter sent me his novel three years ago. I haven't seen Austin Brewbaker since Oxford until today at lunch. There's no connection between Lassiter and his father. It's pure coincidence."

"Then what was his son doing up in your office with his father and your treacherous assistant Natalie? As you Americans are so fond of saying, that's a lot of foxes in the hen house."

"Including you, Alexei."

The Russian took a hefty pull of vodka as his Neanderthal bodyguard Drago stood with his hands crossed in front of him. "Don't you get it?" he said. "They don't care about Beckett. They are after you and me. That's why they broke into your office and probably searched your computer."

"And may I ask what *you* were doing in my office?"

"I wanted to check up on Brewbaker. I knew the moment I met him that he was up to something. You certainly didn't invite him to the party."

"I didn't invite you either, remember?"

"*Da*, but I am not just anyone."

"The police are going to be after you."

"The police think I'm dead."

"How can you be so sure?"

"Because Krishnikov was killed in the crash and he is my double. He carries my identifications on him at all times."

"And why would you have a double?"

"The same reason that Joseph Stalin, Winston Churchill, and Osama bin

Laden did. Because a lot of people want to kill me."

"Well now, you are certainly full of surprises, Alexei."

"When I drive around town or am at a place where I might be at risk, I like to have a double just in case. Krishnikov was my one and only body double, and he is going to be missed. Felix Dadaev did the same thing for Stalin during the war along with three other doubles. Dadaev and his comrades were quite effective. The world didn't even know about him or the others until his autobiography came out in 2008."

"You're even weirder than I thought, Alexei."

The Russian ignored the remark. "I loved Krishnikov like a brother, but the stupid son of a bitch wasn't wearing his seatbelt and he died on impact. He was badly burned in the fire, but he is close to my age and height and with the identifications in his wallet there should be enough to be retrieved to make a positive ID. In any event, we will see if my double is as effective as Dadaev once was for the Man of Steel."

"So your hope is that you've become a ghost. I don't see what that has to do with me."

Popov looked at Drago and they smiled. Then, with surprising calm, the mob boss pulled a custom-designed, baffle-type noise suppressor from his pocket and began threading it into the nose of his Beretta nine-millimeter.

Benedictis said nothing, didn't move a muscle. *Why the fuck is he attaching a silencer to his gun? He needs me alive, right?*

When the Russian was finished, he pointed the gun at him, again.

"I've always liked silencers. They make killing seem so innocuous. Would you agree?"

"You know perfectly well, Alexei, that I—"

Without the slightest hesitation, Popov pulled the trigger. The shot whizzed within an inch of Benedictis's left ear and drove into the thick wood paneling behind him with a dull thud. He didn't even have time to flinch. With the silencer, the shot was no louder than a book being dropped to the floor, and because of the multilayer soundproofing of his thick-walled Dakota apartment, there was no way that the sound could be heard outside the room, especially not with all the commotion on the street below.

The room went deathly silent. Drago smiled.

Benedictis saw his own reflection in the window: embarrassingly, he was as pale as the white marble covering his floor. He felt a twitch of fear as his Russian nemesis trained the muzzle again on his heart. Popov then calmly took another nip of Stoli. Keeping his eyes on the pistol, Benedictis slowly raised his hands above his shoulders.

"I take it that I have your full attention now."

"What do you want from me? Why are you trying to scare the crap out of me?"

"I am not here to scare you. I am here to make sure you are motivated."

"Motivated? I don't know what that—"

The Russian cut him off with an abrupt chop of his gun hand. "As we discussed, tomorrow at lunch at the Victorian Club you will kill Cameron Beckett and Nick Lassiter with the weapons I have provided you. You will make it look like an accident and you will be convincing. There will be eyes upon you. Detective Stafford, Drago here, and my other men will be there to make sure you get the job done and to extract you from the restaurant safely and soundly."

Here he paused, his cold, steely-blue eyes infused with an icy fire.

"If you do this, you and I are even as far as your brother goes. But I will still expect to receive fifty percent of the profits from your new literary role as Cameron Beckett."

"I thought we had agreed to forty."

"I have upped my percentage. I am thinking of expanding my import-export business."

"No, I'm going to need fifty percent minus my agent fee. Acting as my own agent, I still get my fifteen percent cut. That's sixty-five percent for me and thirty-five for you. That's the deal or I—"

The Russian fired another round. This time the shot nicked Benedictis's left ear, tearing off the lower portion of the lobe. He touched his hand to his ear, felt a piece dangling. His fingers came away oozing with blood.

"Jesus Fucking Christ, Alexei? You just shot off my ear, you fuck!"

"Oh, quit your whining. It is only a quarter of an ear…okay maybe a third."

"You're fucking crazy!"

"You should count your blessings that I am allowing you to live."

Benedictis looked at Drago. The son of a bitch was smiling again. He grabbed a couch pillow and pressed it against his bloody, dangling ear. He was in fucking pain and there was no way he was going to pretend that it didn't hurt like hell. When would this nightmare with Popov end?

Would it ever end?

"As I've told you, everyone needs a little motivation now and then," said the Russian in the blandly soothing inflection of a self-help guru. "Perhaps this will persuade you of the seriousness of the situation."

He reached into his pocket, pulled out his phone, pressed a series of buttons, and tossed the phone to Benedictis, who wasn't expecting it and bobbled it in his right hand before pulling it in.

"Say hello to your brother Danny and daughter Rebecca."

What the hell?

He felt a sudden wave of panic. It was bad enough that Popov was messing with Danny; yet, it could be argued that his brother had brought it upon himself by crossing the mob boss in the first place. But his daughter Rebecca? Goddamnit, she was completely innocent and had nothing to do with any of this!

Looking at the Face-Time-enabled iPhone screen, he couldn't believe his eyes. It was a living nightmare. There on the two-inch display was his beloved daughter duct taped to a chair, her eyes blindfolded, and next to her was his brother Danny, fully bound and gagged. They appeared terrified out of their wits, and he was gripped with a sudden urge to kill Popov.

Tossing aside the blood-soaked couch pillow, he stepped forward towards the Russian aggressively. "You monster—you can't take my fucking daughter! She has nothing to do with this!"

SAMUEL MARQUIS

At this, Drago stepped forward to protect his boss, his thick gorilla-like arms ready to snap Benedictis's neck or break his limbs like twigs. But Popov held up his left hand to hold him back and the tattoo-covered bodyguard came to a halt at the edge of the couch.

Popov calmly kept the muzzle of the Beretta trained on Benedictis's heart. "That's where you're wrong, my friend. Your daughter has everything to do with this." He waved the gun menacingly. "Now back the fuck off!"

The literary agent stopped in his tracks and held up his hands in submission. "Okay, okay, but don't you dare lay a finger on her or I'll fucking kill you!"

Now his daughter spoke into the smartphone. "I love you, Daddy...please do as he says or his men are going to kill me and Uncle Danny. Please, Daddy...please just give him what he wants. I'm so scared—"

She was cut off midsentence as a gag was abruptly stuffed into her mouth, a strip of duct tape slapped over the gag, and a black hood thrown over her face.

Benedictis felt like he was about to faint. My God, how had a relatively harmless money-laundering operation to get his brother out of a jam turned into kidnapping and murder? How could he have let himself become a pawn to a Russian mobster? Was it really possible that he, the biggest literary agent on the planet, was a prisoner to a total maniac?

Popov smiled. "I know you weren't expecting such a drastic measure, but you must understand that motivation is a tricky thing. The key is to never let the extent of your own motivation be in doubt to your enemies. It is the reason that I am king in this town. I will tell you what, Anton. Just so you know that I am a man of my word, a man of honor, I will let you have your sixty-five-percent cut. That is only fair since you are both writer and agent. But you must take care of business tomorrow—or face terrible, terrible consequences."

It offended his sense of honor that Popov thought that the money meant anything to him compared to the life of his daughter and brother. "You'd better not lay a fucking finger on either one of them!" he snarled, waving his finger defiantly. "That's the deal—or you might as well just kill me now because I don't want to live if you hurt my baby girl, or my brother!" He felt tears coming to his eyes. "Do you understand me? I don't want to fucking live if you touch a hair on their heads! Do we have a deal?"

The Russian nodded. He then gave a bloodless smile, stepped over to him, and grabbed the phone from him. "*Da*, we have a deal. And I do not think I am going out on a limb when I say that you and I are both now *highly* motivated."

All Benedictis could do was shake his head in disbelief. Phone in hand, Popov returned to the couch and raised the bottle of Stoli in a toast. Again, Drago gave a sinister smile.

"*Privet bratan*—cheers—my good friend, Anton. And tomorrow, may you have happy hunting!"

190

CHAPTER 37

MOUNT SINAI MEDICAL CENTER
1176 FIFTH AVENUE

NICK LASSITER paced the main hallway for the tenth time since arriving at the hospital. He couldn't sit still. Natalie was still in surgery, her life hanging in the balance, and he felt powerless because there was nothing he could do to help her. So, once again, he roamed the aseptic white corridor of the Mount Sinai Medical Center, staring at the cracks and stains in the linoleum floor that were becoming all too familiar to him. His father had already been treated and released for his grazing gunshot wound, but Natalie was still in the operating room and he had yet to hear word of her condition.

He did not want to lose this woman yet again. He had loved her once before and lost her, and now that he seemed to have her back again, he couldn't bear the thought of losing her for good. He loved her and knew that she was the one for him. He realized, finally, what had been patently obvious to everyone else around him for so long. With her life now in jeopardy, the reality of his feelings for her hit him like an epiphany, and the most important thing to him now was not to lose her.

When he compared Natalie to Alexandra, or for that matter to any of the other women he had been with since Natalie, there was no comparison at all. His relationships with Alexandra and the others, he realized, had always been relationships of convenience and nothing more. No one, not even Alexandra, the only woman he had lived with besides Natalie, could hold a candle to the woman who was, at this very moment, fighting for her life in surgery down the hall. It was that simple.

He took a branching hallway and headed towards the oncology ward. *I honestly don't know what I'd do if I lost her again. How could it have come down to this?*

He looked impatiently at his watch. They had been waiting for nearly two hours now. The fact that the surgery was taking so long seemed like a bad omen.

Five minutes later, he headed back down the hallway towards the waiting area. The uncertainty was taking a toll on him. He was forced to step against the wall as a pair of white-sheeted gurneys bearing two comatose teenagers stormed past. They were badly cut and covered with blood. Emergency room technicians and doctors and nurses in surgical greens hurried past.

Another busy night at Mount Sinai.

Once they had passed, he made his way to the waiting area where his father and buddies sat quietly talking. From their faces, he could tell they were as anxious and nerve-wracked as him.

"No news yet?" he asked them for the twentieth time.

"Nothing," said Squelch. "Sorry, Nicky."

His father reached out and touched him on the shoulder reassuringly. "Don't worry. She's going to be okay. She's going to live to be a very old and happy woman, just you wait and see."

God, I hope so, he thought. *I honestly don't know what I'd do if I lost her again. And this time it would be my fault. I shouldn't have flown out here and stirred up this hornet's nest.* He looked at his father. *And you should never have recruited her in the first place. She's not a goddamned secret agent.*

"Hang in there, Nicholas," said Claggebart encouragingly. "It's going to work out. I'm clairvoyant, you know, and I see an amazing future together for you two."

"I pray you're right, Nostradamus."

"I definitely wouldn't bet against me, boy-o."

"Or me," said Bermolito without breaking from typing away on his tablet. "I've checked the survival statistics on these specific types of peri-abdominal and upper-respiratory-system gunshot wounds. The probability distribution is quite favorable. And she's in great hands, Nick. I'm running a quick Monte Carlo analysis just to verify, but I have to say the prognosis looks extremely optimistic."

"Thanks, Berm."

"I'm sorry about the whole thing, Nick," said his father. "I know this is all my fault."

"No, it's mine, Dad. I shouldn't have come to this goddamned town."

"Don't say that, Nicholas—in fact, either of you," said Bermolito. "There's no one to blame. We all knew the risks. We all just wanted to take a stand and make a difference. It's as simple as that."

There were head nods all around. "Berm's right," said Squelch. "But to be completely honest, I also wanted to get out of my goddamned theoretical classroom environment and feel alive again. I know that may sound a little selfish, but it's true."

"Ditto for me, my fellow Brigadiers," declared Claggebart. "I mean, I wanted justice for you, Nicholas, don't get me wrong. But what I think I wanted most of all was to feel involved in something bigger than myself. I wanted to take a stand against injustice, just as Berm says, but I also just wanted to feel passionately alive like the good Dr. Squelch here. And with all of you—the Devil's Brigade—I feel like I've indeed found, to quote Ziggy Marley, that higher vibration."

"I suppose that's why we've all joined this motley crew," said Bermolito.

"It's the same reason, Son, I've been secretly rendezvousing with your mother these past six months. I'm not embarrassed to say it. As bad as I feel for keeping our romance secret from you, I have never felt more alive and happy in a relationship than I have these past few months reconnecting with your mom. I know it may sound cliché, but it's true."

"Mr. B, we love you, man," said Squelch, his voice cracking. Suddenly, he and Claggebart swept in and gave him a big hug. "You are the real deal."

"Okay, I love you too, boys, but let's not get carried away," said his father after a moment as he grappled in vain to break free from their embrace.

"Actually, let's do get carried away," said Lassiter, and he stepped in to join the group hug, as did Bermolito after setting down his tablet. They pulled in tight—all five of them, his father only mildly resisting now—and Lassiter felt the power of the moment, felt the power of the Devil's Brigade. True, he felt a little weird to be hugging four other guys wearing blood-splattered tuxedos in a hospital ward in New York City. But none of them seemed to care. What they had experienced these last two desperate, action-packed days had not been as heroic or dangerous as the First Special Service Force scaling the icy cliffs of Monte La Difensa against dug-in German Panzergrenadiers and a constant barrage of mortar fire, but it had been life-changing and they all realized it. After a minute, they pulled apart and everyone except Lassiter sat back down in their seats. He was still feeling anxious and wanted to be alone to pace the hallway.

He walked up and down the long, wide corridor several times before going to the window and staring out at Central Park. It looked dark and forbidding at night. His thoughts returned to Natalie. She had been a gutsy woman to have agreed to serve as an unofficial government spy these past few months, taking risks that most normal people wouldn't dare take. It was important that she live—not just so he could be with her, but because this messed-up world needed people like Natalie Perkins.

A moment later he started pacing again. Twenty feet down the corridor, the chief surgeon, a tired-looking, middle-aged man in surgical greens, stepped out into the hallway. The surgeon scanned in their direction, making eye contact with him and the others. From his somber face and body language, Lassiter could tell the situation was bleak.

Oh my God, it can't be! he thought in disbelief. He felt his throat go dry and scratchy, and tears came to his eyes.

He started moving towards the surgeon as his dad and the others stood up from their seats. The man plodded along slowly, his head slumped in his shoulders.

"No!" cried Lassiter, dashing down the hallway now. "It can't be!"

The surgeon stopped, his face weary and forlorn as Lassiter came running up to him. His father and buddies quickly formed a circle around him and the surgeon. Looking at the man, he felt all hope sucked out of him.

"I'm afraid I have some bad news."

Squelch's hands flew to his face and tears spilled from his eyes. "Please no! Not sweet Natalie, man!" he mourned.

The weary doctor held up a hand. "Now just hold on a second. She's not dead, but she is still in a blood-loss coma."

"So she's alive," said Lassiter, feeling a modicum of hope. "Is there a chance she could wake up out of the coma?"

"Yes, there's a chance," said the surgeon. "A very small one."

CHAPTER 38

MOUNT SINAI MEDICAL CENTER
1176 FIFTH AVENUE

AUSTIN BREWBAKER saw the crushing look of defeat on his son's face—and just wanted to die. The euphoria they had all experienced only moments earlier during their group hug had been replaced by a despondent gloom that settled over the hospital waiting room like a burial shroud. All of the heads hung low; no one uttered a word. The only sound was the quiet sobbing of Squelch and Claggebart.

His son Nick was too bowled over with shock to even cry. The doctor's words were hardly encouraging. But it was the juxtaposition between the hopefulness of only a minute earlier and the stunned silence of now that made it all seem worse.

He couldn't help but feel responsible for what had happened to the poor girl. She was a literary agent, not a field operative, and yet he had placed her life in jeopardy. Why? What for? To help bring down Popov and Benedictis? Had that been worth risking the young woman's life and getting her most likely killed?

"Again, I'm terribly sorry to have to deliver this news," said the surgeon, looking even more haggard than when he had first made his pronouncement. "If the situation changes, I will let you know. But she is still comatose and in extremely critical condition." He paused, as if unsure what to say next. "I wish I had better news."

He tipped his head lugubriously, turned, and shambled back down the hallway, disappearing into the set of doors at the far end.

Brewbaker turned to his son. "I'm sorry, Nick. This is all my fault."

There were tears in his son's eyes now. "I need a few minutes alone," he said. "I'm going outside."

Brewbaker nodded soberly, feeling all torn up inside. *Goddamnit, just look at him! I am the cause of this!* He shook his head in dismay as his son's friends sank into their chairs like deflated balloons.

It was then his secure, coded mobile vibrated.

He looked at the caller ID: it was his boss, Franklin Harcourt, Deputy Director of the CIA's National Clandestine Service.

Shit! He knew he was in hot water and didn't want to answer it, but he had no choice.

"I've got to take this call," he said to his son's friends. He headed quickly down the hall so he could be out of earshot before answering. "Mr. Deputy Direct—"

"What the fuck have you done, Brewbaker?" Harcourt interrupted him without preamble. "I told you this had to be a one-hundred-percent-clean op with no collateral damage and look what I get: the lead story on the ten o'clock news. Jesus Christ, you might as well have blown up the San Remo—it couldn't have been any worse!"

"I'm afraid it is worse, sir. It's not just the Russians involved in the car crash that are dead. My inside asset, Natalie Perkins, is in critical condition from wounds sustained during the shootout. I'm afraid she's in a blood-loss coma."

"You know that the Company can't stand failure, Austin. And it dislikes public scrutiny even more."

"No one knows of the CIA's involvement except Detective Stafford, and Popov. The latter has been reported as dead by the media, but he is actually alive."

"How do you know he's alive?"

"Because I saw him coming upon the scene in the third Range Rover after the first two had crashed. Contrary to the early reports, the son of a bitch is alive."

"But the police found Popov's identification on one of the bodies. They were able to make a positive ID from that and the remains."

"Yeah well, it's not him. It's someone else."

"Regardless of whose body they found in that burned-out vehicle, this situation is out of control, Austin. And it's all because of you."

"I know the situation is FUBAR, sir. But I did find what I was looking for on Benedictis's hard drive."

"What do you mean you found what you were looking for?"

"I've found out what Popov was searching for on Benedictis's computer. I don't think he got his hands on it two nights ago when he and his men broke into the office because they were interrupted by my asset. But I found what I believe they were looking for in an encrypted file on his hard drive. I've copied it to my portable external hard drive."

"Why didn't you tell me up front what the hell you were after?"

"Because I wasn't quite sure who to trust. But now I know."

"Are you fucking with me, Brewbaker? Whatever intel you think you just got off Benedictis's computer belongs to the United States government. So you'd better tell me right now what it is."

He came to a halt at a large window looking east. The flickering lights of the city and the barges on the Hudson winked across the dark sky. "I'm afraid I can't do that, sir. I still need confirmation."

"Confirmation? What do you mean you need confirmation?"

"I need confirmation from another source. Preferably someone close to Popov."

"Now listen to me very carefully, Austin. You are going to get in touch with our New York office right now and hand over that drive containing the intel. Do you understand me? That's not your personal property to do with as you like. As you've said yourself, this is a national security—"

"But it's not a national security situation, sir. I thought it was too, but it's something else entirely. I was wrong about how Popov fits into the puzzle. It's more complicated than I thought. That's exactly why I'm not handing over my external drive until I've had a chance to go through every file in detail and get independent confirmation."

"You're already in a lot of trouble, Austin. Do you want to lose your job and pension too? Do you really want to have a Senate oversight committee breathing up your ass?"

"Why are you so riled up, Franklin? Has somebody else spoken to you about this?"

"I'm warning you, Austin. Don't go down this road."

He leaned against the window sill. "Are you threatening me, sir?"

"I don't need to tell you what happens to rogue elephants at the Company. It doesn't matter on whose watch."

"You *are* threatening me. Do you have a team in play as we speak?"

Silence.

"Jesus Christ, you've set me up. You wanted me to get what Benedictis had on that computer without drawing attention to yourself or the Company by sending in a large team. You clever bastard, Franklin. I should have known I was in over my head on this case when you gave me black-budget and direct-report authority, as well as my very own New York apartment. You played me. You probably knew about Vivian and me getting back together. Hell, for all I know you're the one who set it all up. My God, is my ex-wife in on this with you? I wouldn't put it past you, Franklin."

"You need to listen to me, Austin. Whatever you think you're doing, you need to stop it right now before…before the situation gets out of hand."

"Are you telling me you've green-lighted a shooter, you bastard? Are you really going to take out one of your own, Mr. Deputy Director?"

"You're not listening, Austin. This is bigger than you, or even me."

"Is that so?"

"You know it is. And you also know there's only one way this can end if you don't hand over that drive and walk away. At this very moment, I can still promise you a golden-parachute retirement package, but only if you stand down."

"And if I don't?"

"I can promise it will end badly for you. It's out of my control."

"Is that what Director Thompkins told you to tell me?"

"No one said anything about the Director of the CIA, Austin. This is about you and me and the proper role of the National Clandestine Service. We don't call it the Directorate of Operations anymore for good reason, Austin. We're supposed to be invisible, to protect our assets at all costs, and to have quality HUMINT— quiet boots on the ground not only in every corner of the world, but right here at home. It's a brave new world, Austin, and it's time you got on board with the program."

"You're full of shit, Franklin. This isn't about us. It's about your boy Popov. So don't try and give me this little Quantico rookie pep talk because I ain't buying."

"You go off the reservation, you know what happens. That's my last warning."

"Why do you care so much about Popov now when the police think he's dead?"

"Don't do this. Hand over the drive and come in. I can protect you."

"Protect me? Jesus Christ, Mr. Deputy Director, that's the last thing you should have said if you wanted me to come in quietly."

"It's out of my hands, Austin. I've given you your last warning."

"Then we have nothing more to discuss, sir." He punched off.

He started walking back to the waiting area. His son was running down the hallway towards him.

Oh my God, he thought. *They're coming after us already? What have I done, what have I done?*

Nick rushed up to him, out of breath.

"What is it? What's happened?" he asked his son.

"Natalie's come out of her coma! She's going to be all right!"

He almost fell to the floor. "Thank God!"

"Her heart actually stopped for three full minutes—but then she suddenly came back to life! Her will to live was just too strong and she came back to us! She came back to me!"

"It's a miracle! It's a goddamn miracle!" he cried, and he pulled his son in a tight embrace.

At that moment, his cell vibrated again. Pulling apart from his son, he looked at the caller ID and saw that he had received a text message. He quickly read the message, his eyes opening wide with surprise. He had definitely not expected this.

"What is it, Dad?"

"You're not going to believe this. It's Cameron Beckett and he wants to talk."

"When?"

"Right now." He paused, preparing himself mentally for what else he had to tell his son now that they were alone away from the others. "I'm afraid that's not all, Nick."

"There's something else?"

"We don't just have to meet with Beckett. We have to meet with some other people."

"Who?"

"That's classified need-to-know—and, unfortunately, you don't need to know. At least not yet."

"But you said there would be no more secrets. You said that now that you were part of our team, you wouldn't hide anything and would be totally up front with us."

"The situation's grown more complicated since then. Much more complicated, in fact. We are now in danger on multiple fronts. But I *can* at least tell you about the intel we've managed to pick up regarding your lunch tomorrow with Beckett and Benedictis."

"What about it?"

"Our camera surveillance and cell phone intercepts of Benedictis indicate that he's planning something big for tomorrow."

"What? What's he planning?"

"You're not going to believe this, but he plans to kill you and Beckett."

197

"What, are you serious?"

"One hundred percent. But, of course, it's not going to happen."

"I certainly hope not. But if Beckett and I are both going to be at the lunch, how exactly is it that Benedictis isn't going to kill us? Are you saying that you're going to use us as bait and then somehow foil his plan?"

He leaned in close to his son's ear, a puissant gleam taking hold of his eyes. "No one is going to be used as bait. We're just going to outright fool the son of a bitch."

"Fool him?"

"Yes, Son. I have a little counterintelligence op of my own planned. And I think you and Beckett are both going to like it."

WEDNESDAY

JUNE 5

CHAPTER 39

BENEDICTIS APARTMENT, THE DAKOTA
1 WEST 72ND STREET

ANTON DE BENEDICTIS hadn't touched his bacon and eggs, English muffin, fresh-squeezed orange juice, or even his cappuccino. He just sat staring at the two guns that Popov had given him—one a Glock, the other a Beretta—resting on the breakfast table.

The pair of gleaming 9mm semiautomatics, two seemingly innocuous hunks of metal, would be used today to murder Cameron Beckett and Nick Lassiter. He wondered which one he should use to kill the bestselling author, a man he had faithfully represented for the past twenty-two years; and which he would use to take out the slush pile interloper that had turned his life upside down. He picked them both up. He liked the feel of the heavier Beretta in his hand and decided that it should be the weapon used to murder his client, whom he would shoot first.

May God help me, he thought as he pictured, in his mind, how it would all unfold. *But I've got to do it for Rebecca and Danny. I have no other choice.*

He was startled by his ringtone. He plucked his iPhone from his pocket, checked the number, and punched the *Answer* button.

"Cameron, is that you? Is everything all right?"

"Yes, I'm fine, mate," answered Beckett in a surprisingly relaxed and cheerful voice. "I just wanted to ring you before our lunch meeting today and tell you that I feel quite good about this."

He couldn't help but feel a wave of guilt slash through him. Jesus, he was about to murder the poor dumb sod in cold blood and here Beckett was calling him to tell him he felt *quite good about this.* Was that irony or what?

"We're going to make everything right. It's going to be my last great act before handing over the reins to you, Anton—or, should I say, Cameron II."

De Benedictis was rendered speechless.

"Is everything all right, mate? I mean, this is a historic day and I need you to be there for me as my literary agent extraordinaire. Anton, are you still there?"

"Yes, yes, of course I'm here. You're right, this is going to be a historic day."

"Are you up to this? I mean, you do realize that, from now on, you're going to have to crank out two or three number one best sellers per year—every year—and be counted on for endless publicity events and book tours all over the world. You'll never again have a moment of free time and your life will be planned down to the last minute. Most importantly, you're going to have to do it up right, like a rock star. Henceforth, when you're not writing or out promoting your books, you'll be staying up late at night carousing with beautiful women, doing endless rails of cocaine and prodigious shots, and generally indulging in things that bugger up your life. But hey, welcome to the big show, mate—you're going to love it. I mean that with all due respect, of course."

"You're fucking with me, right?"

"I'm just blowing off a bit of steam now that I'm about to become a free man. So tell me what was all that fuss about last night at the party? I heard the commotion. What kind of rot have you gotten yourself into with these bloody Russians? They'll be the death of you, you know."

"You let me worry about that. I can take care of myself."

"Can you? It sounded like Gold, Juno, and Sword beaches on June 6, 1944. Quite a bit of running around and shooting. It was all over the news. Strordnary shenanigans to say the least. I'm just saying, mate, Alexei Popov is a very bad bogan to get mixed up with. Are you sure you know what you're doing?"

"Yes, I know what I'm doing. And for God's sake, stop calling me *mate*. You know I've always hated being called that."

"Great, you tell me that after twenty-two years together just before I retire?"

Twenty-two years—and now I'm going to shoot you down like a mangy dingo. Lord, please help me. How am I going to go through with this?

"Maybe it's just my imagination, Anton, but you sound different somehow. Is everything okay, mate?"

"What…I mean, what are you saying?"

"You seem distracted, far away. I know it's because of this reprehensible situation with those damned cheeky Russians, but you don't seem to be at all yourself."

"I'm here, Cam. I'm just tired is all."

"Well, you can't be tired today, mate. Today is the day that we make things right with Nick Lassiter. Today is the day I hand the reins over to you, the new and improved Cameron Beckett. I just spoke with Nick over the phone a few minutes ago and we're all good to go for lunch. You don't know how liberated this makes me feel to be able to put everything behind me."

"You spoke with Nick Lassiter this morning?"

"I wanted to make sure he knew we were being aboveboard. Is there anything wrong with that?"

He hesitated. Was there? "No, of course not," he replied. "It just sounds like you guys are getting a little chummier than I would have expected."

"Well, after today I expect we will be great chums. After all, I am going to be delivering a humble apology and compensating him quite handsomely."

You're not going to be giving him a damned thing because I'm going to kill you, he wanted to say. *Don't you realize you're in danger, mate? Your devoted literary agent* is *a very, very bad man—and now, a very desperate one.*

"I've decided that I'm going to give Nick Lassiter two million dollars, Anton. That clever lad from Dung Heap, Colorado, deserves a heap better treatment than what he's gotten, don't you think, mate? If nothing else, you've got to give him credit for his perseverance. He hasn't been intimidated at all going up against the big boys."

You're going to be dead, so what does it matter? "If you say so, Cam."

"I must say that young man has earned my undying respect. He has proved to be a most formidable opponent. Of course, that has something to do with his bullheaded father and those incorrigible friends of his. But I must say that it is a testament to his character, a testament to his moral fortitude, that he has a coterie that cares so deeply about him."

Yes well, that little coterie of his is about to receive a big shock. In fact, it's going to be the fucking surprise of their lives! Oh God, please help me!

"Well, that's all I wanted to say, Anton. You have been a most remarkable literary agent—the very best, mate, truly strordnary—and I just want to thank you for all the great times. Today, at lunch we are going to do the right thing. Then later at four o'clock the torch will be passed to a new literary lion, a new bestselling author, a new titan of the industry. May the good Lord bless you, my old and great friend, and bring you the same joy that you have, for the past twenty-two years, brought me."

He felt the air leave him all at once, as if he was having an asthma attack. He couldn't breathe!

"Anton, are you all right? Anton, are you there?"

"Yes, yes, I'm fine. I'm just choked up is all—choked up beyond words."

"That is the most wonderful thing anyone has ever said to me. As the great Banjo Paterson is my witness, Anton—and let's not forget the dear poet was born-and-raised in Narrambla just like yours truly—you, my old and great friend, are the greatest literary agent of all time. May both the Heavenly Father and the author of Waltzing Matilda, in their infinite glory, shine a light on you for all eternity. You are the essence of everything that is good and righteous about the human spirit. Cheerio, mate, I will see you at The Victorian Club—at twelve o'clock sharp. Top shelf."

"Yes, I'll see you then, my old friend."

They punched off. Benedictis sat there in a daze, staring out the window at the wind ruffling the billowy trees across the street in Central Park.

May God help me, he thought once again. *For I am—truly—the devil incarnate!*

CHAPTER 40

BREWBAKER FLAT
44 WEST 56TH STREET

"NOW THAT WAS FUN—WHAT A BEAUT," declared Cameron Barnaby Beckett IV as he punched off his cell. "I know I laid it on a little thick, lads, but we are officially a go. *Operation From Russia Without Love* is a bloody go! Oi oi oi!"

Lassiter felt a ripple of nervous excitement as the Australian pumped his fist like an international rugby champion. So that was it then—the game was afoot. The lunch with Benedictis was going ahead as planned, and he and Beckett were now joined at the hip as the two lead actors and primary stunt men in the forthcoming tightly-choreographed melodrama.

He felt the same visceral churning in his stomach that he had in college before lacrosse games. In fact, he was scared shitless, but he tried not to let it show on his face. At least Beckett would be there with him. They would be sharing the same dangers as they attempted to foil Benedictis's plans and lure him and Popov into the clever trap that his father was springing for them.

Operation From Russia Without Love.

He looked at his father. Were they really going to go through with it?

"Are you ready, Son?" said Austin Brewbaker.

"I sure as hell hope so."

"I must confess I'm a bit on edge too," admitted Beckett. "But at the same time, I can't wait for the fireworks to begin. The truth is I've always wanted to do something like this."

"You have?" asked Lassiter. "I've never actually heard of anything like this before."

"That's precisely why it's going to be so exciting. As you well know, Nicholas, it is one thing to write a fictitious gun battle scene by punching away at a computer keyboard—it's quite another to actually stare down the nose of that weapon when the bullets are flying."

"Sounds like last night. Too bad you weren't with us at the Gunfight at the OK Corral in the hallway outside your book party. I don't think I've ever seen so much exploding glass—not even in a disaster movie. But at least this time around we have the advantage of knowing what to expect."

"Yes, mate, thanks to your father's CIA wiretaps and video surveillance cameras we know with one-hundred-percent certainty that Benedictis is planning on shooting us both down like spaniels at high noon today."

"And that Alexei Popov is the one who put him up to it."

"Quite right. It is our very knowing our adversaries' intentions that will be their downfall. Not only do we know what's coming, we know precisely when it's coming. So all we have to do to pull off *Le Sting Deuxième Partie* is follow the scripted plan. Right, Austin?"

"That's right," said his father. "You two have nothing to worry about."

"Come on, Dad, don't bullshit us. You know this is risky as hell."

"Well, it's not going to be a walk in the park. But if you follow the procedures we went over this morning in the preliminary briefing, you're going to be fine. Remember, Benedictis's two guns—the Glock and the Beretta—have been replaced by my infiltration team with weapons that fire only blanks. So Benedictis couldn't shoot either of you even if he wanted to. Like I told you earlier, we made the switch early this morning when Benedictis was at the office. Second, my team will be watching and listening in on you at all times from the surveillance van. You will be captured on both audio and video by your phones and by the transmitters carefully concealed in your clothing. Both of your phones are also equipped with a homing beacon giving your precise GPS position in real time to track your movements, just as a precaution. Just keep your phones on at all times and we'll be able to track you. As I said, my team will be following your movements from the surveillance van. We'll be ready to extract you within seconds if anything starts to go wrong."

"What if Benedictis asks us to power off our phones or remove our SIM cards? What do we do then?"

"Do as he requests as he may have been briefed by Popov outside of our surveillance network. We'll still be able to track you by the cameras and transmitters in your clothing. The phones are just a redundant backup. Any other questions?"

Lassiter looked at Beckett: the Aussie shook his head. "Not at the moment," said Lassiter. "But I'm sure something will come to me in a minute or two."

"All right, in the meantime let's get started." His father gestured towards the two twentysomethings, a woman and a man, to his right. "Ms. Haley and Mr. Motorhead are going to get you outfitted now." He smiled. "And just in case you're wondering, those aren't their real names."

Lassiter looked at the two special-effects techies with their Goth leather outfits, colored punk-rock hairdos, and glittering array of facial and ear rings. They were so vampirishly pale that it looked like they hadn't caught a ray of sunlight in a decade. He found it amusing that his father worked with such unconventional CIA private contractors, and he wondered if they had collaborated together before on other operations.

On the kitchen table next to them, he saw a pair of open leather cases covered with heavy metal and punk stickers and two large nylon bags. Spread out in front of the containers were sealed plastic bag vests, vials of capsules, plastic IV hoses, small explosive devices, clear tape, plastic containers bearing viscous red fluids, nylon rope, Velcro straps, and, last but not least, a pair of handguns.

Jesus, he thought, *I feel like I'm on a Hollywood movie set. Are we really going through with this?*

"All right, you guys," said the woman, Haley. "First take your shirts off."

They did as instructed. She then proceeded to outfit each of them with a clear plastic vest filled with red fluids containing solid chunks, while her partner Motorhead strapped and taped an intricate network of explosive devices, plastic hoses, and smaller fluid bags across their upper backs and necks. Once everything was secure, they put their shirts back on, followed by their jackets, and the two techies thoroughly inspected them.

"You're both good to go," said Haley. "How do the shoulder rigs feel?"

"I barely even notice it's there," admitted Lassiter.

"Same here," said Beckett. "But how are the devices going to be triggered?"

His father stepped forward to answer. "Let's go through it step-by-step," he said in the voice of a Quantico training instructor. "Our friendly U.S. government officer and fake shooter will enter the private dining room prior to Benedictis taking the shot. The shooter will then fire a blank at Nick. Nick's CO_2 cartridge will be sonically triggered by the sound of the first gunshot from the shooter. The explosive device will blow up and away from Nick's body, spattering the fake blood and brain matter against the wall. At the same time, he will bite into his mouth capsule. The blood will cover his face and it will appear as though he has been shot head-on."

"I say, who is Mr. Shooter again?" asked Beckett.

"Nice try, Cameron," said his father with a wry grin. "As I told you during the preliminary briefing, we can't reveal the shooter's identity because we want you to be genuinely surprised. The most important thing about this operation is that it looks totally real. Got it?"

"Yes, I apologize, mate."

His father continued: "The second blank will be fired by Mr. Shooter from Nick's gun once he has recovered it from the floor. This second gunshot will activate Mr. Beckett's CO_2 device. It will appear as though he has been shot in the chest. In both cases, the explosive devices will break the seal in the plastic and release the gore, blowing out a small hole in the back of your jackets and shooting the synthetic blood, brain, and fleshy matter against the wall in a convincingly violent spray. You two don't have to worry about anything except inserting your fake blood capsules into your mouth prior to the shootings, biting down at the moment you are fired upon with the blank, and falling to the floor convincingly, which we're going to teach you how to do.

"The blood from the vest and IV drips will be sound-activated upon the gunshot, so that some of it explodes against the wall as gun spatter and the rest seeps out from your neckline onto the floor to create a puddle. The blood from your mouth will be released once you bite down on the capsule when the blanks are fired. Just let the blood trickle from your open mouth naturally. You don't have to worry about the capsule dissolving in your saliva. These time-release capsules will stay solid for at least fifteen minutes under normal oral temperatures. Once the shots have been fired, Benedictis will be herded quickly out of the room and unable to examine your two bodies up close. Does that about cover it, Haley?"

"You got it, Mr. CIA man. Tarantino's not going to have anything on this baby."

"Oh, this is so fiendishly Hollywood," gushed Beckett. "I absolutely love it."

Lassiter was less sanguine. He was thinking of every possible way the caper could go wrong. He also didn't like keeping Squelch, Claggebart, and Bermolito in the dark about what he was doing. Despite his protests, his father had insisted upon not informing them of the plan so that they would be genuinely surprised when later informed of the two deaths. The goal was to make Benedictis and Popov believe that Benedictis had pulled off the double murder and was set to become the next Cameron Beckett.

"What's the fake blood made out of?" asked Lassiter.

"Maple syrup diluted with water and loaded with tofu chunks and red dye," replied Motorhead. "It's killer stuff, man."

"Let's just hope it's as convincing as you guys think."

"Oh, it will be. It's the same stuff used in *Pulp Fiction*. It's going to look totally real. It's got a lot of chunks."

"The chunks are what are going to sell it," said Haley. "*Operation From Russia Without Love* is going to kick some serious ass. We chunked you guys up real good."

Great, thought Lassiter. *That makes me feel so much better.*

CHAPTER 41

MOUNT SINAI MEDICAL CENTER
1176 FIFTH AVENUE

AN HOUR LATER, Lassiter was flying up the stairs to the second floor of Mount Sinai Medical Center. Natalie had finally been cleared by the doctors to accept visitors and he wanted to see her before his lunch with Benedictis, just in case something went wrong. He didn't know precisely why, but he had a bad feeling about the planned meeting—and over the years he had learned to trust his instincts. Reaching the second floor, he darted anxiously up one hallway, then another, until he found Room 268. He rapped gently on the half-open door. Hearing no response, he stepped inside the room.

Right away, he saw her, but for some trick in the lighting, the figure behind the oxygen mask and beneath the covers appeared too small and fragile to be Natalie. She was asleep, her chest rising and falling in a shallow rhythm. Plastic hoses dangled from her mask, veering off like an array of snaking pipelines to the far side of the bed closest to the window. A clear pouch containing IV fluids hung from a metal stand beside her bed, and a plastic tube trailed beneath the bedcovers to her left arm. There was no doctor or nurse in the room; they were alone.

He sat down quietly in the chair next to the bed so he could watch her. Though she looked tiny and frail, she seemed at peace and was still beautiful as she lay there sleeping. Damnit, did he love her! No, make that he had never stopped loving her! He just hadn't known it until he had reconnected with her here in New York. And now, fortunately, she had survived being shot and he was being granted a second chance to get things right.

He reached out and gently took her hand. *You can't screw it up this time, Nick.* But could he and Natalie really make it work this time around? God, he wanted it to, he thought to himself, as he watched the rhythmic ebb and flow of her chest, as peaceful and natural as the tides.

Her eyes fluttered open and suddenly she was staring at him. Her hand reached up and pulled down her oxygen mask so she could speak.

"You're...you're here." Her face lit up with a gentle glow. Her voice was groggy, but she seemed lucid enough.

Gently, he squeezed her hand. "Yes, I'm here," he said. "We thought we had lost you, but you came back to us. Even the doctors say it was a miracle."

"I don't...remember anything."

"That's probably a good thing. You were between worlds."

She stared off into space for a moment, still collecting herself. He wondered what kind of painkilling medication the doctors had given her; whatever it was, it was potent.

"Thank you for being here when I woke up. Seeing your face is reassuring."

"I called your parents and your office to let them know. Your mother and father are both flying in from Chicago and will be here this evening. I didn't know who else to call so that was pretty much it. You'll probably get bombarded with phone calls and flowers any minute now. And just so you know, the Devil's Brigade is downstairs standing by."

"Standing by?"

"Yes, Lieutenant Perkins, they're awaiting my orders on whether you're greenlit for visitors."

"Lieutenant Perkins? Why can't I be a captain or a major? After being shot in two places, I believe I deserve that much."

He smiled. "All right, Major Perkins it is then. Seriously, how do you feel? Do you want to see the gang or do you need to rest?"

"No, I'd like to see them."

"I still can't believe my father and I got you mixed up in all this."

"I already told you it's not your fault. I wanted to be a secret agent and catch bad guys. I've wanted to do it since I was a little girl. I don't know what else to say because it's the truth."

"My dad loves you, Natalie. Not as much as I love you, of course, but a lot."

She smiled, but he could tell she was still weak from all she had been through. Her recovery was going to take some time, probably weeks. Looking at her in her bed, feeble but alive, he felt himself draw strength from her mental and physical toughness. Her surviving against all odds had brought new meaning to his life, making him feel as if he had a purpose. He wanted to be with her, now and forever. Why in the hell did she almost have to die for him to realize that?

She reached out and gently touched his face. "I love you, Nicky," she said, and there were tears in her eyes. Tears that made him choke up inside and made his brain go all fuzzy and filled him with a sense of longing, the deep insane longing that made you feel alive and vulnerable at the same time. It was a strangely magical feeling, a flutter in his chest, a quickened breath, a taut grip in his gut that had a whiff of euphoric possibility that the world was actually a better place and people were a nobler species than their actual selfish, apish selves. He felt the magic of pure, real emotion. It was the emotion that he had unknowingly yearned for all his life, an emotion he had once had and then lost and now had a chance to reclaim again—that is, if he wasn't too stupid or stubborn to reach out and grab it. She was his soul mate, if there truly ever was such a thing, and he knew he would one day be a lonely old man—a wrinkled, regretful, cantankerous son of bitch—if he didn't act on his impulse at this very moment and ask her to spend the rest of her life with him.

"Natalie, I...I love you more than...will you...I mean, do you think you could ever...would you consider? What I mean to say is, will you, Natalie, marry me and be my wife?"

She looked at him with surprise for a long moment, and he thought he was going to faint. *Oh my God, what did I just do?*

She motioned for him to come closer. He gently leaned down, careful not to disrupt the network of medical tubes in her arms, and she took him in a soft embrace. The warmth of her body was like a freshly lit fire, stirring him inside. She looked up and he gave her a soft kiss on the lips, which were warm and moist. She kissed him back a little harder. They held each other for a moment longer and kissed again before he pulled away, not wanting to accidentally hurt her when she was still in such a fragile state.

Her face shone like the moon.

"Yes, Nick Lassiter, I will marry you," she pronounced. "Under one condition."

"Anything, anything at all," he said. "What is it?"

"That you never grow up."

He laughed. "Now that I can do with no problem."

Suddenly, he heard rejoicing voices behind him. "Oh Great Scott, they're getting married!"

He turned to see his dad and three knuckleheaded buddies jumping up and down and high fiving as if they were at the Super Bowl. So much for an intimate moment of privacy!

"This calls for congratulations, Son!" cried his father. "Would you like a cigar? I happen to have a fresh Cuban right here with me!"

"Here, here!" concurred Claggebart. "A couple of bottles of Dom Perignon and perhaps a tray or two of Clams Casino are certainly in order. I wonder if they can deliver to the hospital!"

"Welcome to the family, Natalie! You know we love you. In fact, Nick's mom and I have always loved you!"

"I can vouch for that," said Lassiter.

"Attaboy, Nicky!" roared Squelch, and he slapped him on the back so hard that it nearly knocked the wind out of him.

"Yes, congratulations, you two!" said Bermolito ebulliently, putting down his tablet and taking off his thick-framed, black-electrician-taped glasses for the first time that Lassiter could remember since fourth or fifth grade. My God, the nerdy fellow was actually quite handsome when he removed his spectacles.

Claggebart was nodding vigorously. "I'd toast your pending nuptials, boy-o and girl-o, if we only had some bloody cocktails! Don't they have a wet bar around here somewhere? Maybe it's on the third floor next to the open heart surgery wing!"

A ripple of laughter echoed through the room before his father waved his hands to silence them. "Now I hate to interrupt all the fun, boys and girls, but I have to borrow Nick here to prep him before his meeting with Beckett and Benedictis. It'll take just a few minutes."

"Wait a second, Nick. You're meeting with Beckett and Benedictis?" asked Natalie, her face showing concern.

He tried not to let the guilt show on his face, but he could tell the instant she looked at him that he had failed. He quickly covered up, cursing himself for not being a better actor. My God, if he couldn't even convince his gunshot, drugged-out fiancée, how was he ever going to fool Benedictis? Jesus, what had he gotten himself into?

SAMUEL MARQUIS

"I told you about the lunch last night at the party," he said to her. "They're going to apologize and offer me a settlement. This time I'm going to take it."

She was still eyeing him worriedly. "I don't know about this. My woman's intuition smells trouble with a capital T."

"There's nothing to worry about. I've got it covered."

"Are you sure you're not trying to pull one over on me?"

He hated himself for lying to her, but he had a chance to take down both Benedictis and Popov once and for all and he intended to do just that. "No, of course not," he replied. "And besides, what could possibly go wrong? We all just want the matter resolved peacefully."

"At least tell me you're going to be careful then. I don't trust these people."

"Don't worry, I'll make sure he's well-prepped and watch his back," said his father, who took him by the elbow and steered him towards the door. "We'll be back in five minutes. You all just celebrate."

"Celebrate!" cried a new voice. "What is going on here? This isn't a cocktail party, this is a hospital!"

A large African-American nurse, wearing a name tag that read ALTHEA like the Grateful Dead song, suddenly stepped into the room and glared at them.

"We were just leaving," said his father, and he quickly escorted Nick past the imposing nurse and down the hallway, out the hospital front door, and into the parking lot, where they came to a halt before a huge, midnight-blue van with a large rooftop antennae. A door slid open to expose two men in dark suits.

He shot his father a look. "What the hell is going on, Dad?"

"Just get in the van, Son. We don't want anyone to see us."

"Who are these guys?"

"They just need to talk to us about something." He motioned him to step in the van. By the serious expression on his face, Lassiter knew it was best not to argue.

"Are you in trouble, Dad?"

"As a matter of fact I am, but fortunately you can help with that. That's why I need you to step into the van and listen to what these gentlemen have to say. They're professionals."

"Professionals? Professionals at what?"

"They're with the CIA here in New York and they're going to be working with us. You see, the situation's changed, Nick. It's highly fluid and we know more now than we did even two hours ago. I'm afraid that's all I can tell you at the moment."

"All right, I just hope you know what you're doing."

"This is counterespionage, kid—no one knows what the fuck they're doing. But since you're about to get married and will soon have plenty of new responsibilities, this will be a good training op for you."

"*From Russia Without Love* is now a training op? Somehow I don't like the sound of that."

"Nick, please just get in the van. We don't want to make a scene."

He looked at the two men: they donned dark mirror sunglasses and looked stiff as wax figures.

210

"Hello, Nick, you can call me Mr. Breeze," said the man to the left, reaching out his hand to help him into the van. "Everything's going to be fine as long as you do as we say."

"And I'm Mr. Quantum, Nick, welcome," said his partner as he shut the door quickly behind them. "If you're ready now, we'll proceed to the rally point."

He looked at his father. "The rally point? But the lunch with Benedictis isn't for another hour and a half, and you just said we'd be back in the hospital room in five minutes."

His father smiled guiltily. "I know, Son, and I'm sorry about that. But the truth is I lied."

CHAPTER 42

THE VICTORIAN CLUB
1 WEST 77TH STREET

SITTING IN A PRIVATE DINING ROOM at The Victorian Club, Anton De Benedictis looked at his Cartier watch for what seemed like the hundredth time. It was 12:13 p.m. What in God's name could be taking Beckett and Lassiter so long? After all, he had spoken with Beckett only a few hours ago and he had seemed exhilarated at the opportunity to finally settle the whole affair. Benedictis had also been concerned about the well-publicized incident with the Russians last night and, therefore, he had called Lassiter an hour ago to personally reassure him about the meeting. It was strictly a chance for the three of them to settle the disagreement once and for all, he had told the kid, and Excalibur and the Russians had nothing to do with it.

So what was taking them so damned long?

He prayed that Lassiter hadn't gotten cold feet and decided to back out at the last second. Or, did he secretly wish that the kid wouldn't show up at all? That way he wouldn't have to perform the grisly deed he had been blackmailed into promising to do. But Popov had Rebecca and Danny, goddamnit, so he had no choice but to go through with it. It was either take care of Lassiter and Beckett—or kiss his beloved daughter and brother goodbye.

Or, was it more complicated than that? Could Popov be trusted at all?

After all, the guy had come by his apartment two hours ago and given him two new murder weapons and some spare magazines to use to kill Lassiter and Beckett. The Russian had insisted that his reason for the last-minute switch was because the old weapons might be able to be traced back to him after all. In contrast, the new Beretta and Glock he claimed would be traceable to one of his competitors, a nasty Latvian that he was particularly anxious to see go down, or at the very least, come under increased police scrutiny. So, courtesy of Popov, the literary agent cum killer now had two new weapons with which to take down his quarry. He couldn't help but feel that the Russian mob boss was acting strangely—why the hell hadn't Popov known that the guns were traceable to begin with?

Suddenly, he felt himself having a panic attack. What in the hell was he even doing here planning to murder two people? He felt for the new Beretta in the left pocket of his Versace jacket, and the new Glock in his right—and he shook his head in dismay. How had he let himself get mixed up with the Russian mob? How had he allowed himself to sink to this desperate criminal state? He frantically loosened his silk tie, feeling as though it was choking him. *Breathe, breathe, you've got to breathe!* He noticed that he was perspiring heavily. Jesus Christ, he was sweating buckets—his goddamned Ermenegildo Zegna was soaked!

He was also on edge because of the tense situation at his literary agency. Because he paid well above his competitors, his staff was assiduously loyal to him, but their loyalty only extended so far. At first, the recent developments with the Devil's Brigade had merely added a layer of intrigue around the office; but after last night's fiasco with the Russians, the gossipy whispers had turned to genuine fear. His senior staff in particular was demanding answers.

So at 10 a.m. this morning, he had given all of his employees the day off, even though it was only Wednesday. All of his staff worked fifty-plus-hour work weeks on a regular basis and deserved a break. But more importantly he didn't want them asking too many questions about what had happened to Natalie, or what was going on with Lassiter or the Russians. He knew he was in way over his head. It was only because he was such a powerful, elite figure in the New York literary establishment, and so feared and respected at his office, that he was surviving such a perilous situation.

All the same, he knew that if he followed through with Popov's dangerous plan, he would be damaged forever. But he could see no other choice. There was no middle ground, no compromise solution, only two forks in the road, and both of them catastrophic and irredeemable. He was completely and utterly fucked no matter which fork he chose. But at the end of the day, if he didn't go through with it, Rebecca and Danny would be killed and he wasn't going to let that happen.

Family came first, goddamnit!

"Hello, my old mate from Snowy River," he heard a suave, erudite Aussie voice say.

He nearly jumped out of his seat and looked up to see Beckett and Nick Lassiter standing there at the door looking at him. *My God, did they come in together? What is that all about?*

"Boy, someone sure is jumpy," said Lassiter, stepping forward and extending his hand. The lanky, sunburnished, outdoorsy American presented a dramatic contrast to the short, pale-faced, bookish Australian.

Jesus Christ, I'm about to kill Mathew McConaughey and Rupert Fucking Murdoch!

"Glad you two could make it," he said, standing up from his chair and shaking Lassiter's hand.

"I'm sorry I'm late, Anton," said Beckett. They all sat down in their curved Victorian-era, velvet-backed chairs fringed in gilded leaf.

"Oh, it's all right, I haven't been waiting long. How is Natalie, Nick? Have you visited her at the hospital?"

"Yes, and luckily she's all right. In fact, we're now engaged."

He wasn't sure he had heard correctly. "Engaged? You're kidding, right?"

"Nope. I popped the question and, surprisingly, she said yes. Of course, she was under the influence of powerful drugs at the time."

"Well, congratulations young lad," said Beckett, beaming.

"Yes, congratulations," said Benedictis, but he suddenly felt dizzy.

This is so wrong. I'm about to kill a kid who's getting married? I don't know that I can do this. And what about Natalie? Hasn't she been through enough? Now she's going to lose her fiancée?

A waiter appeared and Beckett ordered a $200 bottle of Veuve Clicquot champagne for the group. When the waiter shuffled off, they made small talk for a few minutes while perusing the menu. The waiter reappeared, presented the bottle to Beckett and then, with his approval, uncorked it and poured each glass half full before disappearing again.

Beckett raised his champagne glass in a toast. "Here's to you, Master Lassiter!"

"And here's to you two gentlemen for finally doing the right thing!"

They all clinked glasses. To Benedictis's surprise, Beckett and Lassiter quickly tossed back their champagne, refilled their flutes, and each slammed back another round.

"Okay, you two," he said. "This isn't *Animal House.*" Or would it be better that they were drunk when he turned a gun on them?

"Don't be a party pooper, we're just blowing off a little steam," said Beckett with a wild, youthful look in his eyes. He poured himself and Lassiter a third glass.

"I'll drink to that," said the kid.

"Good on you, mate," said the Australian and they tossed back another flute. "Now Nick, you already know how terribly sorry I am for plagiarizing *Blind Thrust.* I know I've bollixed things up quite badly and that you could have sued me and probably won. But for reasons of your own, you have decided not to follow that course of action. So I want to make it up to you. Therefore, as part of my apology here today, I would like to give you compensation as well as a small token of my appreciation." He reached into his jacket pocket, withdrew a manila envelope, and pushed it across the table to Lassiter. "I know that it cannot make up for the pain and suffering you've endured up to now, but I hope that it gives you some sense of closure in the healing process."

Lassiter opened the envelope, pulled out a check, squinted at it, and instantly emitted a gasp of surprise. "Two million dollars? Jesus!"

"It's the least I could do, Nicholas."

"Still, that's a lot of money, Mr. Beckett. Are you sure you want to part with that much? You know that all I ever really wanted was an apology."

"Well then, consider it a wedding gift," said the Australian happily.

"Thank you. I'm deeply moved by your generosity." They raised their glasses again and tossed back more of the bubbly.

The waiter re-emerged to take their lunch orders. Benedictis felt a pang of last-minute doubt. *Should I go through with it? It's not too late to turn back.* He cast a glance at his two victims. *No, no, no, you don't have any choice—Popov will kill Rebecca and Danny if you don't.* All the same, he couldn't help but feel a twinge of guilt at what he was about to do.

"I'll start off first since I didn't get to eat last time," said Lassiter.

"Indeed, you have the honors, mate," exclaimed Beckett, and he poured them each another glass of champagne. "Oh, bloody hell, we're almost out. Another bottle, my good man, and make it quick—we're bloody thirsty!" he bellowed to the waiter.

He and Lassiter laughed uproariously.

My God, they've already drunk the whole damned bottle. What is going on with them? They're both so wasted already they won't even feel it when I shoot them. Shit, what am I talking about? Am I really going to go through with it?

"All right," said Lassiter, "I'm going with what I ordered last time. Let's start with the Oysters Rockefeller, and then proceed with a bowl of lobster bisque and a fresh buffalini mozzarella tomato salad. And for an entrée, I'm going with the pan-seared tuna with toasted black and white sesame seeds, watercress, seaweed salad, teriyaki sauce, and wasabi with a special topping of charred portabella bordelaise. As for my side dishes, I'm going for total debauchery: the five-cheese mac and the sautéed asparagus."

"Strordnary choices," gasped Beckett. "Make that two—give me what he's having across the board." He raised his champagne glass in a toast. "You are a man after my own heart, Sir Nicholas. Do you think, per chance, that you have Australian blood flowing through your veins?"

"I think I must—I've always had a hankering for shrimp on the barbie, potato cakes, and Lamington!"

"Here, here, you young scalawag!" and they clinked glasses and slammed back the last of the champagne.

Benedictis was fast becoming irritated. "Okay, you two, settle down," he said, but then he thought: *Who cares? Let them have their fun. After all, you're about to shoot them down like dogs.*

The waiter took his order—grilled Portobello mushrooms followed by surf and turf of ten ounce prime filet and Brazilian lobster tail with garlic mashed potatoes and creamed spinach—before closing the door to the private room and disappearing again. Two minutes later, the waiter returned with the second bottle of champagne and poured them all a glass. Once again, Beckett and Lassiter pitched in immediately, making outlandish toasts and tossing back the bubbly liquid like bibulous frat boys.

Benedictis shook his head with disapproval. *My God, what has gotten into them? Are they just relieved to have everything behind them and blowing off steam?*

"All right, Cam buddy," said Lassiter. "Before we get too wrecked here, tell me how you two wily sons of bitches did it. Did you rummage through the slush pile until you found the right idea and it just happened to be my novel *Blind Thrust*? Is that how it all went down?"

Benedictis had hoped not to have to go down this road during the luncheon. "I don't think we should get into all that, Nick, when we're trying to put this all behind us. It might stir up resentment."

"Who are you kidding, mate, just tell him the truth? We bloody fucking well stole it, Nick, and that's the bloody fucking truth! That story of yours was like a treasure chest and I jumped on it like Long John Silver himself! Anton plucked the synopsis from the pile and I loved the story from the moment he started reading it aloud!"

"Stop it, Cameron—you're drunk."

"As a matter of a fact, I am. But it's nothing that a little coke can't cure." He pulled out a small glass vial, dug into a mound of fluffy white powder with a miniature gold spoon, and took two quick blasts. "How about you, Nicholas?"

"No thanks, I'm good."

"You most certainly are—you're two million dollars richer!"

"Thanks to you, mate!" He raised his glass and tossed back another jolt of champagne and the author quickly followed suit.

Benedictis couldn't believe what was happening. Had they completely lost their fucking minds? *Jesus, maybe I should just get it over with now?* He felt into his pockets for the Beretta and Glock. He had planned to make his move once lunch was served and the waiter left them alone for a few minutes, but maybe he should go for it now. They were already so drunk they wouldn't know what hit them.

As he contemplated the grisly task that lay before him, his mouth went as dry as a cement kiln. Suddenly, a hundred different worries stampeded through his mind, as he realized the perilous risk he was about to take.

Should I go through with it? What if it doesn't work? What if I get caught? Are Stafford and the others in position? Are they watching me right now? Is the waiter in on it too? Am I going to go to hell? What would Rebecca and Danny think of me if I told them what I've done?

Beckett tossed back more champagne, dribbling some down his chin. Benedictis shook his head in disgust and glanced at Lassiter. The kid was practically falling out of his seat with laughter. Again, he reminded himself that the plan was to take them out after the food arrived, but in the suspense of the moment and with them so intoxicated, he was gripped with an overwhelming urge to act now. Of course, he didn't want to be too rash and blow the whole thing, but the tug he felt inside was almost unbearable.

And then, quite suddenly, everything changed.

CHAPTER 43

THE VICTORIAN CLUB
1 WEST 77TH STREET

"YOU KNOW, NICHOLAS," began Beckett, "that I am retiring as an author. I'm making the announcement at four o'clock this afternoon."

"I don't believe it. You're quitting?"

"Well, yes and no. You see, Anton here has graciously agreed to continue on in my stead. He, of course, will retain the *nom de plume* of Cameron Beckett and continue publishing under my name."

"You're joking, right?"

"I don't think we want to get into all this right now," protested Benedictis, though he wasn't sure why he felt that way when he was going to just shoot them both anyway. "You're supposed to wait for the press conference."

"Oh, it's all right. Nick and I here are fast friends now. Aren't we, Nick?"

It was then Benedictis noticed the sudden change in Lassiter's expression. The young man was gazing at Beckett intently with a dangerous look in his eye. He reached onto the table and picked up the check. "Say, I've got an idea, Cam buddy. Why don't we just tear this up and you anoint me as the new Cameron Beckett instead of him." He nodded dismissively towards Benedictis, who felt a twinge of anger. "I'm a better writer than he is. He's just a literary agent—he's not a real fiction writer. Sure, he's a competent editor, but all he's ever written are stupid-ass *How-To-Be-The-Next-Big-Writer* non-fiction books. Those puppies are a dime a dozen and as worthless as toilet paper for aspiring novelists."

He felt himself stiffen at the affront. Who did this lowly Colorado-cowboy wannabe-author think he was talking to?

"So, what do you say, Cam, why not me instead of this schmuck? At least I'm a real writer and don't have connections with the Russian mob. I'm also young so I won't kick the bucket anytime soon like him. Look at it as if you're passing the torch to a new generation."

Beckett exploded with laughter. "Surely you're not serious."

"Of course I am. I should be the next Cameron Beckett, not him."

"Come on now, let's not get carried away, Nicholas. I mean, your novel was an intriguing concept, but quite frankly you don't have the chops to be a bestseller like me."

"What are you talking about? Your writing sucks!"

The Australian rolled his eyes. "Uh, as if you are qualified to judge *my* work?"

"I'm better than you are. You think because you're a bestseller that you're better than me, but the truth of the matter is you're not. I write like you used to write when you were young and fresh and inspired. Now you're just churning out crap because you have to and because Agent Numb Nuts here"—he tipped his head disdainfully towards Benedictis again—"and the Excalibur Media suits make you do it."

"Nicholas, I think you've had too much to drink."

"No, I'm as clear as a mountain stream, matey. If you want your so-called *brand* and *literary tradition* to carry on with the passion of your earlier works, then you should make me the next Cameron Beckett, not Agent Numb Nuts over here."

Benedictis was in shock. He had not seen this coming. His bony fingers slowly inched towards the Beretta in his pocket. Lassiter and Beckett were so focused on their argument that they hardly noticed him.

Now, the Australian stood up from his chair. "You're not half the writer I am, you redneck twit! Don't you understand your work is unpublished because you're just not bloody good enough! The best you can ever expect to be is freight-class. No, scratch that. You're totally worthless and no one—*No One!*—is ever going to read your work. Unlike me, you will live your whole miserable life and then die in literary obscurity!"

"That may be, but *Blind Thrust* is as good as ninety percent of your novels. It's not as good as *The Silent Assassin* or *Tripoli, Tripoli*, but it's still damned good. It's just that I'm an unpublished author so no one has been willing to take a chance on it."

"Oh no, no, no! You don't have the bloody chops to be a bestselling author. You are a small…a tiny, tiny little man with big dreams and nothing else. There are a million idiots just like you out there publishing their hack spy and romance novels on Amazon and making three dollars and forty-seven cents per week and thinking that they've *made* it. But those nobodies haven't made a bloody fucking thing—except fools out of themselves. They're not published authors—they are typists. All they do is clutter up the publishing world for real novelists like myself. You're one of them, Nick—you're one of those bloody Amazon.com, freight-class losers—and that's all you're ever fucking going to be. I mean, do you actually think I'd be stupid enough to hand over the reins to my Jackson Preston detective series to a hapless redneck from Colorado like you. What do you take me for? A bloody fool!"

They were both red-faced and on their feet now, staring one another down like a pair of gladiators about to do battle.

"You bastard, you stole my fucking book!" Lassiter snarled at Beckett from across the table. "I should have sued your ass to begin with, you Aussie piece of shit!"

"And you—you insignificant little twit—are most certainly no author! You'll never be traditionally published because *you* don't have what it takes!"

This is your chance! You've got to do it now! a voice inside Benedictis screamed. *You have to do this to save Rebecca and Danny! Do it now while they're distracted!*

He listened for any sign of the waiter outside the room and double-checked the door.

No one.

It was now or never.

He discreetly snicked the safety off the Beretta and clasped the pistol in his hand beneath the table. *Okay, this is it, here I—*

He slowly pulled out his Beretta and pointed it at Lassiter.

"Good Lord, Anton!" gasped Beckett. "What the hell are you doing?"

"What does it look like I'm doing? I'm going to shoot him!" Struggling to remain calm, he now pulled the Glock from his coat pocket and held it in his left hand, as he had practiced a dozen times. "And with this other one, I'm going to kill you, you imperious little—"

His words were cut off as the door behind him suddenly flew open, a shot was fired, and Nick Lassiter's face dissolved in a spray of blood and tissue that spattered the far wall.

What the hell! Benedictis screamed to himself as Lassiter collapsed in a heap and a concealed pistol that he hadn't seen fell from Lassiter's right hand onto the floor with a dull thud. *Jesus, he had a gun?*

He wheeled around with the Beretta to protect himself and was shocked to see Detective Stafford filling the doorway, holding a smoking pistol and a small briefcase. The NYPD cop was wearing a pair of black leather gloves and he now slammed the door closed, quickly disarmed Benedictis of both the Beretta and Glock while the literary agent stood there frozen in shock, stuffed the handguns in his briefcase, and dashed over and kneeled down next to the supine body.

"My God is he dead?" asked Beckett.

"Yep, he's gone," answered the detective after checking his pulse. "Good thing I got him. He was about to shoot you, Mr. Benedictis."

The agent couldn't believe his luck. Stafford had just shot and killed Lassiter and now he wouldn't have to kill the young man! But what was he going to do about Beckett?

"I can't believe it. I can't believe you killed him!" shrieked the author, who suddenly looked stone-cold sober.

"It is rather hard to believe, mate, but there it is," replied the detective sarcastically. He then calmly picked up Lassiter's pistol from the floor and pointed it at the bestselling author. "And now it's your turn."

Beckett appeared outraged. "What the hell? Have you gone stark raving—?"

But the Oxford-educated Aussie's voice was cut off as a bullet ripped through his chest. Benedictis was stunned to see blood spurt onto the table and into the author's glass of champagne. Then Beckett wobbled on his beefy legs and fell back into his chair, knocking it over and toppling onto the floor with a loud thump.

Gasping in horror, the agent looked warily at Stafford. *Dear Lord, is he going to kill me too?*

But the detective did no such thing. Instead, he stuffed Lassiter's pistol into the kid's right hand, curled his finger around the trigger, and fired two shots into the maroon-velvet-flocked wall just above where Beckett now lay dead. Then he stuffed the pistol he had used to shoot Lassiter into the Australian's hand and pulled the trigger once. The shot punched into the velvety wallpaper behind

Lassiter with a sickening thud.

"Okay, we're out of here—come on, let's go," commanded Stafford calmly. He picked up the check sitting on the table, studied it for a moment, and stuffed it into his briefcase before stepping towards the wall and popping open a concealed panel.

Good God, so there was one of the secret entrances into the private dining room from the old Cabinet of Curiosity! Still Benedictis hesitated, frozen with fear. There was blood and chunky tissue splattered everywhere, and now, outside the private dining room in the main restaurant beyond, he heard the sound of shuffling feet, shouting voices, and general commotion.

"Don't just stand there. We have to go—now!"

He did as instructed and ducked into the opening in the wall. When Stafford closed the secret door behind him, he couldn't believe that they were actually using one of the storied restaurant's ancient cabinet passageways. The detective led him through a labyrinthine maze covered in dust and cobwebs, until they came to a wine cellar, another corridor, and then a small alcove with a side door that appeared to open out onto West 76th Street, on the south side of the restaurant.

Carefully, Stafford pried the door open and scanned the street. No sign of anyone.

"It's all clear," he said, and he waved him forward.

Benedictis was still in a state of shock. He couldn't believe what had just happened. Had it all been just a crazy dream?

"Where are we going?" he asked. "Won't the waiter remember us?"

"He will but it doesn't matter. He's one of ours."

"He is? Good Lord!"

"Get a grip on yourself, Mr. Benedictis. And stay close behind me—we've still got to get to my goddamned car!"

CHAPTER 44

FROM ACROSS THE STREET, Austin Brewbaker watched as a side door of The Victorian Club opened and Detective Stafford stepped cautiously out onto the sidewalk with Anton De Benedictis. He felt a little jolt of panic. What was going on? What had happened to his son and why weren't they exiting into the back alley from the kitchen as planned?

And then, as Stafford and Benedictis started down the street, he felt even more alarmed. He had the dreadful feeling that he—and they—were being watched.

But by whom?

He scanned the faces of the nearby pedestrians. Nothing unusual there. He then surveyed the neighborhood itself, the upper floors of the buildings, and the rooftops, but he didn't see anything suspicious. Still, he couldn't shake the feeling of being clandestinely observed by someone well-schooled in the art of avoiding detection.

He looked at the front door and then back at the rear kitchen door of the restaurant that led to the back alley, which had been the planned escape route. Something was not right. First, what had happened to Nick? Following the shooting, he was supposed to proceed to the front entrance of The Victorian Club to make simultaneous visual and cell phone contact. So where was he? Second, why in the hell had Stafford and Benedictis exited from the side door instead of behind the kitchen into the alley?

He looked back at Stafford and Benedictis. They were walking quickly down the sidewalk along 76th, looking around every so often to see if they were being followed. Like him, they seemed to sense a disquieting presence. He wished he could put a finger on who exactly was out there. Was it his own people from the Company, the Russians, or perhaps Excalibur's security goons? Or was he just being paranoid?

He started across the street, striding quickly towards Amsterdam Avenue so he could cut Stafford and Benedictis off. His mind was racing. He shouldn't have allowed Nick to meet alone with Beckett and Benedictis. He should have insisted on being close by inside the restaurant during the meeting. Something must have gone awry. Why else would Nick have seemingly disappeared into thin air and still be incommunicado? And why else would Stafford and Benedictis have come out by a side door that hadn't been part of the plan? Why weren't his son and the detective following the goddamned script he had gone over with them in excruciating detail, along with Beckett, before the meeting? Had *Operation From*

Russia Without Love been compromised? Had Benedictis or Stafford somehow used real weapons instead of guns that fired only blanks? Was it possible that Stafford had double-crossed him?

He could feel himself growing frantic. He had been trained to be calm and composed in the field, but right now all of that was out the window. The life of his son was at risk, and Stafford was unpredictable. Did the NYPD VIP officer harbor a secret grudge for how he had been treated at the police station? Had he deliberately botched the covert operation? Was what had happened at The Victorian Club a setup for something bigger, something yet to come? Whatever was going on, Brewbaker had a bad feeling he had been double-crossed by someone.

He continued walking, keeping an eye on the two men. Now the presence he had felt earlier was becoming overpowering. He wasn't just being watched, he was being actively stalked.

He quickly turned around.

There was no one except an elderly woman walking her dog a half block behind him and, further up the street, a pair of young Asian men laughing at a joke. He told himself that he was worrying over nothing and continued on. But he couldn't help but feel a growing uneasiness. He looked at Stafford and Benedictis again across the street and they seemed uncomfortable too, the detective in particular. But thankfully, the cop still hadn't recognized him.

He started off again. But he hadn't gone five paces when he heard the sound of new footsteps behind him. Without stopping, he peered over his shoulder, expecting for someone to appear, but there was no one there.

He stopped, straining his ears to listen, but the footsteps had stopped. Where had they come from? He scanned the building to his left, but there was no sign of anyone in any of the walkways and the old woman and the Asian men were too far behind him. Still, he felt a tickling sensation on the back of his neck, as if he was being closely pursued.

He resumed walking, a little faster now, telling himself that there was a perfectly logical explanation for the noise. But he knew there wasn't.

Instinct told him he was being followed.

He began to walk faster.

To his consternation, he heard a noise again. This time it was unmistakable: the sound of footsteps, coming up fast from behind him.

He turned abruptly. But this time he was too late.

Out of the corner of his eye, he saw a terrible, swift slash of shadow as a man in a dark leather jacket and sunglasses rushed towards him. He heard the sharp crackle of a gunshot followed quickly by two more.

The next thing he knew he was slumped down on the street, the Asian men were hovering over him and calling 911, and the man in the black leather jacket was walking swiftly away from the crime scene.

ψψψ

From a sixth story rooftop, the government assassin raised his Leica range-finding binoculars again and studied his soft target, Austin Brewbaker, walking along the street. He had chosen his current position well. With his M24 sniper rifle, he had a clear line of sight to both the front and rear entrances of The Victorian Club. His intel had indicated this was where the Director of the Russian Counterintelligence Desk would be posted.

He had never received a wet termination order involving such a high-ranking CIA officer, and he felt a rising tension as he watched Brewbaker walking down the street. His soft target was paralleling the movements of the unknown law enforcement figure and Anton De Benedictis across the street. The assassin locked the laser ranging dot on Brewbaker's head to gauge the distance. The invisible ray of laser light struck the target and bounced back instantaneously. He read the red digital readout superimposed, in standard U.S. units, in the upper right hand corner of the image.

One-hundred-and-four yards.

He quickly computed the drift and drop. There was no breeze, so he wouldn't have to correct laterally for windage. He would hold the M24 on the first mil dot below the reticle to account for the bullet's drop over its short flight path.

He brought the stock of the M24 slowly to his shoulder, placing the first mil-dot beneath the crosshairs on his soft target. He wore ultrathin leather gloves to ensure his fingerprints would never be found on the weapon. Through the Leupold Mk 4 LR/T M3 10×40mm fixed-power scope, Austin Brewbaker's image came in clearly as he stopped to look around on the street. It was funny but the CIA director seemed to sense a presence around him as he kept glancing nervously around the street and on the rooftops. But the assassin was deep in the shadows of a pair of building fan turbines and there was no way he was going to let the counterintelligence officer spot him. Even if the guy was, as a Company employee, specifically trained to trust no one and keep an alert eye out at all times.

He held the mil-dot there on his target below with the cool, collected discipline of the professional government assassin that he was. His right index finger slid forward and curled around the trigger. His hands were steady, his muscles tense but precisely controlled. After tracing his soft target for the past two minutes, he was getting a feel for Brewbaker's movements. He was now ready to complete his assignment.

He took one last moment to study his target's face. The image through the scope was clear, unwavering.

A clean kill.

His nerves hardened. His breathing came in a steady rhythm.

He raised the rifle a hair and again the first-mil dot locked onto the soft target's face.

But suddenly something was wrong!

On the street below, a man in a black leather jacket, black Nike running shoes, and dark sunglasses was rushing toward the soft target with a gun. There was a shot followed by two more and, suddenly and unexpectedly, the target was down on the sidewalk. With surprising speed, two young Asian men came to his aid as the man in the leather jacket darted swiftly in the opposite direction, talking into his radio headset.

What the fuck just happened? Who the hell is that!

He set down his rifle, picked up his Leica range-finding binoculars, and focused in on the killer, making a detailed mental note of the way he moved, his clothing, and his pale Slavic facial features. He turned the binoculars onto Brewbaker. The target lay totally still on the pavement with the two Asian Good Samaritans kneeling over him. One of them was calling out for help, while the other was apparently calling 911 on his cell phone. But it would be no use: Brewbaker was clearly stone-cold dead. From across the street, the cop and Benedictis seemed to recognize Brewbaker and they hastened their pace down the street as the man in the leather jacket ran away in the opposite direction, gun held in his right hand.

Suddenly, a black Range Rover squealed onto the scene, the shooter jumped inside, and the car drove away, tires screeching. The government assassin studied the car a moment through his Leica range-finding binoculars, memorizing the plate number and noting the red strip with the word DIPLOMAT stenciled above the license number.

It was all over in less than thirty seconds.

Now, with urgency, the professional assassin broke down his M24 Sniper Weapon System—the rifle muzzle, butt plate, bipod, detachable telescopic sight, and other accessories—and stuffed them in his nylon carrying bag, dashed to the rooftop door, and descended into the echoing stairwell. As he bounded down to ground level, he withdrew his coded mobile, pulled up a contact, and punched in the call.

The voice he wanted to hear on the other end answered after a single ring. "I assume the assignment has been completed to my satisfaction since you are calling me on my secure line."

"It's done all right, but it wasn't me."

"Say again, I don't believe I heard correctly."

"Assignment complete, but it wasn't me. Someone else terminated the target. Three shots, a definite confirmed kill."

"And the shooter's identity?"

"Not yet confirmed. Russian mob, by the looks of him. And the getaway vehicle had diplomatic plates. I got the number if you want to run it."

He quickly gave the man on the other end the tag number, adjusted his sunglasses, opened the door onto the street level, and dashed through the lobby of the hotel.

"All right, get the hell out of there."

"Copy that, already underway. What about the second assignment?"

"That's a red light hold for now. I'll get back to you once the dust has settled."

"But if the Russians are the ones behind this, don't we have to—"

"That's not your call, soldier. Your job is to follow orders. Second target is not greenlit, do you copy?"

"I copy."

"Good, then stay invisible until I call."

"Yes, Mr. Deputy Director, sir. You can count on my discretion."

With approaching sirens now screaming in the distance, the government assassin darted through the front door of the hotel, hit the street, and turned right, walking in the opposite direction of the crowd that had gathered around the lifeless body of the Director of the CIA's Russian Counterintelligence Desk.

CHAPTER 45

MOUNT SINAI MEDICAL CENTER
1176 FIFTH AVENUE

"WE'RE SO SORRY, NATALIE," said Claggebart, standing along the edge of Natalie Perkins's hospital bed. "We shouldn't have let Nick come here to the Big Apple. Then you wouldn't have been shot, and we wouldn't be sitting here worrying about Nick and Mr. B. Let's face it we're in way above our heads. I don't know what we were thinking."

"Speak for yourself, man," countered Squelch. "I'm sorry Natalie was shot too, but we're the Devil's Brigade and this is open warfare. What would have happened if George Washington and his ragtag army of farmers wielding pitchforks had packed it in after Bunker Hill? Where would we be today, huh? We're the Devil's Brigade, people, and we don't surrender to anybody. Especially not with General Frederick and his black-faced marauders with the baggy cargo pants and Tommy-guns looking down at us from heaven, watching our every move, making sure we live up to their lofty standards. By thunder, we came to this glitzy town of megalomaniacs to set things right and we're not leaving until we've finished the job and distinguished ourselves in a manner befitting the original *Schwartzer Teufel!*"

Sitting upright in her hospital bed, Natalie wanted to laugh, but knew it would hurt too much. The pain from her wounds had subsided thanks to the massive doses of painkillers, but the slightest movement still sent shudders of agony through her body. Her only consolation was that she could talk.

"Believe it or not, I agree with the patriotic Dr. Squelch here," she said, feeling proud to be part of such a dedicated team of people, even if they were ridiculously overmatched by their opponents. "We may not have known exactly what we were getting into, but we all wanted to get off our asses and make a difference. And that's exactly what we've done. Even if, in hindsight, what we've been through seems reckless, maybe even crazy—we have fought the good fight."

"Well said, luv," said Bermolito. "And as we speak, Nicky is at The Victorian Club getting justice for the injustices heaped upon him by Beckett and Benedict—"

He stopped right there as everyone had turned towards the open door of the hospital room. Anton De Benedictis and Detective Stafford were both standing there, their expressions as grave as pallbearers.

Natalie had a sudden sick feeling of dread.

Benedictis took a step forward. "I'm sorry for what happened to you last night, Natalie. I also apologize for not coming by sooner. But I'm even sorrier for what I have come here to tell you. I regret to inform you that Nick Lassiter and Austin Brewbaker are dead."

The news floored her; for several seconds she was unable to speak. "W-What did you just say? Did you just walk in here and tell us that Nick and his father are both dead? Why there...there must be some mistake."

She looked at Benedictis, who shook his head somberly, then at Squelch, Claggebart, and Bermolito, who continued to stand there in openmouthed shock.

"I'm afraid it's the truth," the literary agent continued. "I know that you might be inclined to think I had something to do with it. That's why I wanted to tell you face-to-face that I absolutely did not. I have already given my statement to Detective Stafford here and he can fill you in on the circumstances of their deaths. Again, I'm terribly sorry for your loss."

The room went quiet. The heads hung low in shocked silence. Natalie felt tears come to her eyes. Both Nick and his father were dead? How was such a terrible thing possible?

She looked again at Benedictis, then at Stafford, then back at Benedictis, and suddenly she exploded with pent-up emotion.

"You bastard!" she hissed, waving her finger at the renowned literary agent. "You're the one behind this. You're the one that killed Nick and his father! This story you've concocted is something you've cooked up with the detective!"

Stafford stepped forward officially. "Ms. Perkins, that's just not true. Nick Lassiter was shot by Cameron Beckett. They exchanged gunfire during their meeting this afternoon and fatally shot one another. The police crime scene reports will confirm this, I promise you. After the unfortunate incident, I insisted upon escorting Mr. Benedictis here because he wanted to tell you the terrible news in person. I advised him not to come here, but he felt it his personal duty."

"I am truly sorry"—Benedictis looked around the room at everyone—"for your loss. I know you all cared deeply about Nick and his father."

"You monster! You don't know a damned thing about what Nick and his dad meant to us!" shouted Natalie defiantly with tears streaming down her face. "You have no right to be here! Get out of this room right now, goddamn you!"

"Damn right!" echoed Squelch, and he stepped forward and punched Benedictis in the nose, knocking him to the floor.

At that moment, Natalie saw her nurse, Althea—who brooked no opposition here on the second floor, west wing of her medical fiefdom—storm into the room.

"What in the name of Sweet Jesus is going on here? We don't allow no fighting in my hospital unless it's done by me! Now I want everyone out of here this minute!"

"We were just leaving," said Detective Stafford, helping the bloody-nosed Benedictis to his feet.

"I'm terribly sorry about this, Natalie," said her boss, and she could see the genuine contrition in his eyes. "In fact, I'm sorry for everything that's happened. I know that nothing I say can ever bring Nick or Austin back, but I am very sorry."

"Well, sorry doesn't cut it with us, motherfucker!" growled Squelch, and he stepped forward again and gave him a hard shove. "You're bad karma, man, and we're going to get revenge on you for what you've done. This is not the end—this is just the beginning. You, Mr. Big Shot Über Agent, are fucking going down!"

He grabbed him by the collar of his Versace and started to violently shake him, but Stafford was able to pry them apart and shove Benedictis towards the door.

"That's enough!" warned the detective. "You had better watch your step, Dr. Welch, or you could be looking at a lengthy visit to Riker's. Remember, this is my turf and you don't have Nick's father here to protect you anymore. *Capiche?*"

"Now that's where you're wrong, Mr. Big Shot NYPD detective," said big Althea, hands on her hips. "This is my turf and y'all are going to have to move along before I open up a big can of whoop ass. Now get out of my hospital room right now—and that means all of you!"

She aggressively prodded everyone towards the door. Within a matter of seconds, she had cleared the hospital room.

It was now achingly quiet and Natalie wanted to be left alone to cry. Her eyes met Althea's, and she could see from the nurse's sympathetic expression that she had a big heart.

"Sorry about all that ruckus," Althea said as she began checking the vitals instrumentation next to her bed. "You need to rest now, girl. You nearly died last night."

But Natalie had already turned away to stare out the hospital window and wasn't listening. Tears poured from her eyes. She felt old, tired, and utterly alone. So much so that she didn't even want to live.

After all, with Nick gone what was the point?

CHAPTER 46

BENEDICTIS APARTMENT, THE DAKOTA
1 WEST 72ND STREET

ANTON DE BENEDICTIS stared out worriedly at Central Park's Strawberry Fields from the balcony of his Dakota apartment. His battered nose ached and he felt terribly guilty about the killing of Cameron Beckett, Nick Lassiter, and Austin Brewbaker. But what he was most concerned about was the fate of Rebecca and Danny. He still had not gotten them back yet, which was deeply troubling.

He had called Popov repeatedly imploring him to release them, but the despicable mob boss hadn't answered his phone and he had been forced to endure the indignity of leaving a voice message. He had the horrible feeling that even with Beckett and Lassiter dead, Popov would still not be satisfied and demand more from him. Would the Russian renege on his agreement to release Rebecca and Danny? Benedictis could only pray that he wouldn't; but even if Popov kept to his word, he would probably come up with some new way to blackmail him and make his life miserable.

With that in mind, Benedictis wanted to just crawl into bed, pull up the covers, and go to sleep with the hope that it was all just a nightmare, that he would eventually wake up and everything would be all right. But he knew it wouldn't be that easy: he had signed a pact with the devil, and the only chance he had to get his life back was, as radical as it seemed, for Popov to die. With the Russian alive, Benedictis knew he would be a slave to the mob boss for the rest of his life.

But would killing the Russian guarantee his freedom? Wouldn't another Popov just pop up like a jack-in-the-box and take his place? One of his sons perhaps, or maybe an equally dangerous and unpredictable brother, uncle, or nephew?

His smartphone rang, startling him. His precarious predicament was making him jumpy. He looked at the caller ID and instantly recognized the number. He cursed to himself, knowing that the call wasn't from Popov as he had hoped, but rather David Sloan. Reluctantly and with a heavy heart, he hit the green *Accept* button.

"My God, Anton, what the hell is going on?" bristled the Chairman and CEO of Excalibur Publishing Group without preamble.

He took a deep breath to compose himself. He would play the innocent card. "So you've heard about the shooting."

"Yes, and are you fucking kidding me? Cameron Beckett and Nick Lassiter have shot and killed one another—and you didn't think it important enough to call me?"

"Look, David, I've been through a terrible ordeal. I was going to call you, but I had to first contact Cameron's wife, Nicole. She's, understandingly, quite distraught."

"Don't play the sympathy card with me, you ruthless bastard. I know it was you and those damned Russians behind the shootings. This is a fucking disaster. We've both just lost our meal ticket."

"We haven't actually lost anything. A year ago, Cam authorized me to continue all of his series in his stead. It's in his last will and testament."

A stunned silence on the other end.

"David, are you still there?"

"My God, what have you done?"

"I haven't *done* a damned thing. Cameron Beckett has, with proper legal documentation, passed his authorial rights on to me in the event of his unexpected death."

"You fucking bastard, you're behind this! You did this!"

"Calm down, David, you're spouting nonsense. I had nothing to do with their deaths, you fool. Beckett and Lassiter got wildly drunk, started a vicious argument, and went berserk. I had no idea they were both carrying guns; otherwise, I would have called off the meeting. I can guarantee you that I will be acquitted of any wrongdoing, so don't waste any more time with your false accusations."

"My God, this is a disaster. What in the hell was Detective Stafford doing there?"

"To be honest, I don't know. But you should be glad that he was because he got me out of there in a hurry and took my statement. It's his job to handle difficult VIP cases, David, as you damn well know."

"I think you and those goddamned Russians cooked this up. You tricked Beckett into doing this."

"No, like I told you, it's all in his will. As of this moment, I am the new Cameron Beckett. Excalibur can either recognize the new reality and profit from it—or I will be signing elsewhere. You already know that Simon and Schuster and HarperCollins are both offering an extra five percent on domestic sales, a seventy-thirty split on electronic rights, and a half-million more in up-front advances for each novel. Listen, I am giving you the courtesy of knowing that the bidding will start at four o'clock this afternoon when I make my public announcement of Cameron's death, per his wife Nicole's request. I was just about to alert the media and every publisher in the city when you called. But now you're the first to know, David. You have the right of first refusal. What's it going to be? Do I make the announcement two hours from now that I am staying with Excalibur—or do I call Thomas Leibowitz at Simon and Schuster or Catherine Dougherty at HarperCollins and strike a deal with them? Your time is running out, David—the auction *will* soon begin."

"You bastard. I don't know how you deceived Beckett into agreeing to this crazy scheme, but you won't get away with it!"

"I don't think you're in the position to tell me what to do, David. And you can tell Tweedledee and Tweedledum to go fuck themselves."

"You're a monster, Anton, an absolute monster!"

"No, it's you and Excalibur that are the monsters. You're the one who had Lassiter and his father kidnapped by your security people and then thrown out of a car onto the street. How do you think it's going to look for you when that information gets into the hands of the police?"

"You wouldn't dare!"

"The hell I wouldn't! How do I know it wasn't your people that set up the murder of Lassiter and Beckett? Maybe it was a secret ploy to create a scandal, get increased media attention, do away with the meddlesome Lassiter, and launch a new and improved Cameron Beckett? The brand is in place and we all know that authors don't matter. They're a fucking dime a dozen. That's the Big Five's and Amazon's overarching philosophy, you cocksucker, so don't deny it. When the police and public find out about your little security team's threat, they're going to think you orchestrated the whole thing for your precious bottom line."

"You can't do that, Anton! It would ruin us!"

"Then don't fuck with me. I'll be dictating the terms on the new Cameron Beckett contract—or Excalibur is done, kaput, finito. The Beckett franchise alone accounts for more than fifty percent of your company's annual revenues. So don't fuck with me."

"Like I said, you're a ruthless bastard, Anton!"

"What do you expect? I'm a literary agent and I grew up in Hell's Kitchen. By the way, David, I'll need to hear back from you in the next half hour."

"A half hour? I can't possibly—"

"I'm calling Leibowitz and Dougherty right now and see what they're willing to offer. Goodbye, David, and good luck in the bidding process."

"Anton, no, please, you can't—"

But the words were cut off as Benedictis punched off. He took a deep breath to compose himself. Jesus Christ, his heart was quaking in his chest like the disastrous earth tremors in Nick Lassiter's *Blind Thrust*. He felt like he was high on coke.

His phone rang. This time he didn't recognize the number.

He felt a ripple of hope. Could it be Popov with news of Rebecca and Danny?

He hit the *Accept* button on his phone's Face Time and there appeared the thick-necked Russian on his two-inch screen. "I am calling to congratulate my new bestselling author. I don't know how you did it, Anton, but you pulled it off."

He felt a wave of guilty revulsion at what he had witnessed at The Victorian Club, but he was able to suppress his shame. But then he wondered something: How did Popov not know that Stafford had been the one to pull the trigger? Hadn't the detective told him?

Holy shit, he suddenly realized, *something is very wrong.*

"I want Rebecca and Danny handed over to me now. I did what you asked."

"*Da,* you did. And as I am a man of my word, I can promise you that you will see them soon, very soon."

"That's not good enough, Alexei. I want to see them now and make sure they're okay."

231

"I'm afraid that is out of the question."

"But we had a deal, goddamnit!"

"And I told you I would honor our agreement."

"I want to see them for myself—please let me talk to them!"

"As you wish."

There was movement, a squeak of chairs, and then on the small Face Time screen he saw his daughter tied to a chair next to his brother Danny. He felt a wave of relief; at least they were alive.

"Are you okay, honey?" he asked, struggling to hold himself together.

"Yes, I'm fine. I'm just…I'm just really scared, Daddy."

"Everything's going to be all right, I promise. I'm doing everything that they want so you'll be fine. I love you, honey. I love you so much."

"I love you too, Daddy."

"What about Danny? Is he okay?"

"Yes, his eye is badly swollen, but that's—"

The picture suddenly changed and his daughter was no longer there. Benedictis yelled into the phone, but Rebecca was gone and Popov's bloodless face and calm, chilling voice returned.

"As you can see, they are both alive and well. Now shut your mouth and listen up. You have one important step to complete before I can release your two loved ones. You need to send out the message that we agreed upon and remind everyone that the Beckett press conference is still on and that you will be making a formal announcement. You will inform the world of Beckett's untimely death. You will also announce that you will be fulfilling his final wish and taking over for him as author to preserve his legacy for future generations."

"I'll take care of it. But you had better not lay a hand on my daughter or Danny."

"Or else what?"

"Or I'll kill you, I fucking promise!"

"That sounds like an empty threat to me. But to show that I admire your courage, I will bring Rebecca and Danny to this press conference of yours. If you complete the job as I have asked you, I will release them so they can join you at the podium. As you know, I am a family man and it always touches me to see a family reunited."

"Are you fucking with me, Alexei?"

"No, I am not, Mr. New Bestselling Author. I am a man of my word, as you know. You take care of the press conference—and I promise that I will leave you alone to write your novels. With my thirty-five percent cut, I will be content and never bother you or your family again. You will, of course, continue on with the money-laundering service you so efficiently provide. But I will not pester you when it comes to your writing career. I know how touchy authors can be."

"You're a bastard, Alexei. You're never going to let me be free of you, are you?"

"You would miss me too much, Anton. But you could always try killing me—if you have the balls for it."

He laughed cruelly—a real *mooh-rah-rah* laugh that reminded Benedictis of the villains he read about daily in his slush pile—and with that the call ended and the screen went dead.

Benedictis threw the phone across the room where it smashed against the wall and landed with a heavy thud on the floor. Then he knelt down to pray.

Although he had grown up in a deeply religious Catholic household, he had, over the years, given up on God. But right now, he felt weak and desperate and he needed strength to carry on. He fell to his knees and prayed, prayed like the young altar boy he had once been, prayed that nothing would happen to his baby girl Rebecca or brother Danny.

And then, he prayed to God to have mercy on his soul for all of his sins.

There were a shitload of them.

CHAPTER 47

MOUNT SINAI MEDICAL CENTER
1176 FIFTH AVENUE

"WE'VE COME TO BUST YOU OUT, NATALIE—HURRY UP AND GET DRESSED!"

Her first thought, as she stared at Squelch and his two cohorts standing breathlessly before her, was that this was some sort of joke. But something in their eyes—a foolhardy gleam and stubborn insistence—told her that they weren't messing around. Not surprisingly, they had even managed to round up a wheelchair to enable a quick escape.

"What is it? What's happened?" she asked, suddenly feeling alert despite her painkiller-induced grogginess.

"Your boss, Benedictis, has just announced that he's giving a speech at four o'clock," said Claggebart, looking dapper as usual, in a frivolous way, in his blue blazer and flamboyant stars-and-stripes ascot. "It's rumored that he's going to take over as the new Cameron Beckett."

"What? You can't be serious?"

"It's buzzing all over the Net," said Bermolito, scrolling through his tablet. "Benedictis will be speaking in the next twenty-seven minutes."

"Where?"

"The DiMaggio Ballroom of the Excelsior Hotel at 120 Central Park South."

"We need to go there and stop him, Natalie, and we need you to get us in," exhorted Squelch. "That son of a bitch stole Nicky's book then killed him and Beckett so he could become a mega-bestselling author. He's a greedy bastard and we've got to stop him. Goddamnit, we're the Devil's Brigade—we can't let him get away with it!"

"Pup Squelch is right," said Bermolito. "We've come too far together to back out now. We've got to do it for Nicky."

She felt a wave of sadness, but also a lightning bolt of sudden determination. Since learning of Nick's death, she had felt utterly morose and defeated, but now she felt rejuvenated. Squelch and Company were right: they were the Devil's Brigade, and they couldn't quit now. But then, the reality of their predicament sunk in: how, exactly, were they going to stop Benedictis?

"What's your plan?" she asked.

"Uh, I'm afraid we're still working on that," admitted Claggebart. "But we need you, Natalie. You really must hurry."

"All right," she said, "but you're going to have to help me. And someone has to look out for Althea."

"Oh shit, the nurse from hell," said Bermolito. "I knew we should have brought chloroform."

"She definitely rules this roost," observed Squelch. "Yeah, we don't want to mess with that gal."

"I'll keep a lookout," proposed Claggebart.

"Good idea," said Natalie.

While he quickly positioned himself at the door, Squelch and Bermolito disconnected her from the IV and monitoring equipment and helped her from the bed. But as she put her full weight on her feet, she felt a wave of dizziness and nearly collapsed. They gripped her tightly and held her upright. But she wasn't just dizzy; the pain in her chest and ribcage was excruciating.

Jesus, she thought. *To think that I was shot twice just last night and now I'm trying to sneak out of the hospital. What the hell am I doing?*

"Are you all right?" asked Squelch.

"Yes, I'm just lightheaded."

"Oh dear, I think I see our friend Althea down the hallway," warned Claggebart. "Good Lord, those buttocks make J-Lo look positively bottomless. If she sits on us, we are all dead, I can promise you that."

"Is she coming this way?" asked Squelch.

"No, she's haranguing another nurse."

"Good. Now Natalie, can you get dressed?"

"I think so if you can hand me my clothes bag. It's below my bed."

"Uh-oh, no time for dressing—our friend Althea's coming this way!"

"Quick, grab my clothes bag and help me into that wheelchair—I'll have to go like this!"

Squelch snatched the wheelchair, spun it around, and helped her into the seat as Bermolito grabbed her clothing bag and a spare hospital blanket, which he used to cover her up once she was seated.

"We've got to go now!" cried Claggebart, ducking back into the room.

"Quick, you go talk to her to distract her," commanded Squelch.

"All right, I'll use my inestimable charm and powers of persuasion."

"Oh, shit, we're really fucked," said Bermolito.

Claggebart disappeared out the room and headed down the hallway to intercept Althea. Squelch pushed the wheelchair towards the open door. Despite her lightheadedness, Natalie smiled with renewed delight as Squelch peeked cautiously out the door, gave the all-clear sign, and began pushing the wheelchair out into the hallway to make their escape. As they made the turn, she saw Claggebart talking to Althea fifty feet down the hall in front of the nurses' station. He was doing a good job of preoccupying her and blocking her view.

"All right, here we go," whispered Squelch, his eyes filled with a wild gleam. "Damn the torpedoes, man, full speed ahead!"

He swung the wheelchair hard right and they started down the hallway in the opposite direction from Claggebart and Althea, making for the elevators. He made sure to be discreet and not to run, but his Converse All-Stars still made squeaking noises on the spanking-clean, acrylic hospital floor as he propelled her down the hallway in the wheelchair at a brisk walk. Bermolito formed a second rearguard in case Claggebart's inestimable charm and powers of persuasion failed to work on Althea.

Of course, they didn't.

She spotted them before they had gone ten feet. "Hey, where the heck do y'all think you're going!" she shouted to them from down the corridor. "Come back here and I mean right now!"

"Oh, shit, she's caught us red-handed! I don't know who I fear worse, her or Popov!" lamented Bermolito.

Squelch laughed riotously. "The game is afoot, Brigadiers. It's life and liberty—or a slow, painful death from Althea using us a whoopee cushion." He tore into a higher gear, now pushing the wheelchair at a reckless speed in the opposite direction of the booming voice.

"Don't you be thinking you can run away from me! Oh, you's in big trouble now!"

"Watch out, the big girl's going to be coming in hot!" warned Bermolito.

"Keep running, keep running, don't look back!" yelled Claggebart from down the hallway as he struggled to keep Althea at bay. "I've got this!"

Oh dear, what have we done! thought Natalie. Now she could hear shuffling feet, multiple alarmed voices, and the sound of hospital instruments crashing to the floor. Jesus, it sounded like a whole army had mobilized to chase them down!

"I'm sorry we had to do it this way," said Squelch breathlessly as they reached the elevator. "But this is what Nicky would have wanted. Our job's not finished in this town, not yet."

"You're right. We've got to confront Benedictis. We can't let him get away with this."

"Don't worry, we won't." The elevator doors opened up. "We're the Devil's Brigade, man. Commandos extraordinaire. No one messes with us and gets away with it. No one!"

She looked down the hallway as Squelch jammed his foot against the elevator door to keep it from closing. Claggebart and Bermolito were now sprinting for the elevator with Althea and two other nurses, a doctor in a white lab jacket, and a pair of security guards chasing after them, the whole gaggle moving at a surprisingly fast clip.

She looked up at Squelch and smiled. "In sickness and in health, we *are* the Devil's Brigade, right? What I mean to say is, even without Nicky, we're always going to have each other and be part of the Brigade? For the rest of our lives?"

"You betcha, baby. We're going to be kneeling before the altar of Robert T. Frederick and his band of black-devil misfits until we take our last dying breath! And that's a promise!"

He stiffened up ramrod straight and delivered a crisp, punctilious salute that would have made the legendary Fighting General proud as Claggebart and Bermolito came dashing up, panting and laughing hysterically.

"Just in the nick of time, Brigadiers!" cheered Natalie, as Squelch hit the elevator button for the first floor. "Now all we have to do is make it to the getaway car!"

CHAPTER 48

DIMAGGIO BALLROOM, EXCELSIOR HOTEL
120 CENTRAL PARK SOUTH

ANTON DE BENEDICTIS stared out at the large crowd that had packed into the venerable DiMaggio Ballroom on the twentieth floor of the Excelsior Hotel. A moment earlier they had been ensconced in patters and murmurs of gossipy conversation, but now, as he cleared his throat at the podium in preparation for his speech, the crowd deferentially hushed. There were perhaps five hundred people in the audience: reporters, photographers, fellow literary agents, publishers, celebrities, loyal fans, power lawyers, and others he didn't recognize. They were seated in neatly arranged rows and looking up at him with palpable anticipation.

It was the biggest literary event in New York in more than a generation.

Feeling self-conscious, he hoped he was projecting the proper combination of mournful solemnity and professional grace in his conservative, charcoal-gray Brooks Brothers' suit and silk Armani tie. He gulped at the sight of the heavy hitters from the media conglomerates, *New York Times, Wall Street Journal,* and *USA Today* sitting in the first two rows. His eyes then drifted to the foot of the podium where two dozen boom microphones stood poised like javelins. He had given speeches before larger groups than this, but he couldn't remember undergoing this much media scrutiny or feeling this nervous before a speaking engagement in his entire life.

His eyes swept the room a final time. David Sloan and Stanton Greenbourne, Excalibur's in-house lead counsel, sat in the second row glowering at him like pit bulls. Seated all around them was a small army of executives, editors, lawyers, and publicists from the Big Five as well as a dozen elegantly appointed souls from the largest Independents and even—horror of horrors—Amazon. Sloan and Excalibur had made a substantial preemptive offer for him as the new Cameron Beckett, but Benedictis wanted to hold an auction and have the greedy publishers duke it out for the rights to his legally-ironclad authorship for the next decade. After everything he had been through, and especially given his unparalleled track record of success, he was going to push them to the proverbial fucking wall.

At the back of the room, he spotted a wheelchair-bound Natalie Perkins entering the room accompanied by Nick Lassiter's three unruly partners in crime. He wasn't surprised that they were here, but nevertheless he cringed at the thought that they might somehow manage to disrupt the proceedings. He prayed that they didn't have some clever trick up their sleeves to undermine or embarrass him.

At the same time, he felt guilty for what had happened to both Nick and his father. Even though he had been poised to shoot Lassiter and Beckett down like dogs when Stafford had unexpectedly burst into the room, he wondered if he would have been able to go through with actually pulling the trigger. Or, would he have murdered them both in cold blood? To save his daughter and brother, would he actually have gone through with it?

He knew the answer. He knew the answer because the only thing he knew for certain in this crazy fucked-up world was that he absolutely had to get Rebecca and Danny back safely. Like any red-blooded American kid born and raised in Hell's Kitchen before it had become gentrified into a yuppie, metrosexual bag of Manhattan dogshit, he was not about to allow his own flesh and blood to be killed if he could fucking help it.

He watched as the Three Stooges wheeled Natalie all the way up to the front row and took seats off to the far right, leaving her in her wheelchair. My God, was she still wearing a hospital gown? They must have busted her out of the hospital and driven her straight over here for her to be in such a chastened state; he would, indeed, need to keep an alert eye out on her and her cohorts for suspicious activity.

He then spotted Popov and his knot of bodyguards slithering into the auditorium. The people in the crowd gawked at them fearfully and whispered urgently amongst themselves as the mob boss and his motley crew took seats off to the far left in the first row, mirroring Natalie and the others on the other side of the room. As he sat down, Popov smiled menacingly up at him. Benedictis wondered where the son of a bitch was holding Rebecca and Danny, and prayed that nothing had happened to them. Hopefully, they were nearby and he could quickly wrap up his public announcement and secure their release.

He reminded himself that all he had to do was his part and they would be set free, assuming of course that Popov didn't go back on his word and double-cross him. *The bastard.* Benedictis wondered what trick he, too, might have up his sleeve.

Feeling a little prickle of anxiety now with all the key parties assembled, he turned back to face his audience, cleared his throat, and pulled the microphone closer.

"Several hours ago my dear friend and colleague of twenty-two years— Cameron Barnaby Beckett IV—was shot and killed in a tragic shooting. I am not here to comment or give details on the incident, as the police are still investigating. It is a tragedy beyond words. The reason that we are all gathered here is to pay tribute to the man that has brought so much joy to the world with his gripping suspense novels for so many years. He will be greatly missed. If you could all bow your heads now, let's please have a moment of silence for Cameron Beckett, the greatest writer of his generation."

The room went silent as the heads bowed. Several people wept. As the seconds ticked off, the silence seemed interminable to Benedictis. He felt like a snake standing before all of these people, pretending as if he had done nothing wrong when he was an accomplice to double-murder. It was in that self-reflective moment that he spied Detective Stafford walking into the room and taking a seat in the back row.

The NYPD man was alone.

Benedictis continued: "You've already heard fragments about what has happened in the past two days, and many of you want answers. But the only thing I can say is that Cameron Beckett was a great and noble friend, colleague, husband, and father. Indeed, the world will never be the same without him."

He reached into a canvas bag lying on the floor behind him and pulled out the iconic .38-caliber machine-gun pistol that he had taken down from his office wall only this morning. Instantly, murmured voices of panic swept through the room.

He held up his hands in a gesture of mollification. "Please do not be alarmed. This gun belonged to the legendary gangster Baby Face Nelson, Public Enemy #1. The firing pin has been removed and the gun won't even fire." He lifted the weapon for all to see. "I brought this beauty here today because Cameron Beckett gave it to me fifteen years ago to thank me and celebrate the occasion of our tenth *New York Times* bestselling novel together. He gifted it to me along with Nelson's bullet-proof vest because he knew how passionate I was about gangsters when I was growing up in Hell's Kitchen. For the past fifteen years, this machine-gun pistol has been hanging on my wall along with Nelson's bullet-proof vest. I brought it here because I wanted to show it to you all. This is the greatest gift of my life and it was Cameron Beckett who gave it to me."

He set the museum-piece gun down on the podium, feeling himself choking up. With an effort, he forced himself to maintain his composure. He looked at Popov and saw that he was smiling approvingly. The Russian mobster, too, appeared to feel some sort of special kinship with the legendary gangster Baby Face Nelson.

"Cameron and I have talked extensively about what he wanted to do with his stories in the unlikely event of his death or incapacitation. His primary goal was to not be forgotten or leave behind only an enormous backlist that started with *The Quiet Killer* in the early 1990s. More than anything else, he wanted his brand to extend far into his afterlife and he wanted someone he knew well and trusted to carry on his world-renowned tradition of suspense. That person, ladies and gentlemen, is me, his loyal friend, confidant, editor-in-chief, and literary agent for the past twenty-two years: Anton De Benedictis."

The crowd breathed a collective gasp of shock. The reporters began to murmur audibly, chatter amongst themselves, and scratch away at their computers and notepads. His formal announcement, delivered before so many titans of the publishing industry, was big news not just here in New York, but in the global literary marketplace.

"I have here a copy of Cameron's last will and testament," Benedictis continued, pulling out the document. "It states that I am to continue on as the writer under his name as I am the one who loyally guided, nurtured, and served as his editorial consultant for more than two decades. This is the way that Cameron wanted it. I have already spoken to his wife, Nicole, and this is the way she wants it as well. Cam and Nicole both don't want Cameron Beckett's name to disappear. He has spent the past twenty-two years writing the best suspense novels the world has ever seen, and in doing so, he has built up a global fan base of over one hundred million loyal readers. It is for these loyal fans that I will be continuing on Cameron Beckett's great work.

"Of course, there are many precedents to this: Tom Clancy and Vince Flynn; V.C. Andrews and her uncredited authors; Robert Ludlum and Eric Van Lustbader who has continued the Bourne series; and, of course, Ian Fleming and the many writers who have carried on the World War II spymaster's James Bond series, to name just a few. The world's readers expect something special from a Cameron Beckett suspense novel and, by Jove, I am determined to deliver. I promise that the Beckett franchise will continue with all the great characters and spine-tingling suspense the whole world has grown accustomed to. Furthermore, ladies and gentlemen, I am here to inform you that the future publisher of the novels is to be determined here and now in a formal *auction*."

Another rumble of surprise propagated through the stunned crowd like a tsunami. The publishing executives and their well-heeled lackeys were muttering, chattering, and haggling with one another like characters out of a Dickens novel.

It was then he saw Popov smile at him, again. The mobster followed up by raising his hand in what appeared to be a prearranged signal. A moment later, four of the Russian's black-leather-jacketed goons materialized in the back of the room with Rebecca and Danny. To Benedictis's surprise, the goons promptly released them and they started walking cautiously down the main aisle towards the front of the room. He made eye contact again with Popov; the Russian gave a slight nod and again smiled. Feeling a wave of joy and relief, Benedictis dipped his head in thanks as his daughter and brother sat down safely a few rows from the front. Popov cordially bowed his head in reply; fancy that, the son of bitch had kept his word after all!

Now it was time to wrap things up. Rebecca and Danny were free at last!

He breathed a sigh of relief and looked towards the ceiling. *I had no choice in all this. You know that God, right?*

He continued on with his speech: "I know all of this must come as a shock to you," he declared to the audience, feeling a renewed energy with Rebecca and Danny now safe and sound. "But I want you all to know that I am not going to pretend to be Cameron Beckett. It would not be fair to him for me to proclaim myself as the second coming of such a literary icon. My goal is simply to satisfy readers and carry on the proud literary tradition that he has created and sustained for the past three decades. Thank you for your thoughts and prayers and now let us proceed with the auction portion of—"

"Before you do that, my dear fellow, do you mind terribly if I have a quick word," a voice interrupted from the back. "I think I should have some say in all this, considering that reports of my death have been greatly exaggerated."

He looked all the way to the last row of the ballroom. A man with a thick mane of silver hair, a pair of dark reflective sunglasses, and a frumpy Savile Row suit was parting his way through the audience in the back, poking his cane on the floor like an old blind man. Suddenly, the man shed his wig, sunglasses, and frumpy suit jacket—and standing before Benedictis was none other than Cameron Beckett!

"But you're...you're supposed to be—"

"No, I'm not dead, mate." He waved expansively towards the audience. "As you can all see, ladies and gentlemen, the 'Aussie James Patterson' is very much alive."

"But I saw you die. There was…there was blood and chunks…everywhere."

"Well, let's just say blood and chunks can be deceiving. And so can looks. I mean, just look at you, digger. Here all these years I thought you were my good friend and literary agent—but it turns out you're really just a bloody crook!"

"I am not a crook!"

"Of course you aren't—and neither was Richard Millhouse Nixon. You're only working for the Russian mafia and were a split second away from shooting me down in cold blood!"

He felt insane panic. "That's not true!"

"Really? Do you deny pulling a gun on me?"

He didn't respond. This was a disaster and he had no idea what to do. He looked down at Popov, who was muttering something and gesturing frantically at his bodyguards. He then looked at Rebecca and Danny off to his right. With so many people in the room, were they safe? Only as long as Popov and his goons didn't do something crazy.

He could hear his own heart pounding now.

There had to be a way out of this.

Should I make a run for it? But what about Rebecca and Danny? He couldn't just leave them here to fend for themselves. Or could he? He could signal them to follow him and then make a mad dash for one of the exits. No, that was too risky. He couldn't let anything happen to them, not after he had worked so hard to secure their release. They were the two people in the world he cared most about.

Beckett held up a sheath of papers. "By the way, Anton, I also want you to know that I've redone my will and you're no longer in it."

He suddenly felt faint and could hardly breathe.

"But there is someone else present in this room that is in my revised will. Ladies and gentlemen, I give you the new bestselling author operating under the *nom de plume* Cameron Beckett—and his name is Nick Lassiter!"

CHAPTER 49

DIMAGGIO BALLROOM, EXCELSIOR HOTEL
120 CENTRAL PARK SOUTH

LASSITER stood up from his tenth-row seat, peeled off his fake beard and mustache, tossed away his mirror aviator glasses and neck brace, and strode forward towards the stage, moving parallel with Beckett. He had seen Natalie enter the room with his buddies, and he had watched Benedictis lie like the crook he was, and throughout it all he had remained quiet and incognito. But it hadn't been easy. Not when he was desperate to tell his fiancée and friends that he was still alive. And not when he wanted to rip Benedictis's head off. As he strode towards the stage, he heard Squelch, Claggebart, and Bermolito give a rousing cheer. They proceeded to hoist up Natalie in her wheelchair so she could get a good look at him. He gave a thumbs-up sign and grinned triumphantly at them. In response, they beamed back proudly at him.

I love you, he thought, as his and Natalie's eyes caught one another. *I know I've got some serious flaws and I know I should have told you the truth, but I hope you still love me, too.*

"Ladies and gentleman," said Beckett with a P.T. Barnum-like flair for the dramatic. "As I've just said, Nick Lassiter, not Anton De Benedictis, will be taking my place, for I truly am retiring. Nick's first published novel will be *Blind Thrust,* the very novel that Anton and I stole from him three years ago. I made a mistake and now I am attempting to rectify that mistake—in a big, big way."

"This is madness, he's no author!" cried Benedictis. "You always wanted *me* to be the new *you!*"

"That was before you pointed a Beretta at me, mate." He then looked at Lassiter. "I know, Nick, that I shall be the first to read *Blind Thrust,* but what about your father? I should think he would want a go at it. Now that would be top shelf, don't you think?"

From the rear of the auditorium, Lassiter watched as his father, Austin Brewbaker, stepped forward. He commanded a force of more than a dozen armed CIA officers wearing plainclothed suits and a full police SWAT tactical team equipped with raid-gear body armor, dark blue uniforms, and military-style assault rifles. A murmur of surprise rippled through the room at the sight of the small army. Lassiter and Beckett both smiled at one another as another rousing cheer went up from Squelch, Claggebart, and Bermolito.

"Nobody move!" shouted his father. "Anton De Benedictis and Alexei Popov, you are both under arrest! Come with us quietly and no harm will come to you!"

"But you are supposed to be dead!" bellowed Popov in disbelief.

"It appears that, thanks to Kevlar and a little thing called a ballistic trauma plate, news of my demise, too, has been greatly exaggerated. Your man fired three shots and all three burrowed safely into my body armor. He should have been more thorough and checked to make sure I was dead."

The Russian smiled approvingly. "My compliments, Austin. You are one clever bastard."

But it was nothing but a ruse. With surprising speed, Popov dashed to the podium, quickly took Benedictis hostage by putting him in an arm clamp, and pointed a pistol at his head.

An audible gasp echoed through the auditorium.

This was followed by a slew of semiautomatic weapons—from both the plainclothed CIA contingent and the blue-uniformed SWAT team—pointing up at the mob boss.

But they were too late.

"Everyone, stay where you are!" cried Popov, now the one in control as he tightened his grip around Benedictis's throat. "Or I'll kill him where he stands!"

But Brewbaker and his small army of counterintelligence and law enforcement personnel paid him no mind. They encircled and disarmed Popov's stunned bodyguards with alacrity.

"Give it up, Popov!" said his father, his first objective now achieved. "All of your men have been disarmed! Put down your weapon and surrender at once!"

With his men out of the equation and now being handcuffed, the Russian mob boss looked desperately around the room, searching for escape routes.

"I'm warning you to back off!" he hissed to the armed men closing in on the stage. Still clutching Benedictis in a headlock, he slipped his pistol into his pocket, picked up the machine-gun pistol that had belonged to Baby Face Nelson with his free hand, and let loose with a quick spray over their heads to drive them back.

The combined CIA-SWAT team halted in its tracks. Several people at the rear of the auditorium took the opportunity to dash for the exits.

"Well, well," said the Russian when the room had quieted. He had let go of Benedictis for a moment to grab a pair of fresh magazines from the agent's bag with his free hand and was stuffing them into his pockets. "I knew that my friend Anton here hadn't removed the firing pin after all. I mean, what is the point of having a gun that doesn't shoot? That would be un-American. So what were you planning to do with this, Anton? Were you planning on killing me per chance?"

The literary agent didn't reply as Brewbaker and the joint CIA-SWAT team resumed inching its way towards the front of the room. From the other side, Detective Stafford, carrying his NYPD sidearm, also crept towards the stage. Lassiter realized that Benedictis must have planned all along on using the machine-gun pistol to get his daughter and brother back, if things hadn't unfolded according to plan and Popov had gone back on his deal to release them. Kudos to the literary agent for being willing to risk his own life for his family; but unfortunately, his actions had also managed to put a high-capacity weapon in the hands of Popov just as the wily son of a bitch was about to be arrested.

"I told you to stop moving!" snarled the Russian, taking Benedictis hostage again.

"It's over, Popov!" shouted his father. "Put the gun down and step away from Mr. Benedictis!"

"You cannot arrest me. I have diplomatic immunity!"

"There is no diplomatic immunity when it comes to spying on U.S. soil. Now step away from Mr. Benedictis!"

"This is entrapment. You set all this up by faking your deaths."

"Drop the gun now, or we will fire. These men with me are shooters—and I mean they can hit the Romanov Star from a thousand yards. If you value your life, drop your weapon now!"

Popov looked around the room, weighing his options. To Lassiter, time seemed to stand still. He wondered if perhaps it had been an unwise move for his father to attempt the arrest in front of all of these people. But in doing so, he had caught the Russian red-handed at kidnapping. Benedictis's daughter and brother had been released from Popov's captivity minutes earlier just as his father had predicted, which meant that his overall plan to simultaneously secure the hostages and take Popov and Benedictis into custody would have worked if not for the quick-thinking Popov.

Stafford took two steps forward and held up his hands, calling for the mob boss to remain calm. "Put the gun down, Alexei—it's over," he called out. "You are surrounded and have nowhere to go."

"You double-crossed me, you bastard!"

The detective said nothing, keeping his gun pointed at Popov's massive chest. Meanwhile, the combined CIA-SWAT team methodically moved in closer. Lassiter glanced at Natalie. Like everyone else in the room, she looked on with tense anticipation. Keeping the machine-gun pistol pointed at Benedictis's head, Popov started backing up slowly with his captive towards the door behind the stage. Almost imperceptibly, the CIA squad shadowed the Russian's movements and began to fan out towards the stage with their pistols drawn and leveled on him.

"Stop right there, Popov!" commanded his father. "You'll never get out of this room alive! So give it up!"

The Russian continued backing up towards the stage door exit. The room went totally quiet. Anticipating a sudden eruption of violence, most people were crouched down protectively in their seats, mesmerized by the unfolding drama, while a few crawled along the floor or slipped away quietly from the back of the room.

Stafford closed in from the other side. "You have no escape options, Popov. Put the gun down now!"

The Russian smiled insolently, like a man unafraid of death. "I'm afraid you Americans have, as usual, underestimated my—"

His words were cut off as Benedictis jerked away from his grip and grabbed the Glock from his coat pocket. But as he raised the pistol to fire, the Russian opened up with the machine-gun pistol. Benedictis took two bullets in the chest at point-blank range, staggering backwards. Still using the literary agent as a shield, Popov depressed the trigger of the antique weapon in rapid succession, letting loose with a spray at the plainclothed CIA squad and the blue-uniformed SWAT team, mowing down three CIA men in suits up front like a scythe.

Lassiter saw Benedictis fall to the floor and drop the pistol he had managed to wrestle away from Popov. Now both sides opened up. The gunfire roared through the room like a roll of thunder, turning the scene to chaos as people scrambled from the room, dove for cover, and ran into one another trying to escape. Lassiter was relieved when he saw Squelch herd Natalie to the third row to take cover.

Then he looked back at Popov.

The Russian, screaming like a charging Cossack, ripped loose with one final burst, threw open the rear door, and bolted out of the DiMaggio Ballroom.

The chase was on.

CHAPTER 50

THERE WAS A MOMENT OF CONFUSION—his father was mouthing something and gesturing frantically to Stafford and his men—and then they started after Popov. But Lassiter beat them to the door: he wanted the son of a bitch for himself and wasn't about to let the Russian get away.

Earlier in the afternoon, when his father had fully briefed him on the Popov-Benedictis relationship and had scripted out the plan to arrest the two men, Lassiter had felt a sense of impending justice and closure. Both of them would get the punishment they deserved and good would triumph over evil. But now that he saw the damned Russian attempting to steal away from the ballroom, all of that was thrown out the window.

It filled him with volcanic rage.

His father had informed him that Popov was likely being protected not merely through his diplomatic immunity, but from someone high up in the U.S. government. Well, here was his chance to show the Russian mob boss that his special protection was useless. With a little luck, he might be able to get the bastard himself.

Reaching down, he picked up the Glock from the stage floor, shouldered his way through the rear door, and saw Popov dashing down the hallway of the legendary hotel, moving with surprising grace and speed for such a big man. The Russian quickly disappeared around the corner and out of sight.

Lassiter tore off after him, his sneakers burning across the carpet. He was younger and faster, but Popov was a professional criminal and would undoubtedly know how to set a clever trap. Lassiter knew he would have to be careful not to get too close until he had a clean shot.

He darted down the hallway in pursuit, keeping an eye out for trickery.

Up ahead, around the corner, he heard alarmed voices. Taking the corner in an all-out sprint, he saw two hotel guests who had been knocked to the floor scrambling to their feet, and beyond them his target Popov. The Russian was dashing down the hallway towards the fire stairs, the machine-gun pistol clutched tightly in his hands.

"Jesus H. Christ! What kind of hotel is this!" shouted one of the bowled-over guests, shaking his fist angrily.

Lassiter darted past them and drove his shoulder into the heavy steel fire escape door. As he started to enter the stairwell, an eruption of gunfire from above sent him reeling to the concrete floor. In his peripheral vision, he caught a blur of movement and then Popov was gone.

But why was the Russian going up rather than down? Was he laying some sort of trap? Or did he have an escape plan that involved the rooftop?

Rising to his feet, he started after him. When he reached five levels up, he heard a gun blast and a door bang open above him followed by a second door being busted open below. He looked over the railing to see who was coming up behind him.

From several floors below, his father and Stafford peered up at him. They were accompanied by the armed CIA officers and SWAT team.

"Wait, Son! What are you doing!" his father yelled.

Ignoring him, Lassiter dashed on. He felt a powerful need to catch Popov himself, especially after everything the Russian had put Natalie through. When he reached the rooftop door, he saw that the lock had been shot off. He cautiously poked his head through the open door, instantly drawing a blistering fire from his adversary.

He ducked behind the wall and then returned fire, forcing Popov to retreat behind a low balustrade that ran along the middle of the roof. Charging onto the rooftop, he quickly took cover behind a ventilation turbine. Bullets whirred past him like hissing snakes, kicking up gravel from the rooftop and ricocheting off the concrete walls of the stairwell.

At that precise moment, a WABC-TV and Eyewitness News chopper appeared above the skyscrapers to the west, sweeping towards them like a huge dragonfly.

Lassiter popped up like a gopher and opened fire. To his surprise, he caught Popov in the shoulder and the man went down hard on the rooftop.

Jesus, I actually got the son of a bitch?

He heard him groaning and cursing. The Russian then called out to him.

"That was a good shot, Lassiter. But you are a fool for following me up here. Now they will have to kill you."

What in the hell was the guy talking about? "Nice try, Popov. Now why would someone want to kill me?"

"You don't know what all this is about, do you, Nick? My God, what Boy Scouts you and your father are."

Lassiter continued to watch as the news helicopter rumbled in from the west. They were yelling loudly now so their voices weren't drowned out by the chopper. "You're right I don't know what's really going on. So why don't you clue me in."

"I'm a CIA asset, Nick. Just like your father—except that I am a double agent and he is a senior officer at Langley. We are both on the *Company* payroll. The only difference is he has official cover and I do not. But we both work for the same people. Except now I have become an embarrassment."

"You're a CIA asset? Bullshit!"

"Listen to me, you fool. I am not lying. I have no reason to lie to you."

"I don't trust you or believe you. You're a fucking crook."

"I'll admit that I got carried away. But I wouldn't be the first person in this town to abuse my power, now would I? Absolute power corrupts absolutely—haven't you read your Balzac, Nikolai?"

The Russian stood up, and Lassiter realized how close to the edge he was. Jesus, the shot might have sent him toppling over the edge. "All right, you've said your piece. What am I supposed to do about it?"

"Nothing. But your father can do something. For the time being though, I am going to have to make my escape. We Russians always have a backup plan." He nodded towards the approaching helicopter. "My ride is here. Do not try and stop me, Nikolai, or they will open fire on you."

"Have you lost your mind? You're not getting away, goddamnit!"

"Like hell I'm—"

The words died in his mouth as the sound of a single gunshot pierced the air. Suddenly, Popov's face and upper chest opened up, squirting blood like paint splattered across a Jackson Pollack canvas. He reeled backwards, hit the balustrade, and his legs came out from beneath him. His hands reached out and clawed at air as he plunged over the edge of the Excelsior Hotel rooftop. As he fell, he let out an eerie, deafening wail that sounded like it harkened back to the days of Peter the Great.

Lassiter couldn't believe it.

He looked at the helicopter. Framed in the open sliding door was a sniper clutching a rifle with a mounted scope. The dark-haired shooter looked to be a male, but unbeknownst to Lassiter the killer was actually a much-sought after professional female assassin. In fact, the woman was of Italian heritage, but with her routine clever disguises, polyglot mastery of languages, and surgical alteration of her Roman nose, it was never possible to know for sure. Her given name was Angela Valentina Ferrara, but years ago she had become a full-time contract killer and forsaken her real name for aliases. Her current alias was Skyler, no last name. She also had a nom de guerre—Diego Gomez—a fictitious name created by her control agent. The invented Spanish assassin Gomez remained a mystery, a phantom of the files in the hands of the international law enforcement community. For her own security, Skyler was determined to keep it that way.

But Nick Lassiter knew none of this. All he knew was that somehow Popov had been betrayed and the person holding the smoking gun looked to be a dark-haired male sniper in a helicopter. He had no idea that he was staring at one of the most lethal assassins on the planet and a woman he would one day come to work with in international intelligence operations and know well.

Suddenly, the rooftop door banged open behind him. He turned to see his father, Stafford, and a pack of government suits and blue-uniformed SWAT men pouring onto the rooftop. He jumped out from behind the turbine and ran towards them, waving his arms.

"Be careful, there's a sniper in that chopper! He just shot Popov and the Russian fell over the edge!"

His father looked cautiously up at the helicopter, locked eyes for a moment with the shooter, and then the helicopter banked hard right and flew away to the west, no longer posing a threat. Though Lassiter couldn't be sure, he thought he saw a flicker of recognition on his father's face at the sight of the sniper. And then the look vanished as the helicopter arced above the rampart of skyscrapers and disappeared from sight.

Lassiter ran to the edge to ascertain the fate of Popov. Was it possible he could have, like some sort of Rasputin, survived being shot and falling twenty floors to the street below? The answer, he quickly realized, was no. There sprawled out lifelessly on the pavement was the Russian. One of his arms was wrenched back at a grotesque angle. Blood seeped from his head like a giant growing ink blot.

His father peeked over the edge alongside him and, after a few seconds, shook his head in exasperation. He wheeled around and glared at his CIA team and the blue-uniformed SWAT unit.

"Damnit, we needed him alive! Those were my explicit orders!"

A well-honed, silver-haired man wearing a SWAT uniform stepped forward carrying a Heckler & Koch MP5 assault rifle, the same weapon carried by all of his men. "Unfortunately for you and your cohorts, Mr. Director, I have new orders. Drop your weapons, all of you—now!"

Lassiter watched with stunned surprise as the SWAT team in dark blue suddenly turned their automatic rifles on his father and the other CIA officers in civilian clothes, as well as Stafford and two uniformed cops who had arrived on the scene.

"Son of a bitch," said Austin Brewbaker. "I thought I smelled a rat. If you're name's not really David Thomas and you're not a real SWAT commander, who the hell are you?"

"Colonel Jake Wendell Emery, USA Retired. It should come as no surprise to you, Mr. Director, that my men and I, as well as that sniper in the chopper, are not officially attached to the National Clandestine Service formerly known as Operations. We are private contractors. Which is to say that we perform *real* black-on-black instead of just watching it at the multiplex like you folks. You, sir, happen to have made some people above GS-15 very angry back at Langley. Now instruct your men to drop their weapons!"

Lassiter studied the colonel and his hard-looking men, lamenting the sudden change in circumstances. His father—a high-ranking CIA official—had been fooled by his own people. The guys in the blue uniforms and the sniper that had just flown away in the chopper were neither allies nor real officers, but a rogue CIA paramilitary outfit. *Jesus,* he thought bitterly, *we are so fucked.*

"No, I will give them no such order," said his father defiantly.

Emery glowered at him. "A Mexican standoff is it? You sure that's the way you want to play it?" He didn't wait for the answer. He motioned to two of his men in the dark-blue SWAT uniforms and body armor covering Brewbaker's plainclothed CIA team with their assault rifles. "Captain Sheehan and Sergeant Shafroth, please liquidate Director Brewbaker and his men immediately. Do it now. These men pose a direct threat to the national security of the United States!"

The captain and sergeant stepped forward with their rapid-fire weapons.

His father shook his head in disgust. "Americans murdering Americans—I never thought I'd see the terrible day."

"You can say that again," said Lassiter disdainfully. "At least tell us *why* you're doing this?"

Emery considered a moment before shaking his head. "Sorry, no time for chit-chat, gentlemen—we have our orders." The colonel shifted his gaze to his father. "But I will tell you, Director Brewbaker, that you did manage to fool me earlier today outside The Victorian Club. Your little trick of playing possum by pretending to be dead was a clever piece of misdirection. I should have known you'd be wearing a Kevlar vest equipped with a ballistic trauma plate. I was watching you from the rooftop and, I must say, you had me convinced. Perhaps you missed your calling as an actor?"

"I've been with the Company for thirty years and I've never seen a shameful disgrace such as this. This is murder, pure and simple. You know damned well that Deputy Director Harcourt will never get away with this."

"Captain Sheehan and Sergeant Shafroth, if you would please discharge your weapons now. We have a schedule to keep and further discussion is of no strategic value. Now that is a direct order!"

He took a step back, expecting swift compliance.

Lassiter looked at Captain Sheehan, pleading with his eyes. "Why don't you ask Emery why his mandarin bosses at Langley have been protecting a petty Russian mobster all these years and are now poised to kill the head of the CIA's Russian desk? Does that make any fucking sense to you?"

Sheehan and Shafroth just stood there, unable to make a decision.

"Jesus Christ!" he implored them. "Can't you guys think for yourselves? Your orders are total bullshit, can't you see that? You're being ordered to murder American citizens to avoid embarrassment and humiliation from a dead, rogue Russian arms dealer who served as a double agent working for the CIA. Oh yes, that's what Popov told me before that sniper in the chopper took him out, and the Russian had *no reason* to lie to me. He was afraid of the CIA, but not me or my father. In fact, he wanted to surrender only to my dad!"

"That's enough, goddamnit!" snarled Colonel Emery. "Captain Sheehan and Sergeant Shafroth, you two are relieved of command and will face charges." He turned towards two other men. "Corporal Perron and Private Kohnstamm, my order stands. Carry it out at once!"

The two younger men stepped forward.

"Shoot them, goddamnit!"

They hesitated. Then the one to the left, Perron, said, "We can't kill innocent Americans, sir. It's not right."

"That's not your call to make, soldier. All right, if none of you can carry out a direct order, I'm going to do it my—"

"What in the name of General Jack D. Ripper is going on here?"

Lassiter looked up to see Squelch, Claggebart, and Bermolito standing in the shadows of the stairwell door that led to the rooftop.

It was just the distraction he and his father needed.

Suddenly, Austin Brewbaker lunged at Emery, tackling him at the knees at the same time Stafford reached out and tried to knock away his pistol with a well-delivered karate chop. His father and the colonel struggled over the gun, which went off as Lassiter reached out to grab Emery by the arm to help his father. He saw Stafford go down, his shirt and jacket smoldering from the point-blank-range gunshot. Then a second round was fired and Lassiter felt himself driven backwards by the gunshot, followed quickly by a burning sensation in his lungs.

My God, I've been hit! he thought. *Just like Stafford and Natalie!*

He fell to the rooftop next to the still and lifeless Stafford, feeling a searing pain as the world around him erupted in a confused melee. Bodies flew past in a blur. Bursts of automatic weapons fire echoed across the Manhattan skyline. Primitive-sounding screams and grunts added to the orchestra of violence as the two sides—one a rogue CIA paramilitary outfit clad in dark-SWAT-blue, the other his father's genuine NCS team in civilian clothing—battled in close quarters.

Despite his bullet wound, Lassiter rose to his feet and attacked Emery, who had managed to escape from his father's clasp and was crawling towards his pistol. With his father now preoccupied fighting another blue-uniformed enemy combatant, Lassiter attempted a diving tackle and was able to bring the colonel down with a loud thud. He then punched him in the face, drawing blood from Emery's left nostril. As he raised his arm to deliver a second blow, he was kneed in the balls. Unexpectedly, he found himself on top of nothing but the roof and Emery had disappeared. Groaning in agony, he felt a deep, sickening, burning sensation hit him like a sledgehammer.

He looked desperately for the pistol. There it was, only a few feet away.

But now he spotted Emery. He, too, was staring intently at the weapon.

The colonel moved first.

But he was not quick enough. Lassiter knocked him to the rooftop with a fierce body check, dove for the weapon, plucked it up off the gravel, and shot him twice in the chest. The colonel grunted heavily, collapsed onto the rooftop, and went still. Unlike his paramilitary soldiers under him, he was not wearing Kevlar body armor. Now he had paid the price for it.

Feeling exhaustion and traumatic blood loss kicking in, Lassiter took a moment to catch his breath and look around.

He saw a flash of shiny steel in his peripheral vision. A rogue SWAT man wearing full body armor materialized to his left with an assault rifle trained on his father. Lassiter swung Emery's gun to his chest, pointed it, and squeezed the trigger. He saw the SWAT man's face register astonishment as a little red blot appeared at his unprotected neck. He squeezed the trigger two more times and the man staggered and fell to the rooftop, crashing heavily like a slab of beef.

Now Lassiter heard a burst of heavy gunfire to his right. Turning in the direction of the sound, he felt another sharp blow followed by a burning sensation, this time in his shoulder. Shit, he had been hit again! Falling to his knees, he was suddenly blasted with sound from all directions: voices screaming and shouting, feet running towards him, wounded men groaning.

He tried to get to his feet, but failed.

He squeezed his hand against his body to clamp shut the flow of blood, feeling overcome by great weariness. Again, he tried to climb to his feet. This time he collapsed onto the gravel rooftop, unable to move.

The battle quickly came to an end.

He lay there sprawled on the rooftop, blood pouring from his body. The world seemed unusually peaceful as he stared out at the midtown skyline, thinking about how beautiful the city was in early June and how much he would like to take

Natalie on a stroll through Central Park holding hands with her.

Then he heard, or thought he heard, her voice.

"Hold on, Nicky. You're going to make it—just hold on!"

"Natalie, is that you?" he croaked, struggling to bring her into focus. Now he noticed that his father was standing next to her along with Squelch, Claggebart, and Bermolito. Their faces were fuzzy like a dream.

"Yes, it's me," she replied. "Just hang in there."

"Did I tell you I love you?" he said foggily. "In fact, I love all of you guys. If I die, I want you all to know that."

"We love you too, Nicky," said his dad. "And don't even think about dying on us. I'm your father, goddamnit—I can't outlive you."

"I'll try...try my best, Dad," he muttered, and then he was lifted onto a stretcher and carried away by paramedics.

"Hang in there, Nicky. We'll be clinking Harvey Wallbanger glasses and sharing a big, fat Maureen Dowd edible soon enough, I promise you," he heard Squelch say encouragingly, as they started down into the stairwell.

"Thanks...Squelchie. Hey Dad, did we...get the bad guys?"

"Yes, Son, we got them all. You're going to be okay."

"What about that...that sniper? You looked...like...you recognized him."

"We'll talk about that later, Nick. For now, you just hang in there. You're going to be fine."

He wanted to believe him, but he could feel himself getting weaker by the second. He reached out his hand and felt a woman's gentle touch as they bumped and jostled down the stairs.

"Is that you, Natalie?"

"Yes, it's me."

"You shouldn't...shouldn't be out of your wheelchair. You're still hurt."

"I'm a fast healer and my adrenaline is flowing. But most importantly, I want to be here with you. I love you, Nicky."

He heard her quietly sobbing as she spoke. "Don't cry," he said. "You heard my...dad...he said I'm going to be okay."

"He's right, you are," she said, but he could tell she was dreadfully worried about his chances. "I love you, Nicky! I love you!"

"I love you too. If I die, I want you to always remember that."

His vision went blurry again. He felt a sensation of moving faster now. Then he lost consciousness for a moment before coming back. How much time had passed he couldn't tell? Now they were moving down a hallway. He looked up at the faces, but this time they were all fuzzy and unfamiliar. He heard an elevator bell ring and had a fluttery feeling of rapid descent, like he was on a diving small-engine aircraft. He knew that Natalie and the others were no longer with him because he couldn't hear their voices anymore.

Then everything started to slowly go black, the world to slip away.

For the second time in his life, he felt himself dying.

Only this time he knew it was for real.

EPILOGUE – ONE YEAR LATER

LOOKOUT MOUNTAIN CEMETERY
GOLDEN, COLORADO

NATALIE PERKINS, great-granddaughter of legendary book editor Maxwell Perkins, stared down at the granite gravestone of Nicholas Lassiter with tears in her eyes. The cemetery sat atop Lookout Mountain, a massive butte with an elevation of nearly 7,500 feet above sea level that overlooked the small town of Golden and the sprawling Mile High City twelve miles further to the east. Buffalo Bill Cody—the legendary scout, Indian fighter, showman, and friend to Sitting Bull, Teddy Roosevelt, and Generals Sheridan and Custer—was buried here. The promontory's earliest known inhabitants had been the Utes, who prized the mountain as a lookout point for spotting Cheyenne, Arapaho, Kiowa, and Comanche enemies and tracking buffalo along the western edge of the Great Plains.

Natalie Perkins thought it was an appropriate resting spot for the one great love of her life.

She looked up from the gravestone out at the majestic plains to the east. She stood next to Nick's parents, Squelch, Claggebart, and Bermolito, and Cameron Beckett and his wife, Nicole. They were all dressed in funeral black on the first anniversary of what they all called "the New York Affair." As if what had transpired was not a study in wild, violent criminal chaos, but rather a touching golden-era Hollywood movie featuring Cary Grant and Audrey Hepburn. Feeling her throat constrict with sadness, Natalie couldn't believe a whole year had passed since the tragedy. She looked at the pink granite headstone and thought of how much she had loved Nick.

"We all miss you, Son," said Nick's father solemnly.

"Yes, and we will always love and remember you," added Nick's mother, Vivian Lassiter, with feeling.

Squelch, Claggebart, and Bermolito said nothing. But their teary-eyed faces said it all.

"I can't thank you enough. You changed my life, Nicholas," said Cameron Beckett mournfully. He then looked lovingly at his wife, who looked uncannily like Nicole Kidman in the film *Australia*, even down to the corn-silk blonde hair, highborn manner, and ruddy cheeks. "I wouldn't have realized what was most important to me if not for you, mate."

Austin Brewbaker took a step forward. "What you did changed the lives of a lot of people, Nick," he quietly intoned, looking down at the gravestone and talking as if his precious son was still alive. "You were instrumental in helping your country wrap up a most difficult case, a case that has ultimately proved to be one of the biggest intelligence scandals in the nation's history. Now that the dust has settled, we've handed out indictments to more than two dozen CIA officials, agents, and covert operatives as well as broken the back of the powerful Odessa Mafia in Brighton Beach. You helped crack the case for us, Son. By going to New York and stirring things up with *Blind Thrust*, you enabled us to roll up not one, but two, rogue organizations. America owes you a great deal of gratitude, and we all salute you."

With military precision, Natalie and the other members of the Devil's Brigade stood ramrod straight, raised their right arms, and gave crisp salutes.

"We all love you, Nick," she said, the tears cascading down her cheeks. "We will never forget you."

"Amen to that," said Squelch. "The entire Brigade will never forget you, Nicky. We will always love you, man."

"We will indeed. Cheerio, old sport," echoed Claggebart. "May your soul be protected by the Ute spirits on this great mountain for all eternity. You are part of the great bear clan in the sky and you will, now and forever, see with the single eye that is the heart."

Suddenly, he stiffened and looked aghast at everyone.

"Wait a second. Was that way over the top? With my stentorian Indian chief voice, I thought I was on quite a little roll there. But then, I think I somehow crossed the line. I'm so sorry. I don't know what came over—"

"Okay, cut, cut, cut!" cried a new voice.

They all looked up. Squelch and Bermolito suddenly exploded with hysterical laughter.

"I told you, Nicholas, that Claggebart would be the one to blow it!" cried Bermolito.

Nick Lassiter stepped up to the group and lowered his hand-held Sony video camera. "I don't know," he said with a smile that caught Natalie's eye and warmed her inside. "I think it will be enough to fool everyone at the rehearsal dinner party tomorrow night." He walked up and gave her a loving squeeze. "What do you think, babe? Do we have enough?"

She looked down at the weathered nineteenth-century gravestone:

Nicholas "Deadeye" Lassiter
Born June 1, 1859   Died June 1, 1887
He was quick on the draw, but only his mother loved him

She nuzzled up next to him. "I think Claggebart's little mishap is only going to make it funnier."

"Oh dear, you're just trying to make me feel better, aren't you? Well, I must say you have done just that, you comely bride-to-be."

"It all looked very real to me right up to the very end," said Nick with a smile. "I must say those tears of yours Natalie, Mom, and Squelch had me almost believing I was dead. I think the new and improved Devil's Brigade may have missed its calling in Hollywood."

They all laughed and stared out at the peaceful plains below. The wind rustled through the trees and the sun slanted down from the west, covering scenic Lookout Mountain in a golden glow. For a long moment, they were all quiet, taking in the majesty of the natural Western landscape around them and the tranquility of the frontier cemetery.

ψψψ

Nick looked at his mother and father and smiled. There was a philosophical glint in his father's eye as he said, "Looking back on it all one year later, I can honestly say that justice was served across the board. It's true that we weren't able to catch the sniper in the helicopter—we think it was the Spanish contract assassin Diego Gomez—but as I said before, we were able to roll up the rogue CIA element headed by Deputy Director Harcourt and Colonel Emery. Not only that, Popov and his Odessa Mafia have been destroyed and, after six months of legal maneuvering, Benedictis is serving a three-year sentence in Sing Sing. But the best thing is that Nick and Natalie have recovered from their wounds—as has, surprisingly, Detective Stafford—and two days from now the two of them are getting married. And the latest edition to the Devil's Brigade, Cameron Beckett, has retired to Palm Beach, Florida, and is living the dream with his enchanting wife Nicole. I'd say, all things considered, that things turned out pretty damned well."

Beckett cracked a smile. "Aren't you forgetting someone?"

"And who might that be?"

"Why you and Vivian, of course. Let's not forget that it's your wedding this Sunday, too. And you can't bollix it up the second time around, mate."

"I can't? Why the hell not?"

Lassiter watched with amusement as his mom gave his dad a mock admonishing look before laughing, nudging up close to him, and giving him a peck on the cheek.

"You'll have to forgive, Austin," said Vivian Lassiter in a jesting voice. "He still hasn't grown up. He's a bit like his son in that regard."

Lassiter made a face. "Ouch, she's got us both on that one, Dad. I don't think we should take that."

"We have no choice," he replied with a grin. "She's absolutely right."

"Well, well, I'm afraid we're all children at heart," said Claggebart impatiently. "And now, in honor of the occasion and since our esteemed director has ordered 'cut,' I think it's time we allow ourselves the liberty of a libation and a Floridian marine delicacy or two. This way, please."

He led them through a stand of trees to the paired graves of Buffalo Bill and his wife Louisa, who had died in 1921, four years after the legendary frontier scout and showman. On a small table in the shade next to the fenced-in, white-stoned grave site was a silver tray bearing two iced buckets of already uncorked Dom Perignon champagne, a dozen crystal flutes, and silver bowls brimming with Joe's stone crabs and oysters on the half shell with cucumber mignonette.

"Clagge, you clever dog!" cried Lassiter.

"Well, you've certainly made up for your faux pas on film," declared Natalie.

Claggebart fingered his silver ascot, projected his chin in a mock highborn manner, and gave a devilish shrug. "Considering that a rather overdue double wedding is going to take place on Sunday, I decided that there was no time to waste christening the occasion."

"Here, here!" concurred Squelch and Bermolito, and they quickly poured out a dozen glasses of champagne and passed them around.

Cameron Beckett cleared his throat and raised his flute high in the air for a toast. "Here's to Nick and Natalie—and to Austin and Vivian. I wish you all the best from the bottom of my heart. I also thank you for saving my life and helping me see what is most important."

He looked lovingly at his wife Nicole and they smiled.

"Here, here!" echoed the crowd, clinking their glasses in approval.

"And here's also to *Blind Thrust*, which I am pleased to say I have read twice already," said the rejuvenated-looking Aussie. "I just learned this morning that it's sold over a million copies in only a week! Good on you, Nicholas! My first three novels didn't sell that much in six months! And you did it all under your own name—Nicholas Maxwell Lassiter."

"Atta boy, Nicky!" cried Squelch.

"I second that emotion!" agreed Bermolito.

"Oh crikey!" snorted Claggebart. "Thank God I had Joe's stone crabs flown in and we've got ample bubbly!"

"Well done, Son!" congratulated his mother and father.

He felt so blessed that he wanted to burst. *Am I the luckiest guy in the world?* He wished the moment would last forever. But he also knew the real reason for his newfound success.

"Now, before we get too carried away here," he said, holding up his hands, "I need to thank those that have made *Blind Thrust* a success. "First, I couldn't have done it without Cameron Beckett—the good one, that is, not the Dr. Evil who originally stole my book."

"Dr. Evil is long gone, I can assure you, mate," said Beckett good-naturedly.

"But more importantly, I couldn't have done it without the best literary agent in the business, an agent who enjoys, indeed insists upon, genuine high-quality editing and moral support on a daily basis. The person I am talking about is the inheritor to the greatest literary legacy of all time, and it is to this person that I have dedicated my first novel. To the greatest literary confidante and editor since Maxwell Perkins—his own great-granddaughter Natalie!"

"To Natalie!" cheered Squelch, Claggebart, and Bermolito rambunctiously.

She blushed profusely. He leaned down, kissed her, and hugged her tight. When they pulled apart, he saw the tears of joy in her eyes. He felt fortunate indeed to have such a plucky, beautiful, sweet, and devoted partner and literary agent. All she had ever wanted was the same as what he and all of the others wanted—to be appreciated and make a difference. She had never cared about becoming an über-rich, rock-star power agent like Anton De Benedictis. She was a literary agent because she loved reading and editing promising novels and helping make them great. She lived for the thrill of seeing an author break out, of helping nurture and then witnessing the momentous transformation that signaled the dawning of greatness. Just like her great-grandfather before her. Now, working with Nick and her six other clients and living in Colorado, she had everything she wanted.

And so do I, he thought, feeling the power of his emotions swirling through him, as if he was standing on the deck of a great ship on the high seas, watching the rhythmic ebb and flow of the swells.

"I do believe that one additional toast is in order," he said.

"And to what may I inquire, Sir Nicholas?" quipped Claggebart.

"We need to toast the Devil's Brigade."

"Damn straight, Nicky! Damn straight!" snorted Squelch with delight.

There was a brief moment of quiet as they all raised their flutes of champagne.

"To the Devil's Brigade!" roared Lassiter. "The craziest goddamned outfit this side of the Dirty Dozen!"

"Here, here! To the Devil's Brigade!"

They clinked glasses, tipped them back, and broke into a huge cheer that throbbed and echoed across Buffalo Bill's grave site with spirited glee.

In that great moment, a moment that Nick Lassiter would remember for the rest of his life, he could swear he spied the illustrious frontier scout and showman winking down on them all from a little gap in the clouds above.

AUTHOR'S NOTE

THE DEVIL'S BRIGADE is a work of fiction and entertainment and should be read as nothing more. The names, characters, places, government entities, corporations, and incidents are products of the author's imagination or are used fictitiously and are not to be construed as real. Any resemblance to actual events, locales, businesses, companies, organizations, or persons, living or dead, is entirely coincidental.

There is indeed an environmental thriller called *Blind Thrust* featuring a hero named Joe Higheagle and I, Samuel Marquis, wrote the novel. However, to the best of the author's knowledge, there is no literary figure, living or dead, who "stole" the novel from me by infringing on my copyright, borrowed the original idea from me, or appropriated the architecture of the novel by taking *Blind Thrust* from a slush pile or snatching a pirated copy of the novel from me electronically. As such, the fifty-two-time *New York Times* bestselling author Cameron Barnaby Beckett IV—who hails from the legendary Andrew "Banjo" Paterson's birthplace of Narrambla, Australia—is entirely the product of the author's imagination and should not be construed as an attack on Australian authors or culture. I happen to be a great admirer of Australia, one of America's greatest and most longstanding allies, and have always had a deep veneration for its stout defense of freedom and inestimable contributions to literature and cinema.

In a similar vein, New York's very own shining star—über literary agent Anton Fitzgerald De Benedictis—is wholly a creation of the author's imagination. I have had the pleasure of working with two literary agents from two different agencies—Aussie Cherry Weiner of the Cherry Weiner Literary Agency and Christopher Rhodes of the James Fitzgerald Agency—and I can say without a snicker that they bear absolutely no resemblance to Anton De Benedictis from Hell's Kitchen. Similarly, all other traditional publishing figures (literary agents, editors, publishers, publicity reps, security personnel, etc.) depicted as primary or secondary characters in the novel are wholly products of the author's imagination and have no real-life counterpart, at least that the author is aware of.

Denizens of the Mile High City will agree that there is indeed a Buckhorn Exchange Restaurant, a Tivoli Movie Theater, a trendy Lower Downtown district called LoDo, an East and a Kent-Denver High School, and a Denver Police Department. But, to the best of my knowledge, no one named Nick Lassiter or nicknamed Squelch, Claggebart, or Bermolito, or anyone resembling these fictitious literary characters, has ever engaged in fistfights, drunken debauchery, or flights from police officers at these real-life locations.

In the Big Apple, there is no Donald Trump, Jr. Building nor is there a Detective Stafford or NYPD Special Division that handles VIP cases, but there is indeed an American Museum of Natural History, an Uncle Jack's Steakhouse, and a wonderful place of refuge and sanctuary from the tumult of the city called Central Park. Set aside more than a century ago, Central Park does proudly boast such features as Conservatory Pond, Kerbs Memorial Boathouse, Hallett's Nature Sanctuary, Gapstow Bridge, the Victorian Gardens Amusement Park, and prominent statues of the 7th New York Infantry Civil War Memorial and South American General Simon Bolivar. The city also has three famous buildings that are weaved into the plot of the novel: the Plaza Hotel, Dakota, and San Remo. However, to the best of the author's knowledge, no one bearing the slightest resemblance to any of the fictional characters in *The Devil's Brigade* has indulged in car chases, gun battles, or stealthy rooftop sniping activities at any of these real-world locations.

There is no De Benedictis Literary Associates in New York City and no Excalibur Media Group or Excalibur Publishing Group in New York, London, or any other city. Therefore, the literary agency's and publishing house's illicit, shadowy, and threatening activities in the novel have been entirely fictionalized and, in reality, would be unlikely to occur in the real world of book publishing. However, the stealing of the written work and story lines of no-name, deceased, or long-forgotten fiction writers and other creative artists by powerful established writers, publishers, agents, producers, directors, etc., or the companies that these people represent, is a very real problem.

Space does not permit citing all of the relevant cases of large-scale copyright infringement where a big name has stolen from a little guy; a simple Google search will instantly inform the interested party of both the pervasiveness of such intellectual property-rights' infringements and how infrequently the aggrieved little guy with a strong, seemingly irrefutable case receives just compensation for the theft of his creative work. The odds against the real-life Nick Lassiter's of the world succeeding in winning an infringement claim against big-moneyed corporate interests, or big literary/film names that have stolen and plundered their creative works, are both frightening and staggering.

That is the simple, unfortunate truth of it. And that is why *The Devil's Brigade* was written.

ACKNOWLEDGEMENTS

I consulted hundreds of non-fiction books, magazine and newspaper articles, blogs, Web sites, and numerous individuals to develop the story line, characters, and scenes for *The Devil's Brigade* and visited both Denver and New York to properly capture the essence of these two unique settings. All in all, there are too many resources to name here. However, I would be remiss if I didn't give credit to the critical individuals who improved the quality of the manuscript from its initial to its final stage. Any technical mistakes, typographical errors, or examples of overreach due to artistic license, however, are the fault of me and me alone.

I would personally like to thank the following for their support and assistance. First, I would like to thank my wife Christine, an exceptional and highly professional book editor, who painstakingly reviewed and copy-edited the novel. Second, I would like to thank my former literary agent, Christopher Rhodes of the James Fitzgerald Agency, who generously said of the novel: "Fantastic...*Ocean's Eleven* meets *A Night at the Museum*...I really love this project and think it has huge potential." Thanks to Christopher for thoroughly reviewing, vetting, and copy-editing the manuscript, and for making countless improvements to the finished novel before I chose to publish the novel independently due to its iconoclastic, distinctly indie flavor. Third, I would like to thank author James Patterson and author-literary agent Donald Maass for their positive reviews and constructive criticism of my first completed novel, *The Coalition,* the second book in the Nick Lassiter-Skyler International Espionage Series. They took the time to give me genuine feedback and without their encouragement I might not be as determined and resilient an author as I am today. Finally, I would like to thank Austin and Anne Marquis, Governor Roy Romer, Ambassador Marc Grossman, Betsy and Steve Hall, Rik Hall, Christian Fuenfhausen, John Welch, Fred Taylor, Mo Shafroth, Tim and Carey Romer, Peter and Lorrie Frautschi, Deirdre Grant Mercurio, Joe Tallman, Link Nicoll, Toni Conte Augusta Francis, Dawn Ezzo Roseman, Brigid Donnelly Hughes, Peter Brooke, Caroline Fenton Dewey, John and Ellen Aisenbrey, Margot Patterson, Cathy and Jon Jenkins, Danny Bilello and Elena Diaz-Bilello, Charlie and Kay Fial, Vincent Bilello, Elizabeth Gardner, Robin McGehee, Bill Eberhart, Quinn Fitzpatrick, and the other book reviewers and professional contributors large and small who have given generously of their time over the years, as well as to those who have given me loyal support as I have ventured on this incredible odyssey of suspense novel writing.

Lastly, I want to thank anyone and everyone who bought this book and my loyal fans and supporters who helped promote this work. You know who you are and I salute you.

ABOUT THE AUTHOR AND FORTHCOMING TITLES

Samuel Marquis is a bestselling, award-winning suspense author. He works by day as a VP–Principal Hydrogeologist with an environmental firm in Boulder, Colorado, and by night as a spinner of historical and modern suspense yarns. He holds a Master of Science degree in Geology, is a Registered Professional Geologist in eleven states, and is a recognized expert in groundwater contaminant hydrogeology, having served as an expert witness in several class action litigation cases. He also has a deep and abiding interest in military history and intelligence, specifically related to the Golden Age of Piracy, Plains Indian Wars, World War II, and the current War on Terror.

His thrillers have been #1 *Denver Post* bestsellers and received national book award recognition. His first novel, *The Devil's Brigade* (formerly *The Slush Pile Brigade*), was an award-winning finalist in the mystery category of the Beverly Hills Book Awards. His follow-up *Blind Thrust* was the winner of the Foreword Reviews Book of the Year (HM) and Next Generation Indie Book Awards and an award-winning finalist of the USA Best Book and Beverly Hills Book Awards (thriller and suspense). His third novel, *The Coalition*, was the winner of the Beverly Hills Book Awards for a political thriller and an award-winning finalist for the USA Best Book Awards and Colorado Book Awards. *Bodyguard of Deception*, Book 1 of his WWII Series, was an award-winning finalist of the USA Best Book and Foreword Reviews Book Awards in historical fiction. His fifth book, *Cluster of Lies*, won the Beverly Hills Book Awards in the regional fiction: west category and was an award-winning finalist of the USA Best Book and Foreword Reviews Book Awards.

Ambassador Marc Grossman, former U.S. Under Secretary of State, proclaimed, "In his novels *Blind Thrust* and *Cluster of Lies*, Samuel Marquis vividly combines the excitement of the best modern techno-thrillers." Former Colorado Governor Roy Romer said, "*Blind Thrust* kept me up until 1 a.m. two nights in a row. I could not put it down." Kirkus Reviews proclaimed *The Coalition* an "entertaining thriller" and declared that "Marquis has written a tight plot with genuine suspense." James Patterson said *The Coalition* had "a lot of good action and suspense" and compared the novel to *The Day After Tomorrow*, the classic thriller by Allan Folsom. Other book reviewers have compared Marquis's WWII thrillers *Bodyguard of Deception* and *Altar of Resistance* to the epic historical novels of Tom Clancy, John le Carré, Ken Follett, Herman Wouk, Daniel Silva, and Alan Furst.

Below is the list of suspense novels that Samuel Marquis has published or will be publishing in the near future, along with the release dates of both previously published and forthcoming titles.

The World War Two Series
Bodyguard of Deception – March 2016 – Award-Winning Finalist USA Best Book Awards and Foreword Reviews Book Awards
Altar of Resistance – January 2017
Spies of the Midnight Sun – January 2018

The Nick Lassiter – Skyler International Espionage Series
The Devil's Brigade (formerly The Slush Pile Brigade) – September 2015, Reissue April 2017 – The #1 Denver Post Bestseller and Award-Winning Finalist Beverly Hills Book Awards
The Coalition – January 2016, Reissue April 2017 – Winner Beverly Hills Book Awards and Award-Winning Finalist USA Best Book and Colorado Book Awards
The Fourth Pularchek – June 2017

The Joe Higheagle Environmental Sleuth Series
Blind Thrust – October 2015 – The #1 Denver Post Bestseller; Winner Foreword Reviews' Book of the Year (HM) and Next Generation Indie Book Awards; Award-Winning Finalist USA Best Book Awards, Beverly Hills Book Awards, and Next Generation Indie Book Awards
Cluster of Lies – September 2016 – Winner Beverly Hills Book Awards and Award-Winning Finalist USA Best Book and Foreword Review Book Awards

Thank You for Your Support!

To Order Samuel Marquis Books and Contact Samuel:

Visit Samuel Marquis's website, join his mailing list, learn about his forthcoming suspense novels and book events, and order his books at www.samuelmarquisbooks.com. Please send all fan mail (including criticism) to samuelmarquisbooks@gmail.com.

6-12-18

Made in the USA
Middletown, DE
01 April 2018